Vampires, Wine & Roses

Vampires, Wine & Roses

EDITED BY

JOHN RICHARD STEPHENS

BERKLEY BOOKS, NEW YORK

All possible care has been taken to trace the ownership of every selection included and to make full acknowledgment for its use. If any errors have occurred, they will be corrected in subsequent editions provided notification is sent to the publisher.

John Richard Stephens wishes to express his appreciation to Martha and Jim Goodwin; Scott Stephens; Marty Goeller; Mollie Seibert; Joyce Whiteaker and Gary Wood; Terity, Natasha, and Debbie Burbach; Branden, Alisha, and Kathy Hill; Jeff and Carol Whiteaker; Doug and Michelle Whiteaker; Bill and Norene Hilden; Doug and Shirley Strong; Frank and Marybeth DiVito; Stan and Barbara Main; and to his agent, Charlotte Cecil Raymond.

VAMPIRES, WINE & ROSES

A Berkley Book / published by arrangement with the editor

PRINTING HISTORY
Berkley trade paperback edition / February 1997

The Putnam Berkley World Wide Web site address is
http://www.berkley.com/berkley

ISBN: 0-425-15741-5

BERKLEY®
Berkley Books are published by The Berkley Publishing Group,
200 Madison Avenue, New York, New York 10016.
BERKLEY and the "B" design
are trademarks belonging to Berkley Publishing Corporation.

PRINTED IN THE UNITED STATES OF AMERICA

10 9 8 7 6 5 4 3 2 1

This book is dedicated to Jim Goodwin

Contents

UNDER THE INFLUENCE
OF VAMPIRES

FAR FROM BEING A relatively recent phenomenon, vampires have been popular consistently for the past two centuries. Most people believe Bram Stoker's *Dracula* (1897) first brought vampires to the public's attention and that their popularity was kept alive by Bela Lugosi's *Dracula*, followed by Anne Rice's *Interview with the Vampire* (book and movie) and Francis Ford Coppola's version of the Stoker classic.

Actually, many vampire stories were written before *Dracula*, and the vampire motif had a major impact on nineteenth century literature. Even before movies were invented, plays about vampires had appeared on stages almost consistently since the 1820s. Then, more than fifty vampire movies were made before the 1931 Bela Lugosi film. Of course, as the number of movies being made increased, the number of vampire movies also increased. During the seventies alone, over 150 vampire flicks were released. The story is the same in the publishing industry.

While the vampire and similar bloodsucking nightmares have experienced a tremendous surge in popularity over the past two centuries, they have been a part of culture extending far back into human history. The term "vampire" is relatively recent, having probably evolved from the Slavic word *upir*. Before this they were called by many different names in many different languages. Names like *lamia, lilitu, ekimmu, empusa, vroucolaca, strigoi, langsuir, dashnavar, dearg-dul, pamgri, katakhanes, xiang shi, swawmx*, and countless other appellations. Sometimes the characteristics varied a bit, but vampires and their relatives have been with us for a very long time.

In the fifth century B.C., Sophocles wrote in *Oedipus at Colonus* (his sequel to *Oedipus Rex*):

> Then shall my slumbering and buried corpse
> In its cold grave drink their warm life-blood up . . .

There is an interesting vampire story dating from about 217 A.D. written by Philostratus in his *Life of Apollonius of Tyana*. It tells of a young man named Minippus who fell in love with a female vampire from Corinth. At their wedding, Minippus's friends confronted her and "she admitted she was a vampire, and was fattening up Menippus with pleasure before devouring his body, for it was her habit to feed upon young and beautiful bodies, because their blood is pure and strong." The Greek word used in this story is *empusa*, which is usually translated as "vampire." John Keats based his poem "Lamia" on this story.

There is a gap in vampire literature after the Greek and Roman periods, and new literature appears only after Europe moved out of the Dark Ages. Sir Thomas Malory included an encounter between King Arthur's knights and a vampire woman in his *Le Morte D'Arthur* (*The Death of Arthur*). Malory's book, written in the 1460s, is the primary account of King Arthur's exploits, and is actually a synthesis of earlier Arthurian myths.

The famous Swiss philosopher Jean-Jacques Rousseau believed in the actual existence of vampires. A draft of his treatise on education, *Émile*, written in 1758 and 1759, contains the following excerpt:

For some time now, the public news has been concerned with nothing but vampires; there has never been a fact more fully proved *in
law* than their existence, yet despite this, show me a single man of
sense in Europe who believes in vampires or who would even deign
to take the trouble to check the falseness of the facts . . . Who will
venture to tell me exactly how many eyewitnesses are needed to
make a phenomenon credible?

In 1762, Christophe de Beaumont, the Archbishop of Paris, issued a scathing denunciation of *Émile*. Rousseau decided to send
the Archbishop a letter, taking the opportunity to point out some
flaws in the Archbishop's logic—such as the willingness to believe
in miracles, but not vampires. Rousseau wrote:

If ever there was in the world a warranted and proven history, it is
that of vampires: nothing is lacking, official reports, testimonials of
persons of standing, of surgeons, of clergymen, of judges; the ju-
dicial evidence is all-embracing.

It was during this same period that vampire stories found their
way into Western European culture. Since then, their influence
has been widespread. The use of vampiric imagery became very
common in nineteenth-century literature. In fact, it can be found
in some unlikely places, such as *The Rime of the Ancient Mariner*
(1798), where Samuel Taylor Coleridge writes:

> Her lips were red, her looks were free,
> Her locks were yellow as gold:
> Her skin was as white as leprosy,
> The Night–mare LIFE-IN-DEATH was she,
> Who thicks man's blood with cold. . . .
>
> Fear at my heart, as at a cup,
> My life-blood seemed to sip!

Dr. James B. Twichell, an alumni professor of English at the
University of Florida, in his book *The Living Dead: A Study of the
Vampire in Romantic Literature* (1981), writes that even the ancient
mariner himself is "a 'psychic vampire,' who saps the energy of
the Wedding Guest."

In Charlotte Brontë's *Jane Eyre* (1847), Jane's fiancé Rochester keeps his insane first wife hidden away in another part of the house. To Jane, who doesn't know of her existence, Bertha Rochester is more of an apparition. At one point, when Jane has a brief encounter with her, she says:

> I never saw a face like it! It was a discoloured face—it was a savage face. I wish I could forget the roll of the red eyes and the fearful blackened inflation of the lineaments! . . . The lips were swelled and dark; the brow furrowed; the black eyebrows widely raised over bloodshot eyes. Shall I tell you of what it reminded me? . . . of that foul German spectre—the Vampyre.

In *Wuthering Heights* (1847), Emily Brontë subtly uses the vampire metaphor throughout the book. Heathcliff dies emotionally when he discovers Catherine has married someone else. In the last love scene between Heathcliff and Catherine, the servant/housekeeper reports that "my mistress had kissed him first, and I plainly saw that he could hardly bear, for downright agony, to look into her face! The same conviction had stricken him as me, from the instant he beheld her, that there was no prospect of ultimate recovery there—she was fated sure to die."

Shortly after her death, the servant asks Heathcliff, "Is he a ghoul or a vampire?" Later, as he slowly wastes away, he refuses to eat. He goes out at midnight, returning at dawn with "a strange joyful glitter in his eyes." His cheeks become hollow and his eyes red. His calm is "unnatural—[the] appearance of joy under his black brows; the same bloodless hue: and his teeth visible, now and then, in a kind of smile; his frame shivering, not as one shivers from the cold or weakness, but as a tightstretched cord vibrates—a strong thrilling, rather than trembling." After his death, she describes him, saying, "I tried to close his eyes: to extinguish if possible that frightful, life-like gaze of exultation before any one else beheld it. They would not shut: they seemed to sneer at my attempts: and his parted lips and sharp white teeth sneered too!"

There's much, much more to the vampire motif in Emily Brontë's classic masterpiece and some scholarly books that analyze the vampire's influence on literature have devoted entire chapters to *Wuthering Heights*.

D.H. Lawrence dealt with psychic vampirism in his short story "The Lovely Lady." At the request of his old friend Lady Cynthia Asquith, he wrote this story for her murder mystery anthology, *The Black Cap* (1923). Though it's nothing like a traditional murder mystery, it is Lawrence's idea of one. To him, a person's emotional and sexual lives were more important than their physical existence; therefore, a vampire of the emotions was the worst kind of murderer. In this story, the vampire/murderer is a mother whose own emotional life was killed off long ago and who has only survived by sucking out the emotional lives of her two sons. In this murder mystery, it is the murderer who suffers a real death after she is exposed for what she really is, while her second victim is resurrected from his living death through a woman's love.

The vampire motif fit well into Lawrence's world of emotional and sexual intrigue, and he used it often. Scholars point out that it can also be found in *Lady Chatterley's Lover* and in the predatory females of *The Rainbow* and *Women in Love*.

The vampire metaphor even appeared in works of nonfiction, such as in *Das Kapital* (1887), where Karl Marx writes:

> Capital is dead labor, that, vampire-like, only lives by sucking living labor, and lives the more, the more labor it sucks. . . . The prolongation of the working-day beyond the limits of the natural day, into the night, only acts as a palliative. It quenches only in a slight degree the vampire thirst for the living blood of labor.

These are just a few instances of the unexpected influence that vampires have had on literature; but this sampling is far from complete. Dr. Twitchell in *The Living Dead: A Study of the Vampire in Romantic Literature* cites further instances:

> In the works of such artists as Coleridge, Byron, Shelley, Keats, Emily and Charlotte Brontë, Stoker, Wilde, Poe and Lawrence the vampire was variously used to personify the force of maternal attraction/repulsion (Coleridge's Christabel), incest (Byron's Manfred), oppressive paternalism (Shelley's Cenci), adolescent love (Keats' Porphyro), avaricious love (Poe's Morella and Berenice), the struggle for power (E. Brontë's Heathcliff), sexual suppression (C. Brontë's Bertha Rochester), homosexual attraction (Le Fanu's

Carmilla), repressed sexuality (Stoker's Dracula), female domination (D. H. Lawrence's Brangwen women), and, most Romantic of all, the artist himself exchanging energy with aspects of his art (Coleridge's Ancient Mariner, Poe's artist in *The Oval Portrait*, Wordsworth's Leech Gatherer, Wilde's Dorian Gray, and the narrator of James's *The Sacred Fount*).

To this list of literature with vampire imagery, other scholars would include *Beowulf*, Edgar Allan Poe's "The Fall of the House of Usher," William Wordsworth's *Resolution and Independence*, Charles Dickens's *The Old Curiosity Shop* and *Bleak House*, George Eliot's *Middlemarch*, F. Scott Fitzgerald's *Babylon Revisited*, and Virginia Woolf's *To the Lighthouse*. With regard to more contemporary literature, Clive Leatherdale in his book *Dracula: The Novel and the Legend* writes: "And what else is Batman but the Count cleansed of his evil and endowed with a social conscience?" Vampires lend themselves very well as metaphors of society, certain relationships, love, and sex.

The emphasis on pseudo-sexual elements is what has maintained the popularity of vampire imagery throughout the past two centuries. By downplaying the idea that they are essentially cannibalistic corpses and rather presenting them as attractive—but with a selfish, and hence evil, nature—vampires were turned into monsters people could identify and sympathize with. After all, don't we kill animals for our survival? Their attractiveness is further enhanced by the temptation of readers to join them in their victory over the ultimate destruction we are all marching toward—death; even though this method of survival has its drawbacks (not to mention that it can be cut short by any self-appointed savior with a mallet and a stake). Vampires exemplify the most fascinating kind of evil—that which is powerful, sexy, alluring, but also very dangerous.

But even these sexual elements are not new; they actually date back at least to the time of ancient Rome. The sexual nature of the vampire is highlighted in a story from the second century A.D. by Phlegon of Tralles in his *Concerning Wondrous Things*. Unfortunately, the beginning of the story has been lost. It starts with Philinnion, a young woman who was buried about six months earlier, being discovered in bed with a visitor of her family who has fallen in love with her. After her tomb is found empty, the body is discovered in the house, and is subsequently taken out and burned (cremation was the most common method of vampire disposal throughout early history).

Vampires have been with us in one form or another for millennia and they're going to remain with us. In this sense, they are immortal. And there can be no doubt that they've had a major impact on our society.

In this collection of vampire literature by famous authors there are many stories and poems by writers who are not normally associated with the horror genre. In fact, many of these works have never before appeared in any of the dozens of vampire anthologies that have been published over the years. I'm sure even the most avid vampire fanatic will find new, unexpected, and perhaps even surprising material here. Who would have suspected that Woody Allen, Lenny Bruce, and Sting all wrote about vampires? Unfortunately, some of the vampire literature written by famous authors has been forgotten or overlooked because it is part of a larger work. To remedy this, I have included a few of these excerpts. Most stand well on their own since they were written as individual sections within the larger work. Others are presented to show how a particular author deals with the topic. Hopefully these excerpts won't put off those readers who prefer reading a work in its entirety. Since I doubt most enthusiasts would go to the trouble to dig up these buried masterpieces of vampire literature—chances are, they would have trouble finding these works even if they tried—these excerpts are included along with many other overlooked tales to once again make these forgotten vampires accessible to a bloodthirsty public.

William Shakespeare

EXCERPT FROM

ROMEO AND JULIET

———⟫●⟪———

William Shakespeare is described as "the greatest dramatist the
world has ever known and the finest poet who has written in the
English language." Few would expect to find anything of a vampiric nature in his works—particularly in a play as well-known as
Romeo and Juliet. While the play does not contain a vampire, this excerpt does use vampiric language to increase the growing sense of
tension. It was written by Shakespeare in either 1591 or 1596–
1597.

JULIET: Art thou gone so? love, lord, ay, husband, friend!
          I must hear from thee every day in the hour,
          For in a minute there are many days:
          O, by this count I shall be much in years
          Ere I again behold my Romeo!
ROMEO: Farewell!
          I will omit no opportunity
          That may convey my greetings, love, to thee.
JULIET: O think'st thou we shall ever meet again?
ROMEO: I doubt it not; and all these woes shall serve
          For sweet discourses in our time to come.
JULIET: O God, I have an ill-divining soul!
          Methinks I see thee, now thou art below,

As one dead in the bottom of a tomb:
Either my eyesight fails, or thou look'st pale.

ROMEO: And trust me, love, in my eye so do you:
Dry sorrow drinks our blood. Adieu, adieu!

Anne Rice

THE MASTER OF
RAMPLING GATE

Anne Rice's vampires have made her one of America's most popular
horror writers. She is referred to as "the undisputed queen of vampire
literature." Each of her five vampire novels has been a bestseller. *Interview with the Vampire* ranks only behind *Dracula* as the most popular
vampire novel in recent history, and was made into a major motion
picture. Rice's bestselling novels include *The Vampire Lestat, Queen of
the Damned, The Tale of the Body Thief, Cry to Heaven, Feast of All Saints, The
Mummy, Lasher,* and *The Witching Hour.* She has been called "the foremost practitioner of the Gothic style in the modern age." She has written very few short stories. This one was first published in *Redbook*
magazine in February 1984.

SPRING 1888

RAMPLING GATE. IT WAS so real to us in the old pictures, rising like
a fairy-tale castle out of its own dark wood. A wilderness of gables
and chimneys between those two immense towers, gray stone
walls mantled in ivy, mullioned windows reflecting the drifting
clouds.

But why had Father never taken us there? And why, on his
deathbed, had he told my brother that Rampling Gate must be
torn down, stone by stone? "I should have done it, Richard," he

said. "But I was born in that house, as my father was, and his father before him. You must do it now, Richard. It has no claim on you. Tear it down."

Was it any wonder that not two months after Father's passing, Richard and I were on the noon train headed south for the mysterious mansion that had stood upon the rise above the village of Rampling for four hundred years? Surely Father would have understood. How could we destroy the old place when we had never seen it?

But, as the train moved slowly through the outskirts of London I can't say we were very sure of ourselves, no matter how curious and excited we were.

Richard had just finished four years at Oxford. Two whirlwind social seasons in London had proved me something of a shy success. I still preferred scribbling poems and stories in my room to dancing the night away, but I'd kept that a good secret. And though we had lost our mother when we were little, Father had given us the best of everything. Now the carefree years were ended. We had to be independent and wise.

The evening before, we had pored over all the old pictures of Rampling Gate, recalling in hushed, tentative voices the night Father had taken those pictures down from the walls.

I couldn't have been more than six and Richard eight when it happened, yet we remembered well the strange incident in Victoria Station that had precipitated Father's uncharacteristic rage. We had gone there after supper to say farewell to a school friend of Richard's, and Father had caught a glimpse, quite unexpectedly, of a young man at the lighted window of an incoming train. I could remember the young man's face clearly to this day: remarkably handsome, with a head of lustrous brown hair, his large black eyes regarding Father with the saddest expression as Father drew back. "Unspeakable horror!" Father had whispered. Richard and I had been too amazed to speak a word. Later that night, Father and Mother quarreled, and we crept out of our rooms to listen on the stairs.

"That he should dare to come to London!" Father said over and over. "Is it not enough for him to be the undisputed master of Rampling Gate?"

How we puzzled over it as little ones! Who was this stranger, and how could he be master of a house that belonged to our father, a house that had been left in the care of an old, blind housekeeper for years?

But now after looking at the pictures again, it was too dreadful to think of Father's exhortation. And too exhilarating to think of the house itself. I'd packed my manuscripts, for—who knew?—maybe in that melancholy and exquisite setting I'd find exactly the inspiration I needed for the story I'd been writing in my head.

Yet there was something almost illicit about the excitement I felt. I saw in my mind's eye the pale young man again, with his black greatcoat and red woolen cravat. Like bone china, his complexion had been. Strange to remember so vividly. And I realized now that in those few remarkable moments, he had created for me an ideal of masculine beauty that I had never questioned since. But Father had been so angry. I felt an unmistakable pang of guilt.

It was late afternoon when the old trap carried us up the gentle slope from the little railway station and we had our first real look at the house. The sky had paled to a deep rose hue beyond a bank of softly gilded clouds, and the last rays of the sun struck the uppermost panes of the leaded windows and filled them with solid gold.

"Oh, but it's too majestic," I whispered, "too like a great cathedral, and to think that it belongs to us!"

Richard gave me the smallest kiss on the cheek.

I wanted with all my heart to jump down from the trap and draw near on foot, letting those towers slowly grow larger and larger above me, but our old horse was gaining speed.

When we reached the massive front door Richard and I were spirited into the great hall by the tiny figure of the blind housekeeper Mrs. Blessington, our footfalls echoing loudly on the marble tile, and our eyes dazzled by the dusty shafts of light that fell on the long oak table and its heavily carved chairs, on the somber tapestries that stirred ever so slightly against the soaring walls.

"Richard, it is an enchanted place!" I cried, unable to contain myself.

Mrs. Blessington laughed gaily, her dry hand closing tightly on mine.

We found our bedchambers well aired, with snow-white linen on the beds and fires blazing cozily on the hearths. The small, diamond-paned windows opened on a glorious view of the lake and the oaks that enclosed it and the few scattered lights that marked the village beyond.

That night we laughed like children as we supped at the great oak table, our candles giving only a feeble light. And afterward we had a fierce battle of pocket billiards in the game room and a little too much brandy, I fear.

It was just before I went to bed that I asked Mrs. Blessington if there had been anyone in this house since my father left it, years before.

"No, my dear," she said quickly, fluffing the feather pillows. "When your father went away to Oxford, he never came back."

"There was never a young intruder after that? . . ." I pressed her, though in truth I had little appetite for anything that would disturb the happiness I felt. How I loved the Spartan cleanliness of this bedchamber, the walls bare of paper and ornament, the high luster of the walnut-paneled bed.

"A young intruder?" With an unerring certainty about her surroundings, she lifted the poker and stirred the fire. "No, dear. Whatever made you think there was?"

"Are there no ghost stories, Mrs. Blessington?" I asked suddenly, startling myself. *Unspeakable horror.* But what was I thinking—that that young man had not been real?

"Oh, no, darling," she said, smiling. "No ghost would ever dare to trouble Rampling Gate."

Nothing, in fact, troubled the serenity of the days that followed— long walks through the overgrown gardens, trips in the little skiff to and fro across the lake, tea under the hot glass of the empty conservatory. Early evening found us reading and writing by the library fire.

All our inquiries in the village met with the same answers: The villagers cherished the house. There was not a single disquieting legend or tale.

How were we going to tell them of Father's edict? How were we going to remind ourselves?

Richard was finding a wealth of classical material on the library shelves and I had the desk in the corner entirely to myself.

Never had I known such quiet. It seemed the atmosphere of Rampling Gate permeated my simplest written descriptions and wove its way richly into the plots and characters I created. The Monday after our arrival I finished my first real short story, and after copying out a fresh draft, I went off to the village on foot to post it boldly to the editors of *Blackwood's Magazine*.

It was a warm afternoon, and I took my time as I came back. What had disturbed our father so about this lovely corner of England? What had so darkened his last hours that he laid his curse upon this spot? My heart opened to this unearthly stillness, to an indisputable magnificence that caused me utterly to forget myself. There were times here when I felt I was a disembodied intellect drifting through a fathomless silence, up and down garden paths and stone corridors that had witnessed too much to take cognizance of one small and fragile young woman who in random moments actually talked aloud to the suits of armor around her, to the broken statues in the garden, the fountain cherubs who had had no water to pour from their conches for years and years.

But was there in this loveliness some malignant force that was eluding us still, some untold story? *Unspeakable horror . . .* Even in the flood of brilliant sunlight, those words gave me a chill.

As I came slowly up the slope I saw Richard walking lazily along the uneven shore of the lake. Now and then he glanced up at the distant battlements, his expression dreamy, almost blissfully contented.

Rampling Gate had him. And I understood perfectly because it also had me.

With a new sense of determination I went to him and placed my hand gently on his arm. For a moment he looked at me as if he did not even know me, and then he said softly:

"How will I ever do it, Julie? And one way or the other, it will be on my conscience all my life."

"It's time to seek advice, Richard," I said. "Write to our lawyers in London. Write to Father's clergyman, Dr. Matthews. Explain everything. We cannot do this alone."

*   *   *

It was three o'clock in the morning when I opened my eyes. But I had been awake for a long time. And I felt not fear, lying there alone, but something else—some vague and relentless agitation, some sense of emptiness and need that caused me finally to rise from my bed. What was this house, really? A place, or merely a state of mind? What was it doing to my soul?

I felt overwhelmed, yet shut out of some great and dazzling secret. Driven by an unbearable restlessness, I pulled on my woolen wrapper and my slippers and went into the hall.

The moonlight fell full on the oak stairway, and the vestibule far below. Maybe I could write of the confusion I suffered now, put on paper the inexplicable longing I felt. Certainly it was worth the effort, and I made my way soundlessly down the steps.

The great hall gaped before me, the moonlight here and there touching upon a pair of crossed swords or a mounted shield. But far beyond, in the alcove just outside the library, I saw the uneven glow of the fire. So Richard was there. A sense of well-being pervaded me and quieted me. At the same time, the distance between us seemed endless and I became desperate to cross it, hurrying past the long supper table and finally into the alcove before the library doors.

The fire blazed beneath the stone mantelpiece and a figure sat in the leather chair before it, bent over a loose collection of pages that he held in his slender hands. He was reading the pages eagerly, and the fire suffused his face with a warm, golden light.

But it was not Richard. It was the same young man I had seen on the train in Victoria Station fifteen years ago. And not a single aspect of that taut young face had changed. There was the very same hair, thick and lustrous and only carelessly combed as it hung to the collar of his black coat, and those dark eyes that looked up suddenly and fixed me with a most curious expression as I almost screamed.

We stared at each other across that shadowy room, I stranded in the doorway, he visibly and undeniably shaken that I had caught him unawares. My heart stopped.

And in a split second he rose and moved toward me, closing the gap between us, reaching out with those slender white hands.

"Julie!" he whispered, in a voice so low that it seemed my own thoughts were speaking to me. But this was no dream. He was holding me and the scream had broken loose from me, deafening, uncontrollable and echoing from the four walls.

I was alone. Clutching at the door frame, I staggered forward, and then in a moment of perfect clarity I saw the young stranger again, saw him standing in the open door to the garden, looking back over his shoulder; then he was gone.

I could not stop screaming. I could not stop even as I heard Richard's voice calling me, heard his feet pound down that broad, hollow staircase and through the great hall. I could not stop even as he shook me, pleaded with me, settled me in a chair.

Finally I managed to describe what I had seen.

"But you know who it was!" I said almost hysterically. "It was he—the young man from the train!"

"Now, wait," Richard said. "He had his back to the fire, Julie. And you could not see his face clearly—"

"Richard, it was he! Don't you understand? He touched me. He called me Julie," I whispered. "Good God, Richard, look at the fire. I didn't light it—he did. He was here!"

All but pushing Richard out of the way, I went to the heap of papers that lay strewn on the carpet before the hearth. "My story . . ." I whispered, snatching up the pages. "He's been reading my story, Richard. And—dear God—he's read your letters, the letters to Mr. Partridge and Dr. Matthews, about tearing down the house!"

"Surely you don't believe it was the same man, Julie, after all these years . . . ?"

"But he has not changed, Richard, not in the smallest detail. There is no mistake, I tell you. It was the very same man!"

The next day was the most trying since we had come. Together we commenced a search of the house. Darkness found us only half finished, frustrated everywhere by locked doors we could not open and old staircases that were not safe.

And it was also quite clear by suppertime that Richard did not believe I had seen anyone in the study at all. As for the fire—well, he had failed to put it out properly before going to bed; and the pages—well, one of us had put them there and forgotten them, of course . . .

But I knew what I had seen.

And what obsessed me more than anything else was the gentle countenance of the mysterious man I had glimpsed, the innocent eyes that had fixed on me for one moment before I screamed.

"You would be wise to do one very important thing before you retire," I said crossly. "Leave out a note to the effect that you do not intend to tear down the house."

"Julie, you have created an impossible dilemma," Richard declared, the color rising in his face. "You insist we reassure this apparition that the house will not be destroyed, when in fact you verify the existence of the very creature that drove our father to say what he did."

"Oh, I wish I had never come here!" I burst out suddenly.

"Then we should go, and decide this matter at home."

"No—that's just it. I could never go without knowing. I could never go on living without knowing now!"

Anger must be an excellent antidote to fear, for surely something worked to alleviate my natural alarm. I did not undress that night, but rather sat in the darkened bedroom, gazing at the small square of diamond-paned window until I heard the house fall quiet. When the grandfather clock in the great hall chimed the hour of eleven, Rampling Gate was, as usual, fast asleep.

I felt a dark exultation as I imagined myself going out of the room and down the stairs. But I knew I should wait one more hour. I should let the night reach its peak. My heart was beating too fast, and dreamily I recollected the face I had seen, the voice that had said my name.

Why did it seem in retrospect so intimate, that we had known each other before, spoken together a thousand times? Was it because he had read my story, those words that came from my very soul?

"Who are you?" I believe I whispered aloud. "Where are you at this moment?" I uttered the word, "Come."

The door opened without a sound and he was standing there. He was dressed exactly as he had been the night before and his dark eyes were riveted on me with that same obvious curiosity, his mouth just a little slack, like that of a boy.

I sat forward, and he raised his finger as if to reassure me and gave a little nod.

"Ah, it is you!" I whispered.

"Yes," he said in a soft, unobtrusive voice.

"And you are not a spirit!" I looked at his mud-splattered boots, at the faintest smear of dust on that perfect white cheek.

"A spirit?" he asked almost mournfully. "Would that I were that."

Dazed, I watched him come toward me; the room darkened and I felt his cool, silken hands on my face. I had risen. I was standing before him, and I looked up into his eyes.

I heard my own heartbeat. I heard it as I had the night before, right at the moment I had screamed. Dear God, I was talking to him! He was in my room and I was talking to him! And then suddenly I was in his arms.

"Real, absolutely real!" I whispered, and a low, zinging sensation coursed through me so that I had to steady myself.

He was peering at me as if trying to comprehend something terribly important. His lips had a ruddy look to them, a soft look for all his handsomeness, as if he had never been kissed. A slight dizziness came over me, a slight confusion in which I was not at all sure that he was even there.

"Oh, but I am," he said, as if I had spoken my doubt. I felt his breath against my cheek, and it was almost sweet. "I am here, and I have watched you ever since you came."

"Yes . . ."

My eyes were closing. In a dim flash, as of a match being struck, I saw my father, heard his voice. *No, Julie* . . . But that was surely a dream.

"Only a little kiss," said the voice of the one who was really here. I felt his lips against my neck. "I would never harm you. No harm ever for the children of this house. Just the little kiss, Julie, and the understanding that it imparts, that you cannot destroy Rampling Gate, Julie—that you can never, never drive me away."

The core of my being, that secret place where all desires and all commandments are nurtured, opened to him without a struggle or a sound. I would have fallen if he had not held me. My arms closed about him, my hands slipping into the soft, silken mass of his hair.

I was floating, and there was, as there had always been at Rampling Gate, an endless peace. It was Rampling Gate I felt enclosing me; it was that timeless and impenetrable secret that had opened itself at last. . . . *A power within me of enormous ken . . . To see as a god sees, and take the depth of things as nimbly as the outward eyes can size and shape pervade . . .* Yes, those very words from Keats, which I had quoted in the pages of my story that he had read.

But in a violent instant he had released me. "Too innocent," he whispered.

I went reeling across the bedroom floor and caught hold of the frame of the window. I rested my forehead against the stone wall.

There was a tingling pain in my throat where his lips had touched me that was almost pleasurable, a delicious throbbing that would not stop. I knew what he was!

I turned and saw all the room clearly—the bed, the fireplace, the chair. And he stood still exactly as I'd left him and there was the most appalling anguish in his face.

"Something of menace, unspeakable menace," I whispered, backing away.

"Something ancient, something that defies understanding," he pleaded. "Something that can and will go on." But he was shaken and he would not look into my eyes.

I touched that pulsing pain with the tips of my fingers and, looking down at them, saw the blood. "Vampire!" I gasped. "And yet you suffer so, and it is as if you can love!"

"Love? I have loved you since you came. I loved you when I read your secret thoughts and had not yet seen your face."

He drew me to him ever so gently, and slipping his arm around me, guided me to the door.

I tried for one desperate moment to resist him. And as any gentleman might, he stepped back respectfully and took my hand.

Through the long upstairs corridor we passed, and through a small wooden doorway to a screw stair that I had not seen before. I soon realized we were ascending in the north tower, a ruined portion of the structure that had been sealed off years before.

Through one tiny window after another I saw the gently rolling landscape and the small cluster of dim lights that marked the village of Rampling and the pale streak of white that was the London road.

Up and up we climbed, until we reached the topmost chamber, and this he opened with an iron key. He held back the door for me to enter and I found myself in a spacious room whose high, narrow windows contained no glass. A flood of moonlight revealed the most curious mixture of furnishings and objects—a writing-table, a great shelf of books, soft leather chairs, and scores of maps and framed pictures affixed to the walls. Candles all about had dripped their wax on every surface, and in the very midst of this chaos lay my poems, my old sketches—early writings that I had brought with me and never even unpacked.

I saw a black silk top hat and a walking stick, and a bouquet of withered flowers, dry as straw, and daguerreotypes and tintypes in their little velvet cases, and London newspapers and opened books.

There was no place for sleeping in this room.

And when I thought of that, where he must lie when he went to rest, a shudder passed over me and I felt, quite palpably, his lips touching my throat again, and I had the sudden urge to cry.

But he was holding me in his arms; he was kissing my cheeks and my lips ever so softly.

"My father knew what you were!" I whispered.

"Yes," he answered, "and his father before him. And all of them in an unbroken chain over the years. Out of loneliness or rage, I know not which, I always told them. I always made them acknowledge, accept."

I backed away and he didn't try to stop me. He lighted the candles about us one by one.

I was stunned by the sight of him in the light, the gleam in his large black eyes and the gloss of his hair. Not even in the railway station had I seen him so clearly as I did now, amid the radiance of the candles. He broke my heart.

And yet he looked at me as though I were a feast for his eyes, and he said my name again and I felt the blood rush to my face. But there seemed a great break suddenly in the passage of time. What had I been thinking! *Yes, never tell, never disturb . . . something ancient, something greater than good and evil . . .* But no! I felt dizzy again. I heard Father's voice: *Tear it down, Richard, stone by stone.*

He had drawn me to the window. And as the lights of Rampling were subtracted from the darkness below, a great wood stretched out in all directions, far older and denser than the forest of Rampling Gate. I was afraid suddenly, as if I were slipping into a maelstrom of visions from which I could never, of my own will, return.

There was that sense of our talking together, talking and talking in low, agitated voices, and I was saying that I should not give in.

"Bear witness—that is all I ask of you, Julie."

And there was in me some dim certainty that by these visions alone I would be fatally changed.

But the very room was losing its substance, as if a soundless wind of terrific force were blowing it apart. The vision had already begun . . .

We were riding horseback through a forest, he and I. And the trees were so high and so thick that scarcely any sun at all broke through to the fragrant, leaf-strewn ground.

Yet we had no time to linger in this magical place. We had come to the fresh-tilled earth that surrounded a village I somehow knew was called Knorwood, with its gabled roofs and its tiny, crooked streets. We saw the monastery of Knorwood and the little church with the bell chiming vespers under the lowering sky. A great, bustling life resided in Knorwood, a thousand voices rising in common prayer.

Far beyond, on the rise above the forest, stood the round tower of a truly ancient castle; and to that ruined castle—no more than a shell of itself anymore—as darkness fell in earnest we rode. Through its empty chambers we roamed, impetuous children, the horses and the road quite forgotten, and to the lord of the castle, a gaunt and white-skinned creature standing before the roaring fire of the roofless hall, we came. He turned and fixed us with his narrow and glittering eyes. A dead thing he was, I understood, but he carried within himself a priceless magic. And my companion, my innocent young man, stepped forward into the lord's arms.

I saw the kiss. I saw the young man grow pale and struggle and turn away, and the lord retreated with the wisest, saddest smile.

I understood. I knew. But the castle was dissolving as surely as anything in this dream might dissolve, and we were in some damp and close place.

The stench was unbearable to me; it was that most terrible of all stenches, the stench of death. And I heard my steps on the cobblestones and I reached out to steady myself against a wall. The tiny marketplace was deserted; the doors and windows gaped open to the vagrant wind. Up one side and down the other of the crooked street I saw the marks on the houses. And I knew what the marks meant. The Black Death had come to the village of Knorwood. The Black Death had laid it waste. And in a moment of suffocating horror I realized that no one, not a single person, was left alive.

But this was not quite true. There was a young man walking in fits and starts up the narrow alleyway. He was staggering, almost falling, as he pushed in one door after another, and at last came to a hot, reeking place where a child screamed on the floor. Mother and father lay dead in the bed. And the sleek fat cat of the household, unharmed, played with the screaming infant, whose eyes bulged in its tiny, sunken face.

"Stop it!" I heard myself gasp. I was holding my head with both hands. "Stop it—stop it, please!" I was screaming, and my screams would surely pierce the vision and this crude little dwelling would collapse around me and I would rouse the household of Rampling Gate, but I did not. The young man turned and stared at me, and in the close, stinking room I could not see his face.

But I knew it was he, my companion, and I could smell his fever and his sickness, and the stink of the dying infant, and see the gleaming body of the cat as it pawed at the child's outstretched hand.

"Stop it, you've lost control of it!" I screamed, surely with all my strength, but the infant screamed louder. "Make it stop."

"I cannot," he whispered. "It goes on forever! It will never stop!"

And with a great shriek I kicked at the cat and sent it flying out of the filthy room, overturning the milk pail as it went.

Death in all the houses of Knorwood. Death in the cloister, death in the open fields. It seemed the Judgment of God—I was sobbing, begging to be released—it seemed the very end of Creation itself.

But as night came down over the dead village he was alive still, stumbling up the slopes, through the forest, toward that tower where the lord stood at the broken arch of the window, waiting for him to come.

"Don't go!" I begged him. I ran alongside him, crying, but he didn't hear.

The lord turned and smiled with infinite sadness as the young man on his knees begged for salvation, when it was damnation this lord offered, when it was only damnation that the lord would give.

"Yes, damned, then, but living, breathing!" the young man cried, and the lord opened his arms.

The kiss again, the lethal kiss, the blood drawn out of his dying body, and then the lord lifting the heavy head of the young man so the youth could take the blood back again from the body of the lord himself.

I screamed, "Do not—do not drink!" He turned, and his face was now so perfectly the visage of death that I couldn't believe there was animation left in him; yet he asked: "What would you do? Would you go back to Knorwood, would you open those doors one after another, would you ring the bell in the empty church—and if you did, who would hear?"

He didn't wait for my answer. And I had none now to give. He locked his innocent mouth to the vein that pulsed with every semblance of life beneath the lord's cold and translucent flesh. And the blood jetted into the young body, vanquishing in one great burst the fever and the sickness that had wracked it, driving it out along with the mortal life.

He stood now in the hall of the lord alone. Immortality was his, and the blood thirst he would need to sustain it, and that thirst I could feel with my whole soul.

And each and every thing was transfigured in his vision—to the exquisite essence of itself. A wordless voice spoke from the starry veil of heaven; it sang in the wind that rushed through the broken timbers; it sighed in the flames that ate at the sooted stones of the hearth. It was the eternal rhythm of the universe that played beneath every surface as the last living creature in the village—that tiny child—fell silent in the maw of time.

A soft wind sifted and scattered the soil from the newly turned furrows in the empty fields. The rain fell from the black and endless sky.

Years and years passed. And all that had been Knorwood melted into the earth. The forest sent out its silent sentinels, and mighty trunks rose where there had been huts and houses, where there had been monastery walls. And it seemed the horror beyond all horrors that no one should know anymore of those who had lived and died in that small and insignificant village, that not anywhere in the great archives in which all history is recorded should a mention of Knorwood exist.

Yet one remained who knew, one who had witnessed, one who had seen the Ramplings come in the years that followed, seen them raise their house upon the very slope where the ancient castle had once stood, one who saw a new village collect itself slowly upon the unmarked grave of the old.

And all through the walls of Rampling Gate were the stones of that old castle, the stones of the forgotten monastery, the stones of that little church.

We were once again back in the tower.

"It is my shrine," he whispered. "My sanctuary. It is the only thing that endures as I endure. And you love it as I love it, Julie. You have written it . . . You love its grandeur. And its gloom."

"Yes, yes . . . as it's always been . . ." I was crying, though I didn't move my lips.

He had turned to me from the window, and I could feel his endless craving with all my heart.

"What else do you want from me!" I pleaded. "What else can I give?"

A torrent of images answered me. It was beginning again. I was once again relinquishing myself, yet in a great rush of lights and noise I was enlivened and made whole as I had been when we rode together through the forest, but it was into the world of now, this hour, that we passed.

We were flying through the rural darkness along the railway toward London, where the night-time city burst like an enormous bubble in a shower of laughter and motion and glaring light. He was walking with me under the gas lamps, his face all but shimmering with that same dark innocence, that same irresistible warmth. It seemed we were holding tight to each other in the very midst of a crowd. And the crowd was a living thing, a writhing thing, and everywhere there came a dark, rich aroma from it, the aroma of fresh blood. Women in white fur and gentlemen in opera capes swept through the brightly lighted doors of the theater; the blare of the music hall inundated us and then faded away. Only a thin soprano voice was left, singing a high, plaintive song. I was in his arms and his lips were covering mine, and there came that dull, zinging sensation again, that great, uncontrollable opening within myself. Thirst, and the promise of satiation measured only by the intensity of that thirst. Up back staircases we fled together, into high-ceilinged bedrooms papered in red damask, where the loveliest women reclined on brass beds, and the aroma was so strong now that I could not bear it and he said: "Drink. They are your victims! They will give you eternity—you must drink." And I felt the warmth filling me, charging me, blurring my vision until we broke free again, light and invisible, it seemed, as we moved over the rooftops and down again through rain-drenched streets. But the rain did not touch us; the falling snow did not chill us; we had within ourselves a great and indissoluble heat. And together in the carriage we talked to each other in low, exuberant rushes of language; we were lovers; we were constant; we were immortal. We were as enduring as Rampling Gate.

Oh, don't let it stop! I felt his arms around me and I knew we were in the tower room together, and the visions had worked their fatal alchemy.

"Do you understand what I am offering you? To your ancestors I revealed myself, yes; I subjugated them. But I would make you my bride, Julie. I would share with you my power. Come with me. I will not take you against your will, but can you turn away?"

Again I heard my own scream. My hands were on his cool white skin, and his lips were gentle yet hungry, his eyes yielding and ever young. Father's angry countenance blazed before me as if I, too, had the power to conjure. *Unspeakable horror*. I covered my face.

He stood against the backdrop of the window, against the distant drift of pale clouds. The candlelight glimmered in his eyes. Immense and sad and wise, they seemed—and oh, yes, innocent, as I have said again and again. "You are their fairest flower, Julie. To them I gave my protection always. To you I give my love. Come to me, dearest, and Rampling Gate will truly be yours, and it will finally, truly be mine."

*   *   *

Nights of argument, but finally Richard had come round. He would sign over Rampling Gate to me and I should absolutely refuse to allow the place to be torn down. There would be nothing he could do then to obey Father's command. I had given him the legal impediment he needed, and of course I told him I would leave the house to his male heirs. It should always be in Rampling hands.

A clever solution, it seemed to me, since Father had not told me to destroy the place. I had no scruples in the matter now at all.

And what remained was for him to take me to the little railway station and see me off for London, and not worry about my going home to Mayfair on my own.

"You stay here as long as you wish and do not worry," I said. I felt more tenderly toward him than I could ever express. "You knew as soon as you set foot in the place that Father was quite wrong."

The great black locomotive was chugging past us, the passenger cars slowing to a stop.

"Must go now, darling—kiss me," I said.

"But what came over you, Julie—what convinced you so quickly . . . ?"

"We've been through all that, Richard," I said. "What matters is that Rampling Gate is safe and we are both happy, my dear."

I waved until I couldn't see him any more. The flickering lamps of the town were lost in the deep lavender light of the early evening, and the dark hulk of Rampling Gate appeared for one uncertain moment like the ghost of itself on the nearby rise.

I sat back and closed my eyes. Then I opened them slowly, savoring this moment for which I had waited so long.

He was smiling, seated in the far corner of the leather seat opposite, as he had been all along, and now he rose with a swift, almost delicate movement and sat beside me and enfolded me in his arms.

"It's five hours to London," he whispered.

"I can wait," I said, feeling the thirst like a fever as I held tight to him, feeling his lips against my eyelids and my hair. "I want to hunt the London streets tonight," I confessed a little shyly, but I saw only approbation in his eyes.

"Beautiful Julie, my Julie . . ." he whispered.

"You'll love the house in Mayfair," I said.

"Yes . . ." he said.

"And when Richard finally tires of Rampling Gate, we shall go home."

Anne Rice

THE BALLAD OF THE SAD RAT

Anne Rice's vampire classic, *Interview with the Vampire*, was actually inspired by Carlos Castaneda's bestseller *The Teachings of Don Juan: A Yaqui Way of Knowledge*. Castaneda's book is about himself as an anthropologist becoming an apprentice to a Yaqui Indian sorcerer or shaman named Don Juan. Rice said, "I really fell into that book. I was enthralled with the writing and the simplicity of the descriptions and with his tremendous love for the figure of Don Juan as a teacher. That is definitely in *Interview with the Vampire*; the whole concept of Louis learning to be a vampire was influenced by Castaneda." When the movie version of *Interview with the Vampire* was being made, Anne wrote the following song lyrics, which she says you are to sing to the country music of your choice, though it is performed by the Los Angeles-based group Red Heaven and is on their CD. It was published in the first issue of her newsletter *Commotion Strange*. The newsletter is dated January 20, 1995, and the lyrics are dated November 18, 1994. It has this note: "Inspired by and dedicated to Media Mavens who go Bats over Rats."

one, two, three!!!

I'm a lowly rat
in a vampire movie
Oh, woe is me,
Who'll bite me first?

Will it be Tom,
So cute and curly?
Or pretty Brad
Who looks so hurt?

These hunks from hell
are all around me.
And how their fangs
Do make me squeak.

Sweet little Kirsten
won't even pet me
She just says Yuk,
Though she's very sweet.

Oh, thank you, Larry.
Liz Smith, I love you,
and dearest Oprah
how good thou art.

I'm a lowly rat
in a vampire movie
your tender words
do break my heart.

But don't you fret, folks
As you hear my story
We want no tears
On your velvet and lace!

I'm a HOLLYWOOD RAT
in a HOLLYWOOD MOVIE!
WHAT WOULDN'T YOU GIVE
TO TAKE MY PLACE?

Sting

MOON OVER BOURBON STREET

Sting (Gordon Sumner) is one of the most popular contemporary singers, songwriters, and musicians. He is also one of the most talented. These lyrics were inspired by Anne Rice's book *Interview with the Vampire*. The song originally appeared on the album *The Dream of the Blue Turtles* (1985). This was Sting's first solo album after leaving the rock group The Police.

There's a moon over Bourbon Street tonight
I see faces as they pass beneath the pale lamplight.
I've no choice but to follow that call
The bright lights, the people, and the moon and all.
I pray everyday to be strong,
For I know what I do must be wrong.

Oh, you'll never see my shade
Or hear the sound of my feet
While there's a moon
Over Bourbon Street.

It was many years ago that I became what I am.
I was trapped in this life like an innocent lamb.
Now I can never show my face at noon,
And you'll only see me walking by the light of the moon.

The brim of my hat hides the eye of a beast.
I've the face of a sinner but the hands of a priest.

> Oh, you'll never see my shade
> Or hear the sound of my feet
> While there's a moon
> Over Bourbon Street.

She walks every day through the streets of New Orleans.
She's innocent and young from a family of means.
I have stood many times outside her window at night
To struggle with my instinct in the pale moonlight.
How could I be this way when I pray to God above?
I must love what I destroy, and destroy the thing I love.

> Oh, you'll never see my shade
> Or hear the sound of my feet
> While there's a moon
> Over Bourbon Street.

Sir Arthur Conan Doyle

JOHN BARRINGTON COWLES

Scottish author Sir Arthur Conan Doyle is most famous as the creator of Sherlock Holmes. Doyle was a physician who began writing while he was trying to establish his medical practice. He was much more successful as a writer and finally abandoned his practice in 1891, though he took it up again briefly during the Boer War in South Africa. His works include *The Hound of the Baskervilles*, *A Study in Scarlet*, *The Sign of the Four*, and *The White Company*. In one of his Sherlock Holmes stories, "The Adventure of the Sussex Vampire," Holmes is called on to deal with a vampire. Predictably, his response is, "Rubbish, Watson, rubbish! What have we to do with walking corpses who can only be held in their grave by stakes driven through their hearts? It's pure lunacy." In the end, Holmes reveals another, more logical explanation for the behavior of the man falsely accused of being a vampire. This story, "John Barrington Cowles," has more of a supernatural element to it. It was one of Doyle's early stories. It first appeared in *Cassell's Saturday Journal* in April 1884, three years before his first Sherlock Holmes story. This and several of his other stories were published in an anthology titled *Dreamland and Ghostland* (1887), the first time Doyle's work appeared in book form. This story was actually inspired by *Elsie Venner*, a novel by Oliver Wendell Holmes. Holmes was Doyle's favorite author and he named Sherlock after him.

IT MIGHT SEEM RASH of me to say that I ascribe the death of my poor friend, John Barrington Cowles, to any preternatural agency.

25

I am aware that in the present state of public feeling a chain of evidence would require to be strong indeed before the possibility of such a conclusion could be admitted.

I shall therefore merely state the circumstances which led up to this sad event as concisely and as plainly as I can, and leave every reader to draw his own deductions. Perhaps there may be some one who can throw light upon what is dark to me.

I first met Barrington Cowles when I went up to Edinburgh University to take out medical classes there. My landlady in Northumberland Street had a large house, and, being a widow without children, she gained a livelihood by providing accommodation for several students.

Barrington Cowles happened to have taken a bedroom upon the same floor as mine, and when we came to know each other better we shared a small sitting-room, in which we took our meals. In this manner we originated a friendship which was unmarred by the slightest disagreement up to the day of his death.

Cowles' father was the colonel of a Sikh regiment and had remained in India for many years. He allowed his son a handsome income, but seldom gave any other sign of parental affection—writing irregularly and briefly.

My friend, who had himself been born in India, and whose whole disposition was an ardent tropical one, was much hurt by this neglect. His mother was dead, and he had no other relation in the world to supply the blank.

Thus he came in time to concentrate all his affection upon me, and to confide in me in a manner which is rare among men. Even when a stronger and deeper passion came upon him, it never infringed upon the old tenderness between us.

Cowles was a tall, slim young fellow, with an olive, Velasquez-like face, and dark, tender eyes. I have seldom seen a man who was more likely to excite a woman's interest, or to captivate her imagination. His expression was, as a rule, dreamy, and even languid; but if in conversation a subject arose which interested him he would be all animation in a moment. On such occasions his colour would heighten, his eyes gleam, and he could speak with an eloquence which would carry his audience with him.

In spite of these natural advantages he led a solitary life, avoiding female society, and reading with great diligence. He was one of the foremost men of his year, taking the senior medal for anatomy, and the Neil Arnott prize for physics.

How well I can recollect the first time we met her! Often and often I have recalled the circumstances, and tried to remember what the exact impression was which she produced on my mind at the time. After we came to know her my judgement was warped, so that I am curious to recollect what my unbiased instincts were. It is hard, however, to eliminate the feelings which reason or prejudice afterwards raised in me.

It was at the opening of the Royal Scottish Academy in the spring of 1879. My poor friend was passionately attached to art in every form, and a pleasing chord in music or a delicate effect upon canvas would give exquisite pleasure to his highly-strung nature. We had gone together to see the pictures, and were standing in the grand central *salon*, when I noticed an extremely beautiful woman standing at the other side of the room. In my whole life I have never seen such a classically perfect countenance. It was the real Greek type—the forehead broad, very low, and as white as marble, with a cloudlet of delicate locks wreathing round it, the nose straight and clean cut, the lips inclined to thinness, the chin and lower jaw beautifully rounded off, and yet sufficiently developed to promise unusual strength of character.

But those eyes—those wonderful eyes! If I could but give some faint idea of their varying moods, their steely hardness, their feminine softness, their power of command, their penetrating intensity suddenly melting away into an expression of womanly weakness—but I am speaking now of future impressions!

There was a tall, yellow-haired young man with this lady, whom I at once recognised as a law student with whom I had a slight acquaintance.

Archibald Reeves—for that was his name—was a dashing, handsome young fellow, and had at one time been a ringleader in every university escapade; but of late I had seen little of him, and the report was that he was engaged to be married. His companion was, then, I presumed, his *fiancée*. I seated myself upon the velvet settee in the centre of the room, and furtively watched the couple from behind my catalogue.

The more I looked at her the more her beauty grew upon me. She was somewhat short in stature, it is true; but her figure was perfection, and she bore herself in such a fashion that it was only by actual comparison that one would have known her to be under the medium height.

As I kept my eyes upon them, Reeves was called away for some reason, and the young lady was left alone. Turning her back to the pictures, she passed the time until the return of her escort in taking a deliberate survey of the company, without paying the least heed to the fact that a dozen pair of eyes, attracted by her elegance and beauty, were bent curiously upon her. With one of her hands holding the red silk cord which railed off the pictures, she stood languidly moving her eyes from face to face with as little self-consciousness as if she were looking at the canvas creatures behind her. Suddenly, as I watched her, I saw her gaze become fixed, and, as it were, intense. I followed the direction of her looks, wondering what could have attracted her so strongly.

John Barrington Cowles was standing before a picture—one, I think, by Noel Paton—I know that the subject was a noble and ethereal one. His profile was turned towards us, and never have I seen him to such advantage. I have said that he was a strikingly handsome man, but at that moment he looked absolutely magnificent. It was evident that he had momentarily forgotten his surroundings, and that his whole soul was in sympathy with the picture before him. His eyes sparkled, and a dusky pink shone through his clear olive cheeks. She continued to watch him fixedly, with a look of interest upon her face, until he came out of his reverie with a start, and turned abruptly round, so that his gaze met hers. She glanced away at once, but his eyes remained fixed upon her for some moments. The picture was forgotten already, and his soul had come down to earth once more.

We caught sight of her once or twice before we left, and each time I noticed my friend look after her. He made no remark, however, until we got out into the open air, and were walking arm-in-arm along Princes Street.

"Did you notice that beautiful woman, in the dark dress, with the white fur?" he asked.

"Yes, I saw her," I answered.

"Do you know her?" he asked eagerly. "Have you any idea who she is?"

"I don't know her personally," I replied. "But I have no doubt

I could find out all about her, for I believe she is engaged to young Archie Reeves, and he and I have a lot of mutual friends.''

''Engaged!'' ejaculated Cowles.

''Why, my dear boy,'' I said, laughing, ''you don't mean to say you are so susceptible that the fact that a girl to whom you never spoke in your life is engaged is enough to upset you?''

''Well, not exactly to upset me,'' he answered, forcing a laugh. ''But I don't mind telling you, Armitage, that I never was so taken by any one in my life. It wasn't the mere beauty of the face— though that was perfect enough—but it was the character and the intellect upon it. I hope if she is engaged, that it is to some man who will be worthy of her.''

''Why,'' I remarked, ''you speak quite feelingly. It is a clear case of love at first sight, Jack. However, to put your perturbed spirit at rest, I'll make a point of finding out all about her whenever I meet any fellow who is likely to know.''

Barrington Cowles thanked me, and the conversation drifted off into other channels. For several days neither of us made any allusion to the subject, though my companion was perhaps a little more dreamy and distraught than usual. The incident had almost vanished from my remembrance, when one day young Brodie, who is a second cousin of mine, came up to me on the university steps with the face of a bearer of tidings.

''I say,'' he began, ''you know Reeves, don't you?''

''Yes. What of him?''

''His engagement is off.''

''Off!'' I cried. ''Why, I only learned the other day that it was on.''

''Oh, yes—it's all off. His brother told me so. Deucedly mean of Reeves, you know, if he has backed out of it, for she was an uncommonly nice girl.''

''I've seen her,'' I said; ''but I don't know her name.''

''She is a Miss Northcott, and lives with an old aunt of hers in Abercrombie Place. Nobody knows anything about her people, or where she comes from. Anyhow, she is about the most unlucky girl in the world, poor soul!''

''Why unlucky?''

''Well, you know, this was her second engagement,'' said young Brodie, who had a marvellous knack of knowing everything about everybody. ''She was engaged to Prescott—William Prescott, who died. That was a very sad affair. The wedding day was fixed, and the whole thing looked as straight as a die when the smash came."

"What smash?" I asked, with some dim recollection of the circumstances.

"Why, Prescott's death. He came to Abercrombie Place one night, and stayed very late. No one knows exactly when he left, but about one in the morning a fellow who knew him met him walking rapidly in the direction of the Queen's Park. He bade him good night, but Prescott hurried on without heeding him, and that was the last time he was ever seen alive. Three days afterwards his body was found floating in St. Margaret's Loch, under St. Anthony's Chapel. No one could ever understand it, but of course the verdict brought it in as temporary insanity."

"It was very strange," I remarked.

"Yes, and deucedly rough on the poor girl," said Brodie. "Now that this other blow has come it will quite crush her. So gentle and ladylike she is, too!"

"You know her personally, then!" I asked.

"Oh, yes, I know her. I have met her several times. I could easily manage that you should be introduced to her."

"Well," I answered, "it's not so much for my own sake as for a friend of mine. However, I don't suppose she will go out much for some little time after this. When she does I will take advantage of your offer."

We shook hands on this, and I thought no more of the matter for some time.

The next incident which I have to relate as bearing at all upon the question of Miss Northcott is an unpleasant one. Yet I must detail it as accurately as possible, since it may throw some light upon the sequel. One cold night, several months after the conversation with my second cousin which I have quoted above, I was walking down one of the lowest streets in the city on my way back from a case which I had been attending. It was very late, and I was picking my way among the dirty loungers who were clustering round the doors of a great gin-palace, when a man staggered out from among them, and held out his hand to me with a drunken leer. The gaslight fell full upon his face, and, to my intense astonishment, I recognised in the degraded creature before me my former acquaintance, young Archibald Reeves, who had once been famous as one of the most dressy and particular men in the whole college. I was so utterly surprised that for a moment I almost doubted the evidence of my own senses; but there was no mistaking those features, which, though bloated with drink, still retained something of their former comeliness. I was determined to rescue him, for one night at least, from the company into which he had fallen.

"Holloa, Reeves!" I said. "Come along with me. I'm going in your direction."

He muttered some incoherent apology for his condition, and took my arm. As I supported him towards his lodgings I could see that he was not only suffering from the effects of a recent debauch, but that a long course of intemperance had affected his nerves and his brain. His hand when I touched it was dry and feverish, and he started from every shadow which fell upon the pavement. He rambled in his speech, too, in a manner which suggested the delirium of disease rather than the talk of a drunkard.

When I got him to his lodgings I partially undressed him and laid him upon his bed. His pulse at this time was very high, and he was evidently extremely feverish. He seemed to have sunk into a doze; and I was about to steal out of the room to warn his landlady of his condition, when he started up and caught me by the sleeve of my coat.

"Don't go!" he cried. "I feel better when you are here. I am safe from her then."

"From her!" I said. "From whom?"

"Her! her!" he answered peevishly. "Ah! you don't know her. She is the devil! Beautiful—beautiful; but the devil!"

"You are feverish and excited," I said. "Try and get a little sleep. You will wake better."

"Sleep!" he groaned. "How am I to sleep when I see her sitting down yonder at the foot of the bed with her great eyes watching and watching hour after hour? I tell you it saps all the strength and manhood out of me. That's what makes me drink. God help me—I'm half drunk now!"

"You are very ill," I said, putting some vinegar to his temples; "and you are delirious. You don't know what you say."

"Yes, I do," he interrupted sharply, looking up at me. "I know very well what I say. I brought it upon myself. It is my own choice.

But I couldn't—no, by heaven, I couldn't—accept the alternative.
I couldn't keep my faith to her. It was more than man could do.''

I sat by the side of the bed, holding one of his burning hands in
mine, and wondering over his strange words. He lay still for sometime, and then, raising his eyes to me, said in a most plaintive voice—

"Why did she not give me warning sooner? Why did she wait
until I had learned to love her so?''

He repeated this question several times, rolling his feverish head
from side to side, and then he dropped into a troubled sleep. I
crept out of the room, and, having seen that he would be properly
cared for, left the house. His words, however, rang in my ears for
days afterwards, and assumed a deeper significance when taken
with what was to come.

My friend, Barrington Cowles, had been away for his summer
holidays, and I had heard nothing of him for several months.
When the winter session came on, however, I received a telegram
from him, asking me to secure the old rooms in Northumberland
Street for him, and telling me the train by which he would arrive.
I went down to meet him, and was delighted to find him looking
wonderfully hearty and well.

"By the way,'' he said suddenly, that night, as we sat in our
chairs by the fire, talking over the events of the holidays, "you
have never congratulated me yet!''

"On what, my boy?'' I asked.

"What! Do you mean to say you have not heard of my engagement?''

"Engagement! No!'' I answered. "However, I am delighted to
hear it, and congratulate you with all my heart.''

"I wonder it didn't come to your ears,'' he said. "It was the
queerest thing. You remember that girl whom we both admired
so much at the Academy?''

"What!'' I cried, with a vague feeling of apprehension at my
heart. "You don't mean to say that you are engaged to her?''

"I thought you would be surprised,'' he answered. "When I was
staying with an old aunt of mine in Peterhead, in Aberdeenshire,
the Northcotts happened to come there on a visit, and as we had
mutual friends we soon met. I found out that it was a false alarm
about her being engaged, and then—well, you know what it is
when you are thrown into the society of such a girl in a place like

Peterhead. Not, mind you," he added, "that I consider I did a foolish or hasty thing. I have never regretted it for a moment. The more I know Kate the more I admire her and love her. However, you must be introduced to her, and then you will form your own opinion."

I expressed my pleasure at the prospect, and endeavoured to speak as lightly as I could to Cowles upon the subject, but I felt depressed and anxious at heart. The words of Reeves and the unhappy fate of young Prescott recurred to my recollection, and though I could assign no tangible reason for it, a vague, dim fear and distrust of the woman took possession of me. It may be that this was foolish prejudice and superstition upon my part, and that I involuntarily contorted her future doings and sayings to fit into some half-formed wild theory of my own. This has been suggested to me by others as an explanation of my narrative. They are welcome to their opinion if they can reconcile it with the facts which I have to tell.

I went round with my friend a few days afterwards to call upon Miss Northcott. I remember that, as we went down Abercrombie Place, our attention was attracted by the shrill yelping of a dog— which noise proved eventually to come from the house to which we were bound. We were shown upstairs, where I was introduced to old Mrs. Merton, Miss Northcott's aunt, and to the young lady herself. She looked as beautiful as ever, and I could not wonder at my friend's infatuation. Her face was a little more flushed than usual, and she held in her hand a heavy dog-whip, with which she had been chastising a small Scotch terrier, whose cries we had heard in the street. The poor brute was cringing up against the wall, whining piteously, and evidently completely cowed.

"So Kate," said my friend, after we had taken our seats, "you have been falling out with Carlo again."

"Only a very little quarrel this time," she said, smiling charmingly. "He is a dear, good old fellow, but he needs correction now and then." Then, turning to me, "We all do that, Mr. Armitage, don't we? What a capital thing if, instead of receiving a collective punishment at the end of our lives, we were to have one at once, as the dogs do, when we did anything wicked. It would make us more careful, wouldn't it?"

I acknowledged that it would.

"Supposing that every time a man misbehaved himself a gigantic hand were to seize him, and he were lashed with a whip until he fainted"—she clenched her white fingers as she spoke, and cut out viciously with the dog-whip—"it would do more to keep him good than any number of high-minded theories of morality."

"Why, Kate," said my friend, "you are quite savage to-day."

"No, Jack," she laughed. "I'm only propounding a theory for Mr. Armitage's consideration."

The two began to chat together about some Aberdeenshire reminiscence, and I had time to observe Mrs. Merton, who had remained silent during our short conversation. She was a very strange-looking old lady. What attracted attention most in her appearance was the utter want of colour which she exhibited. Her hair was snow-white, and her face extremely pale. Her lips were bloodless, and even her eyes were of such a light tinge of blue that they hardly relieved the general pallor. Her dress was a grey silk, which harmonised with her general appearance. She had a peculiar expression of countenance, which I was unable at the moment to refer to its proper cause.

She was working at some old-fashioned piece of ornamental needlework, and as she moved her arms her dress gave forth a dry, melancholy rustling, like the sound of leaves in the autumn. There was something mournful and depressing in the sight of her. I moved my chair a little nearer, and asked her how she liked Edinburgh, and whether she had been there long.

When I spoke to her she started and looked up at me with a scared look on her face. Then I saw in a moment what the expression was which I had observed there. It was one of fear—intense and overpowering fear. It was so marked that I could have staked my life on the woman before me having at some period of her life been subjected to some terrible experience or dreadful misfortune.

"Oh, yes, I like it," she said, in a soft, timid voice; "and we have been here long—that is, not very long. We move about a great deal." She spoke with hesitation, as if afraid of committing herself.

"You are a native of Scotland, I presume?" I said.

"No—that is, not entirely. We are not natives of any place. We are cosmopolitan, you know." She glanced round in the direction of Miss Northcott as she spoke, but the two were still chatting together near the window. Then she suddenly bent forward to me, with a look of intense earnestness upon her face, and said—

"Don't talk to me any more, please. She does not like it, and I shall suffer for it afterwards. Please, don't do it."

I was about to ask her the reason for this strange request, but when she saw I was going to address her, she rose and walked slowly out of the room. As she did so I perceived that the lovers had ceased to talk, and that Miss Northcott was looking at me with her keen, grey eyes.

"You must excuse my aunt, Mr. Armitage," she said; "she is old, and easily fatigued. Come over and look at my album."

We spent some time examining the portraits. Miss Northcott's father and mother were apparently ordinary mortals enough, and I could not detect in either of them any traces of the character which showed itself in their daughter's face. There was one old daguerreotype, however, which arrested my attention. It represented a man of about the age of forty, and strikingly handsome. He was clean shaven, and extraordinary power was expressed upon his prominent lower jaw and firm, straight mouth. His eyes were somewhat deeply set in his head, however, and there was a snake-like flattening at the upper part of his forehead, which detracted from his appearance. I almost involuntarily, when I saw the head, pointed to it, and exclaimed—

"There is your prototype in your family, Miss Northcott."

"Do you think so?" she said. "I am afraid you are paying me a very bad compliment. Uncle Anthony was always considered the black sheep of the family."

"Indeed," I answered; "my remark was an unfortunate one, then."

"Oh, don't mind that," she said; "I always thought myself that he was worth all of them put together. He was an officer in the Forty-first Regiment, and he was killed in action during the Persian War—so he died nobly, at any rate."

"That's the sort of death I should like to die," said Cowles, his dark eyes flashing, as they would when he was excited; "I often wish I had taken to my father's profession instead of this vile pill compounding drudgery."

"Come, Jack, you are not going to die any sort of death yet," she said, tenderly taking his hand in hers.

I could not understand the woman. There was such an extraordinary mixture of masculine decision and womanly tenderness
about her, with the consciousness of something all her own in the
background, that she fairly puzzled me. I hardly knew, therefore,
how to answer Cowles when, as we walked down the street together, he asked the comprehensive question—

"Well, what do you think of her?"

"I think she is wonderfully beautiful," I answered guardedly.

"That, of course," he replied irritably. "You knew that before
you came!"

"I think she is very clever too," I remarked.

Barrington Cowles walked on for some time, and then he suddenly turned on me with the strange question—

"Do you think she is cruel? Do you think she is the sort of girl
who would take a pleasure in inflicting pain?"

"Well, really," I answered, "I have hardly had time to form an
opinion."

We then walked on for some time in silence.

"She is an old fool," at length muttered Cowles. "She is mad."

"Who is?" I asked.

"Why, that old woman—that aunt of Kate's—Mrs. Merton, or
whatever her name is."

Then I knew that my poor colourless friend had been speaking
to Cowles, but he never said anything more as to the nature of
her communication.

My companion went to bed early that night, and I sat up a long
time by the fire, thinking over all that I had seen and heard. I felt
that there was some mystery about the girl—some dark fatality
so strange as to defy conjecture. I thought of Prescott's interview
with her before their marriage, and the fatal termination of it. I
coupled it with poor drunken Reeves' plaintive cry, "Why did she
not tell me sooner?" and with the other words he had spoken.
Then my mind ran over Mrs. Merton's warning to me, Cowles'
reference to her, and even the episode of the whip and the cringing dog.

The whole effect of my recollections was unpleasant to a degree,
and yet there was no tangible charge which I could bring against
the woman. It would be worse than useless to attempt to warn
my friend until I had definitely made up my mind what I was to

warn him against. He would treat any charge against her with scorn. What could I do? How could I get at some tangible conclusion as to her character and antecedents? No one in Edinburgh knew them except as recent acquaintances. She was an orphan, and as far as I knew she had never disclosed where her former home had been. Suddenly an idea struck me. Among my father's friends there was a Colonel Joyce, who had served a long time in India upon the staff, and who would be likely to know most of the officers who had been out there since the Mutiny. I sat down at once, and, having trimmed the lamp, proceeded to write a letter to the Colonel. I told him that I was very curious to gain some particulars about a certain Captain Northcott, who had served in the Forty-first Foot, and who had fallen in the Persian War. I described the man as well as I could from my recollection of the daguerreotype, and then, having directed the letter, posted it that very night, after which, feeling that I had done all that could be done, I retired to bed, with a mind too anxious to allow me to sleep.

PART II

I got an answer from Leicester, where the Colonel resided, within two days. I have it before me as I write, and copy it verbatim.

"DEAR BOB," it said, "I remember the man well. I was with him at Calcutta, and afterwards at Hyderabad. He was a curious, solitary sort of mortal; but a gallant soldier enough, for he distinguished himself at Sobraon and was wounded, if I remember right. He was not popular in his corps—they said he was a pitiless, cold-blooded fellow, with no geniality in him. There was a rumour, too, that he was a devil-worshipper, or something of that sort, and also that he had the evil eye, which, of course, was all nonsense. He had some strange theories I remember, about the power of the human will and the effects of mind upon matter.

How are you getting on with your medical studies? Never forget, my boy, that your father's son has every claim upon

me, and that if I can serve you in any way I am always at
your command.—Ever affectionately yours,

Edward Joyce

''*P.S.*—By the way, Northcott did not fall in action. He was
killed after peace was declared in a crazy attempt to get some
of the eternal fire from the sunworshippers' temple. There
was considerable mystery about his death.''

I read this epistle over several times—at first with a feeling of
satisfaction, and then with one of disappointment. I had come on
some curious information, and yet hardly what I wanted. He was
an eccentric man, a devil-worshipper, and rumoured to have the
power of the evil eye. I could believe the young lady's eyes, when
endowed with that cold, grey shimmer which I had noticed in
them once or twice, to be capable of any evil which human eye
ever wrought; but still the superstition was an effete one. Was
there not more meaning in that sentence which followed—''He
had theories of the power of the human will and of the effect of
mind upon matter''? I remember having once read a quaint treatise, which I had imagined to be mere charlatanism at the time,
of the power of certain human minds, and of effects produced by
them at a distance. Was Miss Northcott endowed with some exceptional power of the sort? The idea grew upon me, and very
shortly I had evidence which convinced me of the truth of the
supposition.

It happened that at the very time when my mind was dwelling
upon this subject, I saw a notice in the paper that our town was
to be visited by Dr. Messinger, the well-known medium and mesmerist. Messinger was a man whose performance, such as it was,
had been again and again pronounced to be genuine by compe-
tent judges. He was far above trickery, and had the reputation of
being the soundest living authority upon the strange pseudo-
sciences of animal magnetism and electro-biology. Determined,
therefore, to see what the human will could do, even against all
the disadvantages of glaring footlights and a public platform, I took
a ticket for the first night of the performance, and went with several student friends.

We had secured one of the side boxes, and did not arrive until after the performance had begun. I had hardly taken my seat before I recognised Barrington Cowles, with his *fiancée* and old Mrs. Merton, sitting in the third or fourth row of the stalls. They caught sight of me at almost the same moment, and we bowed to each other. The first portion of the lecture was somewhat commonplace, the lecturer giving tricks of pure legerdemain, with one or two manifestations of mesmerism, performed upon a subject whom he had brought with him. He gave us an exhibition of clairvoyance too, throwing his subject into a trance, and then demanding particulars as to the movements of absent friends, and the whereabouts of hidden objects, all of which appeared to be answered satisfactorily. I had seen all this before, however. What I wanted to see now was the effect of the lecturer's will when exerted upon some independent member of the audience.

He came round to that as the concluding exhibition in his performance. "I have shown you," he said, "that a mesmerised subject is entirely dominated by the will of the mesmeriser. He loses all power of volition, and his very thoughts are such as are suggested to him by the master-mind. The same end may be attained without any preliminary process. A strong will can, simply by virtue of its strength, take possession of a weaker one, even at a distance, and can regulate the impulses and the actions of the owner of it. If there was one man in the world who had a very much more highly-developed will than any of the rest of the human family, there is no reason why he should not be able to rule over them all, and to reduce his fellow-creatures to the condition of automatons. Happily there is such a dead level of mental power, or rather of mental weakness, among us that such a catastrophe is not likely to occur; but still within our small compass there are variations which produce surprising effects. I shall now single out one of the audience, and endeavour 'by the mere power of will' to compel him to come upon the platform, and do and say what I wish. Let me assure you that there is no collusion, and that the subject whom I may select is at perfect liberty to resent to the uttermost any impulse which I may communicate to him."

With these words the lecturer came to the front of the platform, and glanced over the first few rows of the stalls. No doubt Cowles' dark skin and bright eyes marked him out as a man of a highly nervous temperament, for the mesmerist picked him out in a moment, and fixed his eyes upon him. I saw my friend give a start of surprise, and then settle down in his chair, as if to express his determination not to yield to the influence of the operator. Messinger was not a man whose head denoted any great brain-power, but his gaze was singularly intense and penetrating. Under the influence of it Cowles made one or two spasmodic motions of his hands, as if to grasp the sides of his seat, and then half rose, but only to sink down again, though with an evident effort. I was watching the scene with intense interest, when I happened to catch a glimpse of Miss Northcott's face. She was sitting with her eyes fixed intently upon the mesmerist, and with such an expression of concentrated power upon her features as I have never seen on any other human countenance. Her jaw was firmly set, her lips compressed, and her face as hard as if it were a beautiful sculpture cut out of the whitest marble. Her eyebrows were drawn down, however, and from beneath them her grey eyes seemed to sparkle and gleam with a cold light.

I looked at Cowles again, expecting every moment to see him rise and obey the mesmerist's wishes, when there came from the platform a short, gasping cry as of a man utterly worn out and prostrated by a prolonged struggle. Messinger was leaning against the table, his hand to his forehead, and the perspiration pouring down his face. "I won't go on," he cried, addressing the audience. "There is a stronger will than mine acting against me. You must excuse me for to-night." The man was evidently ill, and utterly unable to proceed, so the curtain was lowered, and the audience dispersed, with many comments upon the lecturer's sudden indisposition.

I waited outside the hall until my friend and the ladies came out. Cowles was laughing over his recent experience.

"He didn't succeed with me, Bob," he cried triumphantly, as he shook my hand. "I think he caught a Tartar that time."

"Yes," said Miss Northcott, "I think that Jack ought to be very proud of his strength of mind; don't you, Mr. Armitage?"

"It took me all my time, though," my friend said seriously. "You can't conceive what a strange feeling I had once or twice. All the strength seemed to have gone out of me—especially just before he collapsed himself."

I walked round with Cowles in order to see the ladies home.

He walked in front with Mrs. Merton, and I found myself behind with the young lady. For a minute or so I walked beside her without making any remark, and then I suddenly blurted out, in a manner which must have seemed somewhat brusque to her—

"You did that, Miss Northcott."

"Did what?" she asked sharply.

"Why, mesmerised the mesmeriser—I suppose that is the best way of describing the transaction."

"What a strange idea!" she said, laughing. "You give me credit for a strong will then?"

"Yes," I said. "For a dangerously strong one."

"Why dangerous?" she asked, in a tone of surprise.

"I think," I answered, "that any will which can exercise such power is dangerous—for there is always a chance of its being turned to bad uses."

"You would make me out a very dreadful individual Mr. Armitage," she said; and then looking up suddenly in my face—"You have never liked me. You are suspicious of me and distrust me, though I have never given you cause."

The accusation was so sudden and so true that I was unable to find any reply to it. She paused for a moment, and then said in a voice which was hard and cold—

"Don't let your prejudice lead you to interfere with me, however, or say anything to your friend, Mr. Cowles, which might lead to a difference between us. You would find that to be very bad policy."

There was something in the way she spoke which gave an indescribable air of a threat to these few words.

"I have no power," I said, "to interfere with your plans for the future. I cannot help, however, from what I have seen and heard, having fears for my friend."

"Fears!" she repeated scornfully. "Pray what have you seen and heard. Something from Mr. Reeves, perhaps—I believe he is another of your friends?"

"He never mentioned your name to me," I answered, truthfully enough. "You will be sorry to hear that he is dying." As I said it we passed by a lighted window, and I glanced down to see what effect my words had upon her. She was laughing—there was no doubt of it; she was laughing quietly to herself. I could see merriment in every feature of her face. I feared and mistrusted the woman from that moment more than ever.

We said little more that night. When we parted she gave me a quick, warning glance, as if to remind me of what she had said about the danger of interference. Her cautions would have made little difference to me could I have seen my way to benefiting Barrington Cowles by anything which I might say. But what could I say?

I might say that her former suitors had been unfortunate. I might say that I believed her to be a cruel-hearted woman. I might say that I considered her to possess wonderful, and almost preternatural powers. What impression would any of these accusations make upon an ardent lover—a man with my friend's enthusiastic temperament? I felt that it would be useless to advance them, so I was silent.

And now I come to the beginning of the end. Hitherto much has been surmise and inference and hearsay. It is my painful task to relate now, as dispassionately and as accurately as I can, what actually occurred under my own notice, and to reduce to writing the events which preceded the death of my friend.

Towards the end of the winter Cowles remarked to me that he intended to marry Miss Northcott as soon as possible—probably some time in the spring. He was, as I have already remarked, fairly well off, and the young lady had some money of her own, so that there was no pecuniary reason for a long engagement. "We are going to take a little house out at Corstorphine," he said, "and we hope to see your face at our table, Bob, as often as you can possibly come." I thanked him, and tried to shake off my apprehensions, and persuade myself that all would yet be well.

It was about three weeks before the time fixed for the marriage, that Cowles remarked to me one evening that he feared he would be late that night. "I have had a note from Kate," he said, "asking me to call about eleven o'clock to-night, which seems rather a late hour, but perhaps she wants to talk over something quietly after old Mrs. Merton retires."

It was not until after my friend's departure that I suddenly recollected the mysterious interview which I had been told of as preceding the suicide of young Prescott. Then I thought of the ravings of poor Reeves, rendered more tragic by the fact that I had heard that very day of his death. What was the meaning of it all? Had this woman some baleful secret to disclose which must be known before her marriage? Was it some reason which forbade her to marry? Or was it some reason which forbade others to marry her? I felt so uneasy that I would have followed Cowles, even at the risk of offending him, and endeavoured to dissuade him from keeping his appointment, but a glance at the clock showed me that I was too late.

I was determined to wait up for his return, so I piled some coals upon the fire and took down a novel from the shelf. My thoughts proved more interesting than the book, however, and I threw it on one side. An indefinable feeling of anxiety and depression weighed upon me. Twelve o'clock came, and then half-past, without any sign of my friend. It was nearly one when I heard a step in the street outside, and then a knocking at the door. I was surprised, as I knew that my friend always carried a key—however, I hurried down and undid the latch. As the door flew open I knew in a moment that my worst apprehensions had been fulfilled. Barrington Cowles was leaning against the railings outside with his face sunk upon his breast, and his whole attitude expressive of the most intense despondency. As he passed in he gave a stagger, and would have fallen had I not thrown my left arm around him. Supporting him with this, and holding the lamp in my other hand, I led him slowly upstairs into our sitting-room. He sank down upon the sofa without a word. Now that I could get a good view of him, I was horrified to see the change which had come over him. His face was deadly pale, and his very lips were bloodless. His cheeks and forehead were clammy, his eyes glazed, and his whole expression altered. He looked like a man who had gone through some terrible ordeal, and was thoroughly unnerved.

"My dear fellow, what is the matter?" I asked, breaking the silence. "Nothing amiss, I trust? Are you unwell?"

"Brandy!" he gasped. "Give me some brandy!"

I took out the decanter, and was about to help him, when he snatched it from me with a trembling hand, and poured out nearly half a tumbler of the spirit. He was usually a most abstemious man, but he took this off at a gulp without adding any water to it. It seemed to do him good, for the colour began to come back to his face, and he leaned upon his elbow.

"My engagement is off, Bob," he said, trying to speak calmly, but with a tremor in his voice which he could not conceal. "It is all over."

"Cheer up!" I answered, trying to encourage him. "Don't get down on your luck. How was it? What was it all about?"

"About?" he groaned, covering his face with his hands. "If I did tell you, Bob, you would not believe it. It is too dreadful—too horrible—unutterably awful and incredible! O Kate, Kate!" and he rocked himself to and fro in his grief; "I pictured you an angel and I find you a—"

"A what?" I asked, for he had paused.

He looked at me with a vacant stare, and then suddenly burst out, waving his arms: "A fiend!" he cried. "A ghoul from the pit! A vampire soul behind a lovely face! Now, God forgive me!" he went on in a lower tone, turning his face to the wall; "I have said more than I should. I have loved her too much to speak of her as she is. I love her too much now."

He lay still for some time, and I had hoped that the brandy had had the effect of sending him to sleep, when he suddenly turned his face towards me.

"Did you ever read of wehr-wolves?" he asked.

I answered that I had.

"There is a story," he said thoughtfully, "in one of Marryat's books, about a beautiful woman who took the form of a wolf at night and devoured her own children. I wonder what put that idea into Marryat's head?"

He pondered for some minutes, and then he cried out for some more brandy. There was a small bottle of laudanum upon the table, and I managed, by insisting upon helping him myself, to mix about half a drachm with the spirits. He drank it off, and sank his head once more upon the pillow. "Anything better than that," he groaned. "Death is better than that. Crime and cruelty; cruelty and crime. Anything is better than that," and so on, with the monotonous refrain, until at last the words became indistinct, his eyelids closed over his weary eyes, and he sank into a profound slumber. I carried him into his bedroom without arousing him; and making a couch for myself out of the chairs, I remained by his side all night.

In the morning Barrington Cowles was in a high fever. For

weeks he lingered between life and death. The highest medical skill of Edinburgh was called in, and his vigorous constitution slowly got the better of his disease. I nursed him during this anxious time; but through all his wild delirium and ravings he never let a word escape him which explained the mystery connected with Miss Northcott. Sometimes he spoke of her in the tenderest words and most loving voice. At others he screamed out that she was a fiend, and stretched out his arms, as if to keep her off. Several times he cried that he would not sell his soul for a beautiful face, and then he would moan in a most piteous voice, "But I love her—I love her for all that; I shall never cease to love her."

When he came to himself he was an altered man. His severe illness had emaciated him greatly, but his dark eyes had lost none of their brightness. They shone out with startling brilliancy from under his dark, overhanging brows. His manner was eccentric and variable—sometimes irritable, sometimes recklessly mirthful, but never natural. He would glance about him in a strange, suspicious manner, like one who feared something, and yet hardly knew what it was he dreaded. He never mentioned Miss Northcott's name—never until that fatal evening of which I have now to speak.

In an endeavour to break the current of his thoughts by frequent change of scene, I travelled with him through the highlands of Scotland, and afterwards down the east coast. In one of these peregrinations of ours we visited the Isle of May, an island near the mouth of the Firth of Forth, which, except in the tourist season, is singularly barren and desolate. Beyond the keeper of the lighthouse there are only one or two families of poor fisher-folk, who sustain a precarious existence by their nets, and by the capture of cormorants and solan geese. This grim spot seemed to have such a fascination for Cowles that we engaged a room in one of the fishermen's huts, with the intention of passing a week or two there. I found it very dull, but the loneliness appeared to be a relief to my friend's mind. He lost the look of apprehension which had become habitual to him, and became something like his old self. He would wander round the island all day, looking down from the summit of the great cliffs which gird it round, and watching the long green waves as they came booming in and burst in a shower of spray over the rocks beneath.

One night—I think it was our third or fourth on the island—
Barrington Cowles and I went outside the cottage before retiring
to rest, to enjoy a little fresh air, for our room was small, and the
rough lamp caused an unpleasant odour. How well I remember
every little circumstance in connection with that night! It promised to be tempestuous, for the clouds were piling up in the north-
west, and the dark wrack was drifting across the face of the moon,
throwing alternate belts of light and shade upon the rugged surface of the island and the restless sea beyond.

We were standing talking close by the door of the cottage, and
I was thinking to myself that my friend was more cheerful than
he had been since his illness, when he gave a sudden, sharp cry,
and looking round at him I saw, by the light of the moon, an
expression of unutterable horror come over his features. His eyes
became fixed and staring, as if riveted upon some approaching
object, and he extended his long thin forefinger, which quivered
as he pointed.

"Look there!" he cried. "It is she! It is she! You see her there
coming down the side of the brae." He gripped me convulsively
by the wrist as he spoke. "There she is, coming towards us!"

"Who?" I cried, straining my eyes into the darkness.

"She—Kate—Kate Northcott!" he screamed. "She has come for
me. Hold me fast, old friend. Don't let me go!"

"Hold up, old man," I said, clapping him on the shoulder. "Pull
yourself together; you are dreaming; there is nothing to fear."

"She is gone!" he cried, with a gasp of relief. "No, by heaven!
there she is again, and nearer—coming nearer. She told me she
would come for me, and she keeps her word."

"Come into the house," I said. His hand, as I grasped it, was as
cold as ice.

"Ah, I knew it!" he shouted. "There she is, waving her arms.
She is beckoning to me. It is the signal. I must go. I am coming,
Kate; I am coming!"

I threw my arms around him, but he burst from me with su-
perhuman strength, and dashed into the darkness of the night. I
followed him, calling to him to stop, but he ran the more swiftly.
When the moon shone out between the clouds I could catch a
glimpse of his dark figure, running rapidly in a straight line, as if
to reach some definite goal. It may have been imagination, but it

seemed to me that in the flickering light I could distinguish a vague something in front of him—a shimmering form which eluded his grasp and led him onwards. I saw his outlines stand out hard against the sky behind him as he surmounted the brow of a little hill, then he disappeared, and that was the last ever seen by mortal eye of Barrington Cowles.

The fishermen and I walked round the island all that night with lanterns, and examined every nook and corner without seeing a trace of my poor lost friend. The direction in which he had been running terminated in a rugged line of jagged cliffs overhanging the sea. At one place here the edge was somewhat crumbled, and there appeared marks upon the turf which might have been left by human feet. We lay upon our faces at this spot, and peered with our lanterns over the edge, looking down on the boiling surge two hundred feet below. As we lay there, suddenly, above the beating of the waves and the howling of the wind, there rose a strange wild screech from the abyss below. The fishermen—a naturally superstitious race—averred that it was the sound of a woman's laughter, and I could hardly persuade them to continue the search. For my own part I think it may have been the cry of some sea-fowl startled from its nest by the flash of the lantern. However that may be, I never wish to hear such a sound again.

And now I have come to the end of the painful duty which I have undertaken. I have told as plainly and as accurately as I could the story of the death of John Barrington Cowles, and the train of events which preceded it. I am aware that to others the sad episode seemed commonplace enough. Here is the <u>prosaic</u> account which appeared in the *Scotsman* a couple of days afterwards:—

"Sad Occurrence on the Isle of May.—The Isle of May has been the scene of a sad disaster. Mr. John Barrington Cowles, a gentleman well known in University circles as a most distinguished student, and the present holder of the Neil Arnott prize for physics, has been recruiting his health in this quiet retreat. The night before last he suddenly left his friend, Mr. Robert Armitage, and he has not since been heard of. It is almost certain that he has met his death by falling over the cliffs which surround the island. Mr. Cowles' health has been failing for some time, partly from overstudy and partly

from worry connected with family affairs. By his death the University loses one of her most promising alumni.''

I have nothing more to add to my statement. I have unburdened my mind of all that I know. I can well conceive that many, after weighing all that I have said, will see no ground for an accusation against Miss Northcott. They will say that, because a man of a naturally excitable disposition says and does wild things, and even eventually commits self-murder after a sudden and heavy disappointment, there is no reason why vague charges should be advanced against a young lady. To this, I answer that they are welcome to their opinion. For my own part, I ascribe the death of William Prescott, of Archibald Reeves, and of John Barrington Cowles to this woman with as much confidence as if I had seen her drive a dagger into their hearts.

You ask me, no doubt, what my own theory is which will explain all these strange facts. I have none, or, at best, a dim and vague one. That Miss Northcott possessed extraordinary powers over the minds, and through the minds over the bodies, of others, I am convinced, as well as that her instincts were to use this power for base and cruel purposes. That some even more fiendish and terrible phase of character lay behind this—some horrible trait which it was necessary for her to reveal before marriage—is to be inferred from the experience of her three lovers, while the dreadful nature of the mystery thus revealed can only be surmised from the fact that the very mention of it drove from her those who had loved her so passionately. Their subsequent fate was, in my opinion, the result of her vindictive remembrance of their desertion of her, and that they were forewarned of it at the time was shown by the words of both Reeves and Cowles. Above this, I can say nothing. I lay the facts soberly before the public as they came under my notice. I have never seen Miss Northcott since, nor do I wish to do so. If by the words I have written I can save any one human being from the snare of those bright eyes and that beautiful face, then I can lay down my pen with the assurance that my poor friend has not died altogether in vain.

Robert Southey

EXCERPT FROM
THALABA THE DESTROYER

———◦———

The works of Robert Southey fill more than 100 volumes. They include *Joan of Arc*, *The Life of Nelson*, *The Vision of Judgment*, and *The Curse of Kahama*. He became England's poet laureate in 1813 after Sir Walter Scott turned down the honor, and held the position for thirty years. In 1826 he was elected to Parliament without his knowledge, but he turned it down. He was close friends with Sir Walter Scott, William Wordsworth, and Samuel Taylor Coleridge. This excerpt is from a narrative poem that was first published in 1801. The poem has 479 verses. Following are three of them.

> A night of darkness and of storms!
> Into the Chamber of the Tomb
> Thalaba led the Old Man,
> To roof him from the rain.
> A night of storms! the wind
> Swept through the moonless sky,
> And moan'd among the pillar'd sepulchres;
> And in the pauses of its sweep
> They heard the heavy rain
> Beat on the monument above.
> In silence on Oneiza's grave

Her father and her husband sate.
The Cryer from the Minaret
Proclaim'd the midnight hour.
"Now, now!" cried Thalaba;
And o'er the chamber of the tomb
There spread a lurid gleam,

Like the reflection of a sulphur fire;
And in that hideous light
Oneiza stood before them. It was She . . .
Her very lineaments, . . . and such as death
Had changed them, livid cheeks and lips of blue;
But in her eye there dwelt
Brightness more terrible
Than all the loathsomeness of death.
"Still art thou living, wretch?"
In hollow tones she cried to Thalaba;
"And must I nightly leave my grave
To tell thee, still in vain,
God hath abandoned thee?"

"This is not she!" the Old Man exclaim'd;
"A Fiend; a manifest Fiend!"
And to the youth he held his lance;
"Strike and deliver thyself!"
"Strike HER!" cried Thalaba,
And palsied of all power,
Gazed fixedly upon the dreadful form.
"Yea, strike her!" cried a voice, whose tones
Flow'd with such a sudden healing through his soul,
As when the desert shower
From death deliver'd him;
But unobedient to that well-known voice,
His eye was seeking it,
When Moath, firm of heart,
Perform'd the bidding: through the vampire corpse
He thrust his lance; it fell,
And howling with the wound,

Its fiendish tenant fled.
A sapphire light fell on them,
And garmented with glory, in their sight
Oneiza's Spirit stood.

Edgar Allan Poe

LIGEIA

Edgar Allan Poe was born in Boston, but was soon orphaned and subsequently raised by a foster family, which he did not get along well with. While his foster family lived in England for five years, he went to a private school near London. When he returned to the United States, he entered the University of Virginia. He took to gambling to support himself, but his drinking and mounting debts forced him to leave. Poe spent two years in the Army and rose to the rank of Sergeant Major. Shortly after he received an honorable discharge, he entered West Point in an effort to please his foster father. When he realized he would never receive an inheritance, he appeared at a public parade naked, wearing only his white belt, gloves, and rifle. He was promptly thrown out of the academy for "gross neglect of duty." After being refused by the Polish army, he focused more on his writing and began working as a magazine editor. When he was twenty-seven, he married his fourteen-year-old cousin. It was during this period that he wrote his great horror stories, including "The Tell-Tale Heart," "The Pit and the Pendulum," "The Fall of the House of Usher," "The Murders in the Rue Morgue," and his classic poem "The Raven." He is also credited with having invented the detective story. His drinking increased throughout his wife's long illness and eventual death from tuberculosis. Poe was on the way to his wedding with his childhood sweetheart when he disappeared; he was found unconscious several days later. He never regained consciousness, and the cause of his death at the age of forty remains a mystery. Poe's complete works fill seventeen volumes, with only one novel, which is actually more of a novella. Although he was just beginning to be recognized when he died,

Poe is now considered to be one of America's greatest writers and poets. "Ligeia" was first published in the September 1838 issue of *American Museum*. It was "Poe's first undisputed masterpiece and his own personal favorite among his tales."

And the will therein lieth, which dieth not. Who knoweth the mysteries of the will, with its vigor? For God is but a great will pervading all things by nature of its intentness. Man doth not yield himself to the angels, nor unto death utterly, save only through the weakness of his feeble will.

Joseph Glanvill

I CANNOT, FOR MY soul, remember how, when, or even precisely where, I first became acquainted with the lady Ligeia. Long years have since elapsed, and my memory is feeble through much suffering. Or, perhaps, I cannot *now* bring these points to mind, because, in truth, the character of my beloved, her rare learning, her singular yet placid cast of beauty, and the thrilling and enthralling eloquence of her low musical language, made their way into my heart by paces so steadily and stealthily progressive, that they have been unnoticed and unknown. Yet I believe that I met her first and most frequently in some large, old, decaying city near the Rhine. Of her family—I have surely heard her speak. That it is of a remotely ancient date cannot be doubted. Ligeia! Ligeia! Buried in studies of a nature more than all else adapted to deaden impressions of the outward world, it is by that sweet word alone— by Ligeia—that I bring before mine eyes in fancy the image of her who is no more. And now, while I write, a recollection flashes upon me that I have *never known* the paternal name of her who was my friend and my betrothed, and who became the partner of my studies, and finally the wife of my bosom. Was it a playful charge on the part of my Ligeia? or was it a test of my strength of affection, that I should institute no inquiries upon this point? or was it rather a caprice of my own—a wildly romantic offering on the shrine of the most passionate devotion? I but indistinctly recall the fact itself—what wonder that I have utterly forgotten the circumstances which originated or attended it? And, indeed, if ever that spirit which is entitled *Romance*—if ever she, the wan and the misty-winged *Ashtophet* of idolatrous Egypt, presided, as they tell, over marriages ill-omened, then most surely she presided over mine.

There is one dear topic, however, on which my memory fails me not. It is the *person* of Ligeia. In stature she was tall, somewhat slender, and, in her latter days, even emaciated. I would in vain attempt to portray the majesty, the quiet ease of her demeanor, or the incomprehensible lightness and elasticity of her footfall. She came and departed as a shadow. I was never made aware of her entrance into my closed study, save by the dear music of her low sweet voice, as she placed her marble hand upon my shoulder. In beauty of face no maiden ever equalled her. It was the radiance of an opium-dream—an airy and spirit-lifting vision more wildly divine than the phantasies which hovered about the slumbering souls of the daughters of Delos. Yet her features were not of that regular mould which we have been falsely taught to worship in the classical labors of the heathen. "There is no exquisite beauty," says Bacon, Lord Verulam, speaking truly of all the forms and *genera* of beauty, "without some *strangeness* in the proportion." Yet, although I saw that the features of Ligeia were not of a classic regularity—although I perceived that her loveliness was indeed "exquisite," and felt that there was much of "strangeness" pervading it, yet I have tried in vain to detect the irregularity and to trace home my own perception of "the strange." I examined the contour of the lofty and pale forehead—it was faultless—how cold indeed that word when applied to a majesty so divine!—the skin rivalling the purest ivory, the commanding extent and repose, the gentle prominence of the regions above the temples; and then the raven-black, the glossy, the luxuriant, and naturally-curling tresses, setting forth the full force of the Homeric epithet, "hyacinthine!" I looked at the delicate outlines of the nose—and nowhere but in the graceful medallions of the Hebrews had I beheld a similar perfection. There were the same luxurious smoothness of surface, the same scarcely perceptible tendency to the aquiline, the same harmoniously curved nostrils speaking the free spirit. I regarded the sweet mouth. Here was indeed the triumph of all things heavenly—the magnificent turn of the short upper lip—the soft, voluptuous slumber of the under—the dimples which sported, and the color which spoke—the teeth glancing back, with a brilliancy almost startling, every ray of the holy light which fell upon them in her serene and placid yet most exultingly radiant of all smiles. I scrutinized the formation of the chin—and, here too, I found the gentleness of breadth, the softness and the majesty, the fulness and the spirituality, of the Greek—the contour which the god Apollo revealed but in a dream, to Cleomenes, the son of the Athenian. And then I peered into the large eyes of Ligeia.

For eyes we have no models in the remotely antique. It might have been, too, that in these eyes of my beloved lay the secret to which Lord Verulam alludes. They were, I must believe, far larger than the ordinary eyes of our own race. They were even fuller than the fullest of the gazelle eyes of the tribe of the valley of Nourjahad. Yet it was only at intervals—in moments of intense excitement—that this peculiarity became more than slightly no-ticeable in Ligeia. And at such moments was her beauty—in my heated fancy thus it appeared perhaps—the beauty of beings ei-ther above or apart from the earth—the beauty of the fabulous Houri of the Turk. The hue of the orbs was the most brilliant of black, and, far over them, hung jetty lashes of great length. The brows, slightly irregular in outline, had the same tint. The "strangeness," however, which I found in the eyes was of a nature distinct from the formation, or the color, or the brilliancy of the features, and must, after all, be referred to the *expression*. Ah, word of no meaning! behind whose vast latitude of mere sound we intrench our ignorance of so much of the spiritual. The expression of the eyes of Ligeia! How for long hours have I pondered upon it! How have I, through the whole of a midsummer night, strug-gled to fathom it! What was it—that something more profound than the well of Democritus—which lay far within the pupils of my beloved? What *was* it? I was possessed with a passion to dis-cover. Those eyes! those large, those shining, those divine orbs! they became to me twin stars of Leda, and I to them devoutest of astrologers.

There is no point, among the many incomprehensible anoma-lies of the science of mind, more thrillingly exciting than the fact—never, I believe, noticed in the schools—that in our endeavors to recall to memory something long forgotten, we often find ourselves *upon the very verge* of remembrance, without being able, in the end, to remember. And thus how frequently, in my intense scrutiny of Ligeia's eyes, have I felt approaching the full knowledge of their expression—felt it approaching—yet not quite be mine—and so at length entirely depart! And (strange, oh, strangest mystery of all!) I found, in the commonest objects of the universe, a circle of analogies to that expression. I mean to say that, subsequently to the period when Ligeia's beauty passed into my spirit, there dwelling as in a shrine, I derived, from many existences in the material world, a sentiment such as I felt always around, within me, by her large and luminous orbs. Yet not the more could I define that sentiment, or analyze, or even steadily view it. I recognized it, let me repeat, sometimes in the survey of a rapidly growing vine—in the contemplation of a moth, a butterfly, a chrysalis, a stream of running water. I have felt it in the ocean—in the falling of a meteor. I have felt it in the glances of unusually aged people. And there are one or two stars in heaven (one especially, a star of the sixth magnitude, double and changeable, to be found near the large star in Lyra) in a telescopic scrutiny of which I have been made aware of the feeling. I have been filled with it by certain sounds from stringed instruments, and not unfrequently by passages from books. Among innumerable other instances, I well remember something in a volume of Joseph Glanvill, which (perhaps merely from its quaintness—who shall say?) never failed to inspire me with the sentiment: "And the will therein lieth, which dieth not. Who knoweth the mysteries of the will, with its vigor? For God is but a great will pervading all things by nature of its intentness. Man doth not yield him to the angels, nor unto death utterly, save only through the weakness of his feeble will."

Length of years and subsequent reflection have enabled me to trace, indeed, some remote connection between this passage in the English moralist and a portion of the character of Ligeia. An *intensity* in thought, action, or speech was possibly, in her, a result, or at least an index, of that gigantic volition which, during our long intercourse, failed to give other and more immediate evidence of its existence. Of all the women whom I have ever known, she, the outwardly calm, the ever-placid Ligeia, was the most violently a prey to the tumultuous vultures of stern passion. And of such passion I could form no estimate, save by the miraculous expansion of those eyes which at once so delighted and appalled me,—by the almost magical melody, modulation, distinctness, and placidity of her very low voice,—and by the fierce energy (rendered doubly effective by contrast with her manner of utterance) of the wild words which she habitually uttered.

I have spoken of the learning of Ligeia: it was immense—such as I have never known in woman. In the classical tongues was she deeply proficient, and as far as my own acquaintance extended in regard to the modern dialects of Europe, I have never known her at fault. Indeed upon any theme of the most admired because simply the most abstruse of the boasted erudition of the Academy, have I *ever* found Ligeia at fault? How singularly—how thrillingly, this one point in the nature of my wife has forced itself, at this late period only, upon my attention! I said her knowledge was such as I have never known in woman—but where breathes the man who has traversed, and successfully, *all* the wide areas of moral, physical, and mathematical science? I saw not then what I now clearly perceive, that the acquisitions of Ligeia were gigantic, were astounding; yet I was sufficiently aware of her infinite supremacy to resign myself, with a child-like confidence, to her guidance through the chaotic world of metaphysical investigation at which I was most busily occupied during the earlier years of our marriage. With how vast a triumph—with how vivid a delight—with how much of all that is ethereal in hope did I *feel*, as she bent over me in studies but little sought—but less known,— that delicious vista by slow degrees expanding before me, down whose long, gorgeous, and all untrodden path, I might at length pass onward to the goal of a wisdom too divinely precious not to be forbidden!

How poignant, then, must have been the grief with which, after some years, I beheld my well-grounded expectations take wings to themselves and fly away! Without Ligeia I was but as a child groping benighted. Her presence, her readings alone, rendered vividly luminous the many mysteries of the transcendentalism in which we were immersed. Wanting the radiant lustre of her eyes, letters, lambent and golden, grew duller than Saturnian lead. And now those eyes shone less and less frequently upon the pages over which I poured. Ligeia grew ill. The wild eyes blazed with a too-

too glorious effulgence; the pale fingers became of the transparent waxen hue of the grave; and the blue veins upon the lofty forehead swelled and sank impetuously with the tides of the most gentle emotion. I saw that she must die—and I struggled desperately in spirit with the grim Azrael. And the struggles of the passionate wife were, to my astonishment, even more energetic than my own. There had been much in her stern nature to impress me with the belief that, to her, death would have come without its terrors; but not so. Words are impotent to convey any just idea of the fierceness of resistance with which she wrestled with the Shadow. I groaned in anguish at the pitiable spectacle. I would have soothed—I would have reasoned; but in the intensity of her wild desire for life—for life—*but* for life—solace and reason were alike the uttermost of folly. Yet not until the last instance, amid the most convulsive writhings of her fierce spirit, was shaken the external placidity of her demeanor. Her voice grew more gentle— grew more low—yet I would not wish to dwell upon the wild meaning of the quietly uttered words. My brain reeled as I hearkened, entranced to a melody more than mortal—to assumptions and aspirations which mortality had never before known.

That she loved me I should not have doubted; and I might have been easily aware that, in a bosom such as hers, love would have reigned no ordinary passion. But in death only was I fully impressed with the strength of her affection. For long hours, detaining my hand, would she pour out before me the overflowing of a heart whose more than passionate devotion amounted to idolatry. How had I deserved to be so blessed by such confessions?—how had I deserved to be so cursed with the removal of my beloved in the hour of my making them? But upon this subject I cannot bear to dilate. Let me say only, that in Ligeia's more than womanly abandonment to a love, alas! all unmerited, all unworthily bestowed, I at length recognized the principle of her longing with so wildly earnest a desire, for the life which was now fleeing so rapidly away. It is this wild longing—it is this eager vehemence of desire for life—*but* for life—that I have no power to portray—no utterance capable of expressing.

At high noon of the night in which she departed, beckoning me, peremptorily, to her side, she bade me repeat certain verses

composed by herself not many days before. I obeyed her. They
were these:—

>   Lo! 'tis a gala night
>   Within the lonesome latter years!
>   An angel throng, bewinged, <u>bedight</u>
>   In veils, and drowned in tears,
>   Sit in a theatre, to see
>   A play of hopes and fears,
>   While the orchestra breathes fitfully
>   The music of the spheres.
>
>   Mimes, in the form of God on high,
>   Mutter and mumble low,
>   And hither and thither fly;
>   Mere puppets they, who come and go
>   At bidding of vast formless things
>   That shift the scenery to and fro,
>   Flapping from out their condor wings
>   Invisible Woe!
>
>   That motley drama!—oh, be sure
>   It shall not be forgot!
>   With its Phantom chased for evermore,
>   By a crowd that seize it not,
>   Through a circle that ever returneth in
>   To the self-same spot;
>   And much of Madness, and more of Sin
>   And Horror, the soul of the plot!
>
>   But see, amid the mimic rout
>   A crawling shape intrude!
>   A blood-red thing that writhes from out
>   The scenic solitude!
>   It writhes!—it writhes!—with mortal
>   pangs
>   The mimes become its food,
>   And the <u>seraphs</u> sob at vermin fangs
>   In human gore imbued.

> Out—out are the lights—out all!
>   And over each quivering form,
> The curtain, a funeral pall,
>   Comes down with the rush of a storm—
> And the angels, all pallid and wan,
>   Uprising, unveiling, affirm
> That the play is the tragedy, "Man,"
>   And its hero, the conqueror Worm.

"O God!" half shrieked Ligeia, leaping to her feet and extending her arms aloft with a spasmodic movement, as I made an end of these lines—"O God! O Divine Father!—shall these things be undeviatingly so?—shall this conqueror be not once conquered? Are we not part and parcel in Thee? Who—who knoweth the mysteries of the will with its vigor? Man doth not yield him to the angels, *nor unto death utterly*, save only through the weakness of his feeble will."

And now, as if exhausted with emotion, she suffered her white arms to fall, and returned solemnly to her bed of death. And as she breathed her last sighs, there came mingled with them a low murmur from her lips. I bent to them my ear, and distinguished, again, the concluding words of the passage in Glanvill: *"Man doth not yield himself to the angels, nor unto death utterly, save only through the weakness of his feeble will."*

She died: and I, crushed into the very dust with sorrow, could no longer endure the lonely desolation of my dwelling in the dim and decaying city by the Rhine. I had no lack of what the world calls wealth. Ligeia had brought me far more, very far more, than ordinarily falls to the lot of mortals. After a few months, therefore, of weary and aimless wandering, I purchased and put in some repair, an abbey, which I shall not name, in one of the wildest and least frequented portions of fair England. The gloomy and dreary grandeur of the building, the almost savage aspect of the domain, the many melancholy and time-honored memories connected with both, had much in unison with the feelings of utter abandonment which had driven me into that remote and unsocial region of the country. Yet although the external abbey, with its verdant decay hanging about it, suffered but little alteration, I gave way, with a child-like perversity, and perchance with a faint hope of alleviating my sorrows, to a display of more than regal magnificence within. For such follies, even in childhood, I had imbibed a taste, and now they came back to me as if in the dotage of grief. Alas, I feel how much even of incipient madness might have been discovered in the gorgeous and fantastic draperies, in the solemn carvings of Egypt, in the wild cornices and furniture, in the Bedlam patterns of the carpets of tufted gold! I had become a bounden slave in the trammels of opium, and my labors and my orders had taken a coloring from my dreams. But these absurdities I must not pause to detail. Let me speak only of that one chamber, ever accursed, whither, in a moment of mental alienation, I led from the altar as my bride—as the successor of the unforgotten Ligeia—the fair-haired and blue-eyed Lady Rowena Trevanion, of Tremaine.

There is no individual portion of the architecture and decoration of that bridal chamber which is not now visibly before me. Where were the souls of the haughty family of the bride, when, through thirst of gold, they permitted to pass the threshold of an apartment *so* bedecked, a maiden and a daughter so beloved? I have said, that I minutely remember the details of the chamber—yet I am sadly forgetful on topics of deep moment; and here there was no system, no keeping, in the fantastic display, to take hold upon the memory. The room lay in a high turret of the castellated abbey, was pentagonal in shape, and of capacious size. Occupying the whole southern face of the pentagon was the sole window—an immense sheet of unbroken glass from Venice—a single pane, and tinted of a leaden hue, so that the rays of either the sun or moon passing through it, fell with a ghastly lustre on the objects within. Over the upper portion of this huge window, extended the trellis-work of an aged vine, which clambered up the massy walls of the turret. The ceiling, of gloomy-looking oak, was excessively lofty, vaulted, and elaborately fretted with the wildest and most grotesque specimens of a semi-Gothic, semi-Druidical device. From out the most central recess of this melancholy vaulting, depended, by a single chain of gold with long links, a huge censer of the same metal, Saracenic in pattern, and with many perforations so contrived that there writhed in and out of them, as if endued with a serpent vitality, a continual succession of parti-colored fires.

Some few ottomans and golden candelabra, of Eastern figure, were in various stations about; and there was the couch, too—the bridal couch—of an Indian model, and low, and sculptured of solid ebony, with a pall-like canopy above. In each of the angles of the chamber stood on end a gigantic sarcophagus of black granite, from the tombs of the kings over against Luxor, with their aged lids full of immemorial sculpture. But in the draping of the apartment lay, alas! the chief phantasy of all. The lofty walls, gigantic in height—even unproportionably so—were hung from summit to foot, in vast folds, with a heavy and massive looking tapestry—tapestry of a material which was found alike as a carpet on the floor, as a covering for the ottomans and the ebony bed, as a canopy for the bed and as the gorgeous volutes of the curtains which partially shaded the window. The material was the richest cloth of gold. It was spotted all over, at irregular intervals, with arabesque figures, about a foot in diameter, and wrought upon the cloth in patterns of the most jetty black. But these figures partook of the true character of the arabesque only when regarded from a single point of view. By a contrivance now common, and indeed traceable to a very remote period of antiquity, they were made changeable in aspect. To one entering the room, they bore the appearance of simple monstrosities; but upon a farther advance, this appearance gradually departed; and, step by step, as the visitor moved his station in the chamber, he saw himself surrounded by an endless succession of the ghastly forms which belong to the superstition of the Norman, or arise in the guilty slumbers of the monk. The phantasmagoric effect was vastly heightened by the artificial introduction of a strong continual current of wind behind the draperies—giving a hideous and uneasy animation to the whole.

In halls such as these—in a bridal chamber such as this—I passed, with the Lady of Tremaine, the unhallowed hours of the first month of our marriage—passed them with but little disquietude. That my wife dreaded the fierce moodiness of my temper—that she shunned me, and loved me but little—I could not help perceiving; but it gave me rather pleasure than otherwise. I loathed her with a hatred belonging more to demon than to man. My memory flew back (oh, with what intensity of regret!) to Ligeia, the beloved, the august, the beautiful, the entombed. I rev-

elled in recollections of her purity, of her wisdom, of her lofty—
her ethereal nature, of her passionate, her idolatrous love. Now,
then, did my spirit fully and freely burn with more than all the
fires of her own. In the excitement of my opium dreams (for I was
habitually fettered in the shackles of the drug), I would call aloud
upon her name, during the silence of the night, or among the
sheltered recesses of the glens by day, as if, through the wild eagerness, the solemn passion, the consuming ardor of my longing
for the departed, I could restore her to the pathways she had abandoned—ah, *could* it be for ever?—upon the earth.

About the commencement of the second month of the marriage, the Lady Rowena was attacked with sudden illness, from
which her recovery was slow. The fever which consumed her rendered her nights uneasy; and in her perturbed state of half-
slumber, she spoke of sounds, and of motions, in and about the
chamber of the turret, which I concluded had no origin save in
the distemper of her fancy, or perhaps in the phantasmagoric influences of the chamber itself. She became at length convalescent—finally, well. Yet but a brief period elapsed, ere a second
more violent disorder again threw her upon a bed of suffering;
and from this attack her frame, at all times feeble, never altogether
recovered. Her illnesses were, after this epoch, of alarming character, and of more alarming recurrence, defying alike the knowledge and the great exertions of her physicians. With the increase
of the chronic disease, which had thus, apparently, taken too sure
hold upon her constitution to be eradicated by human means, I
could not fail to observe a similar increase in the nervous irritation
of her temperament, and in her excitability by trivial causes of
fear. She spoke again, and now more frequently and pertina-
ciously, of the sounds—of the light sounds—and of the unusual
motions among the tapestries, to which she had formerly alluded.

One night, near the closing in of September, she pressed this
distressing subject with more than usual emphasis upon my attention. She had just awakened from an unquiet slumber, and I
had been watching, with feelings half of anxiety, half of vague
terror, the workings of her emaciated countenance. I sat by the
side of her ebony bed, upon one of the ottomans of India. She
partly arose, and spoke, in an earnest low whisper, of sounds
which she *then* heard, but which I could not hear—of motions

which she *then* saw, but which I could not perceive. The wind was
rushing hurriedly behind the tapestries, and I wished to show her
(what, let me confess it, I could not *all* believe) that those almost
inarticulate breathings, and those very gentle variations of the
figures upon the wall, were but the natural effects of that customary rushing of the wind. But a deadly pallor, overspreading her
face, had proved to me that my exertions to reassure her would
be fruitless. She appeared to be fainting, and no attendants were
within call. I remembered where was deposited a decanter of light
wine which had been ordered by her physicians, and hastened
across the chamber to procure it. But, as I stepped beneath the
light of the censer, two circumstances of a startling nature attracted my attention. I had felt that some palpable although invisible object had passed lightly by my person; and I saw that there
lay upon the golden carpet, in the very middle of the rich lustre
thrown from the censer, a shadow—a faint, indefinite shadow of
angelic aspect—such as might be fancied for the shadow of a
shade. But I was wild with the excitement of an immoderate dose
of opium, and heeded these things but little, nor spoke of them
to Rowena. Having found the wine, I recrossed the chamber, and
poured out a gobletful, which I held to the lips of the fainting
lady. She had now partially recovered, however, and took the
vessel herself, while I sank upon an ottoman near me, with my
eyes fastened upon her person. It was then that I became distinctly
aware of a gentle foot-fall upon the carpet, and near the couch;
and in a second thereafter, as Rowena was in the act of raising
the wine to her lips, I saw, or may have dreamed that I saw, fall
within the goblet, as if from some invisible spring in the atmosphere of the room, three or four large drops of a brilliant and
ruby colored fluid. If this I saw—not so Rowena. She swallowed
the wine unhesitatingly, and I forbore to speak to her of a circumstance which must, after all, I considered, have been but the suggestion of a vivid imagination, rendered morbidly active by the
terror of the lady, by the opium, and by the hour.

Yet I cannot conceal it from my own perception that, immediately subsequent to the fall of the ruby-drops, a rapid change for
the worse took place in the disorder of my wife; so that, on the
third subsequent night, the hands of her menials prepared her for
the tomb, and on the fourth, I sat alone, with her shrouded body,

in that fantastic chamber which had received her as my bride. Wild visions, opium-engendered, flitted, shadow-like, before me. I gazed with unquiet eye upon the sarcophagi in the angles of the room, upon the varying figures of the drapery, and upon the writhing of the parti-colored fires in the censer overhead. My eyes then fell, as I called to mind the circumstances of a former night, to the spot beneath the glare of the censer where I had seen the faint traces of the shadow. It was there, however, no longer; and breathing with greater freedom, I turned my glances to the pallid and rigid figure in the bed. Then rushed upon me a thousand memories of Ligeia—and then came back upon my heart, with the turbulent violence of a flood, the whole of that unutterable woe with which I had regarded *her* thus enshrouded. The night waned; and still, with a bosom full of bitter thoughts of the one only and supremely beloved, I remained gazing upon the body of Rowena.

It might have been midnight, or perhaps earlier, or later, for I had taken no note of time, when a sob, low, gentle, but very distinct, startled me from my revery. I *felt* that it came from the bed of ebony—the bed of death. I listened in an agony of super-stitious terror—but there was no repetition of the sound. I strained my vision to detect any motion in the corpse—but there was not the slightest perceptible. Yet I could not have been de-ceived. I *had* heard the noise, however faint, and my soul was awakened within me. I resolutely and perseveringly kept my at-tention riveted upon the body. Many minutes elapsed before any circumstance occurred tending to throw light upon the mystery. At length it became evident that a slight, a very feeble, and barely noticeable tinge of color had flushed up within the cheeks, and along the sunken small veins of the eyelids. Through a species of unutterable horror and awe, for which the language of mortality has no sufficiently energetic expression, I felt my heart cease to beat, my limbs grow rigid where I sat. Yet a sense of duty finally operated to restore my self-possession. I could no longer doubt that we had been precipitate in our preparations—that Rowena still lived. It was necessary that some immediate exertion be made; yet the turret was altogether apart from the portion of the abbey tenanted by the servants—there were none within call—I had no means of summoning them to my aid without leaving the room for many minutes—and this I could not venture to do. I therefore struggled alone in my endeavors to call back the spirit still hovering. In a short period it was certain, however, that a relapse had taken place; the color disappeared from both eyelid and cheek, leaving a wanness even more than that of marble; the lips became doubly shrivelled and pinched up in the ghastly expression of death; a repulsive clamminess and coldness overspread rapidly at the surface of the body; and all the usual rigorous stiffness immediately supervened. I fell back with a shudder upon the couch from which I had been so startlingly aroused, and again gave myself up to passionate waking visions of Ligeia.

An hour thus elapsed, when (could it be possible?) I was a second time aware of some vague sound issuing from the region of the bed. I listened—in extremity of horror. The sound came again—it was a sigh. Rushing to the corpse, I saw—distinctly saw—a tremor upon the lips. In a minute afterward they relaxed, disclosing a bright line of the pearly teeth. Amazement now struggled in my bosom with the profound awe which had hitherto reigned there alone. I felt that my vision grew dim, that my reason wandered; and it was only by a violent effort that I at length succeeded in nerving myself to the task which duty thus once more had pointed out. There was now a partial glow upon the forehead and upon the cheek and throat; a perceptible warmth pervaded the whole frame; there was even a slight pulsation at the heart. The lady *lived*; and with redoubled ardor I betook myself to the task of restoration. I chafed and bathed the temples and the hands, and used every exertion which experience, and no little medical reading, could suggest. But in vain. Suddenly, the color fled, the pulsation ceased, the lips resumed the expression of the dead, and, in an instant afterward, the whole body took upon itself the icy chilliness, the livid hue, the intense rigidity, the sunken outline, and all the loathsome peculiarities of that which has been, for many days, a tenant of the tomb.

And again I sunk into visions of Ligeia—and again (what marvel that I shudder while I write?), *again* there reached my ears a low sob from the region of the ebony bed. But why shall I pause to relate how, time after time, until near the period of the gray dawn, this hideous drama of revivification was repeated; how each terrific relapse was only into a sterner and apparently more irredeemable death; how each agony wore the aspect of a struggle with some invisible foe; and how each struggle was succeeded by I know not what of wild change in the personal appearance of the corpse? Let me hurry to a conclusion.

The greater part of the fearful night had worn away, and she who had been dead once again stirred—and now more vigorously than hitherto, although arousing from a dissolution more appalling in its utter hopelessness than any. I had long ceased to struggle or to move, and remained sitting rigidly upon the ottoman, a helpless prey to a whirl of violent emotions, of which extreme awe was perhaps the least terrible, the least consuming. The corpse, I repeat, stirred, and now more vigorously than before. The hues of life flushed up with unwonted energy into the countenance— the limbs relaxed—and, save that the eyelids were yet pressed heavily together, and that the bandages and draperies of the grave still imparted their charnel character to the figure, I might have dreamed that Rowena had indeed shaken off, utterly, the fetters of Death. But if this idea was not, even then, altogether adopted, I could at least doubt no longer, when, arising from the bed, tottering, with feeble steps, with closed eyes, and with the manner of one bewildered in a dream, the thing that was enshrouded advanced boldly and palpably into the middle of the apartment.

I trembled not—I stirred not—for a crowd of unutterable fancies connected with the air, the stature, the demeanor, of the figure, rushing hurriedly through my brain, had paralyzed—had chilled me into stone. I stirred not—but gazed upon the apparition. There was a mad disorder in my thoughts—a tumult unappeasable. Could it, indeed, be the *living* Rowena who confronted me? Could it, indeed, be Rowena *at all*—the fair-haired, the blue-eyed Lady Rowena Trevanion of Tremaine? Why, *why* should I doubt it? The bandage lay heavily about the mouth—but then might it not be the mouth of the breathing Lady of Tremaine? And the cheeks—there were the roses as in her noon of life—yes, these might indeed be the fair cheeks of the living Lady of Tremaine. And the chin, with its dimples, as in health, might it not be hers?—but *had she then grown taller since her malady?* What inexpressible madness seized me with that thought? One bound, and I had reached her feet! Shrinking from my touch, she let fall from her head, unloosened, the ghastly cerements which had confined it, and there streamed forth into the rushing atmosphere of the chamber huge masses of long and dishevelled hair; *it was blacker than the raven wings of midnight!* And now slowly opened *the eyes* of the figure which stood before me. "Here then, at least," I shrieked aloud, "can I never—can I never be mistaken—these are the full, and the black, and the wild eyes—of my lost love—of the Lady—of the LADY LIGEIA."

Rudyard Kipling

THE VAMPIRE

Joseph Rudyard Kipling was born in Bombay, India, the son of a clergyman. When he was five years old, he was sent to school in England where he suffered six years of mental torture and beatings from his guardians before his parents moved to England and rescued him. He returned to India as a journalist in 1882 and stayed for eight years before moving back to England. His stories and poems of India made him famous. His works include *Kim*, *The Jungle Book*, *The Light that Failed*, *Plain Tales from the Hills*, and *Captains Courageous*. He also wrote the short story "The Man Who Would be King" and the poem "Gunga Din," both of which were made into movies. In 1907 he was awarded the Nobel Prize for Literature. Kipling published "The Vampire" in 1897. This poem later inspired the movie *A Fool There Was* (1915), which launched the career of Theda Bara, the first vamp; a whole bevy of Hollywood vamps soon followed in her footsteps.

A fool there was and he made his prayer
(Even as you and I!)
To a rag and a bone and a hank of hair,
(We called her the woman who did not care),
But the fool he called her his lady fair—
(Even as you and I!)

Oh, the years we waste and the tears we waste,
And the work of our head and hand
Belong to the woman who did not know

(And now we know that she never could know)
And did not understand!

A fool there was and his goods he spent,
(Even as you and I!)
Honour and faith and a sure intent
(And it wasn't the least what the lady meant),
But a fool must follow his natural bent
(Even as you and I!)

Oh, the toil we lost and the spoil we lost
And the excellent things we planned
Belong to the woman who didn't know why
(And now we know that she never knew why)
And did not understand!

The fool was stripped to his foolish hide,
(Even as you and I!)
Which she might have seen when she threw him aside—
(But it isn't on record the lady tried)
So some of him lived but the most of him died—
(Even as you and I!)

"And it isn't the shame and it isn't the blame
That stings like a white-hot brand—
It's coming to know that she never knew why
(Seeing, at last, she could never know why)
And never could understand!"

Lord Byron

A FRAGMENT OF A TURKISH TALE

———⟫●⟪———

George Gordon Byron was one of the most important poets of the romantic period. Lame from birth, he spent years in poverty before he succeeded to the title of sixth Baron of Byron. He is best known for his masterpiece *Don Juan*. In June of 1816, while staying in Geneva with Percy and Mary Shelley and Dr. John Polidori, Byron proposed that they each write a ghost story. Mary's story was published two years later as *Frankenstein*, and Polidori expanded his tale into the novel *Ernestus Berchtold*. Byron told a vampire story, which inspired Polidori's short story "The Vampyre." When this story was first published without Polidori's knowledge in 1819, it was attributed to Byron. The story was very popular and inspired a flurry of vampire stories and plays. In fact, Goethe said it was the best thing Byron ever wrote. Polidori quickly claimed credit, while Byron denied that the story was Byron's, saying, "I have a personal dislike to Vampires, and the little acquaintance I have with them would by no means induce me to reveal their secrets." Still, that same year Byron published this beginning of his vampire novel as an appendix to his poem *Mazeppa*.

JUNE 17, 1816.

IN THE YEAR 17—, having for some time determined on a journey through countries not hitherto much frequented by travellers, I

71

Lord Byron

set out, accompanied by a friend, whom I shall designate by the name of Augustus Darvell. He was a few years my elder, and a man of considerable fortune and ancient family: advantages which an extensive capacity prevented him alike from undervaluing or overrating. Some peculiar circumstances in his private history had rendered him to me an object of attention, of interest, and even of regard, which neither the reserve of his manners, nor occasional indications of an inquietude at times nearly approaching to alienation of mind, could extinguish.

I was yet young in life, which I had begun early; but my intimacy with him was of a recent date: we had been educated at the same schools and university; but his progress through these had preceded mine, and he had been deeply initiated into what is called the world, while I was yet in my novitiate. While thus engaged, I heard much both of his past and present life; and, although in these accounts there were many and irreconcilable contradictions, I could still gather from the whole that he was a being of no common order, and one who, whatever pains he might take to avoid remark, would still be remarkable. I had cultivated his acquaintance subsequently, and endeavoured to obtain his friendship, but this last appeared to be unattainable; whatever affections he might have possessed seemed now, some to have been extinguished, and others to be concentred: that his feelings were acute, I had sufficient opportunities of observing; for, although he could control, he could not altogether disguise them: still he had a power of giving to one passion the appearance of another, in such a manner that it was difficult to define the nature of what was working within him; and the expressions of his features would vary so rapidly, though slightly, that it was useless to trace them to their sources. It was evident that he was a prey to some cureless disquiet; but whether it arose from ambition, love, remorse, grief, from one or all of these, or merely from a morbid temperament akin to disease, I could not discover: there were circumstances alleged which might have justified the application to each of these causes; but, as I have before said, these were so contradictory and contradicted, that none could be fixed upon with accuracy. Where there is mystery, it is generally supposed that there must also be evil: I know not how this may be, but in him there certainly was the one, though I could not ascertain the extent of the other—and felt loth, as far as regarded himself, to believe in its existence. My advances were received with sufficient coolness: but I was young, and not easily discouraged, and at length succeeded in obtaining, to a certain degree, that common-place intercourse and moderate confidence of common and every-day concerns, created and cemented by similarity of pursuit and frequency of meeting, which is called intimacy, or friendship, according to the ideas of him who uses those words to express them.

Darvell had already travelled extensively; and to him I had applied for information with regard to the conduct of my intended journey. It was my secret wish that he might be prevailed on to accompany me; it was also a probable hope, founded upon the shadowy restlessness which I observed in him, and to which the animation which he appeared to feel on such subjects, and his apparent indifference to all by which he was more immediately surrounded, gave fresh strength. This wish I first hinted, and then expressed: his answer, though I had partly expected it, gave me all the pleasure of surprise—he consented; and, after the requisite arrangement, we commenced our voyages. After journeying through various countries of the south of Europe, our attention was turned towards the East, according to our original destination; and it was in my progress through these regions that the incident occurred upon which will turn what I may have to relate.

The constitution of Darvell, which must from his appearance have been in early life more than usually robust, had been for some time gradually giving away, without the intervention of any apparent disease: he had neither cough nor hectic, yet he became daily more enfeebled; his habits were temperate, and he neither declined nor complained of fatigue; yet he was evidently wasting away: he became more and more silent and sleepless, and at length so seriously altered, that my alarm grew proportionate to what I conceived to be his danger.

We had determined, on our arrival at Smyrna, on an excursion to the ruins of Ephesus and Sardis, from which I endeavoured to dissuade him in his present state of indisposition—but in vain: there appeared to be an oppression on his mind, and a solemnity in his manner, which ill corresponded with his eagerness to proceed on what I regarded as a mere party of pleasure little suited to a valetudinarian; but I opposed him no longer—and in a few days we set off together, accompanied only by a serrugee and a single janizary.

We had passed halfway towards the remains of Ephesus, leaving behind us the more fertile environs of Smyrna, and were entering upon that wild and tenantless tract through the marshes and defiles which lead to the few huts yet lingering over the broken columns of Diana the roofless walls of expelled Christianity, and the still more recent but complete desolation of abandoned mosques—when the sudden and rapid illness of my companion obliged us to halt at a Turkish cemetery, the turbaned tombstones of which were the sole indication that human life had ever been a sojourner in this wilderness. The only caravanserai we had seen was left some hours behind us, not a vestige of a town or even cottage was within sight or hope, and this "city of the dead" appeared to be the sole refuge of my unfortunate friend, who seemed on the verge of becoming the last of its inhabitants.

In this situation, I looked round for a place where he might most conveniently repose: contrary to the usual aspect of Mahometan burial-grounds, the cypresses were in this few in number, and these thinly scattered over its extent; the tombstones were mostly fallen, and worn with age: upon one of the most considerable of these, and beneath one of the most spreading trees, Darvell supported himself, in a half-reclining posture, with great difficulty. He asked for water. I had some doubts of our being able to find any, and prepared to go in search of it with hesitating despondency: but he desired me to remain; and turning to Suleiman, our janizary, who stood by us smoking with great tranquillity, he said, "Suleiman, verban su" (*i.e.* "bring some water") and went on describing the spot where it was to be found with great minuteness, at a small well for camels, a few hundred yards to the right: the janizary obeyed. I said to Darvell, "How did you know this?" He replied, "From our situation; you must perceive that this place was once inhabited, and could not have been so without springs: I have also been here before."

"You have been here before! How came you never to mention this to me? and what could you be doing in a place where no one would remain a moment longer than they could help it?"

To this question I received no answer. In the mean time Suleiman returned with the water, leaving the serrugee and the horses at the fountain. The quenching of his thirst had the appearance of reviving him for a moment; and I conceived hopes of his being able to proceed, or at least to return, and I urged the attempt. He was silent—and appeared to be collecting his spirits for an effort to speak. He began:

"This is the end of my journey, and of my life; I came here to die; but I have a request to make, a command—for such my last words must be. You will observe it?"

"Most certainly; but I have better hopes."

"I have no hopes, nor wishes, but this—conceal my death from every human being."

"I hope there will be no occasion; that you will recover, and—"

"Peace! it must be so: promise this."

"I do."

"Swear it, by all that—" He here dictated an oath of great solemnity.

"There is no occasion for this. I will observe your request; and to doubt me is—"

"It cannot be helped—you must swear."

I took the oath, it appeared to relieve him. He removed a seal ring from his finger, on which were some Arabic characters, and presented it to me. He proceeded:

"On the ninth day of the month, at noon precisely (what month you please, but this must be the day), you must fling this ring into the salt springs which run into the Bay of Eleusis; the day after, at the same hour, you must repair to the ruins of the temple of Ceres, and wait one hour."

"Why?"

"You will see."

"The ninth day of the month, you say?"

"The ninth."

As I observed that the present was the ninth day of the month, his countenance changed, and he paused. As he sat, evidently becoming more feeble, a stork, with a snake in her beak, perched upon a tombstone near us; and, without devouring her prey, appeared to be steadfastly regarding us. I know not what impelled me to drive it away, but the attempt was useless; she made a few circles in the air, and returned exactly to the same spot. Darvell

pointed to it, and smiled—he spoke—I know not whether to himself or to me—but the words were only, " 'Tis well!"

"What is well? What do you mean?"

"No matter; you must bury me here this evening, and exactly
where that bird is now perched. You know the rest of my injunc-
tions."

He then proceeded to give me several directions as to the manner in which his death might be best concealed. After these were
finished, he exclaimed, "You perceive that bird?"

"Certainly."

"And the serpent writhing in her beak?"

"Doubtless: there is nothing uncommon in it; it is her natural
prey. But it is odd that she does not devour it."

He smiled in a ghastly manner, and said faintly, "It is not yet
time!" As he spoke, the stork flew away. My eyes followed it for
a moment—it could hardly be longer than ten might be counted.
I felt Darvell's weight, as it were, increase upon my shoulder, and,
turning to look upon his face, perceived that he was dead!

I was shocked with the sudden certainty which could not be
mistaken—his countenance in a few minutes became nearly
black. I should have attributed so rapid a change to poison, had I
not been aware that he had no opportunity of receiving it unper-
ceived. The day was declining, the body was rapidly altering, and
nothing remained but to fulfil his request. With the aid of Suleiman's yagatan and my own sabre, we scooped a shallow grave
upon the spot which Darvell had indicated: the earth easily gave
way, having already received some Mahometan tenant. We dug
as deeply as the time permitted us, and throwing the dry earth
upon all that remained of the singular being departed, we cut a
few sods of greener turf from the less withered soil around us, and
laid them upon his sepulchre.

Between astonishment and grief, I was tearless.

In the introduction to *Ernestus Berchtold*, Dr. John Polidori outlines Byron's story, saying, "Two friends were to travel from
England into Greece; while there one of them should die, but
before his death, should obtain from his friend an oath of secrecy with regard to his decease. Some short time after, the re-

maining traveler returning to his native country, should be startled at perceiving his former companion moving about in society, and should be horrified at finding that he made love to his former friend's sister." Unfortunately, Byron never finished his novel.

Lord Byron

EXCERPT FROM
THE GIAOUR

———⇒⊃●⊂⇐———

This is one completed segment of the incomplete ballad "The Giaour."
Giaour, meaning "infidel," is a Turkish term for a non-Muslim, especially a Christian. When it was first published, the ballad contained
an introductory note that explained that the completed story would
have concerned the adventures of a female slave who, in accordance
with Muslim customs, was thrown into the sea because of infidelity
and how she was avenged by her lover, a young Venetian. It's set in
Greece in the late eighteenth century during the Greek Revolution
when part of that country was controlled by the Republic of Venice
and part by the Ottoman Empire. It was a time when, as Byron put it,
"the cruelty exercised on all sides was unparalleled even in the annals
of the faithful." In the following segment, someone curses the Giaour,
wishing that he become a vampire. This was published in 1813, three
years before Lord Byron wrote the fragment of the vampire novel that
appears in the previous chapter.

> But thou, false Infidel! shalt writhe
> Beneath avenging Monkir's scythe;
> And from its torment 'scape alone
> To wander round lost Eblis' throne;
> And fire unquench'd, unquenchable—

Around—within—thy heart shall dwell,
Nor ear can hear, nor tongue can tell
The tortures of that inward hell!—
But first, on earth as Vampire sent,
Thy cor[p]se shall from its tomb be rent;
Then ghastly haunt thy native place,
And suck the blood of all thy race,
There from thy daughter, sister, wife,
At midnight drain the stream of life;
Yet loathe the banquet which perforce
Must feed thy livid living cor[p]se;
Thy victims ere they yet expire
Shall know the dæmon for their sire,
As cursing thee, thou cursing them,
Thy flowers are wither'd on the stem.
But one that for thy crime must fall—
The youngest—most belov'd of all,
Shall bless thee with a *father's* name—
That word shall wrap thy heart in flame!
Yet must thou end thy task, and mark
Her cheek's last tinge, her eye's last spark,
And the last glassy glance must view
Which freezes o'er its lifeless blue;
Then with unhallowed hand shalt tear
The tresses of her yellow hair,
Of which in life a lock when shorn,
Affection's fondest pledge was worn;
But now is borne away by thee,
Memorial of thine agony!
Wet with thine own best blood shall drip,
Thy gnashing tooth and haggard lip;
Then stalking to thy sullen grave—
Go—and with Gouls and Afrits rave;
Till these in horror shrink away
From spectre more accursed than they!

H. G. Wells

THE FLOWERING OF THE STRANGE ORCHID

A Tale of an Orchid Enthusiast

⋯⟫●⟪⋯

Herbert George Wells is considered to be the father of modern science fiction. Born to a working-class family in Britain, he went through several changes in careers before becoming a teacher and marrying his cousin. Several years later, he gave up both his career and his wife, and ran away with one of his students, whom he married in 1895. That same year he published *The Time Machine*, which was quickly followed by *The Island of Dr. Moreau*, *The Invisible Man*, and *The War of the Worlds*. In all, he wrote 156 books and hundreds of short stories and articles. This story was first published in the April 1905 issue of *Pearson's Magazine*.

THE BUYING OF ORCHIDS always has in it a certain speculative flavour. You have before you the brown shrivelled lump of tissue, and for the rest you must trust your judgement, or the auctioneer, or your good-luck, as your taste may incline. The plant may be moribund or dead, or it may be just a respectable purchase, fair value for your money, or perhaps—for the thing has happened again and again—there slowly unfolds before the delighted eyes of the happy purchaser, day after day, some new variety, some novel richness, a strange twist of the labellum, or some subtler coloration or unexpected mimicry. Pride, beauty, and profit blossom together on one delicate green spike, and, it may be, even immortality. For the new miracle of Nature may stand in need of a new specific name, and what so convenient as that of its discoverer? "Johnsmithia!" There have been worse names.

It was perhaps the hope of some such happy discovery that made Winter-Wedderburn such a frequent attendant at these sales—that hope, and also, maybe, the fact that he had nothing else of the slightest interest to do in the world. He was a shy, lonely, rather ineffectual man, provided with just enough income to keep off the spur of necessity, and not enough nervous energy to make him seek any exacting employments. He might have collected stamps or coins, or translated Horace, or bound books, or invented new species of diatoms. But, as it happened, he grew orchids, and had one ambitious little hothouse.

"I have a fancy," he said over his coffee, "that something is going to happen to me to-day." He spoke—as he moved and thought—slowly.

"Oh, don't say *that!*" said his housekeeper—who was also his remote cousin. For "something happening" was a euphemism that meant only one thing to her.

"You misunderstand me. I mean nothing unpleasant—though what I do mean I scarcely know.

"To-day," he continued after a pause, "Peters' are going to sell a batch of plants from the Andamans and the Indies. I shall go up and see what they have. It may be I shall buy something good, unawares. That may be it."

He passed his cup for his second cupful of coffee.

"Are these the things collected by that poor young fellow you told me of the other day?" asked his cousin as she filled his cup.

"Yes," he said, and became meditative over a piece of toast.

"Nothing ever does happen to me," he remarked presently, beginning to think aloud. "I wonder why? Things enough happen to other people. There is Haney. Only the other week, on Monday he picked up sixpence, on Wednesday his chicks all had the staggers, on Friday his cousin came home from Australia, and on Saturday he broke his ankle. What a whirl of excitement!—compared to me."

"I think I would rather be without so much excitement," said his housekeeper. "It can't be good for you."

"I suppose it's troublesome. Still—you see, nothing ever happens to me. When I was a little boy I never had accidents. I never fell in love as I grew up. Never married—I wonder how it feels to have something happen to you, something really remarkable.

"That orchid-collector was only thirty-six—twenty years younger than myself—when he died. And he had been married twice and divorced once; he had had malarial fever four times, and once he broke his thigh. He killed a Malay once, and once he was wounded by a poisoned dart. And in the end he was killed by jungle-leeches. It must have all been very troublesome, but then it must have been very interesting, you know—except, perhaps, the leeches."

"I am sure it was not good for him," said the lady, with conviction.

"Perhaps not." And then Wedderburn looked at his watch. "Twenty-three minutes past eight. I am going up by the quarter to twelve train, so that there is plenty of time. I think I shall wear my alpaca jacket—it is quite warm enough—and my grey felt hat and brown shoes. I suppose—"

He glanced out of the window at the serene sky and sunlit garden, and then nervously at his cousin's face.

"I think you had better take an umbrella if you are going to London," she said in a voice that admitted of no denial. "There's all between here and the station coming back."

When he returned he was in a state of mild excitement. He had made a purchase. It was rare that he could make up his mind quickly enough to buy, but this time he had done so.

"There are Vandas," he said, "and a Dendrobe and some Palæonophis." He surveyed his purchases lovingly as he consumed his soup. They were laid out on the spotless tablecloth before him, and he was telling his cousin all about them as he slowly meandered through his dinner. It was his custom to live all his visits to London over again in the evening for her and his own entertainment.

"I knew something would happen to-day. And I have bought all these. Some of them—some of them—I feel sure, do you know, that some of them will be remarkable. I don't know how it is, but

I feel just as sure as if some one had told me that some of these will turn out remarkable.

"That one"—he pointed to a shrivelled rhizome—"was not identified. It may be a Palæonophis—or it may not. It may be a new species, or even a new genus. And it was the last that poor Batten ever collected."

"I don't like the look of it," said his housekeeper. "It's such an ugly shape."

"To me it scarcely seems to have a shape."

"I don't like those things that stick out," said his housekeeper.

"It shall be put away in a pot to-morrow."

"It looks," said the housekeeper, "like a spider shamming dead."

Wedderburn smiled and surveyed the root with his head on one side. "It is certainly not a pretty lump of stuff. But you can never judge of these things from their dry appearance. It may turn out to be a very beautiful orchid indeed. How busy I shall be to-morrow! I must see to-night just exactly what to do with these things, and to-morrow I shall set to work.

"They found poor Batten lying dead, or dying, in a mangrove swamp—I forget which," he began again presently, "with one of these very orchids crushed up under his body. He had been unwell for some days with some kind of native fever, and I suppose he fainted. These mangrove swamps are very unwholesome. Every drop of blood, they say, was taken out of him by the jungle-leeches. It may be that very plant that cost him his life to obtain."

"I think none the better of it for that."

"Men must work though women may weep," said Wedderburn, with profound gravity.

"Fancy dying away from every comfort in a nasty swamp! Fancy being ill of fever with nothing to take but chlorodyne and quinine—if men were left to themselves they would live on chlorodyne and quinine—and no one round you but horrible natives! They say the Andaman islanders are most disgusting wretches—and, anyhow, they can scarcely make good nurses, not having the necessary training. And just for people in England to have orchids!"

"I don't suppose it was comfortable, but some men seem to enjoy that kind of thing," said Wedderburn. "Anyhow, the natives of his party were sufficiently civilised to take care of all his collection until his colleague, who was an ornithologist, came back again from the interior; though they could not tell the species of the orchid, and had let it wither. And it makes these things more interesting."

"It makes them disgusting. I should be afraid of some of the malaria clinging to them. And just think, there has been a dead body lying across that ugly thing! I never thought of that before. There! I declare I cannot eat another mouthful of dinner."

"I will take them off the table if you like, and put them in the window-seat. I can see them just as well there."

The next few days he was indeed singularly busy in his steamy little hothouse, fussing about with charcoal, lumps of teak, moss, and all the other mysteries of the orchid cultivator. He considered he was having a wonderfully eventful time. In the evening he would talk about these new orchids to his friends, and over and over again he reverted to his expectation of something strange.

Several of the Vandas and the Dendrobium died under his care, but presently the strange orchid began to show signs of life. He was delighted, and took his housekeeper right away from jam-making to see it at once, directly he made the discovery.

"That is a bud," he said, "and presently there will be a lot of leaves there, and those little things coming out here are aerial rootlets."

"They look to me like little white fingers poking out of the brown. I don't like them," said his housekeeper.

"Why not?"

"I don't know. They look like fingers trying to get at you. I can't help my likes and dislikes."

"I don't know for certain, but I don't *think* there are any orchids I know that have aerial rootlets quite like that. It may be my fancy, of course. You see they are a little flattened at the ends."

"I don't like 'em," said his housekeeper, suddenly shivering and turning away. "I know it's very silly of me—and I'm very sorry, particularly as you like the thing so much. But I can't help thinking of that corpse."

"But it may not be that particular plant. That was merely a guess of mine."

His housekeeper shrugged her shoulders.

"Anyhow I don't like it," she said.

Wedderburn felt a little hurt at her dislike to the plant. But that did not prevent his talking to her about orchids generally, and this orchid in particular, whenever he felt inclined.

"There are such queer things about orchids," he said one day; "such possibilities of surprises. You know, Darwin studied their fertilisation, and showed that the whole structure of an ordinary orchid-flower was contrived in order that moths might carry the pollen from plant to plant. Well, it seems that there are lots of orchids known the flower of which cannot possibly be used for fertilisation in that way. Some of the Cypripediums, for instance; there are no insects known that can possibly fertilise them, and some of them have never been found with seed."

"But how do they form new plants?"

"By runners and tubers, and that kind of outgrowth. That is easily explained. The puzzle is, what are the flowers for?"

"Very likely," he added, "*my* orchid may be something extraordinary in that way. If so, I shall study it. I have often thought of making researches as Darwin did. But hitherto I have not found the time, or something else has happened to prevent it. The leaves are beginning to unfold now. I do wish you would come and see them!"

But she said that the orchid-house was so hot it gave her the headache. She had seen the plant once again, and the aerial rootlets, which were now some of them more than a foot long, had unfortunately reminded her of tentacles reaching out after something; and they got into her dreams, growing after her with incredible rapidity. So that she had settled to her entire satisfaction that she would not see that plant again, and Wedderburn had to admire its leaves alone. They were of the ordinary broad form, and a deep glossy green, with splashes and dots of deep red towards the base. He knew of no other leaves quite like them. The plant was placed on a low bench near the thermometer, and close by was a simple arrangement by which a tap dripped on the hot-water pipes and kept the air steamy. And he spent his afternoons now with some regularity meditating on the approaching flowering of this strange plant.

And at last the great thing happened. Directly he entered the little glass house he knew that the spike had burst out, although his great *Palæonophis Lowii* hid the corner where his new darling stood. There was a new odour in the air, a rich, intensely sweet scent, that overpowered every other in that crowded, steaming little greenhouse.

Directly he noticed this as he hurried down to the strange orchid. And, behold! the trailing green spikes bore now three great splashes of blossom, from which this overpowering sweetness proceeded. He stopped before them in an ecstasy of admiration.

The flowers were white, with streaks of golden orange upon the petals; the heavy labellum was coiled into an intricate projection, and a wonderful bluish purple mingled there with the gold. He could see at once that the genus was altogether a new one. And the insufferable scent! How hot the place was! The blossoms swam before his eyes.

He would see if the temperature was right. He made a step towards the thermometer. Suddenly everything appeared unsteady. The bricks on the floor were dancing up and down. Then the white blossoms, the green leaves behind them, the whole greenhouse, seemed to sweep sideways, and then in a curve upward.

At half-past four his cousin made the tea, according to their invariable custom. But Wedderburn did not come in for his tea.

"He is worshipping that horrid orchid," she told herself, and waited ten minutes. "His watch must have stopped. I will go and call him."

She went straight to the hothouse, and, opening the door, called his name. There was no reply. She noticed that the air was very close, and loaded with an intense perfume. Then she saw something lying on the bricks between the hot-water pipes.

For a minute, perhaps, she stood motionless.

He was lying, face upward, at the foot of the strange orchid. The tentacle-like aerial rootlets no longer swayed freely in the air, but were crowded together, a tangle of grey ropes, and stretched tight with their ends closely applied to his chin and neck and hands.

She did not understand. Then she saw from under one of the exultant tentacles upon his cheek there trickled a little thread of blood.

With an inarticulate cry she ran towards him, and tried to pull him away from the leech-like suckers. She snapped two of these tentacles, and their sap dripped red.

Then the overpowering scent of the blossom began to make her head reel. How they clung to him! She tore at the tough ropes, and he and the white inflorescence swam about her. She felt she was fainting, knew she must not. She left him and hastily opened the nearest door, and, after she had panted for a moment in the fresh air, she had a brilliant inspiration. She caught up a flower-pot and smashed in the windows at the end of the greenhouse. Then she re-entered. She tugged now with renewed strength at Wedderburn's motionless body, and brought the strange orchid crashing to the floor. It still clung with the grimmest tenacity to its victim. In a frenzy, she lugged it and him into the open air.

Then she thought of tearing through the sucker rootlets one by one, and in another minute she had released him and was dragging him away from the horror.

He was white and bleeding from a dozen circular patches.

The odd-job man was coming up the garden, amazed at the smashing of glass, and saw her emerge, hauling the inanimate body with red-stained hands. For a moment he thought impossible things.

"Bring some water!" she cried, and her voice dispelled his fancies. When, with unnatural alacrity, he returned with the water, he found her weeping with excitement, and with Wedderburn's head upon her knee, wiping the blood from his face.

"What's the matter?" said Wedderburn, opening his eyes feebly, and closing them again at once.

"Go and tell Annie to come out here to me, and then go for Dr. Haddon at once," she said to the odd-job man so soon as he brought the water; and added, seeing he hesitated, "I will tell you all about it when you come back."

Presently Wedderburn opened his eyes again, and, seeing that he was troubled by the puzzle of his position, she explained to him, "You fainted in the hothouse."

"And the orchid?"

"I will see to that," she said.

Wedderburn had lost a good deal of blood, but beyond that he had suffered no very great injury. They gave him brandy mixed with some pink extract of meat, and carried him upstairs to bed.

His housekeeper told her incredible story in fragments to Dr. Haddon. "Come to the orchid-house and see," she said.

The cold outer air was blowing in through the open door, and the sickly perfume was almost dispelled. Most of the torn aerial rootlets lay already withered amidst a number of dark stains upon the bricks. The stem of the inflorescence was broken by the fall of the plant, and the flowers were growing limp and brown at the edges of the petals. The doctor stooped towards it, then saw that one of the aerial rootlets still stirred feebly, and hesitated.

The next morning the strange orchid still lay there, black now and putrescent. The door banged intermittently in the morning breeze, and all the array of Wedderburn's orchids was shrivelled and prostrate. But Wedderburn himself was bright and garrulous upstairs in the story of his strange adventure.

Ray Bradbury

THE HOMECOMING

Ray Bradbury is one of the greatest and most popular science fiction writers in the world. He started out writing for pulp magazines in the 1940s, and gradually gained in popularity. His books include such classics as *The Martian Chronicles, Fahrenheit 451, R is for Rocket, The Illustrated Man*, plus two of my favorites—*Dandelion Wine* and *Something Wicked This Way Comes*. Many of his short stories have been dramatized in the television series *Ray Bradbury Theater*, hosted, of course, by Ray Bradbury himself. His works are in a large way responsible for bringing science fiction to a mainstream audience, though he has never restricted himself to this genre. This story, first published in *Mademoiselle* in 1946, was selected for the *O. Henry Awards Prize of 1947*. It also appeared in Bradbury's first book, *Dark Carnival* (1947), and then in *The October Country* (1955).

"HERE THEY COME," SAID Cecy, lying there flat in her bed.

"Where are they?" cried Timothy from the doorway.

"Some of them are over Europe, some over Asia, some of them over the Islands, some over South America!" said Cecy, her eyes closed, the lashes long, brown, and quivering.

Timothy came forward upon the bare plankings of the upstairs room. "Who are they?"

"Uncle Einar and Uncle Fry, and there's Cousin William, and I see Frulda and Helgar and Aunt Morgiana and Cousin Vivian, and I see Uncle Johann! They're all coming fast!''

"Are they up in the sky?'' cried Timothy, his little gray eyes flashing. Standing by the bed, he looked no more than his four-teen years. The wind blew outside, the house was dark and lit only by starlight.

"They're coming through the air and traveling along the ground, in many forms,'' said Cecy, in her sleeping. She did not move on the bed; she thought inward on herself and told what she saw. "I see a wolflike thing coming over a dark river—at the shallows—just above a waterfall, the starlight shining up his pelt. I see a brown oak leaf blowing far up in the sky. I see a small bat flying. I see many other things, running through the forest trees and slipping through the highest branches; and they're *all* coming this way!''

"Will they be here by tomorrow night?'' Timothy clutched the bedclothes. The spider on his lapel swung like a black pendulum, excitedly dancing. He leaned over his sister. "Will they all be here in time for the Homecoming?''

"Yes, yes, Timothy, yes,'' sighed Cecy. She stiffened. "Ask no more of me. Go away now. Let me travel in the places I like best.''

"Thanks, Cecy,'' he said. Out in the hall, he ran to his room. He hurriedly made his bed. He had just awakened a few minutes ago, at sunset, and as the first stars had risen, he had gone to let his excitement about the party run with Cecy. Now she slept so quietly there was not a sound. The spider hung on a silvery lasso about Timothy's slender neck as he washed his face. "Just think, Spid, tomorrow night is Allhallows Eve!''

He lifted his face and looked into the mirror. His was the only mirror allowed in the house. It was his mother's concession to his illness. Oh if only he were not so afflicted! He opened his mouth, surveyed the poor, inadequate teeth nature had given him. No more than so many corn kernels—round, soft and pale in his jaws. Some of the high spirit died in him.

It was now totally dark and he lit a candle to see by. He felt exhausted. This past week the whole family had lived in the fash-ion of the old country. Sleeping by day, rousing at sunset to move about. There were blue hollows under his eyes. "Spid, I'm no good," he said, quietly, to the little creature. "I can't even get used to sleeping days like the others."

He took up the candleholder. Oh, to have strong teeth, with incisors like steel spikes. Or strong hands, even, or a strong mind. Even to have the power to send one's mind out, free, as Cecy did. But, no, he was the imperfect one, the sick one. He was even— he shivered and drew the candle flame closer—afraid of the dark. His brothers snorted at him. Bion and Leonard and Sam. They laughed at him because he slept in a bed. With Cecy it was different; her bed was part of her comfort for the composure necessary to send her mind abroad to hunt. But Timothy, did he sleep in the wonderful polished boxes like the others? He did not! Mother let him have his own bed, his own room, his own mirror. No wonder the family skirted him like a holy man's crucifix. If only the wings would sprout from his shoulder blades. He bared his back, stared at it. And sighed again. No chance. Never.

Downstairs were exciting and mysterious sounds, the slithering black crape going up in all the halls and on the ceilings and doors. The sputter of burning black tapers in the banistered stairwell. Mother's voice, high and firm. Father's voice, echoing from the damp cellar. Bion walking from outside the old country house lugging vast two-gallon jugs.

"I've just got to go to the party, Spid," said Timothy. The spider whirled at the end of its silk, and Timothy felt alone. He would polish cases, fetch toadstools and spiders, hang crape, but when the party started he'd be ignored. The less seen or said of the imperfect son the better.

All through the house below, Laura ran.

"The Homecoming!" she shouted gaily. "The Homecoming!" Her footsteps everywhere at once.

Timothy passed Cecy's room again, and she was sleeping quietly. Once a month she went belowstairs. Always she stayed in bed. Lovely Cecy. He felt like asking her, "Where are you now, Cecy? And *in* who? And what's happening? Are you beyond the hills? And what goes on there?" But he went on to Ellen's room instead.

Ellen sat at her desk, sorting out many kinds of blonde, red and black hair and little scimitars of fingernails gathered from her manicurist job at the Mellin Village beauty parlor fifteen miles over. A sturdy mahogany case lay in one corner with her name on it.

"Go away," she said, not even looking at him. "I can't work with you gawking."

"Allhallows Eve, Ellen; just think!" he said, trying to be friendly.

"Hunh!" She put some fingernail clippings in a small white sack, labeled them. "What can it mean to you? What do you know of it? It'll scare hell out of you. Go back to bed."

His cheeks burned. "I'm needed to polish and work and help serve."

"If you don't go, you'll find a dozen raw oysters in your bed tomorrow," said Ellen, matter-of-factly. "Good-by, Timothy."

In his anger, rushing downstairs, he bumped into Laura.

"Watch where you're going!" she shrieked from clenched teeth.

She swept away. He ran to the open cellar door, smelled the channel of moist earthy air rising from below. "Father?"

"It's about time," Father shouted up the steps. "Hurry down, or they'll be here before we're ready!"

Timothy hesitated only long enough to hear the million other sounds in the house. Brothers came and went like trains in a station, talking and arguing. If you stood in one spot long enough the entire household passed with their pale hands full of things. Leonard with his little black medical case, Samuel with his large, dusty ebon-bound book under his arm, bearing more black crape, and Bion excursioning to the car outside and bringing in many more gallons of liquid.

Father stopped polishing to give Timothy a rag and a scowl. He thumped the huge mahogany box. "Come on, shine this up, so we can start on another. Sleep your life away."

While waxing the surface, Timothy looked inside.

"Uncle Einar's a big man, isn't he, Papa?"

"Unh."

"How big is he?"

"The size of the box'll tell you."

"I was only asking. Seven feet tall?"
"You talk a lot."

About nine o'clock Timothy went out into the October weather. For two hours in the now-warm, now-cold wind he walked the meadows collecting toadstools and spiders. His heart began to beat with anticipation again. How many relatives had Mother said would come? Seventy? One hundred? He passed a farmhouse. If only you knew what was happening at our house, he said to the glowing windows. He climbed a hill and looked at the town, miles away, settling into sleep, the town-hall clock, high and round, white in the distance. The town did not know, either. He brought home many jars of toadstools and spiders.

In the little chapel belowstairs a brief ceremony was celebrated. It was like all the other rituals over the years, with Father chanting the dark lines, Mother's beautiful white ivory hands moving in the reverse blessings, and all the children gathered except Cecy, who lay upstairs in bed. But Cecy was present. You saw her peering, now from Bion's eyes, now Samuel's, now Mother's, and you felt a movement and now she was in you, fleetingly, and gone.

Timothy prayed to the Dark One with a tightened stomach. "Please, please, help me grow up, help me be like my sisters and brothers. Don't let me be different. If only I could put the hair in the plastic images as Ellen does, or make people fall in love with me as Laura does with people, or read strange books as Sam does, or work in a respected job like Leonard and Bion do. Or even raise a family one day, as Mother and Father have done. . . ."

At midnight a storm hammered the house. Lightning struck outside in amazing, snow-white bolts. There was a sound of an approaching, probing, sucking tornado, funneling and nuzzling the moist night earth. Then the front door, blasted half off its hinges, hung stiff and discarded, and in trooped Grandmama and Grandpapa, all the way from the old country!

From then on people arrived each hour. There was a flutter at the side window, a rap on the front porch, a knock at the back. There were fey noises from the cellar; autumn wind piped down the chimney throat, chanting. Mother filled the large crystal punch bowl with a scarlet fluid poured from the jugs Bion had

carried home. Father swept from room to room lighting more tapers. Laura and Ellen hammered up more wolfsbane. And Timothy stood amidst this wild excitement, no expression to his face,
his hands trembling at his sides, gazing now here, now there.
Banging of doors, laughter, the sound of liquid pouring, darkness,
sound of wind, the webbed thunder of wings, the padding of feet,
the welcoming bursts of talk at the entrances, the transparent rat-
tlings of casements, the shadows passing, coming, going, waver-
ing.

"Well, well, and *this* must be Timothy!"

"What?"

A chilly hand took his hand. A long hairy face leaned down
over him. "A good lad, a fine lad," said the stranger.

"Timothy," said his mother. "This is Uncle Jason."

"Hello, Uncle Jason."

"And over here—" Mother drifted Uncle Jason away. Uncle
Jason peered back at Timothy over his caped shoulder, and
winked.

Timothy stood alone.

From off a thousand miles in the candled darkness, he heard a
high fluting voice; that was Ellen. "And my brothers, they *are*
clever. Can you guess their occupations, Aunt Morgiana?"

"I have no idea."

"They operate the undertaking establishment in town."

"What!" A gasp.

"Yes!" Shrill laughter. "Isn't that priceless!"

Timothy stood very still.

A pause in the laughter. "They bring home sustenance for
Mama, Papa and all of us," said Laura. "Except, of course, Timothy. . . ."

An uneasy silence. Uncle Jason's voice demanded, "Well?
Come now. What about Timothy?"

"Oh, Laura, your tongue," said Mother.

Laura went on with it. Timothy shut his eyes. "Timothy
doesn't—well—doesn't *like* blood. He's delicate."

"He'll learn," said Mother. "He'll learn," she said very firmly.
"He's my son, and he'll learn. He's only fourteen."

"But I was raised on the stuff," said Uncle Jason, his voice passing from one room on into another. The wind played the trees

outside like harps. A little rain spatted on the windows—"raised on the stuff," passing away into faintness.

Timothy bit his lips and opened his eyes.

"Well, it was all my fault." Mother was showing them into the kitchen now. "I tried forcing him. You can't force children, you only make them sick, and then they never get a taste for things. Look at Bion, now, he was thirteen before he . . ."

"I understand," murmured Uncle Jason. "Timothy will come around."

"I'm sure he will," said Mother, defiantly.

Candle flames quivered as shadows crossed and recrossed the dozen musty rooms. Timothy was cold. He smelled the hot tallow in his nostrils and instinctively he grabbed at a candle and walked with it around and about the house, pretending to straighten the crape.

"*Timothy*," someone whispered behind a patterned wall, hissing and sizzling and sighing the words, "*Timothy is afraid of the dark.*"

Leonard's voice. Hateful Leonard!

"I like the candle, that's all," said Timothy in a reproachful whisper.

More lightning, more thunder. Cascades of roaring laughter. Bangings and clickings and shouts and rustles of clothing. Clammy fog swept through the front door. Out of the fog, settling his wings, stalked a tall man.

"Uncle Einar!"

Timothy propelled himself on his thin legs, straight through the fog, under the green webbing shadows. He threw himself across Einar's arms. Einar lifted him.

"You've wings, Timothy!" He tossed the boy light as thistles. "Wings, Timothy: fly!" Faces wheeled under. Darkness rotated. The house blew away. Timothy felt breezelike. He flapped his arms. Einar's fingers caught and threw him once more to the ceiling. The ceiling rushed down like a charred wall. "Fly, Timothy!" shouted Einar, loud and deep. "Fly with wings! Wings!"

He felt an exquisite ecstasy in his shoulder blades, as if roots grew, burst to explode and blossom into new, moist membrane. He babbled wild stuff; again Einar hurled him high.

The autumn wind broke in a tide on the house, rain crashed down, shaking the beams, causing chandeliers to tilt their enraged candle lights. And the one hundred relatives peered out from every black, enchanted room, circling inward, all shapes and sizes, to where Einar balanced the child like a baton in the roaring spaces.

"Enough!" shouted Einar, at last.

Timothy, deposited on the floor timbers, exaltedly, exhaustedly fell against Uncle Einar, sobbing happily. "Uncle, uncle, uncle!"

"Was it good, flying? Eh, Timothy?" said Uncle Einar, bending down, patting Timothy's head. "Good, good."

It was coming toward dawn. Most had arrived and were ready to bed down for the daylight, sleep motionlessly with no sound until the following sunset, when they would shout out of their mahogany boxes for the revelry.

Uncle Einar, followed by dozens of others, moved toward the cellar. Mother directed them downward to the crowded row on row of highly polished boxes. Einar, his wings like sea-green tarpaulins tented behind him, moved with a curious whistling down the passageway; where his wings touched they made a sound of drumheads gently beaten.

Upstairs, Timothy lay wearily thinking, trying to like the darkness. There was so much you could do in darkness that people couldn't criticize you for, because they never saw you. He *did* like the night, but it was a qualified liking: sometimes there was so much night he cried out in rebellion.

In the cellar, mahogany doors sealed downward, drawn in by pale hands. In corners, certain relatives circled three times to lie, heads on paws, eyelids shut. The sun rose. There was a sleeping.

Sunset. The revel exploded like a bat nest struck full, shrieking out, fluttering, spreading. Box doors banged wide. Steps rushed up from cellar damp. More late guests, kicking on front and back portals, were admitted.

It rained, and sodden visitors laid their capes, their water-pelleted hats, their sprinkled veils upon Timothy who bore them to a closet. The rooms were crowd-packed. The laughter of one cousin, shot from one room, angled off the wall of another, ricocheted, banked, and returned to Timothy's ears from a fourth room, accurate and cynical.

A mouse ran across the floor.

"I know you, Niece Leibersrouter!" exclaimed Father, around him but not to him. The dozens of towering people pressed in against him, elbowed him, ignored him.

Finally, he turned and slipped away up the stairs.

He called softly. "Cecy. Where are you now, Cecy?"

She waited a long while before answering. "In the Imperial Valley," she murmured faintly. "Beside the Salton Sea, near the mud pots and the steam and the quiet. I'm inside a farmer's wife. I'm sitting on a front porch. I can make her move if I want, or do anything or think anything. The sun's going down."

"What's it like, Cecy?"

"You can hear the mud pots hissing," she said, slowly, as if speaking in a church. "Little gray heads of steam push up the mud like bald men rising in the thick syrup, head first, out in the boiling channels. The gray heads rip like rubber fabric, collapse with noises like wet lips moving. And feathery plumes of steam escape from the ripped tissue. And there is a smell of deep sulphurous burning and old times. The dinosaur has been abroiling here ten million years."

"Is he done yet, Cecy?"

The mouse spiraled three women's feet and vanished into a corner. Moments later a beautiful woman rose up out of nothing and stood in the corner, smiling her white smile at them all.

Something huddled against the flooded pane of the kitchen window. It sighed and wept and tapped continually, pressed against the glass, but Timothy could make nothing of it, he saw nothing. In imagination he was outside staring in. The rain was on him, the wind at him, and the taper-dotted darkness inside was inviting. Waltzes were being danced; tall thin figures pirouetted to outlandish music. Stars of light flickered off lifted bottles; small clods of earth crumbled from casques, and a spider fell and went silently legging over the floor.

Timothy shivered. He was inside the house again. Mother was calling him to run here, run there, help, serve, out to the kitchen now, fetch this, fetch that, bring the plates, heap the food—on and on—the party happened.

"Yes, he's done. Quite done." Cecy's calm sleeper's lips turned up. The languid words fell slowly from her shaping mouth. "Inside this woman's skull I am, looking out, watching the sea that does not move, and is so quiet it makes you afraid. I sit on the porch and wait for my husband to come home. Occasionally, a fish leaps, falls back, starlight edging it. The valley, the sea, the few cars, the wooden porch, my rocking chair, myself, the silence."

"What now, Cecy?"

"I'm getting up from my rocking chair," she said.

"Yes?"

"I'm walking off the porch, toward the mud pots. Planes fly over, like primordial birds. Then it is quiet, so quiet."

"How long will you stay inside her, Cecy?"

"Until I've listened and looked and felt enough: until I've changed her life some way. I'm walking off the porch and along the wooden boards. My feet knock on the planks, tiredly, slowly."

"And now?"

"Now the sulphur fumes are all around me. I stare at the bubbles as they break and smooth. A bird darts by my temple, shrieking. Suddenly I am in the bird and fly away! And as I fly, inside my new small glass-bead eyes I see a woman below me, on a boardwalk, take one two three steps forward into the mud pots. I hear a sound as of a boulder plunged into molten depths. I keep flying, circle back. I see a white hand, like a spider, wriggle and disappear into the gray lava pool. The lava seals over. Now I'm flying home, swift, swift, swift!"

Something clapped hard against the window. Timothy started.

Cecy flicked her eyes wide, bright, full, happy, exhilarated.

"Now I'm *home*!" she said.

After a pause, Timothy ventured, "The Homecoming's on. And everybody's here."

"Then why are you upstairs?" She took his hand. "Well, ask me." She smiled slyly. "Ask me what you came to ask."

"I didn't come to ask anything," he said. "Well, almost nothing. Well—oh, Cecy!" It came from him in one long rapid flow. "I want to do something at the party to make them look at me, something to make me good as them, something to make me belong, but there's nothing I can do and I feel funny and, well, I thought you might . . ."

"I might," she said, closing her eyes, smiling inwardly. "Stand up straight. Stand very still." He obeyed. "Now, shut your eyes and blank out your thought."

He stood very straight and thought of nothing, or at least thought of thinking nothing.

She sighed. "Shall we go downstairs now, Timothy?" Like a hand into a glove, Cecy was within him.

"Look everybody!" Timothy held the glass of warm red liquid. He held up the glass so that the whole house turned to watch him. Aunts, uncles, cousins, brothers, sisters!

He drank it straight down.

He jerked a hand at his sister Laura. He held her gaze, whispering to her in a subtle voice that kept her silent, frozen. He felt tall as the trees as he walked to her. The party now slowed. It waited on all sides of him, watching. From all the room doors the faces peered. They were not laughing. Mother's face was astonished. Dad looked bewildered, but pleased and getting prouder every instant.

He nipped Laura, gently, over the neck vein. The candle flames swayed drunkenly. The wind climbed around on the roof outside. The relatives stared from all the doors. He popped toadstools into his mouth, swallowed, then beat his arms against his flanks and circled. "Look, Uncle Einar! I can fly, at last!" Beat went his hands. Up and down pumped his feet. The faces flashed past him.

At the top of the stairs, flapping, he heard his mother cry, "Stop, Timothy!" far below. "Hey!" shouted Timothy, and leaped off the top of the well, thrashing.

Halfway down, the wings he thought he owned dissolved. He screamed. Uncle Einar caught him.

Timothy flailed whitely in the receiving arms. A voice burst out of his lips, unbidden. "This is Cecy! This is Cecy! Come see me, all of you, upstairs, first room on the left!" Followed by a long trill of high laughter. Timothy tried to cut it off with his tongue.

Everybody was laughing. Einar set him down. Running through the crowding blackness as the relatives flowed upstairs toward Cecy's room to congratulate her, Timothy banged the front door open.

"Cecy, I hate you, I hate you!"

By the sycamore tree, in deep shadow, Timothy spewed out his dinner, sobbed bitterly and thrashed in a pile of autumn leaves. Then he lay still. From his blouse pocket, from the protection of the matchbox he used for his retreat, the spider crawled forth. Spid walked along Timothy's arm. Spid explored up his neck to his ear and climbed in the ear to tickle it. Timothy shook his head. "Don't, Spid. Don't."

The feathery touch of a tentative feeler probing his eardrum set Timothy shivering. "Don't, Spid!" He sobbed somewhat less.

The spider traveled down his cheek, took a station under the boy's nose, looked up into the nostrils as if to seek the brain, and then clambered softly up over the rim of the nose to sit, to squat there peering at Timothy with green-gem eyes until Timothy filled with ridiculous laughter. "Go away, Spid!"

Timothy sat up, rustling the leaves. The land was very bright with the moon. In the house he could hear the faint ribaldry as Mirror, Mirror was played. Celebrants shouted, dimly muffled, as they tried to identify those of themselves whose reflections did not, had not ever, appeared in a glass.

"Timothy." Uncle Einar's wings spread and twitched and came in with a sound like kettledrums. Timothy felt himself plucked up like a thimble and set upon Einar's shoulder. "Don't feel badly, Nephew Timothy. Each to his own, each in his own way. How much better things are for you. How rich. The world's dead for us. We've seen so much of it, believe me. Life's best to those who live the least of it. It's worth more per ounce, Timothy, remember that."

The rest of the black morning, from midnight on, Uncle Einar led him about the house, from room to room, weaving and singing. A horde of late arrivals set the entire hilarity off afresh. Great-great-great-great and a thousand more great-greats Grandmother was there, wrapped in Egyptian cerements. She said not a word, but lay straight as a burnt ironing board against the wall, her eye hollows cupping a distant, wise, silent glimmering. At the break-fast, at four in the morning, one-thousand-odd-greats Grand-mama was stiffly seated at the head of the longest table.

The numerous young cousins caroused at the crystal punch bowl. Their shiny olive-pit eyes, their conical, devilish faces and curly bronze hair hovered over the drinking table, their hard-soft, half-girl half-boy bodies wrestling against each other as they got unpleasantly, sullenly drunk. The wind got higher, the stars burned with fiery intensity, the noises redoubled, the dances quickened, the drinking became more positive. To Timothy there were thousands of things to hear and watch. The many darknesses roiled, bubbled, the many faces passed and repassed. . . .

"Listen!"

The party held its breath. Far away the town clock struck its chimes, saying six o'clock. The party was ending. In time to the rhythm of the striking clock, their one hundred voices began to sing songs that were four hundred years old, songs Timothy could not know. Arms twined, circling slowly, they sang, and somewhere in the cold distance of morning the town clock finished out its chimes and quieted.

Timothy sang. He knew no words, no tune, yet the words and tune came round and high and good. And he gazed at the closed door at the top of the stairs.

"Thanks, Cecy," he whispered. "You're forgiven. Thanks."

Then he just relaxed and let the words move, with Cecy's voice, free from his lips.

Good-bys were said, there was a great rustling. Mother and Father stood at the door to shake hands and kiss each departing relative in turn. The sky beyond the open door colored in the east. A cold wind entered. And Timothy felt himself seized and settled in one body after another, felt Cecy press him into Uncle Fry's head so he stared from the wrinkled leather face, then leaped in a flurry of leaves up over the house and awakening hills. . . .

Then, loping down a dirt path, he felt his red eyes burning, his fur pelt rimed with morning, as inside Cousin William he panted through a hollow and dissolved away. . . .

Like a pebble in Uncle Einar's mouth, Timothy flew in a webbed thunder, filling the sky. And then he was back, for all time, in his own body.

In the growing dawn, the last few were embracing and crying and thinking how the world was becoming less a place for them. There had been a time when they had met every year, but now decades passed with no reconciliation. "Don't forget," someone cried, "we meet in Salem in 1970!"

Salem. Timothy's numbed mind turned the words over. Salem, 1970. And there would be Uncle Fry and a thousand-times-great Grandmother in her withered cerements, and Mother and Father and Ellen and Laura and Cecy and all the rest. But would he be there? Could he be certain of staying alive until then?

With one last withering blast, away they all went, so many scarves, so many fluttery mammals, so many sere leaves, so many whining and clustering noises, so many midnights and insanities and dreams.

Mother shut the door. Laura picked up a broom. "No," said Mother. "We'll clean tonight. Now we need sleep." And the family vanished down cellar and upstairs. And Timothy moved in the crape-littered hall, his head down. Passing a party mirror, he saw the pale mortality of his face all cold and trembling.

"Timothy," said Mother.

She came to touch her hand on his face. "Son," she said, "we love you. Remember that. We all love you. No matter how different you are, no matter if you leave us one day." She kissed his cheek. "And if and when you die, your bones will lie undisturbed, we'll see to that. You'll lie at ease forever, and I'll come visit every Allhallows Eve and tuck you in the more secure."

The house was silent. Far away the wind went over a hill with its last cargo of dark bats, echoing, chittering.

Timothy walked up the steps, one by one, crying to himself all the way.

Sir Walter Scott

EXCERPT FROM

ROKEBY

———⊱◈⊰———

Sir Walter Scott (1771–1832), one of Scotland's most famous authors and a leading romantic writer, invented the historical novel and was the first to portray peasant characters sympathetically and realistically. His many works include the *Waverley* novels, *Ivanhoe*, *Rob Roy*, *The Black Dwarf*, *The Heart of Midlothian*, *The Talisman*, and the narrative poems *The Lay of the Last Minstrel* and *The Lady of the Lake*. His death in 1832 marks the end of the romantic age of English literature. This narrative poem is set in 1644 during England's civil war. Most of the story takes place at the estate called Rokeby and at Barnard Castle, both in Yorkshire, England. It was first published in 1813. These are two of its 168 verses.

Wilfrid must love and woo the bright
Matilda, heir of Rokeby's knight.
To love her was an easy hest,
The secret empress of his breast;
To woo her was a harder task
To one that durst not hope or ask.
Yet all Matilda could she gave
In pity to her gentle slave;
Friendship, esteem, and fair regard,

And praise, the poet's best reward!
She read the tales his taste approved,
And sung the lays he framed or loved;
Yet, loath to nurse the fatal flame
Of hopeless love in friendship's name,
In kind caprice she oft withdrew
The favouring glance to friendship due,
Then I grieved to see her victim's pain,
And gave the dangerous smiles again. . . .

More wouldst thou know—yon tower survey,
Yon couch unpressed since parting day,
Yon untrimmed lamp, whose yellow gleam
Is mingling with the cold moonbeam,
And yon thin form!—the hectic red
On his pale cheek unequal spread;
The head reclined, the loosened hair,
The limbs relaxed, the mournful air.—
See, he looks up;—a woeful smile
Lightens his woe-worn cheek a while,—
'Tis Fancy wakes some idle thought,
To gild the ruin she has wrought;
For, like the bat of Indian brakes,
Her pinions fan the wound she makes,
And, soothing thus the dreamer's pain,
She drinks his life-blood from the vein.
Now to the lattice turn his eyes,
Vain hope! to see the sun arise.
The moon with clouds is still o'ercast,
Still howls by fits the stormy blast;
Another hour must wear away
Ere the east kindle into day,
And hark! to waste that weary hour,
He tries the minstrel's magic power.

Ivan Turgenev

PHANTOMS

Ivan Turgenev (1818–1883) was one of the most important of Russia's novelists and the first to gain popularity outside his country. Like Charles Dickens, Turgenev wrote about the harsh lives of the lower classes. This often brought him into conflict with the government, which once banished him to his estate for a year. He finally became fed up and left Russia forever, settling in Germany. As the author of *Liza*, *Smoke*, *Fathers and Sons*, and *Torrents of Spring*, he was more famous than Leo Tolstoy and Dostoyevsky during his lifetime, though this situation has reversed since his death. Nevertheless, his works are still considered major Russian classics. The following supernatural tale was published in 1864, just a few months after he left Russia.

FOR A LONG TIME I could not get to sleep, and kept turning from side to side. "Confound this foolishness about table-turning!" I thought. "It simply upsets one's nerves.". . . Drowsiness began to overtake me at last . . .

Suddenly it seemed to me as though there were the faint and plaintive sound of a harp-string in the room.

I raised my head. The moon was low in the sky, and looked me straight in the face. White as chalk lay its light upon the floor . . . The strange sound was distinctly repeated.

I leaned on my elbow. A faint feeling of awe plucked at my

heart. A minute passed, another . . . Somewhere, far away, a cock crowed; another answered still more remote.

I let my head sink back on the pillow. "See what one can work oneself up to," I thought again, . . . "there's a singing in my ears."

After a little while I fell asleep—or I thought I fell asleep. I had an extraordinary dream. I fancied I was lying in my room, in my bed—and was not asleep, could not even close my eyes. And again I heard the sound . . . I turned over . . . The moonlight on the floor began softly to lift, to rise up, to round off slightly above . . . Before me, impalpable as mist, a white woman was standing motionless.

"Who are you?" I asked with an effort.

A voice made answer, like the rustle of leaves: "It is I . . . I . . . I . . . I have come for you."

"For me? But who are you?"

"Come by night to the edge of the wood where there stands an old oak-tree. I will be there."

I tried to look closely into the face of the mysterious woman— and suddenly I gave an involuntary shudder: there was a chilly breath upon me. And then I was not lying down, but sitting up in my bed; and where, as I fancied, the phantom had stood, the moonlight lay in a long streak of white upon the floor.

The day passed somehow. I tried, I remember, to read, to work . . . everything was a failure. The night came. My heart was throbbing within me, as though it expected something. I lay down, and turned with my face to the wall.

"Why did you not come?" sounded a distinct whisper in the room.

I looked around quickly.

Again she . . . again the mysterious phantom. Motionless eyes in a motionless face, and a gaze full of sadness.

"Come!" I heard the whisper again.

"I will come," I replied with instinctive horror. The phantom bent slowly forward, and undulating faintly like smoke, melted away altogether. And again the moon shone white and untroubled on the smooth floor.

*   *   *

I passed the day in unrest. At supper I drank almost a whole bottle
of wine, and all but went out on to the steps; but I turned back
and flung myself into my bed. My blood was pulsing painfully.

Again the sound was heard . . . I started, but did not look round.
All at once I felt that someone had tight hold of me from behind,
and was whispering in my very ear: "Come, come, come.". . .
Trembling with terror, I moaned out: "I will come!" and sat up.

A woman stood stooping close to my very pillow. She smiled
dimly and vanished. I had time, though, to make out her face. It
seemed to me I had seen her before—but where, when? I got up
late, and spent the whole day wandering about the country. I
went to the old oak at the edge of the forest, and looked carefully
all around.

Towards evening I sat at the open window in my study. My old
housekeeper set a cup of tea before me, but I did not touch it . . .
I kept asking myself in bewilderment: "Am not I going out of my
mind?" The sun had just set: and not the sky alone was flushed
with red; the whole atmosphere was suddenly filled with an almost unnatural purple. The leaves and grass never stirred, stiff as
though freshly coated with varnish. In their stony rigidity, in the
vivid sharpness of their outlines, in this combination of intense
brightness and death-like stillness, there was something weird and
mysterious. A rather large gray bird suddenly flew up without a
sound and settled on the very window sill . . . I looked at it, and
it looked at me sideways with its round, dark eye. "Were you sent
to remind me, then?" I wondered.

At once the bird fluttered its soft wings, and without a sound—
as before—flew away. I sat a long time still at the window, but I
was no longer a prey to uncertainty. I had, as it were, come within
the enchanted circle, and I was borne along by an irresistible
though gentle force, as a boat is borne along by the current long
before it reaches the waterfall. I started up at last. The purple had
long vanished from the air, the colors were darkened, and the
enchanted silence was broken. There was the flutter of a gust of
wind, the moon came out brighter and brighter in the sky that
was growing bluer, and soon the leaves of the trees were weaving
lighted candle, but there was a draught from the window and the

flame went out. I could restrain myself no longer. I jumped up, clapped on my cap, and set off to the corner of the forest, to the old oak-tree.

This oak had, many years before, been struck by lightening; the top of the tree had been shattered, and was withered up, but there was still life left in it for centuries to come. As I was coming up to it, a cloud passed over the moon: it was very dark under its thick branches. At first I noticed nothing special; but I glanced on one side, and my heart fairly failed me—a white figure was standing motionless beside a tall bush between the oak and the forest. My hair stood upright on my head, but I plucked up my courage and went towards the forest.

Yes, it was she, my visitor of the night. As I approached her, the moon shone out again. She seemed all, as it were, spun out of half-transparent, milky mist,—through her face I could see a branch faintly stirring in the wind; only the hair and eyes were a little dark, and on one of the fingers of her clasped hands a slender ring shone with a gleam of pale gold. I stood still before her, and tried to speak; but the voice died away in my throat, though it was no longer fear exactly I felt. Her eyes were turned upon me; their gaze expressed neither distress nor delight, but a sort of life-less attention. I waited to see whether she would utter a word, but she remained motionless and speechless, and still gazed at me with her deathly intent eyes. Dread came over me again.

"I have come!" I cried at last with an effort. My voice sounded muffled and strange to me.

"I love you," I heard her whisper.

"You love me!" I repeated in amazement.

"Give yourself up to me," was whispered me again in reply.

"Give myself up to you! But you are a phantom; you have no body even." A strange animation came upon me. "What are you—smoke, air, vapor? Give myself up to you! Answer me first, Who are you? Have you lived upon the earth? Whence have you come?"

"Give yourself up to me. I will do you no harm. Only say two words: 'Take me.' "

I looked at her. "What is she saying?" I thought. "What does it all mean? And how can she take me? Shall I try?"

"Very well," I said, and unexpectedly loudly, as though someone had given me a push from behind; "take me!"

I had hardly uttered these words when the mysterious figure, with a sort of inward laugh, which set her face quivering for an instant, bent forward, and stretched out her arms wide apart . . . I tried to dart away, but I was already in her power. She seized me, my body rose a foot from the ground, and we both floated smoothly and not too swiftly over the wet, still grass.

At first I felt giddy, and instinctively I closed my eyes . . . A minute later I opened them again. We were floating as before; but the forest was now nowhere to be seen. Under us stretched a plain, spotted here and there with dark patches. With horror I felt that we had risen to a fearful height.

"I am lost; I am in the power of Satan," flashed through me like lightning. Till that instant the idea of a temptation of the evil one, of the possibility of perdition, had never entered my head. We still whirled on, and seemed to be mounting higher and higher.

"Where will you take me?" I moaned at last.

"Where you like," my companion answered. She clung close to me; her face was almost resting upon my face. But I was scarcely conscious of her touch.

"Let me sink down to the earth, I am giddy at this height."

"Very well; only shut your eyes and hold your breath."

I obeyed, and at once felt that I was falling like a stone flung from the hand . . . the air whistled in my ears. When I could think again, we were floating smoothly once more just above the earth, so that we caught our feet in the tops of the tall grass.

"Put me on my feet," I began. "What pleasure is there in flying? I'm not a bird."

"I thought you would like it. We have no other pastime."

"You? Then what are you?"

There was no answer.

"You don't dare to tell me that?"

The plaintive sound which had awakened me the first night

quivered in my ears. Meanwhile we were still, scarcely perceptibly, moving in the damp night air.

"Let me go!" I said. My companion moved slowly away, and I
found myself on my feet. She stopped before me and again folded
her hands. I grew more composed and looked into her face; as
before, it expressed submissive sadness.

"Where are we?" I asked. I did not recognize the country about
me.

"Far from your home, but you can be there in an instant."

"How can that be done? By trusting myself to you again?"

"I have done you no harm and will do you none. Let us fly till
dawn, that is all. I can bear you away wherever you fancy—to the
ends of the earth. Give yourself up to me! Say only: 'Take me!' "

"Well . . . take me!"

She again pressed close to me, again my feet left the earth—
and we were flying.

"Which way?" she asked me.

"Straight on, keep straight on."

"But here is a forest."

"Lift us over the forest, only slower."

We darted upwards like a wild snipe flying up into a birch-tree,
and again flew on in a straight line. Instead of grass, we caught
glimpses of tree-tops just under our feet. It was strange to see the
forest from above, its bristling back lighted up by the moon. It
looked like some huge slumbering wild beast, and accompanied
us with a vast unceasing murmur, like some inarticulate roar. In
one place we crossed a small glade; intensely black was the jagged
streak of shadow along one side of it. Now and then there was
the plaintive cry of a hare below us; above us the owl hooted,
plaintively too; there was a scent in the air of mushrooms, buds,
and dawn-flowers; the moon fairly flooded everything on all sides
with its cold, hard light; the Pleiades gleamed just over our heads.
And now the forest was left behind; a streak of fog stretched out
across the open country; it was the river. We flew along one of its
banks, above the bushes, still and weighed down with moisture.
The river's waters at one moment glimmered with a flash of blue,
at another flowed on in darkness, as it were, in wrath. Here and

there a delicate mist moved strangely over the water, and the
water-lilies' cups shone white in maiden pomp with every petal
open to its full, as though they knew their safety out of reach. I
longed to pick one of them, and behold, I found myself at once
on the river's surface . . . The damp air struck me an angry blow
in the face, just as I broke the thick stalk of a great flower. We
began to fly across from bank to bank, like the water-fowl we were
continually waking up and chasing before us. More than once we
chanced to swoop down on a family of wild ducks, settled in a
circle on an open spot among the reeds, but they did not stir; at
most one of them would thrust out its neck from under its wing,
stare at us, and anxiously poke its beak away again in its fluffy
feathers, and another faintly quacked, while its body twitched a
little all over. We startled one heron; it flew up out of a willow
bush, brandishing its legs and fluttering its wings with clumsy
eagerness: it struck me as remarkably like a German. There was
not the splash of a fish to be heard, they too were asleep. I began
to get used to the sensation of flying, and even to find a pleasure
in it; any one will understand me, who has experienced flying in
dreams. I proceeded to scrutinize with close attention the strange
being, by whose good offices such unlikely adventures had befallen me.

She was a woman with a small un-Russian face. Grayish-white,
half-transparent, with scarcely marked shades, she reminded one
of the alabaster figures on a vase lighted up within, and again her
face seemed familiar to me.

"Can I speak with you?" I asked.

"Speak."

"I see a ring on your finger; you have lived then on the earth,
you have been married?"

I waited . . . There was no answer.

"What is your name, or, at least, what was it?"

"Call me Alice."

"Alice! That's an English name! Are you an Englishwoman? Did
you know me in former days?"

"No."

"Why is it then you have come to me?"

"I love you."

"And are you content?"

"Yes; we float, we whirl together in the fresh air."

"Alice!" I said all at once, "you are perhaps a sinful, condemned soul?"

My companion's head bent towards me. "I don't understand you," she murmured.

"I adjure you in God's name . . ." I was beginning.

"What are you saying?" she put in in perplexity. "I don't understand."

I fancied that the arm that lay like a chilly girdle about my waist softly trembled . . .

"Don't be afraid," said Alice, "don't be afraid, my dear one!" Her face turned and moved towards my face . . . I felt on my lips a strange sensation, like the faintest prick of a soft and delicate sting . . . Leeches might prick so in a mild and drowsy mood.

I glanced downwards. We had now risen again to a considerable height. We were flying over some provincial town I did not know, situated on the side of a wide slope. Churches rose up high among the dark mass of wooden roofs and orchards; a long bridge stood out black at the bend of a river; everything was hushed, buried in slumber. The very crosses and cupolas seemed to gleam with a silent brilliance; silently stood the tall posts of the wells beside the round tops of the willows; silently the straight whitish road darted arrow-like into one end of the town, and silently it ran out again at the opposite end on to the dark waste of monotonous fields.

"What town is this?" I asked.

"X . . ."

"X . . . in Y . . . province?"

"Yes."

"I'm a long distance indeed from home!"

"Distance is not for us."

"Really?" I was fired by a sudden recklessness. "Then take me to South America!"

"To America I cannot. It's daylight there by now."

"And we are night-birds. Well, anywhere, where you can, only far, far away."

"Shut your eyes and hold your breath," answered Alice, and

we flew along with the speed of a whirlwind. With a deafening noise the air rushed into my ears. We stopped, but the noise did not cease. On the contrary, it changed to a sort of menacing roar, the roll of thunder . . .

"Now you can open your eyes," said Alice.

I obeyed . . . Good God, where was I?

Overhead, ponderous, smoke-like storm-clouds; they huddled, they moved on like a herd of furious monsters . . . and there below, another monster; a raging, yes, raging, sea . . . The white foam gleamed with spasmodic fury, and surged up in hillocks upon it, and hurling up shaggy billows, it beat with a sullen roar against a huge cliff, black as pitch. The howling of the tempest, the chilling gasp of the storm-rocked abyss, the weighty splash of the breakers, in which from time to time one fancied something like a wail, like distant cannon-shots, like a bell ringing—the tearing crunch and grind of the shingle on the beach, the sudden shriek of an unseen gull, on the murky horizon the disabled hulk of a ship—on every side death, death and horror . . . Giddiness overcame me, and I shut my eyes again with a sinking heart . . .

"What is this? Where are we?"

"On the south coast of the Isle of Wight opposite the Blackgang cliff where ships are so often wrecked," said Alice, speaking this time with peculiar distinctness, and as it seemed to me with a certain malignant pleasure . . .

"Take me away, away from here . . . home! home!" I shrank up, hid my face in my hands . . . I felt that we were moving faster than before, the wind now was not roaring or moaning, it whistled in my hair, in my clothes . . . I caught my breath . . .

"Stand on your feet now," I heard Alice's voice saying. I tried to master myself, to regain consciousness . . . I felt the earth under the soles of my feet and I heard nothing, as though everything had swooned away about me . . . only in my temples the blood throbbed irregularly, and my head was still giddy with a faint ringing in my ears. I drew myself up and opened my eyes.

We were on the bank of my pond. Straight before me there were glimpses through the pointed leaves of the willows of its broad surface with threads of fluffy mist clinging here and there upon it. To the right a held of rye shone dimly; on the left stood up my orchard trees, tall, rigid, drenched it seemed in dew . . . The breath of the morning was already upon them. Across the pure gray sky stretched like streaks of smoke, lay two or three slanting clouds; they had a yellowish tinge, the first faint glow of dawn fell on them; one could not say whence it came; the eye could not detect on the horizon, which was gradually growing lighter, the spot where the sun was to rise. The stars had disappeared; nothing was astir yet, though everything was already on the point of awakening in the enchanted stillness of the morning twilight.

"Morning! see, it is morning!" cried Alice in my ear. "Farewell till tomorrow."

I turned round . . . Lightly rising from the earth, she floated by, and suddenly she raised both hands above her head. The head and hands and shoulders glowed for an instant with warm corporeal light; living sparks gleamed in the dark eyes; a smile of mysterious tenderness stirred the reddening lips . . . A lovely woman had suddenly arisen before me . . . But as though dropping into a swoon, she fell back instantly and melted away like vapor.

I remained passive.

When I recovered myself and looked round me, it seemed to me that the corporeal, pale-rosy color that had flitted over the figure of my phantom had not yet vanished, and was enfolding me, diffused in the air . . . It was the flush of dawn. All at once I was conscious of extreme fatigue and turned homewards. As I passed the poultry-yard, I heard the first morning cackling of the geese (no birds wake earlier than they do); along the roof at the end of each beam sat a rook, and they were all busily and silently pluming themselves, standing out in sharp outline against the milky sky. From time to time they all rose at once, and after a short flight, settled again in a row, without uttering a caw . . . From the wood close by came twice repeated the drowsy, fresh chuck-chuck of the black-cock, beginning to fly into the dewy grass, overgrown by brambles . . . With a faint tremor all over me I made my way to my bed, and soon fell into a sound sleep.

*　　　*　　　*

The next night, as I was approaching the old oak, Alice moved to meet me, as if I were an old friend. I was not afraid of her as I had been the day before, I was almost rejoiced at seeing her; I did not even attempt to comprehend what was happening to me; I was simply longing to fly farther to interesting places.

Alice's arm again twined about me, and we took flight again.

"Let us go to Italy," I whispered in her ear.

"Wherever you wish, my dear one," she answered solemnly and slowly, and slowly and solemnly she turned her face towards me. It struck me as less transparent than on the eve; more woman-like and more imposing; it recalled to me the being I had had a glimpse of in the early dawn at parting.

"This night is a great night," Alice went on. "It comes rarely— when seven times thirteen . . ."

At this point I could not catch a few words.

"Tonight we can see what is hidden at other times."

"Alice!" I implored, "but who are you, tell me at last?"

Silently she lifted her long white hand. In the dark sky, where her finger was pointing, a comet flashed, a reddish streak among the tiny stars.

"How am I to understand you?" I began, "Or, as that comet floats between the planets and the sun, do you float among men . . . or what?"

But Alice's hand was suddenly passed before my eyes . . . It was as though a white mist from the damp valley had fallen on me . . .

"To Italy! to Italy!" I heard her whisper. "This night is a great night!"

The mist cleared away from before my eyes, and I saw below me an immense plain. But already, by the mere breath of the warm soft air upon my cheeks, I could tell I was not in Russia; and the plain, too, was not like our Russian plains. It was a vast dark expanse, apparently desert and not overgrown with grass; here and there over its whole extent gleamed pools of water, like broken pieces of looking-glass; in the distance could be dimly descried a noiseless motionless sea. Great stars shone bright in the spaces between the big beautiful clouds; the murmur of thousands, subdued but never-ceasing, rose on all sides, and very strange was this shrill but drowsy chorus, this voice of the darkness and the desert . . .

"The Pontine marshes," said Alice. "Do you hear the frogs? do you smell the sulphur?"

"The Pontine marshes . . ." I repeated, and a sense of grandeur and of desolation came upon me. "But why have you brought me here, to this gloomy forsaken place? Let us fly to Rome instead."

"Rome is near," answered Alice . . . "Prepare yourself!"

We sank lower, and flew along an ancient Roman road. A bullock slowly lifted from the slimy mud its shaggy monstrous head, with short tufts of bristles between its crooked backward-bent horns. It turned the whites of its dull malignant eyes askance, and sniffed a heavy snorting breath into its wet nostrils, as though scenting us.

"Rome, Rome is near . . ." whispered Alice. "Look, look in front . . ."

I raised my eyes.

What was the blur of black on the edge of the night sky? Were these the lofty arches of an immense bridge? What river did it span? Why was it broken down in parts? No, it was not a bridge, it was an ancient aqueduct. All around was the holy ground of the Campagna, and there, in the distance, the Albanian hills, and their peaks and the gray ridge of the old aqueduct gleamed dimly in the beams of the rising moon . . .

We suddenly darted upwards, and floated in the air before a deserted ruin. No one could have said what it had been: sepulcher, palace, or castle . . . Dark ivy encircled it all over in its deadly clasp, and below gaped yawning a half-ruined vault. A heavy underground smell rose in my face from this heap of tiny closely-fitted stones, whence the granite facing of the wall had long crumbled away.

"Here," Alice pronounced, and she raised her hand: "Here! call aloud three times running the name of the mighty Roman!"

"What will happen?"

"You will see."

I wondered. *"Divus Caius Julius Caesar!"* I cried suddenly; *"divus Caius Julius Caesar!"* I repeated deliberately; *"Caesar!"*

*　　*　　*

The last echoes of my voice had hardly died away, when I heard . . .

It is difficult to say what I did hear. At first there reached me a confused din the ear could scarcely catch, the endlessly-repeated clamor of the blare of trumpets, and the clapping of hands. It seemed that somewhere, immensely far away, at some fathomless depth, a multitude innumerable was suddenly astir, and was rising up, rising up in agitation, calling to one another, faintly, as if muffled in sleep, the suffocating sleep of ages. Then the air began moving in dark currents over the ruin . . . Shades began flitting before me, myriads of shades, millions of outlines, the rounded curves of helmets, the long straight lines of lances; the moonbeams were broken into momentary gleams of blue upon these helmets and lances, and all this army, this multitude, came closer and closer, and grew, in more and more rapid movement . . . An indescribable force, a force fit to set the whole world moving, could be felt in it; but not one figure stood out clearly . . . And suddenly I fancied a sort of tremor ran all round, as if it were the rush and rolling apart of some huge waves . . . "*Caesar, Caesar venit!*" sounded voices, like the leaves of a forest when a storm has suddenly broken upon it . . . a muffled shout thundered through the multitude, and a pale stern head, in a wreath of laurel, with downcast eyelids, the head of the emperor, began slowly to rise out of the ruin . . .

There is no word in the tongue of man to express the horror which clutched at my heart . . . I felt that were that head to raise its eyes, to part its lips, I must perish on the spot! "Alice!" I moaned, "I won't, I can't, I don't want Rome, coarse, terrible Rome . . . Away, away from here!"

"Coward!" she whispered, and away we flew. I just had time to hear behind me the iron voice of the legions, like a peal of thunder . . . then all was darkness.

"Look round," Alice said to me, "and don't fear."

I obeyed—and, I remember, my first impression was so sweet that I could only sigh. A sort of smoky-gray, silvery-soft, half-light, half-mist, enveloped me on all sides. At first I made out nothing: I was dazzled by this azure brilliance; but little by little began to emerge the outlines of beautiful mountains and forests; a lake lay at my feet, with stars quivering in its depths, and the musical splash of waves. The fragrance of orange flowers met me with a rush, and with it—and also as it were with a rush—came floating the pure powerful notes of a woman's young voice. This fragrance, this music, fairly drew me downwards, and I began to sink . . . to sink down towards a magnificent marble palace, which stood, invitingly white, in the midst of a wood of cypress. The music flowed out from its wide open windows, the waves of the lake, flecked with the pollen of flowers, splashed upon its walls, and just opposite, all clothed in the dark green of orange flowers and laurels, enveloped in shining mist, and studded with statues, slender columns, and the porticoes of temples, a lofty round island rose out of the water . . .

"Isola Bella!" said Alice. . . . "Lago Maggiore . . ."

I murmured only "Ah!" and continued to drop. The woman's voice sounded louder and clearer in the palace; I was irresistibly drawn towards it . . . I wanted to look at the face of the singer, who, in such music, gave voice to such a night. We stood still before the window.

In the center of a room, furnished in the style of Pompeii, and more like an ancient temple than a modern drawing-room, surrounded by Greek statues, Etruscan vases, rare plants, and precious stuffs, lighted up by the soft radiance of two lamps enclosed in crystal globes, a young woman was sitting at the piano. Her head slightly bowed and her eyes half-closed, she sang an Italian melody; she sang and smiled, and at the same time her face wore an expression of gravity, almost of sternness . . . a token of perfect rapture! She smiled . . . and Praxiteles' Faun, indolent, youthful as she, effeminate, and voluptuous, seemed to smile back at her from a corner, under the branches of an oleander, across the delicate smoke that curled upwards from a bronze censer on an antique tripod. The beautiful singer was alone. Spell-bound by the music, her beauty, the splendor and sweet fragrance of the night, moved to the heart by the picture of this youthful, serene, and untroubled happiness, I utterly forgot my companion, I forgot the strange way in which I had become a witness of this life, so remote, so completely apart from me, and I was on the point of tapping at the window, of speaking . . .

I was set trembling all over by a violent shock—just as though I had touched a galvanic battery. I looked round . . . The face of Alice was—for all its transparency—dark and menacing; there was a dull glow of anger in her eyes, which were suddenly wide and round . . .

"Away!" she murmured wrathfully, and again whirling and darkness and giddiness . . . Only this time not the shout of legions, but the voice of the singer, breaking on a high note, lingered in my ears . . .

We stopped. The high note, the same note was still ringing and did not cease to ring in my ears, though I was breathing quite a different air, a different scent . . . a breeze was blowing upon me, fresh and invigorating, as though from a great river, and there was a smell of hay, smoke and hemp. The long-drawn-out note was followed by a second, and a third, but with an expression so unmistakable, a trill so familiar, so peculiarly our own, that I said to myself at once: "That's a Russian singing a Russian song!" and at that very instant everything grew clear about me.

We found ourselves on a flat riverside plain. To the left, newly-mown meadows, with rows of huge haystacks, stretched endlessly till they were lost in the distance; to the right extended the smooth surface of a vast mighty river, till it too was lost in the distance. Not far from the bank, big dark barges slowly rocked at anchor, slightly tilting their slender masts, like pointing fingers. From one of these barges came floating up to me the sounds of a liquid voice, and a fire was burning in it, throwing a long red light that danced and quivered on the water. Here and there, both on the river and in the fields other lights were glimmering, whether close at hand or far away, the eye could not distinguish; they shrank together, then suddenly lengthened out into great blurs of light; grasshoppers innumerable kept up an unceasing churr, persistent as the frogs of the Pontine marshes; and across the cloudless, but dark lowering sky floated from time to time the cries of unseen birds.

"Are we in Russia?" I asked of Alice.

"It is the Volga," she answered.

We flew along the river-bank. "Why did you tear me away from there, from that lovely country?'' I began. ''Were you envious, or was it jealousy in you?''

The lips of Alice faintly stirred, and again there was a menacing light in her eyes . . . But her whole face grew stony again at once.

''I want to go home,'' I said.

''Wait a little, wait a little,'' answered Alice. ''Tonight is a great night. It will not soon return. You may be a spectator . . . Wait a little.''

And we suddenly flew across the Volga in a slanting direction, keeping close to the water's surface, with the low impetuous flight of swallows before a storm. The broad waves murmured heavily below us, the sharp river breeze beat upon us with its strong cold wing . . . the high right bank began soon to rise up before us in the half-darkness. Steep mountains appeared with great ravines between. We came near to them.

''Shout: 'Lads, to the barges!' '' Alice whispered to me. I remembered the terror I had suffered at the apparition of the Roman phantoms. I felt weary and strangely heavy, as though my heart were ebbing away within me. I wished not to utter the fatal words; I knew beforehand that in response to them there would appear, as in the wolves' valley of the Freischuitz, some monstrous thing; but my lips parted against my will, and in a weak forced voice I shouted, also against my will: ''Lads, to the barges!''

At first all was silence, even as it was at the Roman ruins, but suddenly I heard close to my very ear a coarse bargeman's laugh, and with a moan something dropped into the water and a gurgling sound followed . . . I looked round: no one was anywhere to be seen, but from the bank the echo came bounding back, and at once from all sides rose a deafening din. There was a medley of everything in this chaos of sound: shouting and whining, furious abuse and laughter, laughter above everything; the plash of oars and the cleaving of hatchets, a crash as of the smashing of doors and chests, the grating of rigging and wheels, and the neighing of horses, and the clang of the alarm bell and the clink of chains, the roar and crackle of fire, drunken songs and quick, gnashing chatter, weeping inconsolable, plaintive despairing prayers, and shouts of command, the dying gasp and the reckless whistle, the guffaw and the thud of the dance . . . "Kill them! Hang them! Drown them! rip them up! bravo! bravo! don't spare them!" could be heard distinctly; I could even hear the hurried breathing of men panting. And meanwhile all around, as far as the eye could reach, nothing could be seen, nothing was changed; the river rolled by mysteriously, almost sullenly, the very bank seemed more deserted and desolate—that was all.

I turned to Alice, but she put her finger to her lips . . .

"Stepan Timofeitch! Stepan Timofeitch is coming!" was shouted noisily all round; "he is coming, our father, our ataman, our breadgiver!" As before I saw nothing but it seemed to me as though a huge body were moving straight at me . . . "Frolka! where art thou, dog?" thundered an awful voice. "Set fire to every corner at once—and to the hatchet with them, the white-handed scoundrels!"

I felt the hot breath of the flame close by, and tasted the bitter savor of the smoke; and at the same instant something warm like blood spurted over my face and hands . . . A savage roar of laughter broke out all—round . . .

I lost consciousness, and when I came to myself, Alice and I were gliding along beside the familiar bushes that bordered my wood, straight towards the old oak . . .

"Do you see the little path?" Alice said to me, "where the moon shines dimly and where are two birch-trees overhanging? Will you go there?"

But I felt so shattered and exhausted that I could only say in reply: "Home! home!"

"You are at home," replied Alice.

I was in fact standing at the very door of my house—alone. Alice had vanished. The yard-dog was about to approach, he scanned me suspiciously—and with a bark ran away.

With difficulty I dragged myself up to my bed and fell asleep without undressing.

All the following morning my head ached, and I could scarcely move my legs; but I cared little for my bodily discomfort; I was devoured by regret, overwhelmed with vexation.

I was excessively annoyed with myself. "Coward!" I repeated

incessantly; "yes—Alice was right. What was I frightened of? how could I miss such an opportunity? . . . I might have seen Caesar himself—and I was senseless with terror, I whimpered and turned away, like a child at the sight of the rod. Razin, now—that's another matter. As a nobleman and landowner . . . though, indeed, even then what had I really to fear? Coward! coward! . . . "

"But wasn't it all a dream?" I asked myself at last. I called my housekeeper.

"Marfa, what o'clock did I go to bed yesterday—do you remember?"

"Why, who can tell, master? . . . Late enough, surely. Before it was quite dark you went out of the house; and you were tramping about in your bedroom when the night was more than half over. Just on morning—yes. And this is the third day it's been the same. You've something on your mind, it's easy to see."

"Aha-ha!" I thought. "Then there's no doubt about the flying. Well, and how do I look today?" I added aloud.

"How do you look? Let me have a look at you. You've got thinner a bit. Yes, and you're pale, master; to be sure, there's not a drop of blood in your face."

I felt a slight twinge of uneasiness . . . I dismissed Marfa.

"Why, going on like this, you'll die, or go out of your mind, perhaps," I reasoned with myself, as I sat deep in thought at the window. "I must give it all up. It's dangerous. And now my heart beats so strangely. And when I fly, I keep feeling as though someone were sucking at it, or as it were drawing something out of it—as the spring sap is drawn out of the birch-tree, if you stick an ax into it. I'm sorry, though. And Alice too . . . She is playing cat and mouse with me . . . still she can hardly wish me harm. I will give myself up to her for the last time—and then . . . But if she is drinking my blood? That's awful. Besides, such rapid locomotion cannot fail to be injurious; even in England, I'm told, on the railways, it's against the law to go more than one hundred miles an hour . . ."

So I reasoned with myself—but at ten o'clock in the evening, I was already at my post before the old oak tree.

*　　*　　*

The night was cold, dull, gray; there was a feeling of rain in the air. To my amazement, I found no one under the oak; I walked several times round it, went up to the edge of the wood, turned back again, peered anxiously into the darkness . . . All was emptiness. I waited a little, then several times I uttered the name, Alice, each time a little louder, . . . but she did not appear. I felt sad, almost sick at heart; my previous apprehensions vanished; I could not resign myself to the idea that my companion would not come back to me again.

"Alice! Alice! come! Can it be you will not come?" I shouted, for the last time.

A crow, who had been waked by my voice, suddenly darted upwards into a tree-top close by, and catching in the twigs, fluttered his wings . . . But Alice did not appear.

With downcast head, I turned homewards. Already I could discern the black outlines of the willows on the pond's edge, and the light in my window peeped out at me through the apple-trees in the orchard—peeped at me, and hid again, like the eye of some man keeping watch on me—when suddenly I heard behind me the faint swish of the rapidly parted air, and something at once embraced and snatched me upward, as a buzzard pounces on and snatches up a quail . . . It was Alice sweeping down upon me. I felt her cheek against my cheek, her enfolding arm about my body, and like a cutting cold her whisper pierced to my ear, "Here I am." I was frightened and delighted both at once . . . We flew at no great height above the ground.

"You did not mean to come today?" I said.

"And you were dull without me? You love me? Oh, you are mine!"

The last words of Alice confused me . . . I did not know what to say. "I was kept," she went on; "I watched."

"Who could keep you?"

"Where would you like to go?" inquired Alice, as usual not answering my question.

"Take me to Italy—to that lake, you remember."

Alice turned a little away, and shook her head in refusal. At that point I noticed for the first time that she had ceased to be transparent. And her face seemed tinged with color; there was a faint glow of red over its misty whiteness. I glanced at her eyes . . . and felt a pang of dread; in those eyes something was astir—with the slow, continuous, malignant movement of the benumbed snake, twisting and turning as the sun begins to thaw it.

"Alice," I cried, "who are you? Tell me who you are."

Alice simply shrugged her shoulders.

I felt angry . . . I longed to punish her; and suddenly the idea occurred to me to tell her to fly with me to Paris. "That's the place for you to be jealous," I thought. "Alice," I said aloud, "you are not afraid of big towns—Paris, for instance?"

"No."

"Not even those parts where it is as light as in the boulevards?"

"It is not the light of day."

"Good; then take me at once to the Boulevard des Italiens."

Alice wrapped the end of her long hanging sleeve about my head. I was at once enfolded in a sort of white vapor full of the drowsy fragrance of the poppy. Everything disappeared at once; every light, every sound, and almost consciousness itself. Only the sense of being alive remained, and that was not unpleasant.

Suddenly the vapor vanished; Alice took her sleeve from my head, and I saw at my feet a huge mass of closely packed buildings, brilliant light, movement, noisy traffic . . . I saw Paris.

I had been in Paris before, and so I recognized at once the place to which Alice had directed her course. It was the Garden of the Tuileries with its old chestnut-trees, its iron railings, its fortress moat, and its brutal-looking Zouave sentinels. Passing the palace, passing the Church of St. Roche, on the steps of which the first Napoleon for the first time shed French blood, we came to a halt high over the Boulevard des Italiens, where the third Napoleon did the same thing and with the same success. Crowds of people, dandies young and old, workmen in blouses, women in gaudy dresses, were thronging on the pavements; the gilded restaurants and cafés were flaring with lights; omnibuses, carriages of all sorts and shapes, moved to and fro along the boulevard; everything was bustle, everything was brightness, wherever one chanced to look . . . But, strange to say, I had no inclination to forsake my pure dark airy height. I had no inclination to get nearer to this human ant-hill. It seemed as though a hot, heavy, reddish vapor rose from it, half-fragrance, half-stench; so many lives were flung struggling in one heap together there. I was hesitating . . . But suddenly, sharp as the clang of iron bars, the voice of a harlot of the streets floated up to me; like an insolent tongue, it was thrust out, this voice; it stung me like the sting of a viper. At once I saw in imagination the strong, heavy-jawed, greedy, flat Parisian face, the mercenary eyes, the paint and powder, the frizzed hair, and the nosegay of gaudy artificial flowers under the high-pointed hat, the polished nails like talons, the hideous crinoline . . . I could fancy too one of our sons of the steppes running with pitiful eagerness after the doll put up for sale . . . I could fancy him with clumsy coarseness and violent stammering, trying to imitate the manners of the waiters at Véfour's, mincing, flattering, wheedling . . . and a feeling of loathing gained possession of me . . . "No," I thought, "here Alice has no need to be jealous . . ."

Meanwhile I perceived that we had gradually begun to descend . . . Paris was rising to meet us with all its din and odor . . .

"Stop," I said to Alice. "Are you not stifled and oppressed here?"

"You asked me to bring you here yourself."

"I am to blame, I take back my word. Take me away, Alice, I beseech you. To be sure, here is Prince Kulmametov hobbling along the boulevard; and his friend, Serge Varaksin, waves to him, shouting: "Ivan Stepanitch, *allons souper,* make haste, zhay angazha Rigol-bouche itself!" Take me away from these furnished apartments and *maisons dorées*, from the Jockey Club and the Figaro, from close-shaven military heads and varnished barracks, from sergents-de-ville with Napoleonic beards, and from glasses of muddy absinthe, from gamblers playing dominoes at the cafés, and gamblers on the Bourse, from red ribbons in button-holes, from M. de Four, inventor of "matrimonial specialities," and the gratuitous consultations of Dr. Charles Albert, from liberal lectures and government pamphlets, from Parisian comedies and Parisian operas, from Parisian wit and Parisian ignorance . . . Away! away! away!"

"Look down," Alice answered; "you are not now in Paris."

I lowered my eyes . . . It was true. A dark plain, intersected here and there by the whitish lines of roads, was rushing rapidly by below us, and only behind us on the horizon, like the reflection of an immense conflagration, rose the great glow of the innumerable lights of the capital of the world.

Again a veil fell over my eyes . . . Again I lost consciousness. The veil was withdrawn at last. What was it down there below? What was this part, with avenues of lopped lime-trees, with isolated fir-trees of the shape of parasols, with porticoes and temples in the Pompadour style, with statues of satyrs and nymphs of the Bernini school, with rococo tritons in the midst of meandering lakes, closed in by low parapets of blackened marble? Wasn't it Versailles? No, it was not Versailles. A small palace, also rococo, peeped out behind a clump of bushy oaks. The moon shone dimly, shrouded in mist, and over the earth there was, as it were spread out, a delicate smoke. The eye could not decide what it was, whether moonlight or fog. On one of the lakes a swan was asleep; its long back was white as the snow of the frost-bound steppes, while glow-worms gleamed like diamonds in the bluish shadow at the base of a statue.

"We are near Mannheim," said Alice; "this is the Schwetzingen garden."

"We are in Germany," I thought, and I fell to listening. All was silence, except somewhere, secluded and unseen, the splash and babble of falling water. It seemed continually to repeat the same words: "Aye, aye, aye, for aye, aye." And all at once I fancied that in the very center of one of the avenues, between clipped walls of green, a cavalier came tripping along in red-heeled boots, a gold-braided coat, with lace ruffs at his wrists, a light steel rapier at his thigh, smilingly offering his arm to a lady in a powdered wig and a gay chintz . . . Strange, pale faces . . . I tried to look into them . . . But already everything had vanished, and as before there was nothing but the babbling water.

"Those are dreams wandering," whispered Alice; "yesterday there was much—oh, much—to see; today, even the dreams avoid man's eyes. Forward! forward!"

We soared higher and flew farther on. So smooth and easy was our flight that it seemed that we moved not, but everything moved to meet us. Mountains came into view, dark, undulating, covered with forest; they rose up and swam towards us . . . And now they were slipping by beneath us, with all their windings, hollows, and narrow glades, with gleams of light from rapid brooks among the slumbering trees at the bottom of the dales; and in front of us more mountains sprung up again and floated towards us . . . We were in the heart of the Black Forest.

Mountains, still mountains . . . and forest, magnificent, ancient, stately forest. The night sky was clear; I could recognize some kinds of trees, especially the splendid firs, with their straight white trunks. Here and there on the edge of the forest, wild goats could be seen; graceful and alert, they stood on their slender legs and listened, turning their heads prettily and pricking up their great funnel-shaped ears. A ruined tower, sightless and gloomy, on the crest of a bare cliff, laid bare its crumbling turrets; above the old forgotten stones, a little golden star was shining peacefully. From a small almost black lake rose, like a mysterious wail, the plaintive croak of tiny frogs. I fancied other notes, long-drawn-out, languid like the strains of an Æolian harp . . . Here we were in the home of legend! The same delicate moonlight mist, which had struck me in Schwetzingen, was shed here on every side, and the farther away the mountains, the thicker was this mist. I counted up five, six, ten different tones of shadow at different heights on the mountain slopes, and over all this realm of varied silence the moon queened it pensively. The air blew in soft, light currents. I felt myself a lightness at heart, and, as it were, a lofty calm and melancholy . . .

"Alice, you must love this country!"

"I love nothing."

"How so? Not me?"

"Yes . . . you!" she answered indifferently.

It seemed to me that her arm clasped my waist more tightly than before.

"Forward! forward!" said Alice, with a sort of cold fervor.

"Forward!" I repeated.

A loud, thrilling cry rang out suddenly over our heads, and was at once repeated a little in front.

"Those are belated cranes flying to you, to the north," said Alice; "would you like to join them?"

"Yes, yes! raise me up to them."

We darted upwards and in one instant found ourselves beside the flying flock.

The big handsome birds (there were thirteen of them) were flying in a triangle, with slow sharp flaps of their hollow wings; with their heads and legs stretched rigidly out, and their breasts stiffly pressed forward, they pushed on persistently and so swiftly that the air whistled about them. It was marvelous at such a height, so remote from all things living, to see such passionate, strenuous life, such unflinching will, untiringly cleaving their triumphant way through space. The cranes now and then called to one another, the foremost to the hindmost; and there was a certain pride, dignity, and invincible faith in these loud cries, this converse in the clouds. "We shall get there, be sure, hard though it be," they seemed to say, cheering one another on. And then the thought came to me that men, such as these birds—in Russia—nay, in the whole world, are few.

"We are flying towards Russia now," observed Alice. I noticed now, not for the first time, that she almost always knew what I was thinking of. "Would you like to go back?"

"Let us go back . . . or no! I have been in Paris; take me to Petersburg."

"Now?"

"At once . . . Only wrap my head in your veil, or it will go ill with me."

Alice raised her hand . . . but before the mist enfolded me, I had time to feel on my lips the contact of that soft, dull sting . . .

"Li-i-isten!" sounded in my ears a long-drawn-out cry. "Li-i-isten!" was echoed back with a sort of desperation in the distance. "Li-i-isten!" died away somewhere far, far away. I started. A tall golden spire flashed on my eyes; I recognized the fortress of St. Peter and St. Paul.

A northern, pale night! But was it night at all? Was it not rather a pallid, sickly daylight? I never liked Petersburg nights; but this time the night seemed even fearful to me; the face of Alice had vanished completely, melted away like the mist of morning in the July sun, and I saw her whole body clearly, as it hung, heavy and solitary on a level with the Alexander column. So here was Petersburg! Yes, it was Petersburg, no doubt. The wide empty gray streets; the grayish-white, and yellowish-gray and grayish-lilac houses, covered with stucco, which was peeling off, with their sunken windows, gaudy sign-boards, iron canopies over steps, and wretched little greengrocer's shops; the facades, inscriptions, sentry-boxes, troughs; the golden cap of St. Isaac's; the senseless motley Bourse; the granite walls of the fortress, and the broken wooden pavement; the barges loaded with hay and timber; the smell of dust, cabbage, matting, and hemp; the stony-faced dvorniks in sheepskin coats, with high collars; the cab-drivers, huddled up dead asleep on their decrepit cabs—yes, this was Petersburg, our northern Palmyra. Everything was visible; everything was clear—cruelly clear and distinct—and everything was mournfully sleeping, standing out in strange huddled masses in the dull clear air. The flush of sunset—a hectic flush—had not yet gone, and would not be gone till morning from the white starless sky; it was reflected on the silken surface of the Neva, while faintly gurgling and faintly moving, the cold blue waves hurried on . . .

"Let us fly away," Alice implored.

And without waiting for my reply, she bore me away across the Neva, over the palace square to Liteiny Street. Steps and voices were audible beneath us; a group of young men, with worn faces, came along the street talking about dancing-classes. "Sub-lieutenant Stolpakov's seventh!" shouted suddenly a soldier standing half-asleep on guard at a pyramid of rusty bullets; and a little farther on, at an open window in a tall house, I saw a girl in a creased silk dress, without cuffs, with a pearl net on her hair, and a cigarette in her mouth. She was reading a book with reverent attention; it was a volume of the works of one of our modern Juvenals.

"Let us fly away!" I said to Alice.

One instant more, and there were glimpses below us of the rotting pine copses and mossy bogs surrounding Petersburg. We bent our course straight to the south; sky, earth, all grew gradually darker and darker. The sick night; the sick daylight; the sick town—all were left behind us.

*   *   *

We flew more slowly than usual, and I was able to follow with my eyes the immense expanse of my native land gradually unfolding before me, like the unrolling of an endless panorama. Forests, copses, fields, ravines, rivers—here and there villages and churches—and again fields and forests and copses and ravines . . . Sadness came over me, and a kind of indifferent dreariness. And I was not sad and dreary simply because it was Russia I was flying over. No. The earth itself, this flat surface which lay spread out beneath me; the whole earthly globe, with its populations, multitudinous, feeble, crushed by want, grief and diseases, bound to a clod of pitiful dust; this brittle, rough crust, this shell over the fiery sands of our planet, overspread with the mildew we call the organic, vegetable kingdom; these human flies, a thousand times paltrier than flies; their dwellings glued together with filth, the pitiful traces of their tiny, monotonous bustle, of their comic struggle with the unchanging and inevitable, how revolting it all suddenly was to me. My heart turned slowly sick, and I could not bear to gaze longer on these trivial pictures, on this vulgar show . . . Yes, I felt dreary, worse than dreary. Even pity I felt nothing of for my brother men: all feelings in me were merged in one which I scarcely dare to name: a feeling of loathing, and stronger than all and more than all within me was the loathing—for myself.

"Cease," whispered Alice, "cease, or I cannot carry you. You have grown heavy."

"Home," I answered her in the very tone in which I used to say the word to my coachman, when I came out at four o'clock at night from some Moscow friends, where I had been talking since dinner-time of the future of Russia and the significance of the commune. "Home," I repeated, and closed my eyes.

But I soon opened them again. Alice seemed huddling strangely up to me; she was almost pushing against me. I looked at her and my blood froze at the sight. One who has chanced to behold on the face of another a sudden look of intense terror, the cause of which he does not suspect, will understand me. By terror, overmastering terror, the pale features of Alice were drawn and contorted, almost effaced. I had never seen anything like it even on a living human face. A lifeless, misty phantom, a shade, . . . and this deadly horror . . .

"Alice, what is it?" I said at last.

"She . . . she . . ." she answered with an effort. "She."

"She? Who is she?"

"Do not utter her name, not her name," Alice faltered hurriedly. "We must escape, or there will be an end to everything, and for ever . . . Look, over there!"

I turned my head in the direction in which her trembling hand was pointing, and discerned something . . . something horrible indeed.

This something was the more horrible that it had no definite shape. Something bulky, dark, yellowish-black, spotted like a lizard's belly, not a storm-cloud, and not smoke, was crawling with a snake-like motion over the earth. A wide rhythmic undulating movement from above downwards, and from below upwards, an undulation recalling the malignant sweep of the wings of a vulture seeking its prey; at times an indescribably revolting groveling on the earth, as of a spider stooping over its captured fly . . . Who are you, what are you, menacing mass? Under her influence, I saw it, I felt it—all sank into nothingness, all was dumb . . .

A putrefying, pestilential chill came from it. At this chill breath the heart turned sick, and the eyes grew dim, and the hair stood up on the head. It was a power moving; that power which there is no resisting, to which all is subject, which sightless, shapeless, senseless, sees all, knows all, and like a bird of prey picks out its victims, like a snake, stifles them and stabs them with its frozen sting . . .

"Alice! Alice!" I shrieked like one in frenzy. "It is death! death itself!"

The wailing sound I had heard before broke from Alice's lips; this time it was more like a human wail of despair, and we flew. But our flight was strangely and alarmingly unsteady; Alice turned over in the air, fell, rushed from side to side like a partridge mortally wounded, or trying to attract a dog away from her young. And meanwhile in pursuit of us, parting from the indescribable mass of horror, rushed sort of long undulating tentacles, like outstretched arms, like talons . . . Suddenly a huge shape, a muffled figure on a pale horse, sprang up and flew upwards into the very

heavens . . . Still more fearfully, still more desperately Alice struggled. "She has seen! All is over! I am lost!" I heard her broken
whisper. "Oh, I am miserable! I might have profited, have won
life, . . . and now . . . Nothingness, nothingness!" It was too unbearable . . . I lost consciousness.

When I came to myself, I was lying on my back in the grass, feeling
a dull ache all over me, as from a bad bruise. The dawn was beginning in the sky: I could clearly distinguish things. Not far off,
alongside a birch copse, ran a road planted with willows: the country seemed familiar to me. I began to recollect what had happened
to me, and shuddered all over directly my mind recalled the last,
hideous apparition . . .

"But what was Alice afraid of?" I thought. "Can she too be
subject to that power? Is she not immortal? Can she too be in
danger of annihilation, dissolution? How is it possible?"

A soft moan sounded close by me. I turned my head. Two paces
from me lay stretched out motionless a young woman in a white
gown, with thick disordered tresses, with bare shoulders. One arm
was thrown behind her head, the other had fallen on her bosom.
Her eyes were closed, and on her tightly shut lips stood a fleck of
crimson stain. Could it be Alice? But Alice was a phantom, and I
was looking upon a living woman. I crept up to her, bent
down . . .

"Alice, it is you?" I cried. Suddenly, slowly quivering, the wide
eyelids rose; dark piercing eyes were fastened upon me, and at
the same instant lips too fastened upon me, warm, moist, smelling
of blood . . . soft arms twined tightly round my neck, a burning,
full heart pressed convulsively to mine. "Farewell, farewell for
ever!" the dying voice uttered distinctly, and everything vanished.

I got up, staggering like a drunken man, and passing my hands
several times over my face, looked carefully about me. I found
myself near the high road, a mile and a half from my own place.
The sun had just risen when I got home.

All the following nights I awaited—and I confess not without
alarm—the appearance of my phantom; but it did not visit me
again. I even set off one day, in the dusk, to the old oak, but
nothing took place there out of the common. I did not, however,

overmuch regret the discontinuance of this strange acquaintance. I reflected much and long over this inexplicable, almost unintelligible phenomenon; and I am convinced that not only science cannot explain it, but that even in fairy tales and legends nothing like it is to be met with. What was Alice, after all? An apparition, a restless soul, an evil spirit, a sylphide, a vampire, or what? Sometimes it struck me again that Alice was a woman I had known at some time or other, and I made tremendous efforts to recall where I had seen her . . . Yes, yes, I thought sometimes, directly, this minute, I shall remember . . . In a flash everything had melted away again like a dream. Yes, I thought a great deal, and, as is always the way, came to no conclusion. The advice or opinion of others I could not bring myself to invite; fearing to be taken for a madman. I gave up all reflection upon it at last; to tell the truth, I had no time for it. For one thing, the emancipation had come along with the redistribution of property, etc.; and for another, my own health failed; I suffered with my chest, with sleeplessness, and a cough. I got thin all over. My face was yellow as a dead man's. The doctor declares I have too little blood, calls my illness by the Greek name, "anemia," and is sending me to Gastein. The arbitrator swears that without me there's no coming to an understanding with the peasants. Well, what's one to do?

But what is the meaning of the piercingly-pure, shrill notes, the notes of an harmonica, which I hear directly any one's death is spoken of before me? They keep growing louder, more penetrating . . . And why do I shudder in such anguish at the mere thought of annihilation?

Robert Louis Stevenson

OLALLA

———⟐———

Robert Louis Stevenson (1850–1894) was born into a family of Scottish lighthouse engineers. Because he suffered from tuberculosis as a child, his education was somewhat neglected. However, he did study engineering, and later became a lawyer—both to please his parents— but what he really wanted to do was write. He never practiced law, but rather worked at establishing himself in print. It took several years before his work was recognized. He went on to write the classics *Treasure Island, Kidnapped*, "The Body Snatcher," and *The Strange Case of Dr. Jekyll and Mr. Hyde*. Stevenson eventually moved to Samoa and, by the time of his death, had become one of the most popular British writers. This story first appeared in *The Court and Society Review* in December, 1885—two years after *Treasure Island*, and a year before *Jekyll and Hyde*. It was later included in his book *The Merry Men, and Other Tales and Fables* (1887).

"Now," SAID THE DOCTOR, "my part is done, and, I may say, with some vanity, well done. It remains only to get you out of this cold and poisonous city and to give you two months of a pure air and an easy conscience. The last is your affair. To the first I think I can help you. It falls indeed rather oddly; it was but the other day the Padre came in from the country; and as he and I are old friends, although of contrary professions, he applied to me in a matter of distress among some of his parishioners. This was a family—but you are ignorant of Spain, and even the names of our grandees are hardly known to you; suffice it, then, that they were once great people, and are now fallen to the brink of destitution. Nothing now belongs to them but the residencia, and certain leagues of desert mountain, in the greater part of which not even a goat could support life. But the house is a fine old place, and stands at a great height among the hills, and most salubriously; and I had no sooner heard my friend's tale, than I remembered you. I told him I had a wounded officer, wounded in the good cause, who was now able to make a change; and I proposed that his friends should take you for a lodger. Instantly the Padre's face grew dark, as I had maliciously foreseen it would. It was out of the question, he said. Then let them starve, said I, for I have no sympathy with tatterdemalion pride. Thereupon we separated, not very content with one another; but yesterday, to my wonder, the Padre returned and made a submission: the difficulty, he said, he had found upon inquiry to be less than he had feared; or, in other words, these proud people had put their pride in their pocket. I closed with the offer; and, subject to your approval, I have taken rooms for you in the residencia. The air of these mountains will renew your blood; and the quiet in which you will there live is worth all the medicines in the world."

"Doctor," said I, "you have been throughout my good angel, and your advice is a command. But tell me, if you please, something of the family with which I am to reside."

"I am coming to that," replied my friend; "and, indeed, there is a difficulty in the way. These beggars are, as I have said, of very high descent and swollen with the most baseless vanity; they have lived for some generations in a growing isolation, drawing away, on either hand, from the rich who had now become too high for them, and from the poor, whom they still regarded as too low; and even to-day, when poverty forces them to unfasten their door to a guest, they cannot do so without a most ungracious stipulation. You are to remain, they say, a stranger; they will give you attendance, but they refuse from the first the idea of the smallest intimacy."

I will not deny that I was piqued, and perhaps the feeling

strengthened my desire to go, for I was confident that I could break down that barrier if I desired. "There is nothing offensive in such a stipulation," said I; "and I even sympathise with the feeling that inspired it."

"It is true they have never seen you," returned the doctor politely; "and if they knew you were the handsomest and the most pleasant man that ever came from England (where I am told that handsome men are common, but pleasant ones not so much so), they would doubtless make you welcome with a better grace. But since you take the thing so well, it matters not. To me, indeed, it seems discourteous. But you will find yourself the gainer. The family will not much tempt you. A mother, a son, and a daughter; an old woman said to be half witted, a country lout, and a country girl, who stands very high with her confessor, and is, therefore," chuckled the physician, "most likely plain; there is not much in that to attract the fancy of a dashing officer."

"And yet you say they are high-born," I objected.

"Well, as to that, I should distinguish," returned the doctor. "The mother is, not so the children. The mother was the last representative of a princely stock, degenerate both in parts and fortune. Her father was not only poor, he was mad: and the girl ran wild about the residencia till his death. Then, much of the fortune having died with him, and the family being quite extinct, the girl ran wilder than ever, until at last she married, Heaven knows whom, a muleteer some say, others a smuggler; while there are some who uphold there was no marriage at all, and that Felipe and Olalla are bastards. The union, such as it was, was tragically dissolved some years ago; but they live in such seclusion, and the country at that time was in so much disorder, that the precise manner of the man's end is known only to the priest—if even to him."

"I begin to think I shall have strange experiences," said I.

"I would not romance, if I were you," replied the doctor; "you will find, I fear, a very grovelling and commonplace reality. Felipe, for instance, I have seen. And what am I to say? He is very rustic, very cunning, very loutish, and, I should say, an innocent; the others are probably to match. No, no, Señor commandante, you must seek congenial society among the great sights of our mountains; and in these at least, if you are at all a lover of the works of nature, I promise you will not be disappointed.''

The next day Felipe came for me in a rough country cart, drawn by a mule; and a little before the stroke of noon, after I had said farewell to the doctor, the innkeeper, and different good souls who had befriended me during my sickness, we set forth out of the city by the eastern gate, and began to ascend into the Sierra. I had been so long a prisoner, since I was left behind for dying after the loss of the convoy, that the mere smell of the earth set me smiling. The country through which we went was wild and rocky, partially covered with rough woods, now of the cork-tree, and now of the great Spanish chestnut, and frequently intersected by the beds of mountain torrents. The sun shone, the wind rustled joyously; and we had advanced some miles, and the city had already shrunk into an inconsiderable knoll upon the plain behind us, before my attention began to be diverted to the companion of my drive. To the eye, he seemed but a diminutive, loutish, well-made country lad, such as the doctor had described, mighty quick and active, but devoid of any culture; and this first impression was with most observers final. What began to strike me was familiar, chattering talk; so strangely inconsistent with the terms on which I was to be received; and partly from his imperfect enunciation, partly from the sprightly incoherence of the matter, so very difficult to follow clearly without an effort of the mind. It is true I had before talked with persons of a similar mental constitution; persons who seemed to live (as he did) by the senses, taken and possessed by the visual object of the moment and unable to discharge their minds of that impression. His seemed to me (as I sat, distantly giving ear) a kind of conversation proper to drivers, who pass much of their time in a great vacancy of the intellect and threading the sights of a familiar country. But this was not the case of Felipe; by his own account, he was a homekeeper. ''I wish I was there now,'' he said; and then spying a tree by the wayside, he broke off to tell me that he had once seen a crow among its branches.

''A crow?'' I repeated, struck by the ineptitude of the remark, and thinking I had heard imperfectly.

But by this time he was already filled with a new idea; hearkening with a rapt intentness, his head on one side, his face puckered; and he struck me rudely, to make me hold my peace. Then he smiled and shook his head.

"What did you hear?" I asked.

"O, it is all right," he said; and began encouraging his mule with cries that echoed unhumanly up the mountain walls.

I looked at him more closely. He was superlatively well-built, light, and lithe and strong; he was well-featured; his yellow eyes were very large, though, perhaps, not very expressive; take him altogether, he was a pleasant-looking lad, and I had no fault to find with him, beyond that he was of a dusky hue, and inclined to hairiness; two characteristics that I disliked. It was his mind that puzzled, and yet attracted me. The doctor's phrase—an innocent—came back to me; and I was wondering if that were, after all, the true description, when the road began to go down into the narrow and naked chasm of a torrent. The waters thundered tumultuously in the bottom; and the ravine was filled full of the sound, the thin spray, and the claps of wind, that accompanied their descent. The scene was certainly impressive, but the road was in that part very securely walled in; the mule went steadily forward; and I was astonished to perceive the paleness of terror in the face of my companion. The voice of that wild river was inconstant, now sinking lower as if in weariness, now doubling its hoarse tones; momentary freshets seemed to swell its volume, sweeping down the gorge, raving and booming against the barrier walls; and I observed it was at each of these accessions to the clamour, that my driver more particularly winced and blanched. Some thoughts of Scottish superstition and the river Kelpie passed across my mind; I wondered if perchance the like were prevalent in that part of Spain; and turning to Felipe, sought to draw him out.

"What is the matter?" I asked.

"O, I am afraid," he replied.

"Of what are you afraid?" I returned. "This seems one of the safest places on this very dangerous road."

"It makes a noise," he said, with a simplicity of awe that set my doubts at rest.

The lad was but a child in intellect; his mind was like his body, active and swift, but stunted in development; and I began from that time forth to regard him with a measure of pity, and to listen, at first with indulgence, and at last even with pleasure, to his disjointed babble.

By about four in the afternoon we had crossed the summit of the mountain line, said farewell to the western sunshine, and began to go down upon the other side, skirting the edge of many ravines and moving through the shadow of dusky woods. There rose upon all sides the voice of falling water, not condensed and formidable as in the gorge of the river, but scattered and sounding gaily and musically from glen to glen. Here, too, the spirits of my driver mended, and he began to sing aloud in a falsetto voice, and with a singular bluntness of musical perception, never true either to melody of key, but wandering at will, and yet somehow with an effect that was natural and pleasing, like that of the song of birds. As the dusk increased, I fell more and more under the spell of this artless warbling, listening and waiting for some articulate air, and still disappointed; and when at last I asked him what it was he sang—"O," cried he, "I am just singing!" Above all, I was taken with a trick he had of unweariedly repeating the same note at little intervals; it was not so monotonous as you would think, or, at least, not disagreeable; and it seemed to breathe a wonderful contentment with what is, such as we love to fancy in the attitude of trees, or the quiescence of a pool.

Night had fallen dark before we came out upon a plateau, and drew up, a little after, before a certain lump of superior blackness which I could only conjecture to be the residencia. Here, my guide, getting down from the cart, hooted and whistled for a long time in vain; until at last an old peasant man came towards us from somewhere in the surrounding dark, carrying a candle in his hand. By the light of this I was able to perceive a great arched doorway of a Moorish character: it was closed by iron-studded gates, in one of the leaves of which Felipe opened a wicket. The peasant carried off the cart to some out-building; but my guide and I passed through the wicket, which was closed again behind us; and by the glimmer of the candle, passed through a court, up a stone stair, along a section of an open gallery, and up more stairs again, until we came at last to the door of a great and somewhat bare apartment. This room, which I understood was to be mine, was pierced by three windows, lined with some lustrous wood disposed in panels, and carpeted with the skins of many savage animals. A bright fire burned in the chimney, and shed abroad a changeable flicker; close up to the blaze there was drawn a table, laid for supper; and in the far end a bed stood ready. I was pleased by these preparations, and said so to Felipe; and he, with the same simplicity of disposition that I had already remarked in him, warmly re-echoed my praises. "A fine room," he said; "a very fine room. And fire, too; fire is good; it melts out the pleasure in your bones. And the bed," he continued, carrying over the candle in that direction—"see what fine sheets—how soft, how smooth, smooth"; and he passed his hand again and again over their texture, and then laid down his head and rubbed his cheeks among them with a grossness of content that somehow offended me. I took the candle from his hand (for I feared he would set the bed on fire) and walked back to the supper-table, where, perceiving a measure of wine, I poured out a cup and called to him to come and drink of it. He started to his feet at once and ran to me with a strong expression of hope; but when he saw the wine, he visibly shuddered.

"Oh, no," he said, "not that; that is for you. I hate it."

"Very well, Señor," said I; "then I will drink to your good health, and to the prosperity of your house and family. Speaking of which," I added, after I had drunk, "shall I not have the pleasure of laying my salutations in person at the feet of the Señora, your mother?"

But at these words all the childishness passed out of his face, and was succeeded by a look of indescribable cunning and secrecy. He backed away from me at the same time, as though I were an animal about to leap or some dangerous fellow with a weapon, and when he had got near the door, glowered at me sullenly with contracted pupils. "No," he said at last, and the next moment was gone noiselessly out of the room; and I heard his footing die away down-stairs as light as rainfall, and silence closed over the house.

After I had supped I drew up the table nearer to the bed and began to prepare for rest; but in the new position of the light, I was struck by a picture on the wall. It represented a woman, still young. To judge by her costume and the mellow unity which reigned over the canvas, she had long been dead; to judge by the vivacity of the attitude, the eyes and the features, I might have been beholding in a mirror the image of life. Her figure was very slim and strong, and of a just proportion; red tresses lay like a crown over her brow; her eyes, of a very golden brown, held mine with a look; and her face, which was perfectly shaped, was yet marred by a cruel, sullen, and sensual expression. Something in both face and figure, something exquisitely intangible, like the echo of an echo, suggested the features and bearing of my guide; and I stood awhile, unpleasantly attracted and wondering at the oddity of the resemblance. The common, carnal stock of that race, which had been originally designed for such high dames as the one now looking on me from the canvas, had fallen to baser uses, wearing country clothes, sitting on the shaft and holding the reins of a mule cart, to bring home a lodger. Perhaps an actual link subsisted; perhaps some scruple of the delicate flesh that was once clothed upon with the satin and brocade of the dead lady, now winced at the rude contact of Felipe's frieze.

The first light of the morning shone full upon the portrait, and, as I lay awake, my eyes continued to dwell upon it with growing complacency; its beauty crept about my heart insidiously, silencing my scruples one after another; and while I knew that to love such a woman were to sign and seal one's own sentence of degeneration, I still knew that, if she were alive, I should love her. Day after day the double knowledge of her wickedness and of my weakness grew clearer. She came to be the heroine of many daydreams, in which her eyes led on to, and sufficiently rewarded, crimes. She cast a dark shadow on my fancy; and when I was out in the free air of heaven, taking vigorous exercise and healthily renewing the current of my blood, it was often a glad thought to me that my enchantress was safe in the grave, her wand of beauty broken, her lips closed in silence, her philtre spilt. And yet I had a half-lingering terror that she might not be dead after all, but re-arisen in the body of some descendant.

Felipe served my meals in my own apartment; and his resemblance to the portrait haunted me. At times it was not at times, upon some change of attitude or flash of expression, it would leap out upon me like a ghost. It was above all in his ill tempers that the likeness triumphed. He certainly liked me; he was proud of my notice, which he sought to engage by many simple and child-like devices; he loved to sit close before my fire, talking his broken talk or singing his odd, endless, wordless songs, and sometimes drawing his hand over my clothes with an affectionate manner of caressing that never failed to cause in me an embarrassment of which I was ashamed. But for all that, he was capable of flashes of causeless anger and fits of sturdy sullenness. At a word of reproof, I have seen him upset the dish of which I was about to eat, and this not surreptitiously, but with defiance; and similarly at a hint of inquisition. I was not unnaturally curious, being in a strange place and surrounded by strange people, but at the shadow of a question, he shrank back, lowering and dangerous. Then it was that, for a fraction of a second, this rough lad might have been the brother of the lady in the frame. But these humours were swift to pass; and the resemblance died along with them.

In these first days I saw nothing of any one but Felipe, unless the portrait is to be counted; and since the lad was plainly of weak mind, and had moments of passion, it may be wondered that I bore his dangerous neighbourhood with equanimity. As a matter of fact, it was for some time irksome; but it happened before long that I obtained over him so complete a mastery as set my disquietude at rest.

It fell in this way. He was by nature slothful, and much of a vagabond, and yet he kept by the house, and not only waited upon my wants, but laboured every day in the garden or small farm to the south of the residencia. Here he would be joined by the peasant whom I had seen on the night of my arrival, and who dwelt at the far end of the enclosure, about half a mile away, in a rude out-house; but it was plain to me that, of these two, it was Felipe who did most; and though I would sometimes see him throw down his spade and go to sleep among the very plants he had been digging, his constancy and energy were admirable in themselves, and still more so since I was well assured they were foreign to his disposition and the fruit of an ungrateful effort. But while I admired, I wondered what had called forth in a lad so shuttle-witted this enduring sense of duty. How was it sustained? I asked myself, and to what length did it prevail over his instincts? The priest was possibly his inspirer; but the priest came one day to the residencia. I saw him both come and go after an interval of close upon an hour, from a knoll where I was sketching, and all that time Felipe continued to labour undisturbed in the garden.

At last, in a very unworthy spirit, I determined to debauch the lad from his good resolutions, and, waylaying him at the gate, easily persuaded him to join me in a ramble. It was a fine day, and the woods to which I led him were green and pleasant and sweet-smelling and alive with the hum of insects. Here he discovered himself in a fresh character, mounting up to heights of gaiety that abashed me, and displaying an energy and grace of movement that delighted the eye. He leaped, he ran round me in mere glee; he would stop, and look and listen, and seemed to drink in the world like a cordial; and then he would suddenly spring into a tree with one bound, and hang and gambol there like one at home. Little as he said to me, and that of not much import, I have rarely enjoyed more stirring company; the sight of his delight was a continual feast: the speed and accuracy of his movements pleased me to the heart; and I might have been so thoughtlessly unkind as to make a habit of these walks, had not chance prepared a very rude conclusion to my pleasure. By some swiftness or dexterity the lad captured a squirrel in a tree-top. He was then some way ahead of me, but I saw him drop to the ground and crouch there, crying aloud for pleasure like a child. The sound stirred my sympathies, it was so fresh and innocent; but as I bettered my pace to draw near, the cry of the squirrel knocked upon my heart. I have heard and seen much of the cruelty of lads, and above all of peasants; but what I now beheld struck me into a passion of anger. I thrust the fellow aside, plucked the poor brute out of his hands, and with swift mercy killed it. Then I turned upon the torturer, spoke to him long out of the heat of my indignation, calling him names at which he seemed to wither; and at length, pointing towards the residencia, bade him begone and leave me, for I chose to walk with men, not with vermin. He fell upon his knees, and, the words coming to him with more clearness than usual, poured out a stream of the most touching supplications, begging me in mercy to forgive him, to forget what he had done, to look to the future. "O, I try so hard," he said. "O, commandante, bear with Felipe this once; he will never be a brute again!" Thereupon, much more affected than I cared to show, I suffered myself to be persuaded, and at last shook hands with him and made it up. But the squirrel, by way of penance, I made him bury; speaking of the poor thing's beauty, telling him what pains it had suffered, and how base a thing was the abuse of strength. "See,

Felipe," said I, "you are strong indeed; but in my hands you are as helpless as that poor thing of the trees. Give me your hand in mine. You cannot remove it. Now suppose that I were cruel like you, and took a pleasure in pain. I only tighten my hold, and see how you suffer." He screamed aloud, his face stricken ashy and dotted with needle points of sweat; and when I set him free, he fell to the earth and nursed his hand and moaned over it like a baby. But he took the lesson in good part; and whether from that, or from what I had said to him, or the higher notion he now had of my bodily strength, his original affection was changed into a dog-like, adoring fidelity.

Meanwhile I gained rapidly in health. The residencia stood on the crown of a stony plateau; on every side the mountains hemmed it about; only from the roof, where was a bartizan, there might be seen between two peaks, a small segment of plain blue, with extreme distance. The air in these altitudes moved freely and largely; great clouds congregated there, and were broken up by the wind and left in tatters on the hill-tops; a hoarse and yet faint rumbling of torrents rose from all round; and one could there study all the ruder and more ancient characters of nature in something of their pristine force. I delighted from the first in the vigorous scenery and changeful weather; nor less in the antique and dilapidated mansion where I dwelt. This was a large oblong, flanked at two opposite corners by bastion-like projections, one of which commanded the door, while both were loopholed for musketry. The lower storey was, besides, naked of windows, so that the building, if garrisoned, could not be carried without artillery. It enclosed an open court planted with pomegranate trees. From this a broad flight of marble stairs ascended to an open gallery, running all round and resting, towards the court, on slender pillars. Thence again, several enclosed stairs led to the upper storeys of the house, which were thus broken up into distinct divisions. The windows, both within and without, were closely shuttered; some of the stonework in the upper parts had fallen; the roof, in one place, had been wrecked in one of the flurries of wind which were common in these mountains; and the whole house, in the strong, beating sunlight, and standing out above a grove of stunted cork-trees, thickly laden and discoloured with dust, looked like the sleeping palace of the legend. The court, in particular, seemed the very home of slumber. A hoarse cooing of doves haunted about the eaves; the winds were excluded, but when they blew outside, the mountain dust fell here as thick as rain, and veiled the red bloom of the pomegranates; shuttered windows and the closed doors of numerous cellars, and the vacant arches of the gallery, enclosed it; and all day long the sun made broken profiles on the four sides, and paraded the shadow of the pillars on the gallery floor. At the ground level there was, how-ever, a certain pillared recess, which bore the marks of human habitation. Though it was open in front upon the court, it was yet provided with a chimney, where a wood fire would be always prettily blazing; and the tile floor was littered with the skins of animals.

It was in this place that I first saw my hostess. She had drawn one of the skins forward and sat in the sun, leaning against a pillar. It was her dress that struck me first of all, for it was rich and brightly coloured, and shone out in that dusty courtyard with something of the same relief as the flowers of the pomegranates. At a second look it was her beauty of person that took hold of me. As she sat back—watching me, I thought, though with invisible eyes—and wearing at the same time an expression of almost im-becile good-humour and contentment, she showed a perfectness of feature and a quiet nobility of attitude that were beyond a sta-tue's. I took off my hat to her in passing, and her face puckered with suspicion as swiftly and lightly as a pool ruffles in the breeze; but she paid no heed to my courtesy. I went forth on my custom-ary walk a trifle daunted, her idol-like impassivity haunting me; and when I returned, although she was still in much the same posture, I was half surprised to see that she had moved as far as the next pillar, following the sunshine. This time, however, she addressed me with some trivial salutation, civilly enough con-ceived, and uttered in the same deep-chested, and yet indistinct and lisping tones, that had already baffled the utmost niceness of my hearing from her son. I answered rather at a venture; for not only did I fail to take her meaning with precision, but the sudden disclosure of her eyes disturbed me. They were unusually large, the iris golden like Felipe's, but the pupil at that moment so dis-tended that they seemed almost black; and what affected me was not so much their size as (what was perhaps its consequence) the singular insignificance of their regard. A look more blankly stupid I have never met. My eyes dropped before it even as I spoke, and I went on my way up-stairs to my own room, at once baffled and embarrassed. Yet, when I came there and saw the face of the portrait, I was again reminded of the miracle of family descent. My hostess was, indeed, both older and fuller in person; her eyes were of a different colour; her face, besides, was not only free from the ill-significance that offended and attracted me in the painting; it was devoid of either good or bad—a moral blank expressing literally naught. And yet there was a likeness, not so much speaking as immanent, not so much in any particular feature as upon the whole. It should seem, I thought, as if when the master set his signature to that grave canvas, he had not only caught the image of one smiling and false-eyed woman, but stamped the essential quality of a race.

From that day forth, whether I came or went, I was sure to find the Señora seated in the sun against a pillar, or stretched on a rug before the fire; only at times she would shift her station to the top round of the stone staircase, where she lay with the same nonchalance right across my path. In all these days, I never knew her to display the least spark of energy beyond what she expended in brushing and re-brushing her copious copper-coloured hair, or in lisping out, in the rich and broken hoarseness of her voice, her customary idle salutations to myself. These, I think, were her two chief pleasures, beyond that of mere quiescence. She seemed always proud of her remarks, as though they had been witticisms: and, indeed, though they were empty enough, like the conversation of many respectable persons, and turned on a very narrow range of subjects, they were never meaningless or incoherent; nay, they had a certain beauty of their own, breathing as they did, of her entire contentment. Now she would speak of the warmth in which (like her son) she greatly delighted; now of the flowers of the pomegranate trees, and now of the white doves and long-winged swallows that fanned the air of the court. The birds excited her. As they raked the eaves in their swift flight, or skimmed sidelong past her with a rush of wind, she would sometimes stir, and sit a little up, and seem to awaken from her doze of satisfaction. But for the rest of her days she lay luxuriously folded on herself and sunk in sloth and pleasure. Her invincible content at first annoyed me, but I came gradually to find repose in the spectacle, until at last it grew to be my habit to sit down beside her four times in the day, both coming and going, and to talk with her sleepily, I scarce knew of what. I had come to like her dull, almost animal neighbourhood; her beauty and her stupidity soothed and amused me. I began to find a kind of transcendental good-sense in her remarks, and her unfathomable good-nature moved me to admiration and envy. The liking was returned; she enjoyed my presence half unconsciously, as a man in deep meditation may enjoy the babbling of a brook. I can scarce say she brightened when I came, for satisfaction was written on her face eternally, as on some foolish statue's; but I was made conscious of her pleasure by some more intimate communication than the sight. And one day, as I sat within reach of her on the marble step, she suddenly shot forth one of her hands and patted mine. The thing was done, and she was back in her accustomed attitude, before my mind had received intelligence of the caress; and when I turned to look her in the face I could perceive no answerable sentiment. It was plain she attached no moment to the act, and I blamed myself for my own more uneasy consciousness.

The sight and (if I may so call it) the acquaintance of the mother confirmed the view I had already taken of the son. The family blood had been impoverished, perhaps by long inbreeding, which I knew to be a common error among the proud and the exclusive. No decline, indeed, was to be traced in the body, which had been handed down unimpaired in shapeliness and strength; and the faces of to-day were struck as sharply from the mint as the face of two centuries ago that smiled upon me from the portrait. But the intelligence (that more precious heirloom) was degenerate; the treasure of ancestral memory ran low; and it had required the potent, plebeian crossing of a muleteer or mountain contrabandista to raise what approached hebetude in the mother into the active oddity of the son. Yet, of the two, it was the mother I preferred. Of Felipe, vengeful and placable, full of starts and shyings, inconstant as a hare, I could even conceive as a creature possibly noxious. Of the mother I had no thoughts but those of kindness. And, indeed, as spectators are apt ignorantly to take sides, I grew something of a partisan in the enmity which I perceived to smoulder between them. True, it seemed mostly on the mother's part.

She would sometimes draw in her breath as he came near, and the pupils of her vacant eyes would contract with horror or fear. Her emotions, such as they were, were much upon the surface and readily shared; and this latent repulsion occupied my mind, and kept me wondering on what grounds it rested, and whether the son was certainly in fault.

I had been about ten days in the residencia, when there sprang up a high and harsh wind, carrying clouds of dust. It came out of malarious lowlands, and over several snowy sierras. The nerves of those on whom it blew were strung and jangled; their eyes smarted with the dust; their legs ached under the burthen of their body; and the touch of one hand upon another grew to be odious. The wind, besides, came down the gullies of the hills and stormed about the house with a great, hollow buzzing and whistling that was wearisome to the ear and dismally depressing to the mind. It did not so much blow in gusts as with the steady sweep of a waterfall, so that there was no remission of discomfort while it blew. But higher upon the mountain, it was probably of a more variable strength, with accesses of fury; for there came down at times a far-off wailing, infinitely grievous to hear; and at times, on one of the high shelves or terraces, there would start up, and then disperse, a tower of dust, like the smoke of an explosion.

I no sooner awoke in bed than I was conscious of the nervous tension and depression of the weather, and the effect grew stronger as the day proceeded. It was in vain that I resisted; in vain that I set forth upon my customary morning's walk; the irrational, unchanging fury of the storm had soon beat down my strength and wrecked my temper; and I returned to the residencia, glowing with dry heat, and foul and gritty with dust. The court had a forlorn appearance; now and then a glimmer of sun fled over it; now and then the wind swooped down upon the pomegranates, and scattered the blossoms, and set the window shutters clapping on the wall. In the recess the Señora was pacing to and fro with a flushed countenance and bright eyes; I thought, too, she was speaking to herself, like one in anger. But when I addressed her with my customary salutation, she only replied by a sharp gesture and continued her walk. The weather had distempered even this impassive creature; and as I went on up-stairs I was the less ashamed of my own discomposure.

All day the wind continued; and I sat in my room and made a feint of reading, or walked up and down, and listened to the riot overhead. Night fell, and I had not so much as a candle. I began to long for some society, and stole down to the court. It was now plunged in the blue of the first darkness; but the recess was redly lighted by the fire. The wood had been piled high, and was crowned by a shock of flames, which the draught of the chimney brandished to and fro. In this strong and shaken brightness the Señora continued pacing from wall to wall with disconnected gestures, clasping her hands, stretching forth her arms, throwing back her head as in appeal to heaven. In these disordered movements the beauty and grace of the woman showed more clearly; but there was a light in her eye that struck on me unpleasantly; and when I had looked on awhile in silence, and seemingly unobserved, I turned tail as I had come, and groped my way back again to my own chamber.

By the time Felipe brought my supper and lights, my nerve was utterly gone; and, had the lad been such as I was used to seeing him, I should have kept him (even by force had that been necessary) to take off the edge from my distasteful solitude. But on Felipe, also, the wind had exercised its influence. He had been feverish all day; now that the night had come he was fallen into a low and tremulous humour that reacted on my own. The sight of his scared face, his starts and pallors and sudden hearkenings, unstrung me; and when he dropped and broke a dish, I fairly leaped out of my seat.

"I think we are all mad to-day," said I, affecting to laugh.

"It is the black wind," he replied dolefully. "You feel as if you must do something, and you don't know what it is."

I noted the aptness of the description; but, indeed, Felipe had sometimes a strange felicity in rendering into words the sensations of the body. "And your mother, too," said I; "she seems to feel this weather much. Do you not fear she may be unwell?"

He stared at me a little, and then said, "No," almost defiantly; and the next moment, carrying his hand to his brow, cried out lamentably on the wind and the noise that made his head go round like a mill-wheel. "Who can be well?" he cried; and, indeed, I could only echo his question, for I was disturbed enough myself.

I went to bed early, wearied with day-long restlessness; but the poisonous nature of the wind, and its ungodly and unintermittent uproar, would not suffer me to sleep. I lay there and tossed, my nerves and senses on the stretch. At times I would dose, dream horribly, and wake again; and these snatches of oblivion confused me as to time. But it must have been late on in the night, when I was suddenly startled by an outbreak of pitiable and hateful cries. I leaped from my bed, supposing I had dreamed; but the cries still continued to fill the house, cries of pain, I thought, but certainly of rage also, and so savage and discordant that they shocked the heart. It was no illusion; some living thing, some lunatic or some wild animal, was being foully tortured. The thought of Felipe and the squirrel flashed into my mind, and I ran to the door, but it had been locked from the outside; and I might shake it as I pleased, I was a fast prisoner. Still the cries continued. Now they would dwindle down into a moaning that seemed to be articulate, and at these times I made sure they must be human; and again they would break forth and fill the house with ravings worthy of hell. I stood at the door and gave ear to them, till at last they died away. Long after that, I still lingered and still continued to hear them mingle in fancy with the storming of the wind; and when at last I crept to my bed, it was with a deadly sickness and a blackness of horror on my heart.

It was little wonder if I slept no more. Why had I been locked in? What had passed? Who was the author of these indescribable and shocking cries? A human being? It was inconceivable. A beast? The cries were scarce quite bestial; and what animal, short of a lion or a tiger, could thus shake the solid walls of the residencia? And while I was thus turning over the elements of the mystery, it came into my mind that I had not yet set eyes upon the daughter of the house. What was more probable than that the daughter of the Señora, and the sister of Felipe, should be herself insane? Or, what more likely than that these ignorant and half-witted people should seek to manage an afflicted kinswoman by violence? Here was a solution; and yet when I called to mind the cries (which I never did without a shuddering chill) it seemed altogether insufficient: not even cruelty could wring such cries from madness. But of one thing I was sure: I could not live in a house where such a thing was half conceivable and not probe the matter home and, if necessary, interfere.

The next day came, the wind had blown itself out, and there was nothing to remind me of the business of the night. Felipe came to my bedside with obvious cheerfulness; as I passed through the court, the Señora was sunning herself with her accustomed immobility; and when I issued from the gateway, I found the whole face of nature austerely smiling, the heavens of a cold blue, and sown with great cloud islands, and the mountain-sides mapped forth into provinces of light and shadow. A short walk restored me to myself, and renewed within me the resolve to plumb this mystery; and when, from the vantage of my knoll, I had seen Felipe pass forth to his labours in the garden, I returned at once to the residencia to put my design in practice. The Señora appeared plunged in slumber; I stood awhile and marked her, but she did not stir; even if my design were indiscreet I had little to fear from such a guardian; and turning away, I mounted to the gallery and began my exploration of the house.

All morning I went from one door to another, and entered spacious and faded chambers, some rudely shuttered, some receiving their full charge of daylight, all empty and unhomely. It was a rich house, on which Time had breathed his tarnish and dust had scattered disillusion. The spider swung there; the bloated tarantula scampered on the cornices; ants had their crowded highways on the floor of halls of audience; the big and foul fly, that lives on carrion and is often the messenger of death, had set up his nest in the rotten woodwork, and buzzed heavily about the rooms. Here and there a stool or two, a couch, a bed, or a great carved chair remained behind, like islets on the bare floors, to testify of man's by-gone habitation; and everywhere the walls were set with the portraits of the dead. I could judge, by these decaying effigies, in the house of what a great and what a handsome race I was then wandering. Many of the men wore orders on their breasts, and had the port of noble officers; the women were all richly attired; the canvases most of them by famous hands. But it was not so much these evidences of greatness that took hold upon my mind, even contrasted, as they were, with the present depopulation and decay of that great house. It was rather the parable of family life that I read in this succession of fair faces and shapely bodies. Never before had I so realised the miracle of the continued race, the creation and recreation, the weaving and changing and handing down of fleshy elements. That a child should be born of its mother, that it should grow and clothe itself (we know not how) with humanity, and put on inherited looks, and turn its head with the manner of one ascendant, and offer its hand with the gesture of another, are wonders dulled for us by repetition. But in the singular unity of look, in the common features and common bearing, of all these painted generations on the walls of the residencia, the miracle started out and looked me in the face. And an ancient mirror falling opportunely in my way, I stood and read my own features a long while, tracing out on either hand the filaments of descent and the bonds that knit me with my family.

At last, in the course of these investigations, I opened the door of a chamber that bore the marks of habitation. It was of large proportions and faced to the north, where the mountains were most wildly figured. The embers of a fire smouldered and smoked upon the hearth, to which a chair had been drawn close. And yet the aspect of the chamber was ascetic to the degree of sternness; the chair was uncushioned; the floor and walls were naked; and beyond the books which lay here and there in some confusion, there was no instrument of either work or pleasure. The sight of books in the house of such a family exceedingly amazed me; and I began with a great hurry, and in momentary fear of interruption, to go from one to another and hastily inspect their character. They were of all sorts, devotional, historical, and scientific, but mostly of a great age and in the Latin tongue. Some I could see to bear the marks of constant study; others had been torn across and tossed aside as if in petulance or disapproval. Lastly, as I cruised about that empty chamber, I espied some papers written upon with pencil on a table near the window. An unthinking curiosity led me to take one up. It bore a copy of verses, very roughly metred in the original Spanish, and which I may render somewhat thus—

> Pleasure approached with pain and shame,
> Grief with a wreath of lilies came.
> Pleasure showed the lovely sun;
> Jesu dear, how sweet it shone!

Grief with her worn hand pointed on,
Jesu dear, to thee!

Shame and confusion at once fell on me; and, laying down the paper, I beat an immediate retreat from the apartment. Neither Felipe nor his mother could have read the books nor written these rough but feeling verses. It was plain I had stumbled with sacrilegious feet into the room of the daughter of the house. God knows, my own heart most sharply punished me for my indiscretion. The thought that I had thus secretly pushed my way into the confidence of a girl so strangely situated, and the fear that she might somehow come to hear of it, oppressed me like guilt. I blamed myself besides for my suspicions of the night before; wondered that I should ever have attributed those shocking cries to one of whom I now conceived as of a saint, spectral of mien, wasted with maceration, bound up in the practices of a mechanical devotion, and dwelling in a great isolation of soul with her incongruous relatives; and as I leaned on the balustrade of the gallery and looked down into the bright close of pomegranates and at the gaily dressed and somnolent woman, who just then stretched herself and delicately licked her lips as in the very sensuality of sloth, my mind swiftly compared the scene with the cold chamber looking northward on the mountains, where the daughter dwelt.

That same afternoon, as I sat upon my knoll, I saw the Padre enter the gate of the residencia. The revelation of the daughter's character had struck home to my fancy, and almost blotted out the horrors of the night before; but at sight of this worthy man the memory revived. I descended, then, from the knoll, and making a circuit among the woods, posted myself by the wayside to await his passage. As soon as he appeared I stepped forth and introduced myself as the lodger of the residencia. He had a very strong, honest countenance, on which it was easy to read the mingled emotions with which he regarded me, as a foreigner, a heretic, and yet one who had been wounded for the good cause. Of the family at the residencia he spoke with reserve, and yet with respect. I mentioned that I had not yet seen the daughter, whereupon he remarked that that was as it should be, and looked at me a little askance. Lastly, I plucked up courage to refer to the cries that had disturbed me in the night. He heard me out in silence, and then stopped and partly turned about, as though to mark beyond doubt that he was dismissing me.

"Do you take tobacco powder?" said he, offering his snuffbox; and then, when I had refused, "I am an old man," he added, "and I may be allowed to remind you that you are a guest."

"I have, then, your authority," I returned, firmly enough, although I flushed at the implied reproof, "to let things take their course, and not to interfere?"

He said "yes," and with a somewhat uneasy salute turned and left me where I was. But he had done two things: he had set my conscience at rest, and he had awakened my delicacy. I made a great effort, once more dismissed the recollections of the night, and fell once more to brooding on my saintly poetess. At the same time, I could not quite forget that I had been locked in, and that night when Felipe brought me my supper I attacked him warily on both points of interest.

"I never see your sister," said I casually.

"Oh, no," said he; "she is a good, good girl," and his mind instantly veered to something else.

"Your sister is pious, I suppose," I asked in the next pause.

"Oh," he cried, joining his hands with extreme fervour, "a saint; it is she that keeps me up."

"You are very fortunate," said I, "for the most of us, I am afraid, and myself among the number, are better at going down."

"Señor," said Felipe earnestly, "I would not say that. You should not tempt your angel. If one goes down, where is he to stop?"

"Why, Felipe," said I, "I had no guess you were a preacher, and I may say a good one; but I suppose that is your sister's doing?"

He nodded at me with round eyes.

"Well, then," I continued, "she has doubtless reproved you for your sin of cruelty?"

"Twelve times!" he cried; for this was the phrase by which the odd creature expressed the sense of frequency. "And I told her you had done so—I remembered that," he added proudly—"and she was pleased."

"Then, Felipe," said I, "what were those cries that I heard last night? for surely they were cries of some creature in suffering."

"The wind," returned Felipe, looking in the fire.

I took his hand in mine, at which, thinking it to be a caress, he smiled with a brightness of pleasure that came near disarming my resolve. But I trod the weakness down. "The wind," I repeated; "and yet I think it was this hand," holding it up, "that had first locked me in." The lad shook visibly, but answered never a word. "Well," said I, "I am a stranger and a guest. It is not my part either to meddle or to judge in your affairs; in these you shall take your sister's counsel, which I cannot doubt to be excellent. But in so far as concerns my own I will be no man's prisoner, and I demand that key." Half an hour later my door was suddenly thrown open, and the key tossed ringing on the floor.

A day or two after I came in from a walk a little before the point of noon. The Señora was lying lapped in slumber on the threshold of the recess; the pigeons dozed below the eaves like snowdrifts; the house was under a deep spell of noontide quiet; and only a wandering and gentle wind from the mountain stole round the galleries, rustled among the pomegranates, and pleasantly stirred the shadows. Something in the stillness moved me to imitation, and I went very lightly across the court and up the marble staircase. My foot was on the topmost round, when a door opened, and I found myself face to face with Olalla. Surprise transfixed me; her loveliness struck to my heart; she glowed in the deep shadow of the gallery, a gem of colour; her eyes took hold upon mine and clung there, and bound us together like the joining of hands; and the moments we thus stood face to face, drinking each other in, were sacramental and the wedding of souls. I know not how long it was before I awoke out of a deep trance, and, hastily bowing, passed on into the upper stair. She did not move, but followed me with her great, thirsting eyes; and as I passed out of sight it seemed to me as if she paled and faded.

In my own room, I opened the window and looked out, and could not think what change had come upon that austere field of mountains that it should thus sing and shine under the lofty heaven. I had seen her—Olalla! And the stone crags answered, Olalla! and the dumb, unfathomable azure answered, Olalla! The pale saint of my dreams had vanished for ever; and in her place I beheld this maiden on whom God had lavished the richest colours and the most exuberant energies of life, whom he had made active as a deer, slender as a reed, and in whose great eyes he had lighted the torches of the soul. The thrill of her young life, strung like a wild animal's, had entered into me; the force of soul that had looked out from her eyes and conquered mine, mantled about my heart and sprang to my lips in singing. She passed through my veins: she was one with me.

I will not say that this enthusiasm declined; rather my soul held out in its ecstasy as in a strong castle, and was there besieged by cold and sorrowful considerations. I could not doubt but that I loved her at first sight, and already with a quivering ardour that was strange to my experience. What then was to follow? She was the child of an afflicted house, the Señora's daughter, the sister of Felipe; she bore it even in her beauty. She had the lightness and swiftness of the one, swift as an arrow, light as dew; like the other, she shone on the pale background of the world with the brilliancy of flowers. I could not call by the name of brother that half-witted lad, nor by the name of mother that immovable and lovely thing of flesh, whose silly eyes and perpetual simper now recurred to my mind like something hateful. And if I could not marry, what then? She was helplessly unprotected; her eyes, in that single and long glance which had been all our intercourse, had confessed a weakness equal to my own; but in my heart I knew her for the student of the cold northern chamber, and the writer of the sorrowful lines; and this was a knowledge to disarm a brute. To flee was more than I could find courage for; but I registered a vow of unsleeping circumspection.

As I turned from the window, my eyes alighted on the portrait. It had fallen dead, like a candle after sunrise; it followed me with eyes of paint. I knew it to be like, and marvelled at the tenacity of type in that declining race; but the likeness was swallowed up in difference. I remembered how it had seemed to me a thing unapproachable in the life, a creature rather of the painter's craft than of the modesty of nature, and I marvelled at the thought, and exulted in the image of Olalla. Beauty I had seen before, and not been charmed, and I had been often drawn to women, who were not beautiful except to me; but in Olalla all that I desired and had not dared to imagine was united.

I did not see her the next day, and my heart ached and my eyes longed for her, as men long for morning. But the day after, when

I returned, about my usual hour, she was once more on the gallery, and our looks once more met and embraced. I would have spoken, I would have drawn near to her; but strongly as she plucked at my heart, drawing me like a magnet, something yet more imperious withheld me; and I could only bow and pass by; and she, leaving my salutation unanswered, only followed me with her noble eyes.

I had now her image by rote, and as I conned the traits in memory it seemed as if I read her very heart. She was dressed with something of her mother's coquetry, and love of positive colour. Her robe, which I knew she must have made with her own hands, clung about her with a cunning grace. After the fashion of that country, besides, her bodice stood open in the middle, in a long slit, and here, in spite of the poverty of the house, a gold coin, hanging by a ribbon, lay on her brown bosom. These were proofs, had any been needed, of her inborn delight in life and her own loveliness. On the other hand, in her eyes, that hung upon mine, I could read depth beyond depth of passion and sadness, lights of poetry and hope, blacknesses of despair, and thoughts that were above the earth. It was a lovely body, but the inmate, the soul, was more than worthy of that lodging. Should I leave this incomparable flower to wither unseen on these rough mountains? Should I despise the great gift offered me in the eloquent silence of her eyes? Here was a soul immured; should I not burst its prison? All side considerations fell off from me; were she the child of Herod I swore I should make her mine; and that very evening I set myself, with a mingled sense of treachery and disgrace, to captivate the brother. Perhaps I read him with more favourable eyes, perhaps the thought of his sister always summoned up the better qualities of that imperfect soul; but he had never seemed to me so amiable, and his very likeness to Olalla, while it annoyed, yet softened me.

A third day passed in vain—an empty desert of hours. I would not lose a chance, and loitered all afternoon in the court where (to give myself a countenance) I spoke more than usual with the Señora. God knows it was with a most tender and sincere interest that I now studied her; and even as for Felipe, so now for the mother, I was conscious of a growing warmth of toleration. And yet I wondered. Even while I spoke with her, she would doze off into a little sleep, and presently awake again without embarrassment; and this composure staggered me. And again, as I marked her make infinitesimal changes in her posture, savouring and lingering on the bodily pleasure of the moment, I was driven to wonder at this depth of passive sensuality. She lived in her body; and her consciousness was all sunk into and disseminated her members, where it luxuriously dwelt. Lastly, I could not grow accustomed to her eyes. Each time she turned on me these great, beautiful, and meaningless orbs, wide open to the day, but closed against human inquiry—each time I had occasion to observe the lively changes of her pupils which expanded and contracted in a breath—I know not what it was came over me, I can find no name for the mingled feeling of disappointment, annoyance, and distaste that jarred along my nerves. I tried her on a variety of subjects, equally in vain; and at last led the talk to her daughter. But even there she proved indifferent; said she was pretty, which (as with children) was her highest word of commendation, but was plainly incapable of any higher thought; and when I remarked that Olalla seemed silent, merely yawned in my face and replied that speech was of no great use when you had nothing to say. "People speak much, very much," she added, looking at me with expanded pupils; and then again yawned, and again showed me a mouth that was as dainty as a toy. This time I took the hint, and, leaving her to her repose, went up into my own chamber to sit by the open window, looking on the hills and not beholding them, sunk in lustrous and deep dreams, and hearkening in fancy to the note of a voice that I had never heard.

I awoke on the fifth morning with a brightness of anticipation that seemed to challenge fate. I was sure of myself, light of heart and foot, and resolved to put my love incontinently to the touch of knowledge. It should lie no longer under the bonds of silence, a dumb thing, living by the eye only, like the love of beasts; but should now put on the spirit, and enter upon the joys of the complete human intimacy. I thought of it with wild hopes, like a voyager to El Dorado; into that unknown and lovely country of her soul, I no longer trembled to adventure. Yet when I did indeed encounter her, the same force of passion descended on me and at once submerged my mind; speech seemed to drop away from me like a childish habit; and I but drew near to her as the giddy man draws near to the margin of a gulf. She drew back from me a little as I came: but her eyes did not waver from mine, and these lured me forward. At last, when I was already within reach of her, I stopped. Words were denied me; if I advanced I could but clasp her to my heart in silence; and all that was sane in me, all that was still unconquered, revolted against the thought of such an accost. So we stood for a second, all our life in our eyes, exchanging salvos of attraction and yet each resisting; and then, with a great effort of the will, and conscious at the same time of a sudden bitterness of disappointment, I turned and went away in the same silence.

What power lay upon me that I could not speak? And she, why was she also silent? Why did she draw away before me dumbly, with fascinated eyes? Was this love? or was it a mere brute attraction, mindless and inevitable, like that of the magnet for the steel? We had never spoken, we were wholly strangers; and yet an influence, strong as the grasp of a giant, swept us silently together. On my side, it filled me with impatience; and yet I was sure that she was worthy; I had seen her books, read her verses, and thus, in a sense, divined the soul of my mistress. But on her side, it struck me almost cold. Of me, she knew nothing but my bodily favour; she was drawn to me as stones fall to earth; the laws that rule the earth conducted her, unconsenting, to my arms; and I drew back at the thought of such a bridal, and began to be jealous for myself. It was not thus that I desired to be loved. And then I began to fall into a great pity for the girl herself. I thought how sharp must be her mortification, that she, the student, the recluse, Felipe's saintly monitress, should have thus confessed an overweening weakness for a man with whom she had never exchanged a word. And at the coming of pity, all other thoughts were swallowed up; and I longed only to find and console and reassure her; to tell her how wholly her love was returned on my side, and how her choice, even if blindly made, was not unworthy.

The next day it was glorious weather; depth upon depth of blue over-canopied the mountains; the sun shone wide; and the wind in the trees and the many falling torrents in the mountains filled the air with delicate and haunting music. Yet I was prostrated with sadness. My heart wept for the sight of Olalla, as a child weeps for its mother. I sat down on a boulder on the verge of the low cliffs that bound the plateau to the north. Thence I looked down into the wooded valley of a stream, where no foot came. In the mood I was in, it even touching to behold the place untenanted; it lacked Olalla; and I thought of the delight and glory of a life passed wholly with her in that strong air, and among these rugged and lovely surroundings, at first with a whimpering sentiment, and then again with such a fiery joy that I seemed to grow in strength and stature, like a Samson.

And then suddenly I was aware of Olalla drawing near. She appeared out of a grove of cork-trees, and came straight towards me; and I stood up and waited. She seemed in her walking a creature of such life and fire and lightness as amazed me; yet she came quietly and slowly. Her energy was in the slowness; but for inimitable strength, I felt she would have run, she would have flown to me. Still, as she approached, she kept her eyes lowered to the ground; and when she had drawn quite near, it was without one glance that she addressed me. At the first note of her voice I started. It was for this I had been waiting; this was the last test of my love. And lo, her enunciation was precise and clear, not lisping and incomplete like that of her family; and the voice, though deeper than usual with women, was still both youthful and womanly. She spoke in a rich chord; golden contralto strains mingled with hoarseness, as the red threads were mingled with the brown among her tresses. It was not only a voice that spoke to my heart directly; but it spoke to me of her. And yet her words immediately plunged me back upon despair.

"You will go away," she said, "to-day."

Her example broke the bonds of my speech; I felt as lightened of a weight, or as if a spell had been dissolved. I know not in what words I answered; but, standing before her on the cliffs, I poured out the whole ardour of my love, telling her that I lived upon the thought of her, slept only to dream of her loveliness, and would gladly forswear my country, my language, and my friends, to live for ever by her side. And then, strongly commanding myself, I changed the note; I reassured, I comforted her; I told her I had divined in her a pious and heroic spirit, with which I was worthy to sympathise, and which I longed to share and lighten. "Nature," I told her, "was the voice of God, which men disobey at peril; and if we were thus dumbly drawn together, ay, even as by a miracle of love, it must imply a divine fitness in our souls; we must be made," I said—"made for one another. We should be mad rebels," I cried out—"mad rebels against God, not to obey this instinct."

She shook her head. "You will go to-day," she repeated, and then with a gesture, and in a sudden, sharp note—"no, not to-day," she cried, "to-morrow."

But at this sign of relenting, power came in upon me in a tide. I stretched out my arms and called upon her name; and she leaped to me and clung to me. The hills rocked about us, the earth quailed; a shock as of a blow went through me and left me blind and dizzy. And the next moment, she had thrust me back, broken rudely from my arms, and fled with the speed of a deer among the cork-trees.

I stood and shouted to the mountains; I turned and went back towards the residencia, walking upon air. She sent me away, and yet I had but to call upon her name and she came to me. These were but the weaknesses of girls, from which even she, the strangest of her sex, was not exempted. Go? Not I, Olalla—O, not I, Olalla, my Olalla! A bird sang near by; and in that season, birds were rare. It bade me be of good cheer. And once more the whole countenance of nature, from the ponderous and stable mountains down to the lightest leaf and the smallest darting fly in the shadow of the groves began to stir before me and to put on the lineaments of life and wear a face of awful joy. The sunshine struck upon the hills, strong as a hammer on the anvil, and the hills shook; the earth, under that vigorous insolation, yielded up heady scents; the woods smouldered in the blaze. I felt a thrill of travail and delight run through the earth. Something elemental, something rude, violent, and savage, in the love that sang in my heart, was like a key to nature's secrets; and the very stones that rattled under my feet appeared alive and friendly. Olalla! Her touch had quickened, and renewed, and strung me up to the old pitch of concert with the rugged earth, to a swelling of the soul that men learn to forget in their polite assemblies. Love burned in me like rage; tenderness waxed fierce; I hated, I adored, I pitied, I revered her with ecstasy. She seemed the link that bound me in with dead things on the one hand, and with our pure and pitying God upon

the other; a thing brutal and divine, and akin at once to the innocence and to the unbridled forces of the earth.

My head thus reeling, I came into the courtyard of the residencia, and the sight of the mother struck me like a revelation. She
sat there, all sloth and contentment, blinking under the strong
sunshine, branded with a passive enjoyment, a creature set quite
apart, before whom my ardour fell away like a thing ashamed. I
stopped a moment, and, commanding such shaken tones as I was
able, said a word or two. She looked at me with her unfathomable
kindness; her voice in reply sounded vaguely out of the realm of
peace in which she slumbered, and there fell on my mind, for the
first time, a sense of respect for one so uniformly innocent and
happy, and I passed on in a kind of wonder at myself, that I should
be so much disquieted.

On my table there lay a piece of the same yellow paper I had
seen in the north room; it was written on with pencil in the same
hand, Olalla's hand, and I picked it up with a sudden sinking of
alarm, and read, "If you have any kindness for Olalla, if you have
any chivalry for a creature sorely wrought, go from here to-day;
in pity, in honour, for the sake of Him who died, I supplicate that
you shall go." I looked at this awhile in mere stupidity, then I
began to awaken to a weariness and horror of life; the sunshine
darkened outside on the bare hills, and I began to shake like a
man in terror. The vacancy thus suddenly opened in my life unmanned me like a physical void. It was not my heart, it was not
my happiness, it was life itself that was involved. I could not lose
her. I said so, and stood repeating it. And then, like one in a dream,
I moved to the window, put forth my hand to open the casement,
and thrust it through the pane. The blood spirited from my wrist;
and with an instantaneous quietude and command of myself, I
pressed my thumb on the little leaping fountain, and reflected
what to do. In that empty room there was nothing to my purpose;
I felt, besides, that I required assistance. There shot into my mind
a hope that Olalla herself might be my helper, and I turned and
went down-stairs, still keeping my thumb upon the wound.

There was no sign of either Olalla or Felipe, and I addressed
myself to the recess, whither the Señora had now drawn quite
back and sat dozing close before the fire, for no degree of heat
appeared too much for her.

"Pardon me," said I, "if I disturb you, but I must apply to you for help."

She looked up sleepily and asked me what it was, and with the very words, I thought she drew in her breath with a widening of the nostrils and seemed to come suddenly and fully alive.

"I have cut myself," I said, "and rather badly. See!" And I held out my two hands from which the blood was oozing and dripping.

Her great eyes opened wide, the pupils shrank into points; a veil seemed to fall from her face, and leave it sharply expressive and yet inscrutable. And as I still stood, marvelling a little at her disturbance, she came swiftly up to me, and stooped and caught me by the hand; and the next moment my hand was at her mouth, and she had bitten me to the bone. The pang of the bite, the sudden spiriting of blood, and the monstrous horror of the act, flashed through me all in one, and I beat her back; and she sprang at me again and again, with bestial cries, cries that I recognised, such cries as had awakened me on the night of the high wind. Her strength was like that of madness; mine was rapidly ebbing with the loss of blood; my mind besides was whirling with the abhorrent strangeness of the onslaught, and I was already forced against the wall, when Olalla ran betwixt us, and Felipe, following at a bound, pinned down his mother on the floor.

A trance-like weakness fell upon me; I saw, heard, and felt, but I was incapable of movement. I heard the struggle roll to and fro upon the floor, the yells of that catamount ringing up to Heaven as she strove to reach me. I felt Olalla clasp me in her arms, her hair falling on my face, and, with the strength of a man, raise and half drag, half carry me up stairs into my own room, where she cast me down upon the bed. Then I saw her hasten to the door and lock it, and stand an instant listening to the savage cries that shook the residencia. And then, swift and light as a thought, she was again beside me, binding up my hand, laying it in her bosom, moaning and mourning over it with dove-like sounds. They were not words that came to her, they were sounds more beautiful than speech, infinitely touching, infinitely tender; and yet as I lay there, a thought stung to my heart, a thought wounded me like a sword, a thought, like a worm in a flower, profaned the holiness of my love. Yes, they were beautiful sounds, and they were inspired by human tenderness; but was their beauty human?

All day I lay there. For a long time the cries of that nameless female thing, as she struggled with her half-witted whelp, resounded through the house, and pierced me with despairing sorrow and disgust. They were the death-cry of my love; my love was murdered; it was not only dead, but an offence to me; and yet, think as I pleased, feel as I must, it still swelled within me like a storm of sweetness, and my heart melted at her looks and touch. This horror that had sprung out, this doubt upon Olalla, this savage and bestial strain that ran not only through the whole behaviour of her family, but found a place in the very foundations and story of our love—though it appalled, though it shocked and sickened me, was yet not of power to break the knot of my infatuation.

When the cries had ceased, there came the scraping at the door, by which I knew Felipe was without; and Olalla went and spoke to him—I know not what. With that exception, she stayed close beside me, now kneeling by my bed and fervently praying, now sitting with her eyes upon mine. So then, for these six hours I drank in her beauty, and silently perused the story in her face. I saw the golden coin hover on her breaths; I saw her eyes darken and brighten, and still speak no language but that of an unfathomable kindness; I saw the faultless face, and, through the robe, the lines of the faultless body. Night came at last, and in the growing darkness of the chamber, the sight of her slowly melted; but even then the touch of her smooth hand lingered in mine and talked with me. To lie thus in deadly weakness and drink in the traits of the beloved, is to re-awake to love from whatever shock of disillusion. I reasoned with myself; and I shut my eyes on horrors, and again I was very bold to accept the worst. What mattered it, if that imperious sentiment survived; if her eyes still beckoned and attached me; if now, even as before, every fibre of my dull body yearned and turned to her? Late on in the night some strength revived in me, and I spoke.

"Olalla," I said, "nothing matters; I ask nothing; I am content; I love you."

She knelt down awhile and prayed, and I devoutly respected her devotions. The moon had begun to shine in upon one side of each of the three windows, and make a misty clearness in the room, by which I saw her indistinctly. When she re-arose she made the sign of the cross.

"It is for me to speak," she said, "and for you to listen. I know; you can but guess. I prayed, how I prayed for you to leave this place. I begged it of you, and I know you would have granted me even this; or if not, O let me think so!"

"I love you," I said.

"And yet you have lived in the world," she said, after a pause, "you are a man and wise; and I am but a child. Forgive me, if I seem to teach, who am as ignorant as the trees of the mountain; but those who learn much do but skim the face of knowledge; they seize the laws, they conceive the dignity of the design—the horror of the living fact fades from their memory. It is we who sit at home with evil who remember, I think, and are warned and pity. Go, rather, go now, and keep me in mind. So I shall have a life in the cherished places of your memory: a life as much my own, as that which I lead in this body."

"I love you," I said once more; and reaching out my weak hand, took hers, and carried it to my lips, and kissed it. Nor did she resist, but winced a little; and I could see her look upon me with a frown that was not unkindly, only sad and baffled. And then it seemed she made a call upon her resolution; plucked my hand towards her, herself at the same time leaning somewhat forward, and laid it on the beating of her heart. "There!" she cried, "you feel the very footfall of my life. It only moves for you; it is yours. But is it even mine? It is mine indeed to offer you, as I might take the coin from my neck, as I might break a live branch from a tree, and give it you. And yet not mine! I dwell, or I think I dwell (if I exist at all), somewhere apart, an impotent prisoner, and carried about and deafened by a mob that I disown. This capsule, such as throbs against the sides of animals, knows you at a touch for its master; ay, it loves you! But my soul, does my soul? I think not; I know not, fearing to ask. Yet when you spoke to me your words were of the soul; it is of the soul that you ask—it is only from the soul that you would take me."

"Olalla," I said, "the soul and the body are one, and mostly so in love. What the body chooses, the soul loves; where the body clings, the soul cleaves; body for body, soul to soul they come together at God's signal; and the lower part (if we can call aught low) is only the footstool and foundation of the highest."

"Have you," she said, "seen the portraits in the house of my fathers? Have you looked at my mother or at Felipe? Have your eyes ever rested on that picture that hangs by your bed? She who sat for it died ages ago; and she did evil in her life. But look again: there is my hand to the least line, there are my eyes and my hair. What is mine, then, and what am I? If not a curve in this poor body of mine (which you love, and for the sake of which you dotingly dream that you love me), not a gesture that I can frame, not a tone of my voice, not any look from my eyes, no, not even now when I speak to him I love, but has belonged to others? Others, ages dead, have wooed other men with my eyes; other men have heard the pleading of the same voice that now sounds in your ears. The hands of the dead are in my bosom; they move me, they pluck me, they guide me; I am a puppet at their command; and I but reinform features and attributes that have long been laid aside from evil in the quiet of the grave. Is it me you love, friend? or the race that made me? The girl who does not know and cannot answer for the least portion of herself? or the stream of which she is a transitory eddy, the tree of which she is the passing fruit? The race exists; it is old, it is ever young, it carries its eternal destiny in its bosom; upon it, like waves upon the sea, individual succeeds to individual, mocked with a semblance of self-control, but they are nothing. We speak of the soul, but the soul is in the race."

"You fret against the common law," I said. "You rebel against the voice of God, which he has made so winning to convince, so imperious to command. Hear it, and how it speaks between us! Your hand clings to mine, your heart leaps at my touch, the unknown elements of which we are compounded awake and run together at a look; the clay of the earth remembers its independent life and yearns to join us; we are drawn together as the stars are turned about in space, or as the tides ebb and flow, by things older and greater than we ourselves."

"Alas!" she said, "what can I say to you? My fathers, eight hundred years ago, ruled all this province: they were wise, great, cunning, and cruel; they were a picked race of the Spanish; their flags led in war; the king called them his cousin; the people, when the rope was slung for them or when they returned and found their hovels smoking, blasphemed their name. Presently a change began. Man has risen; if he has sprung from the brutes, he can descend again to the same level. The breath of weariness blew on their humanity and the cords relaxed; they began to go down; their minds fell on sleep, their passions awoke in gusts, heady and senseless like the wind in the gutters of the mountains; beauty was still handed down, but no longer the guiding wit nor the human heart; the seed passed on, it was wrapped in flesh, the flesh covered the bones, but they were the bones and the flesh of brutes, and their mind was as the mind of flies. I speak to you as I dare; but you have seen for yourself how the wheel has gone backward with my doomed race. I stand, as it were, upon a little rising ground in this desperate descent, and see both before and behind, both what we have lost and to what we are condemned to go farther downward. And shall I—I that dwell apart in the house of the dead, my body, loathing its ways—shall I repeat the spell? Shall I bind another spirit, reluctant as my own, into this bewitched and tempest-broken tenement that I now suffer in? Shall I hand down this cursed vessel of humanity, charge it with fresh life as with fresh poison, and dash it, like a fire, in the faces of posterity? But my vow has been given; the race shall cease from off the earth. At this hour my brother is making ready; his foot will soon be on the stair; and you will go with him and pass out of my sight for ever. Think of me sometimes as one to whom the lesson of life was very harshly told, but who heard it with courage; as one who loved you indeed, but who hated herself so deeply that her love was hateful to her; as one who sent you away and yet would have longed to keep you for ever; who had no dearer hope than to forget you, and no greater fear than to be forgotten.''

She had drawn towards the door as she spoke, her rich voice sounding softer and farther away; and with the last word, she was gone, and I lay alone in the moonlit chamber. What I might have done had not I lain bound by my extreme weakness, I know not; but as it was there fell upon me a great and blank despair. It was not long before there shone in at the door the ruddy glimmer of a lantern, and Felipe coming, charged me without a word upon his shoulders, and carried me down to the great gate, where the cart was waiting. In the moonlight the hills stood out sharply, as if they were of cardboard; on the glimmering surface of the plateau, and from among the low trees which swung together and sparkled in the wind, the great black cube of the residencia stood out bulkily, its mass only broken by three dimly lighted windows in the northern front above the gate. They were Olalla's windows, and as the cart jolted onwards I kept my eyes fixed upon them till, where the road dipped into a valley, they were lost to my view for ever. Felipe walked in silence beside the shafts, but from time to time he would check the mule and seem to look back upon me; and at length drew quite near and laid his hand upon my head. There was such kindness in the touch, and such a simplicity, as of the brutes, that tears broke from me like the bursting of an artery.

"Felipe," I said, "take me where they will ask no questions."

He said never a word, but he turned his mule about, end for end, retraced some part of the way we had gone, and, striking into another path, led me to the mountain village, which was, as we say in Scotland, the kirkton of that thinly peopled district. Some broken memories dwell in my mind of the day breaking over the plain, of the cart stopping, of arms that helped me down, of a bare room into which I was carried, and of a swoon that fell upon me like sleep.

The next day and the days following, the old priest was often at my side with his snuff-box and prayer-book, and after awhile, when I began to pick up strength, he told me that I was now on a fair way to recovery, and must as soon as possible hurry my departure; whereupon, without naming any reason, he took snuff and looked at me sideways. I did not affect ignorance. I knew he must have seen Olalla. "Sir," said I, "you know that I do not ask in wantonness. What of that family?"

He said they were very unfortunate; that it seemed a declining race, and that they were very poor and had been much neglected.

"But she has not," I said. "Thanks, doubtless, to yourself, she is instructed and wise beyond the use of women."

"Yes," he said, "the Señorita is well informed. But the family has been neglected."

"The mother?" I queried.

"Yes, the mother too," said the Padre, taking snuff. "But Felipe is a well-intentioned lad."

"The mother is odd?" I asked.

"Very odd," replied the priest.

"I think, sir, we beat about the bush," said I. "You must know more of my affairs than you allow. You must know my curiosity to be justified on many grounds. Will you not be frank with me?"

"My son," said the old gentleman, "I will be very frank with you on matters within my competence; on those of which I know nothing it does not require much discretion to be silent. I will not fence with you, I take your meaning perfectly; and what can I say, but that we are all in God's hands, and that His ways are not as our ways? I have even advised with my superiors in the church, but they, too, were dumb. It is a great mystery."

"Is she mad?" I asked.

"I will answer you according to my belief. She is not," returned the Padre, "or she was not. When she was young—God help me, I fear I neglected that wild lamb—she was surely sane; and yet, although it did not run to such heights, the same strain was already notable; it had been so before her in her father, ay, and before him, and this inclined me, perhaps, to think too lightly of it. But these things go on growing, not only in the individual but in the race."

"When she was young," I began, and my voice failed me for a moment, and it was only with a great effort that I was able to add, "was she like Olalla?"

"Now God forbid!" exclaimed the Padre. "God forbid that any man should think so slightingly of my favourite penitent! No, no; the Señorita (but for her beauty, which I wish most honestly she had less of) has not a hair's resemblance to what her mother was at the same age. I could not bear to have you think so; though, Heaven knows, it were, perhaps, better that you should."

At this, I raised myself in bed, and opened my heart to the old man; telling him of our love and of her decision, owning my own horrors, my own passing fancies, but telling him that these were at an end; and with something more than a purely formal submission, appealing to his judgement.

He heard me very patiently and without surprise; and when I had done, he sat for some time silent. Then he began: "The church," and instantly broke off again to apologise. "I had forgotten, my child, that you were not a Christian," said he. "And indeed, upon a point so highly unusual, even the church can scarce be said to have decided. But would you have my opinion? The Señorita is, in a matter of this kind, the best judge; I would accept her judgement."

On the back of that he went away, nor was he thenceforward so assiduous in his visits; indeed, even when I began to get about again, he plainly feared and deprecated my society, not as in distaste but much as a man might be disposed to flee from the riddling sphinx. The villagers, too, avoided me; they were unwilling to be my guides upon the mountain. I thought they looked at me askance, and I made sure that the more superstitious crossed themselves on my approach. At first I set this down to my heretical opinions; but it began at length to dawn upon me that if I was thus redoubted it was because I had stayed at the residencia. All men despise the savage notions of such peasantry; and yet I was conscious of a chill shadow that seemed to fall and dwell upon my love. It did not conquer, but I may not deny that it restrained my ardour.

Some miles westward of the village there was a gap in the sierra, from which the eye plunged direct upon the residencia; and thither it became my daily habit to repair. A wood crowned the summit; and just where the pathway issued from its fringes, it was overhung by a considerable shelf of rock, and that, in its turn, was surmounted by a crucifix of the size of life and more than usually painful in design. This was my perch; thence, day after day, I looked down upon the plateau, and the great old house, and could see Felipe, no bigger than a fly, going to and fro about the garden. Sometimes mists would draw across the view, and be broken up again by mountain winds; sometimes the plain slumbered below me in unbroken sunshine; it would sometimes be all blotted out by rain. This distant post, these interrupted sights of the place where my life had been so strangely changed suited the indecision of my humour. I passed whole days there, debating with myself the various elements of our position; now leaning to the suggestions of love, now giving an ear to prudence, and in the end halting irresolute between the two.

One day, as I was sitting on my rock, there came by that way a somewhat gaunt peasant wrapped in a mantle. He was a stranger, and plainly did not know me even by repute; for, instead of keeping the other side, he drew near and sat down beside me, and we had soon fallen in talk. Among other things he told me he had been a muleteer, and in former years had much frequented these mountains; later on, he had followed the army with his mules, had realised a competence, and was now living retired with his family.

"Do you know that house?" I inquired, at last, pointing to the residencia, for I readily wearied of any talk that kept me from the thought of Olalla.

He looked at me darkly and crossed himself.

"Too well," he said, "it was there that one of my comrades sold himself to Satan; the Virgin shield us from temptations! He has paid the price; he is now burning in the reddest place in Hell!"

A fear came upon me; I could answer nothing; and presently the man resumed, as if to himself. "Yes," he said, "O yes, I know it. I have passed its doors. There was snow upon the pass, the wind was driving it; sure enough there was death that night upon the mountains, but there was worse beside the hearth. I took him by the arm, Señor, and dragged him to the gate; I conjured him, by all he loved and respected, to go forth with me; I went on my knees before him in the snow; and I could see he was moved by my entreaty. And just then she came out on the gallery, and called him by his name; and he turned, and there was she standing with a lamp in her hand and smiling on him to come back. I cried out aloud to God, and threw my arms about him, but he put me by, and left me alone. He had made his choice; God help us. I would pray for him, but to what end? there are sins that not even the Pope can loose."

"And your friend," I asked, "what became of him?"

"Nay, God knows," said the muleteer. "If all be true that we hear, his end was like his sin, a thing to raise the hair."

"Do you mean that he was killed?" I asked.

"Sure enough, he was killed," returned the man. "But how? Ay, how? But these are things that it is sin to speak of."

"The people of that house . . ." I began.

But he interrupted me with a savage outburst.

"The people?" he cried. "What people? There are neither men nor women in that house of Satan's! What? have you lived here so long, and never heard?" And here he put his mouth to my ear and whispered, as if even the fowls of the mountain might have overheard and been stricken with horror.

What he told me was not true, nor was it even original; being, indeed, but a new edition, vamped up again by village ignorance and superstition, of stories nearly as ancient as the race of man. It was rather the application that appalled me. In the old days, he said, the church would have burned out that nest of basilisks; but the arm of the church was now shortened; his friend Miguel had been unpunished by the hands of men, and left to the more awful judgement of an offended God. This was wrong; but it should be so no more. The Padre was sunk in age; he was even bewitched himself; but the eyes of his flock were now awake to their own danger; and some day—ay, and before long—the smoke of that house should go up to heaven.

He left me filled with horror and fear. Which way to turn I knew not; whether first to warn the Padre, or to carry my ill-news direct to the threatened inhabitants of the residencia Fate was to decide for me; for, while I was still hesitating, I beheld the veiled figure of a woman drawing near to me up the pathway. No veil could deceive my penetration; by every line and every movement I recognised Olalla; and keeping hidden behind a corner of the rock, I suffered her to gain the summit. Then I came forward. She knew me and paused, but did not speak; I, too, remained silent; and we continued for some time to gaze upon each other with a passionate sadness.

"I thought you had gone," she said at length. "It is all that you can do for me—to go. It is all I ever asked of you. And you still stay. But do you know, that every day heaps up the peril of death, not only on your head, but on ours? A report has gone about the mountain; it is thought you love me, and the people will not suffer it."

I saw she was already informed of her danger, and I rejoiced at it. "Olalla," I said, "I am ready to go this day, this very hour, but not alone."

She stepped aside and knelt down before the crucifix to pray, and I stood by and looked now at her and now at the object of her adoration, now at the living figure of the penitent, and now at the ghastly, daubed countenance, the painted wounds, and the projected ribs of the image. The silence was only broken by the wailing of some large birds that circled sidelong, as if in surprise or alarm, about the summit of the hills. Presently Olalla rose again, turned towards me, raised her veil, and, still leaning with one hand on the shaft of the crucifix, looked upon me with a pale and sorrowful countenance.

"I have laid my hand upon the cross," she said. "The Padre says you are no Christian; but look up for a moment with my eyes, and behold the face of the Man of Sorrows. We are all such as He was—the inheritors of sin; we must all bear and expiate a past which was not ours; there is in all of us—ay, even in me—a sparkle of the divine. Like Him, we must endure for a little while, until morning returns bringing peace. Suffer me to pass on upon my way alone; it is thus that I shall be least lonely, counting for my friend Him who is the friend of all the distressed; it is thus that I shall be the most happy, having taken my farewell of earthly happiness, and willingly accepted sorrow for my portion."

I looked at the face of the crucifix, and, though I was no friend to images, and despised that imitative and grimacing art of which it was a rude example, some sense of what the thing implied was carried home to my intelligence. The face looked down upon me with a painful and deadly contraction: but the rays of a glory encircled it, and reminded me that the sacrifice was voluntary. It stood there, crowning the rock, as it still stands on so many highway-sides, vainly preaching to passers-by, an emblem of sad and noble truths; that pleasure is not an end, but an accident; that pain is the choice of the magnanimous; that it is best to suffer all things and do well. I turned and went down the mountain in silence; and when I looked back for the last time before the wood closed about my path, I saw Olalla still leaning on the crucifix.

Baudelaire

THE VAMPIRE

(Translated by Philip Higson)

———⟫●⟪———

Charles Baudelaire's life was miserable, marked by poverty and disease. He contracted syphilis when young, and the intense pain forced him to resort to alcohol and opium for relief. Baudelaire was a French poet, critic, and short story writer. During his lifetime he was best known for translating Edgar Allan Poe's works into French. His own works show Poe's influence. It wasn't until after his death that his poetry received recognition. According to the *Encyclopedia Americana*, Baudelaire was "the most influential of all the modern poets." *Les Fleurs du Mal* (*Flowers of Evil*) is considered his masterpiece. "Le Vampire" ("The Vampire") is from this book, which was published in 1857. The vampire here was his mistress, Jeanne Duval. At the bottom of one of his sketches of her, Baudelaire wrote, "Seeking whom she may devour."

> You that have, like a dagger-blade,
> Transfixed my heart that mourned,
> Who, strong as countless demons made,
> Came, reckless, gay-adorned,
>
> And in my downcast spirit found
> Your bed and your domain;

—Vile wretch to whom I'm tightly bound:
A convict on his chain,

A stubborn gambler with his bets,
A drunkard with his brew,
A carcass with its wormy pets,
—Accursed accursed be you!

I begged the swift-descending sword
To grant me my release,
And treacherous poison, too, implored
To aid my cowardice.

Alas! The poison and the blade
Proclaimed contemptuously:
"You are not worthy to be made
From cursed thralldom free,

You fool!—were we to liberate
You rudely from her sway,
Your kisses would resuscitate
Your vampire's lifeless clay!"

Jules Verne

EXCERPT FROM

THE CARPATHIAN CASTLE

———❖———

Jules Verne was the first modern science fiction writer. Among his many classic works are *Around the World in Eighty Days*, *Voyage to the Center of the Earth*, *Twenty Thousand Leagues Under the Sea*, and *Mysterious Island*. His books anticipated many scientific discoveries and inventions, such as submarines and spaceships. In 1892, Verne published the Gothic novel, *Le Château des Carpethes* (*The Carpathian Castle*). This hard-to-find book tells the story of forester Nic Deck and a local "doctor," who decide to investigate a long-deserted—and reputedly haunted—castle in Transylvania after a newly purchased telescope discovers smoke rising from one of its chimneys. The following excerpt is the most striking—and most vampiric—scene in the novel. While Verne's book is somewhat reminiscent of *Dracula*, it was actually published five years before Stoker's novel.

THE THIN CRESCENT OF the moon, looking like a silver sickle, disappeared almost as soon as the sun set. A few clouds, coming from the west, extinguished one by one the last gleams of twilight. Darkness gradually rose from below and covered everything. The circle of mountains was blotted out in the shadows and the castle itself soon disappeared.

If the night threatened to be very dark, nothing suggested that it would be troubled by any atmospheric disturbance, gale, rain or storm. This was lucky for Nic Deck and his companion, who were going to camp in the open air.

On this barren plateau of Orgall there were no clumps of trees. Here and there were a few lowly shrubs, which gave no shelter against the nocturnal cold. There were rocks in plenty, some half-buried in the ground, others hardly in equilibrium so that the slightest push would have sent them rolling down into the fir-woods.

It was now a matter of finding somewhere to spend the night and of seeking shelter against the fall in temperature, which is remarkable in these altitudes.

"We've got plenty of choice—where to be miserable!" murmured Doctor Patak.

"Are you grumbling, then?" asked Nic Deck.

"Yes, I am! What a splendid place to catch a fine cold or the rheumatism, which I don't know I'll ever get cured of!"

A very artless confession on the part of the old quarantine officer. Oh, how he regretted his comfortable little house at Werst, with its room so snug and its bed so well furnished with pillows and counterpane!

Among the stones on the Orgall plateau one had to be chosen whose position offered the best shelter against the south-west wind, which was beginning to get biting. This was what Nic Deck did, and soon the doctor joined him behind a large rock, as flat as a table on its upper surface.

This was one of those stone benches which are frequently found buried amid the scabious and saxifrage at the turnings of the Wallachian roads. While the traveler sits on them he can quench his thirst with the water contained in a vase placed on them, and which is every day refilled by the country people. When Baron Rodolphe de Gortz lived at the castle, this bench had borne a bowl which servants of the family took care never to leave empty. But now it was dirty and worn and covered with a greenish moss, and the slightest shock would have reduced it to dust.

At the end of the seat rose a granite shaft, the remains of an ancient cross; nothing was left of the arms although a half-effaced groove in the upright showed where they had been.

As a freethinker, Doctor Patak could not admit that this cross could protect him against supernatural apparitions. But by an anomaly common to a good many of the incredulous, although he did not believe in God, he was not very far from believing in the devil. In his heart he believed the Chort[1] was not far away; it was he that haunted the castle, and it was neither the closed gate nor the raised drawbridge, nor the lofty wall, nor the deep moat that would keep him from emerging if the fancy took him, to come and wring both their necks.

And when the doctor saw that he had to spend a whole night under these conditions, he shuddered with terror. No! This was too much to ask of any human creature, and it would be more than the most energetic of characters could bear.

And then an idea came to him somewhat late in the day—an idea he had not thought of before he left Werst. It was Tuesday evening, and on that day the local people took care never to go out after sundown. Tuesday, they knew, was an ill-omened day. Their legends told them that if they ventured abroad on that day, they ran the risk of meeting with some evil spirit. And so, on Tuesday, nobody traveled on the roads and by-ways after night-fall.

And here Doctor Patak found himself not only far from home, but close to a haunted castle, two or three miles from the village. And here he would have to stay until the dawn came—if ever it came again! Really, this was simply tempting the devil!

Deep in these thoughts, the doctor saw the forester calmly taking a piece of cold meat out of his wallet, after having a good mouthful from his flask. The best thing, it occurred to him, was to do likewise, and that was what he did. A leg of a goose, a thick slice of bread, the whole well moistened with rakiou, was the least he could take to revive his strength. But if that calmed his hunger, it did not calm his fears.

"Now let's go to sleep," Nic Deck suggested, as soon as he had put his wallet at the foot of the stone.

"Sleep, forester?"

"Good-night, doctor."

"Good-night—that's easy to say, but I'm afraid all this will end badly."

[1]The devil.

Nic Deck, being in no humor for conversation, made no reply. Accustomed by his vocation to sleep in the midst of the woods, he threw himself down beside the stone seat and was not slow in falling into a deep sleep. And all the doctor could do was to grumble between his teeth when he heard his companion's regular breathing.

As for him, it was impossible for him even for a few minutes to deaden his senses of hearing and seeing. In spite of his fatigue he never stopped looking and listening. His brain was a prey to those extravagant visions which give rise to the troubles of sleeplessness.

What was he trying to look for in the darkness of the shadows? Everything and nothing; the hazy shapes of the objects around him, the scattered clouds across the sky, the almost imperceptible mass of the castle. Then it was the rocks on the Orgall plateau which seemed to be moving in a sort of infernal saraband. Suppose they were to collapse on their bases, slip down the slope, roll on to the two adventurers, and crush them at the castle gate whose entrance was denied them!

The unhappy doctor got up; he listened to the noises which are ever present on lofty table-lands—those disquieting murmurs which seem to whisper and groan and sigh. He heard the nyctalops[2] brushing the rocks with frenzied wing, the stryges [vampires][3] in their nocturnal flight, and two or three pairs of funereal owls whose hooting sounded like a cry of pain. Then all his muscles contracted at once, and his body shivered, bathed in icy sweat.

Thus the long hours flowed by until midnight. If the doctor had been able to talk, to exchange a few words now and again, to give free vent to his complaints, he would have been less afraid. But Nic Deck was asleep, plunged into a deep slumber.

Midnight—that terrible hour for all, the hour of apparitions, the hour of evil!

What would happen now?

[2]Something afflicted with night blindness.
[3]Earlier in the book it talks of how "vampires known as stryges, because they shrieked like stryges, quenched their thirst on human blood." *Stryge* and *strygoï* are Romanian words for "vampire," though these are not the "living dead" we're familiar with. A *stryge* is a blood-sucking entity that looks like a woman with the body of a bird. Here the word is used interchangably with "vampire."

The doctor had just got up once more. He was asking himself whether he were awake, or whether he were suffering from a nightmare.

Overhead he thought he saw—no! he really did see—strange shapes, lit by a spectral light, pass from one horizon to the other, rise, fall, and drift down with the clouds. They looked like monsters, dragons with serpents' tails, hippogryphs with huge wings, gigantic krakens, enormous vampires, fighting to seize him in their talons or swallow him in their jaws.

Then, everything on the Orgall plateau was in movement—the rocks, the trees which rose at its edge. And very distinctly at short intervals a clanging reached his ear.

"The bell!" he murmured, "the castle bell!"

Yes! It was indeed the bell of the old chapel, and not that of the church at Vulkan, which the wind would have borne in the opposite direction.

And now the strokes became more hurried. The hand that struck them was no longer tolling a funeral knell. No! It was an alarm, whose urgent strokes were awaking the echoes of the Transylvanian frontier.

As he listened to these dismal vibrations, Doctor Patak was seized with a convulsive fear, an insurmountable anguish, an irresistible terror, which made the whole of his flesh creep.

But the forester had been awakened by the alarming clang of the bell. He rose while Doctor Patak seemed to be getting beside himself. He listened, and his eyes tried to pierce the deep shadows which overhung the castle.

"That bell! That bell!" Doctor Patak repeated. "It's the Chort that's ringing it!"

Certainly the poor terrified doctor now believed more than ever in the devil.

The forester stood motionless, and did not reply.

Suddenly a series of roars like those of a foghorn at the entrance to a harbor broke forth in tumultuous undulations. Far around space was shaken by its deafening howl.

Then a light shot from the central donjon,[4] an intense light, from which leapt flashes of penetrating clearness and blinding cor-

[4]A fortified inner tower or keep of a castle.

uscations. What hearth could produce this powerful light, whose irradiations were spreading in long sheets over the surface of the Orgall plateau? From what furnace came this photogenic stream, which seemed to embrace the rocks even as it bathed them with a strange lividness?

"Nic—Nic!" exclaimed the doctor. "Look at me! Am I nothing but a corpse like you?"

They had, indeed, both assumed a cadaverous aspect. Their faces were pallid; their eyes seemed to have gone, the orbits apparently empty; their cheeks were grayish-green, like the mosses which according to the legend grow on the skulls of men that have been hanged.

Nic Deck was astounded at what he saw, at what he heard. Doctor Patak was in the last stage of fright: his muscles retracted, his skin bristling, his pupils dilated, his body as rigid as if he were a victim of tetanus. As Victor Hugo puts it in his poem *Contemplations* "he breathed fright."

A minute—a minute at most—this terrifying phenomenon lasted. Then the strange light gradually faded, the roaring ceased, and the Orgall plateau returned to silence and darkness.

Neither of the men thought any more of sleep. The doctor overwhelmed with stupor, the forester upright against the stone seat, awaited the return of dawn.

After Nic enters the castle, he discovers that it is being used by scientists for their experiments and far-reaching discoveries in electronics, chemistry, and physics. The scientists—one of whom is vampire-like Baron de Gortz, the owner of the castle who had disappeared years earlier—take advantage of the people's superstitions to keep their work secret. Jules Verne's novels are famous for their incorporation of inventions that were yet to be invented. Here, the scientists use sirens operated by compressed air to broadcast the foghorn-like sounds, and they project outlines of creatures on the clouds. They also record sound, have a video-telephone with a speaker, and they even bug a nearby tavern to keep tabs on what is going on in the village. All this is pretty amazing, considering this novel was written less than five years after Thomas Edison made his first lightbulb.

Voltaire

VAMPIRES

———◦———

Voltaire, whose real name was François Marie Arouet, was a leading figure of the Enlightenment. He was from a middle-class family and gave up studying law to write. His poor health forced him to temperance during a period of French history when excess was popular. Twice he was unjustly thrown in prison, and he spent a number of years in exile. Some of his works were considered subversive by the government and were censored. He often launched attacks on the excesses of religion (primarily in the Catholic Church); he courageously intervened to save freethinkers and Protestants from being persecuted or martyred; and he actively fought for political and social reform. Voltaire was a strong advocate of free thought and religious tolerance and is now considered one of the world's greatest philosophers. This nonfiction entry on vampires (actually more of an essay) is from his *Dictionaire Philosophique* (*Philosophical Dictionary*), which was published in 1764.

WHAT! IS IT IN our eighteenth century that vampires exist? Is it after the reigns of Locke, Shaftesbury, Trenchard, and Collins? Is it under those of d'Alembert, Diderot, St. Lambert, and Duclos that we believe in vampires, and that the reverend father Dom

Calmet,[1] Benedictine priest of the congregation of St. Vannes, and St. Hidulphe, abbé of Senon—an abbey of a hundred thousand livres a year, in the neighborhood of two other abbeys of the same revenue—has printed and reprinted the history of vampires, with the approbation of the [doctors at] Sorbonne,[2] signed Marcilli?

These vampires were corpses, who went out of their graves at night to suck the blood of the living, either at their throats or stomachs, after which they returned to their cemeteries. The persons so sucked waned, grew pale, and fell into consumption; while the sucking corpses grew fat, got rosy, and enjoyed an excellent appetite. It was in Poland, Hungary, Silesia, Moravia, Austria, and Lorraine, that the dead made this good cheer. We never heard a word of vampires in London, nor even at Paris. I confess that in both these cities there were stock-jobbers, brokers, and men of business, who sucked the blood of the people in broad daylight; but they were not dead, though corrupted. These true suckers lived not in cemeteries, but in very agreeable palaces.

Who would believe that we derive the idea of vampires from Greece? Not from the Greece of Alexander, Aristotle, Plato, Epicurus, and Demosthenes; but from Christian Greece, unfortunately schismatic. For a long time Christians of the Greek rite have imagined that the bodies of Christians of the Latin church, buried in Greece, do not decay, because they are excommunicated. This is precisely the contrary to that of us Christians of the Latin church, who believe that corpses which do not corrupt are marked with the seal of eternal beatitude. So much so, indeed, that when we have paid a hundred thousand crowns to Rome, to give them a saint's brevet, we adore them with the worship of *"dulia."*

The Greeks are persuaded that these dead are sorcerers; they call them *"broucolacas,"* or *"vroucolacas,"* according as they pronounce the second letter of the alphabet. The Greek corpses go into houses to suck the blood of little children, to eat the supper of the fathers and mothers, drink their wine, and break all the

---

[1]Philosopher John Locke; Locke's pupil Anthony Ashley Cooper, 3rd Earl of Shaftesbury; theologian Anthony Collins; Jean Le Rond d'Alembert; Denis Diderot; Jean François St. Lambert; Charles Pinot Duclos; and Dom Augustin Calmet.

[2]At the University of Paris.

furniture. They can only be put to rights by burning them when they are caught. But the precaution must be taken of not putting them into the fire until after their hearts are torn out, which must be burned separately. The celebrated Tournefort, sent into the Levant by Louis XIV., as well as so many other virtuosi, was witness of all the acts attributed to one of these *"broucolacas,"* and to this ceremony.

After slander, nothing is communicated more promptly than superstition, fanaticism, sorcery, and tales of those raised from the dead. There were *"broucolacas"* in Wallachia, Moldavia, and some among the Polanders, who are of the Romish church. This superstition being absent, they acquired it, and it went through all the east of Germany. Nothing was spoken of but vampires, from 1730 to 1735; they were laid in wait for, their hearts torn out and burned. They resembled the ancient martyrs—the more they were burned, the more they abounded.

Finally, Calmet became their historian, and treated vampires as he treated the Old and New Testaments, by relating faithfully all that has been said before him.

The most curious things, in my opinion, were the verbal suits juridically conducted, concerning the dead who went from their tombs to suck the little boys and girls of their neighborhood. Calmet relates that in Hungary two officers, delegated by the emperor Charles VI., assisted by the bailiff of the place and an executioner, held an inquest on a vampire, who had been dead six weeks, and who had sucked all the neighborhood. They found him in his coffin, fresh and jolly, with his eyes open, and asking for food. The bailiff passed his sentence; the executioner tore out the vampire's heart, and burned it, after which he feasted no more.

Who, after this, dares to doubt of the resuscitated dead, with which our ancient legends are filled, and of all the miracles related by Bollandus, and the sincere and revered Dom Ruinart? You will find stories of vampires in the "Jewish Letters" of d'Argens,[3] whom the Jesuit authors of the "Journal of Trevoux" have accused of believing nothing. It should be observed how they triumph in the history of the vampire of Hungary; how they thanked God and the Virgin for having at last converted this poor d'Argens,

[3]*Lettres Juives (Jewish Letters)* by Jean-Baptiste Boyer, the Marquis d'Argens.

the chamberlain of a king who did not believe in vampires. "Behold," said they, "this famous unbeliever, who dared to throw doubts on the appearance of the angel to the Holy Virgin; on the star which conducted the magi; on the cure of the possessed; on the immersion of two thousand swine in a lake; on an eclipse of the sun at the full moon; on the resurrection of the dead who walked in Jerusalem—his heart is softened, his mind is enlightened; he believes in vampires."

There no longer remained any question, but to examine whether all these dead were raised by their own virtue, by the power of God, or by that of the devil. Several great theologians of Lorraine, of Moravia, and Hungary, displayed their opinions and their science. They related all that St. Augustine, St. Ambrose, and so many other saints, had most unintelligibly said on the living and the dead. They related all the miracles of St. Stephen, which are found in the seventh book of the works of St. Augustine. This is one of the most curious of them: In the city of Aubzal in Africa, a young man was crushed to death by the ruins of a wall; the widow immediately invoked St. Stephen, to whom she was very much devoted. St. Stephen raised him. He was asked what he had seen in the other world. "Sirs," said he, "when my soul quitted my body, it met an infinity of souls, who asked it more questions about this world than you do of the other. I went I know not whither, when I met St. Stephen, who said to me, 'Give back that which thou hast received.' I answered, 'What should I give back? you have given me nothing.' He repeated three times, 'Give back that which thou hast received.' Then I comprehended that he spoke of the credo; I repeated my credo to him, and suddenly he raised me." Above all, they quoted the stories related by Sulpicius Severus, in the life of St. Martin. They proved that St. Martin, with some others, raised up a condemned soul.

But all these stories, however true they might be, had nothing in common with the vampires who rose to suck the blood of their neighbors, and afterwards replaced themselves in their coffins. They looked if they could not find in the Old Testament, or in the mythology, some vampire whom they could quote as an example; but they found none. It was proved, however, that the dead drank and ate, since in so many ancient nations food was placed on their tombs.

The difficulty was to know whether it was the soul or the body of the dead which ate. It was decided that it was both. Delicate and unsubstantial things, as sweetmeats, whipped cream, and melting fruits, were for the soul, and roast beef and the like were for the body.

The kings of Persia were, said they, the first who caused themselves to be served with viands after their death. Almost all the kings of the present day imitate them; but they are the monks who eat their dinner and supper, and drink their wine. Thus, properly speaking, kings are not vampires; the true vampires are the monks, who eat at the expense of both kings and people.

It is very true that St. Stanislaus, who had bought a considerable estate from a Polish gentleman, and not paid him for it, being brought before King Boleslaus by his heirs, raised up the gentleman; but this was solely to get quittance. It is not said that he gave a single glass of wine to the seller, who returned to the other world without having eaten or drunk. They afterwards treated of the grand question, whether a vampire could be absolved who died excommunicated, which comes more to the point.

I am not profound enough in theology to give my opinion on this subject; but I would willingly be for absolution, because in all doubtful affairs we should take the mildest part. *"Odia restringenda, favores ampliandi."*

The result of all this is that a great part of Europe has been infested with vampires for five or six years, and that there are now no more; that we have had Convulsionaries in France for twenty years, and that we have them no longer; that we have had demoniacs for seventeen hundred years, but have them no longer; that the dead have been raised ever since the days of Hippolytus, but that they are raised no longer; and, lastly, that we have had Jesuits in Spain, Portugal, France, and the two Sicilies, but that we have them no longer.

John Keats

LAMIA

John Keats was an English poet of the romantic period who has been considered by many to be a poetic genius. His work had a major influence on Victorian poetry, particularly that of Tennyson and the Pre-Raphaelites. His most famous poems include *Endymion*, "Hyperion," "Ode to a Grecian Urn," "Ode to a Nightingale," "To Autumn," "La Belle Dame sans Merci," and "Lamia." The last of these is presented here. Based on a story by Philostratus from the third century A.D., by way of Robert Burton's *Anatomy of Melancholy*. Set in Corinth, a young man falls in love with and marries a beautiful woman, who turns out to be a lamia (the lamia were an early form of vampire). According to Philostratus, "They are wont to lust not for love but for flesh: and they particularly seek human flesh and by arousing sexual desire they seek to devour whom they wish." These winged serpent-women would usually fly around at night seeking victims, from which they often sucked blood. They also enjoyed stealing children and tearing them apart. In this poem, Keats chose to emphasize the more sensual side of the lamia—just as most nineteenth and twentieth-century writers have done with the vampire. It was written in 1819 and published the following year in *Lamia, Isabella, The Eve of St. Agnes, and Other Poems*. Of this poem, Keats said, "There is that sort of fire in it which must take hold of people in some way—give them either pleasant or unpleasant sensation."

PART I

Upon a time, before the faery broods
Drove Nymph and Satyr from the prosperous woods,
Before King Oberon's bright diadem,
Sceptre, and mantle, clasp'd with dewy gem,
Frighted away the Dryads and the Fauns
From rushes green, and brakes, and cowslip'd lawns,
The ever-smitten Hermes empty left
His golden throne, bent warm on amorous theft:
From high Olympus had he stolen light,
On this side of Jove's clouds, to escape the sight
Of his great summoner, and made retreat
Into a forest on the shores of Crete.
For somewhere in that sacred island dwelt
A nymph, to whom all hoofed Satyrs knelt;
At whose white feet the languid Tritons poured
Pearls, while on land they wither'd and adored.
Fast by the springs where she to bathe was wont,
And in those meads where sometime she might haunt,
Were strewn rich gifts, unknown to any Muse,
Though Fancy's casket were unlock'd to choose.
Ah, what a world of love was at her feet!
So Hermes thought, and a celestial heat
Burnt from his winged heels to either ear,
That from a whiteness, as the lily clear,
Blush'd into roses 'mid his golden hair,
Fallen in jealous curls about his shoulders bare.

From vale to vale, from wood to wood, he flew,
Breathing upon the flowers his passion new,
And wound with many a river to its head,
To find where this sweet nymph prepar'd her secret bed:
In vain; the sweet nymph might nowhere be found,
And so he rested, on the lonely ground,
Pensive, and full of painful jealousies
Of the Wood-Gods, and even the very trees.
There as he stood, he heard a mournful voice,

Such as once heard, in gentle heart, destroys
All pain but pity: thus the lone voice spake:
"When from this wreathed tomb shall I awake!
When move in a sweet body fit for life,
And love, and pleasure, and the ruddy strife
Of hearts and lips! Ah, miserable me!"
The God, dove-footed, glided silently
Round bush and tree, soft-brushing, in his speed,
The taller grasses and full-flowering weed,
Until he found a palpitating snake,
Bright, and cirque-couchant in a dusky brake.

   She was a gordian shape of dazzling hue,
Vermilion-spotted, golden, green, and blue;
Striped like a zebra, freckled like a pard,
Eyed like a peacock, and all crimson barr'd;
And full of silver moons, that, as she breathed,
Dissolv'd, or brighter shone, or interwreathed
Their lustres with the gloomier tapestries—
So rainbow-sided, touch'd with miseries,
She seem'd, at once, some penanced lady elf,
Some demon's mistress, or the demon's self.
Upon her crest she wore a wannish fire
Sprinkled with stars, like Ariadne's tiar:
Her head was serpent, but ah, bitter-sweet!
She had a woman's mouth with all its pearls complete:
And for her eyes: what could such eyes do there
But weep, and weep, that they were born so fair?
As Proserpine still weeps for her Sicilian air.
Her throat was serpent, but the words she spake
Came, as through bubbling honey, for Love's sake,
And thus; while Hermes on his pinions lay,
Like a stoop'd falcon ere he takes his prey.

   "Fair Hermes, crown'd with feathers, fluttering light,
I had a splendid dream of thee last night:
I saw thee sitting, on a throne of gold,
Among the Gods, upon Olympus old,
The only sad one; for thou didst not hear
The soft, lute-finger'd Muses chaunting clear,

Nor even Apollo when he sang alone,
Deaf to his throbbing throat's long, long melodious moan.
I dreamt I saw thee, robed in purple flakes,
Break amorous through the clouds, as morning breaks,
And, swiftly as a bright Phœbean dart,
Strike for the Cretan isle; and here thou art!
Too gentle Hermes, hast thou found the maid?''
Whereat the star of Lethe not delay'd
His rosy eloquence, and thus inquired:
"Thou smooth-lipp'd serpent, surely high inspired!
Thou beauteous wreath, with melancholy eyes,
Possess whatever bliss thou canst devise,
Telling me only where my nymph is fled,—
Where she doth breathe!'' "Bright planet, thou hast said,''
Return'd the snake, "but seal with oaths, fair God!''
"I swear,'' said Hermes, "by my serpent rod,
And by thine eyes, and by thy starry crown!''
Light flew his earnest words, among the blossoms blown.
Then thus again the brilliance feminine:
"Too frail of heart! for this lost nymph of thine,
Free as the air, invisibly, she strays
About these thornless wilds; her pleasant days
She tastes unseen; unseen her nimble feet
Leave traces in the grass and flowers sweet;
From weary tendrils, and bow'd branches green,
She plucks the fruit unseen, she bathes unseen:
And by my power is her beauty veil'd
To keep it unaffronted, unassail'd
By the love-glances of unlovely eyes,
Of Satyrs, Fauns, and blear'd Silenus' sighs.
Pale grew her immortality, for woe
Of all these lovers, and she grieved so
I took compassion on her, bade her steep
Her hair in weïrd syrops, that would keep
Her loveliness invisible, yet free
To wander as she loves, in liberty.
Thou shalt behold her, Hermes, thou alone,
If thou wilt, as thou swearest, grant my boon!''
Then, once again, the charmed God began

An oath, and through the serpent's ears it ran
Warm, tremulous, devout, psalterian.
Ravish'd, she lifted her Circean head,
Blush'd a live damask, and swift-lisping said,
"I was a woman, let me have once more
A woman's shape, and charming as before.
I love a youth of Corinth—O the bliss!
Give me my woman's form, and place me where he is.
Stoop, Hermes, let me breathe upon thy brow,
And thou shalt see thy sweet nymph even now."
The God on half-shut feathers sank serene,
She breath'd upon his eyes, and swift was seen
Of both the guarded nymph near-smiling on the green.
It was no dream; or say a dream it was,
Real are the dreams of Gods, and smoothly pass
Their pleasures in a long immortal dream.
One warm, flush'd moment, hovering, it might seem
Dash'd by the wood-nymph's beauty, so he burn'd;
Then, lighting on the printless verdure, turn'd
To the swoon'd serpent, and with languid arm,
Delicate, put to proof the lythe Caducean charm.
So done, upon the nymph his eyes he bent
Full of adoring tears and blandishment,
And towards her stept: she, like a moon in wane,
Faded before him, cower'd, nor could restrain
Her fearful sobs, self-folding like a flower
That faints into itself at evening hour:
But the God fostering her chilled hand,
She felt the warmth, her eyelids open'd bland,
And, like new flowers at morning song of bees,
Bloom'd, and gave up her honey to the lees.
Into the green-recessed woods they flew;
Nor grew they pale, as mortal lovers do.

   Left to herself, the serpent now began
To change; her elfin blood in madness ran,
Her mouth foam'd, and the grass, therewith besprent,
Wither'd at dew so sweet and virulent;
Her eyes in torture fix'd, and anguish drear,

Hot, glaz'd, and wide, with lid-lashes all sear,
Flash'd phosphor and sharp sparks, without one cooling tear.
The colours all inflam'd throughout her train,
She writh'd about, convuls'd with scarlet pain:
A deep volcanian yellow took the place
Of all her milder-mooned body's grace;
And, as the lava ravishes the mèad,
Spoilt all her silver mail, and golden brede;
Made gloom of all her frecklings, streaks and bars,
Eclips'd her crescents, and lick'd up her stars:
So that, in moments few, she was undrest
Of all her sapphires, greens, and amethyst,
And rubious-argent: of all these bereft,
Nothing but pain and ugliness were left.
Still shone her crown; that vanish'd, also she
Melted and disappear'd as suddenly;
And in the air, her new voice luting soft,
Cried, "Lycius! gentle Lycius!"—Borne aloft
With the bright mists about the mountains hoar
These words dissolv'd: Crete's forests heard no more.

Whither fled Lamia, now a lady bright,
A full-born beauty new and exquisite?
She fled into that valley they pass o'er
Who go to Corinth from Cenchreas' shore;
And rested at the foot of those wild hills,
The rugged founts of the Peræan hills,
And of that other ridge whose barren back
Stretches, with all its mist and cloudy rack,
South-westward to Cleone. There she stood
About a young bird's flutter from a wood,
Fair, on a sloping green of mossy tread,
By a clear pool, wherein she passioned
To see herself escap'd from so sore ills,
While her robes flaunted with the daffodils.

Ah, happy Lycius!—for she was a maid
More beautiful than ever twisted braid,
Or sigh'd, or blush'd, or on spring-flowered lea
Spread a green kirtle to the minstrelsy:

A virgin purest lipp'd, yet in the lore
Of love deep learned to the red heart's core:
Not one hour old, yet of sciential brain
To unperplex bliss from its neighbour pain;
Define their pettish limits, and estrange
Their points of contact, and swift counterchange;
Intrigue with the specious chaos, and dispart
Its most ambiguous atoms with sure art;
As though in Cupid's college she had spent
Sweet days a lovely graduate, still unshent,
And kept his rosy terms in idle languishment.

　　Why this fair creature chose so fairily
By the wayside to linger, we shall see;
But first 'tis fit to tell how she could muse
And dream, when in the serpent prison-house,
Of all she list, strange or magnificent:
How, ever, where she will'd, her spirit went;
Whether to faint Elysium, or where
Down through tress-lifting waves the Nereids fair
Wind into Thetis' bower by many a pearly stair;
Or where God Bacchus drains his cups divine,
Stretch'd out, at ease, beneath a glutinous pine;
Or where in Pluto's gardens palatine
Mulciber's columns gleam in far piazzian line.
And sometimes into cities she would send
Her dream, with feast and rioting to blend;
And once, while among mortals dreaming thus,
She saw the young Corinthian Lycius
Charioting foremost in the envious race,
Like a young Jove with calm uneager face,
And fell into a swooning love of him.
Now on the moth-time of that evening dim
He would return that way, as well she knew,
To Corinth from the shore; for freshly blew
The eastern soft wind, and his galley now
Grated the quaystones with her brazen prow
In port Cenchreas, from Egina isle
Fresh anchor'd; whither he had been awhile

To sacrifice to Jove, whose temple there
Waits with high marble doors for blood and incense rare.
Jove heard his vows, and better'd his desire;
For by some freakful chance he made retire
From his companions, and set forth to walk,
Perhaps grown wearied of their Corinth talk:
Over the solitary hills he fared,
Thoughtless at first, but ere eve's star appeared
His phantasy was lost, where reason fades,
In the calm'd twilight of Platonic shades.
Lamia beheld him coming, near, more near—
Close to her passing, in indifference drear,
His silent sandals swept the mossy green;
So neighbour'd to him, and yet so unseen
She stood: he pass'd, shut up in mysteries,
His mind wrapp'd like his mantle, while her eyes
Follow'd his steps, and her neck regal white
Turn'd—syllabling thus, "Ah, Lycius bright,
And will you leave me on the hills alone?
Lycius, look back! and be some pity shown."
He did; not with cold wonder fearingly,
But Orpheus-like at an Eurydice;
For so delicious were the words she sung,
It seem'd he had lov'd them a whole summer long:
And soon his eyes had drunk her beauty up,
Leaving no drop in the bewildering cup,
And still the cup was full,—while he, afraid
Lest she should vanish ere his lip had paid
Due adoration, thus began to adore;
Her soft look growing coy, she saw his chain so sure:
"Leave thee alone! Look back! Ah, Goddess, see
Whether my eyes can ever turn from thee!
For pity do not this sad heart belie—
Even as thou vanishest so I shall die.
Stay! though a Naiad of the rivers, stay!
To thy far wishes will thy streams obey:
Stay! though the greenest woods be thy domain,
Alone they can drink up the morning rain:
Though a descended Pleiad, will not one

Of thine harmonious sisters keep in tune
Thy spheres, and as thy silver proxy shine?
So sweetly to these ravish'd ears of mine
Came thy sweet greeting, that if thou shouldst fade
Thy memory will waste me to a shade:—
For pity do not melt!''—''If I should stay,''
Said Lamia, ''here, upon this floor of clay,
And pain my steps upon these flowers too rough,
What canst thou say or do of charm enough
To dull the nice remembrance of my home?
Thou canst not ask me with thee here to roam
Over these hills and vales, where no joy is,—
Empty of immortality and bliss!
Thou art a scholar, Lycius, and must know
That finer spirits cannot breathe below
In human climes, and live: Alas! poor youth,
What taste of purer air hast thou to soothe
My essence? What serener palaces,
Where I may all my many senses please,
And by mysterious sleights a hundred thirsts appease?
It cannot be—Adieu!'' So said, she rose
Tiptoe with white arms spread. He, sick to lose
The amorous promise of her lone complain,
Swoon'd, murmuring of love, and pale with pain.
The cruel lady, without any show
Of sorrow for her tender favourite's woe,
But rather, if her eyes could brighter be,
With brighter eyes and slow amenity,
Put her new lips to his, and gave afresh
The life she had so tangled in her mesh:
And as he from one trance was wakening
Into another, she began to sing,
Happy in beauty, life, and love, and every thing,
A song of love, too sweet for earthly lyres,
While, like held breath, the stars drew in their panting fires.
And then she whisper'd in such trembling tone,
As those who, safe together met alone
For the first time through many anguish'd days,
Use other speech than looks; bidding him raise

His drooping head, and clear his soul of doubt,
For that she was a woman, and without
Any more subtle fluid in her veins
Than throbbing blood, and that the self-same pains
Inhabited her frail-strung heart as his.
And next she wonder'd how his eyes could miss
Her face so long in Corinth, where, she said,
She dwelt but half retir'd, and there had led
Days happy as the gold coin could invent
Without the aid of love; yet in content
Till she saw him, as once she pass'd him by,
Where 'gainst a column he leant thoughtfully
At Venus' temple porch, 'mid baskets heap'd
Of amorous herbs and flowers, newly reap'd
Late on that eve, as 'twas the night before
The Adonian feast; whereof she saw no more,
But wept alone those days, for why should she adore?
Lycius from death awoke into amaze,
To see her still, and singing so sweet lays;
Then from amaze into delight he fell
To hear her whisper woman's lore so well;
And every word she spake entic'd him on
To unperplex'd delight and pleasure known.
Let the mad poets say whate'er they please
Of the sweets of Fairies, Peris, Goddesses,
There is not such a treat among them all,
Haunters of cavern, lake, and waterfall,
As a real woman, lineal indeed
From Pyrrha's pebbles or old Adam's seed.
Thus gentle Lamia judg'd, and judg'd aright,
That Lycius could not love in half a fright,
So threw the goddess off, and won his heart
More pleasantly by playing woman's part,
With no more awe than what her beauty gave,
That, while it smote, still guaranteed to save.
Lycius to all made eloquent reply,
Marrying to every word a twinborn sigh;
And last, pointing to Corinth, ask'd her sweet,
If 'twas too far that night for her soft feet.

The way was short, for Lamia's eagerness
Made, by a spell, the triple league decrease
To a few paces; not at all surmised
By blinded Lycius, so in her comprized.
They pass'd the city gates, he knew not how,
So noiseless, and he never thought to know.

As men talk in a dream, so Corinth all,
Throughout her palaces imperial,
And all her populous streets and temples lewd,
Mutter'd, like tempest in the distance brew'd,
To the wide-spreaded night above her towers.
Men, women, rich and poor, in the cool hours,
Shuffled their sandals o'er the pavement white,
Companion'd or alone; while many a light
Flared, here and there, from wealthy festivals,
And threw their moving shadows on the walls,
Or found them cluster'd in the corniced shade
Of some arch'd temple door, or dusky colonnade.

Muffling his face, of greeting friends in fear,
Her fingers he press'd hard, as one came near
With curl'd gray beard, sharp eyes, and smooth bald crown,
Slow-stepp'd, and robed in philosophic gown:
Lycius shrank closer, as they met and past,
Into his mantle, adding wings to haste,
While hurried Lamia trembled: "Ah," said he,
"Why do you shudder, love, so ruefully?
Why does your tender palm dissolve in dew?"—
"I'm wearied," said fair Lamia: "tell me who
Is that old man? I cannot bring to mind
His features:—Lycius! wherefore did you blind
Yourself from his quick eyes?" Lycius replied,
" 'Tis Apollonius sage, my trusty guide
And good instructor; but to-night he seems
The ghost of folly haunting my sweet dreams."

While yet he spake they had arrived before
A pillar'd porch, with lofty portal door,
Where hung a silver lamp, whose phosphor glow

Reflected in the slabbed steps below,
Mild as a star in water; for so new,
And so unsullied was the marble hue,
So through the crystal polish, liquid fine,
Ran the dark veins, that none but feet divine
Could e'er have touch'd there. Sounds Æolian
Breath'd from the hinges, as the ample span
Of the wide doors disclos'd a place unknown
Some time to any, but those two alone,
And a few Persian mutes, who that same year
Were seen about the markets: none knew where
They could inhabit; the most curious
Were foil'd, who watch'd to trace them to their house:
And but the flitter-winged verse must tell,
For truth's sake, what woe afterwards befel,
'Twould humour many a heart to leave them thus,
Shut from the busy world of more incredulous.

Part II

Love in a hut, with water and a crust,
Is—Love, forgive us!—cinders, ashes, dust;
Love in a palace is perhaps at last
More grievous torment than a hermit's fast:—
That is a doubtful tale from faery land,
Hard for the non-elect to understand.
Had Lycius liv'd to hand his story down,
He might have given the moral a fresh frown,
Or clench'd it quite: but too short was their bliss
To breed distrust and hate, that make the soft voice hiss.
Besides, there, nightly, with terrific glare,
Love, jealous grown of so complete a pair,
Hover'd and buzz'd his wings, with fearful roar,
Above the lintel of their chamber door,
And down the passage cast a glow upon the floor.

   For all this came a ruin: side by side
They were enthroned, in the even tide,

Upon a couch, near to a curtaining
Whose airy texture, from a golden string,
Floated into the room, and let appear
Unveil'd the summer heaven, blue and clear,
Betwixt two marble shafts:—there they reposed,
Where use had made it sweet, with eyelids closed,
Saving a tythe which love still open kept,
That they might see each other while they almost slept;
When from the slope side of a suburb hill,
Deafening the swallow's twitter, came a thrill
Of trumpets—Lycius started—the sounds fled,
But left a thought, a buzzing in his head.
For the first time, since first he harbour'd in
That purple-lined palace of sweet sin,
His spirit pass'd beyond its golden bourn
Into the noisy world almost forsworn.
The lady, ever watchful, penetrant,
Saw this with pain, so arguing a want
Of something more, more than her empery
Of joys; and she began to moan and sigh
Because he mused beyond her, knowing well
That but a moment's thought is passion's passing bell.
"Why do you sigh, fair creature?" whisper'd he:
"Why do you think?" return'd she tenderly:
"You have deserted me;—where am I now?
Not in your heart while care weighs on your brow:
No, no, you have dismiss'd me; and I go
From your breast houseless: ay, it must be so."
He answer'd, bending to her open eyes,
Where he was mirror'd small in paradise,
"My silver planet, both of eve and morn!
Why will you plead yourself so sad forlorn,
While I am striving how to fill my heart
With deeper crimson, and a double smart?
How to entangle, trammel up and snare
Your soul in mine, and labyrinth you there
Like the hid scent in an unbudded rose?
Ay, a sweet kiss—you see your mighty woes.
My thoughts! shall I unveil them? Listen then!

What mortal hath a prize, that other men
May be confounded and abash'd withal,
But lets it sometimes pace abroad majestical,
And triumph, as in thee I should rejoice
Amid the hoarse alarm of Corinth's voice.
Let my foes choke, and my friends shout afar,
While through the thronged streets your bridal car
Wheels round its dazzling spokes.''—The lady's cheek
Trembled; she nothing said, but, pale and meek,
Arose and knelt before him, wept a rain
Of sorrows at his words; at last with pain
Beseeching him, the while his hand she wrung,
To change his purpose. He thereat was stung,
Perverse, with stronger fancy to reclaim
Her wild and timid nature to his aim:
Besides, for all his love, in self despite,
Against his better self, he took delight
Luxurious in her sorrows, soft and new.
His passion, cruel grown, took on a hue
Fierce and sanguineous as 'twas possible
In one whose brow had no dark veins to swell.
Fine was the mitigated fury, like
Apollo's presence when in act to strike
The serpent—Ha, the serpent! certes, she
Was none. She burnt, she lov'd the tyranny,
And, all subdued, consented to the hour
When to the bridal he should lead his paramour.
Whispering in midnight silence, said the youth,
''Sure some sweet name thou hast, though, by my truth,
I have not ask'd it, ever thinking thee
Not mortal, but of heavenly progeny,
As still I do. Hast any mortal name,
Fit appellation for this dazzling frame?
Or friends or kinsfolk on the citied earth,
To share our marriage feast and nuptial mirth?''
''I have no friends,'' said Lamia, ''no, not one;
My presence in wide Corinth hardly known:
My parents' bones are in their dusty urns
Sepulchred, where no kindled incense burns,

Seeing all their luckless race are dead, save me,
And I neglect the holy rite for thee.
Even as you list invite your many guests;
But if, as now it seems, your vision rests
With any pleasure on me, do not bid
Old Apollonius—from him keep me hid."
Lycius, perplex'd at words so blind and blank,
Made close inquiry; from whose touch she shrank,
Feigning a sleep; and he to the dull shade
Of deep sleep in a moment was betray'd.

It was the custom then to bring away
The bride from home at blushing shut of day,
Veil'd, in a chariot, heralded along
By strewn flowers, torches, and a marriage song,
With other pageants: but this fair unknown
Had not a friend. So being left alone,
(Lycius was gone to summon all his kin)
And knowing surely she could never win
His foolish heart from its mad pompousness,
She set herself, high-thoughted, how to dress
The misery in fit magnificence.
She did so, but 'tis doubtful how and whence
Came, and who were her subtle servitors.
About the halls, and to and from the doors,
There was a noise of wings, till in short space
The glowing banquet-room shone with wide-arched grace.
A haunting music, sole perhaps and lone
Supportress of the faery-roof, made moan
Throughout, as fearful the whole charm might fade.
Fresh carved cedar, mimicking a glade
Of palm and plantain, met from either side,
High in the midst, in honour of the bride:
Two palms and then two plantains, and so on,
From either side their stems branch'd one to one
All down the aisled place, and beneath all
There ran a stream of lamps straight on from wall to wall.
So canopied, lay an untasted feast
Teeming with odours. Lamia, regal drest,

Silently paced about, and as she went,
In pale contented sort of discontent
Mission'd her viewless servants to enrich
The fretted splendour of each nook and niche.
Between the tree-stems, marbled plain at first,
Came jasper pannels; then, anon, there burst
Forth creeping imagery of slighter trees,
And with the larger wove in small intricacies.
Approving all, she faded at self-will,
And shut the chamber up, close, hush'd and still,
Complete and ready for the revels rude,
When dreadful guests would come to spoil her solitude.

    The day appear'd, and all the gossip rout.
O senseless Lycius! Madman! wherefore flout
The silent-blessing fate, warm cloister'd hours,
And show to common eyes these secret bowers?
The herd approach'd; each guest, with busy brain,
Arriving at the portal, gaz'd amain,
And enter'd marveling: for they knew the street,
Remember'd it from childhood all complete
Without a gap, yet ne'er before had seen
That royal porch, that high-built fair demesne;
So in they hurried all, maz'd, curious and keen:
Save one, who look'd thereon with eye severe,
And with calm-planted steps walk'd in austere;
'Twas Apollonius: something too he laugh'd,
As though some knotty problem, that had daft
His patient thought, had now begun to thaw,
And solve and melt:—'twas just as he foresaw.

    He met within the murmurous vestibule
His young disciple. " 'Tis no common rule,
Lycius," said he, "for uninvited guest
To force himself upon you, and infest
With an unbidden presence the bright throng
Of younger friends; yet must I do this wrong,
And you forgive me." Lycius blush'd, and led
The old man through the inner doors broad-spread;

With reconciling words and courteous mien
Turning into sweet milk the sophist's spleen.

   Of wealthy lustre was the banquet-rooms
Fill'd with pervading brilliance and perfume:
Before each lucid pannel fuming stood
A censer fed with myrrh and spiced wood,
Each by a sacred tripod held aloft,
Whose slender feet wide-swerv'd upon the soft
Wool-woofed carpets: fifty wreaths of smoke
From fifty censers their light voyage took
To the high roof, still mimick'd as they rose
Along the mirror'd walls by twin-clouds odorous.
Twelve sphered tables, by silk seats insphered,
High as the level of a man's breast rear'd
On libbard's paws, upheld the heavy gold
Of cups and goblets, and the store thrice told
Of Ceres' horn, and, in huge vessels, wine
Come from the gloomy tun with merry shine.
Thus loaded with a feast the tables stood,
Each shrining in the midst the image of a God.

   When in an antichamber every guest
Had felt the cold full sponge to pleasure press'd,
By minist'ring slaves, upon his hands and feet,
And fragrant oils with ceremony meet
Pour'd on his hair, they all mov'd to the feast
In white robes, and themselves in order placed
Around the silken couches, wondering
Whence all this mighty cost and blaze of wealth could spring.

   Soft went the music the soft air along,
While fluent Greek a vowel'd undersong
Kept up among the guests, discoursing low
At first, for scarcely was the wine at flow;
But when the happy vintage touch'd their brains,
Louder they talk, and louder come the strains
Of powerful instruments:—the gorgeous dyes,
The space, the splendour of the draperies,
The roof of awful richness, nectarous cheer,

Beautiful slaves, and Lamia's self, appear,
Now, when the wine has done its rosy deed,
And every soul from human trammels freed,
No more so strange; for merry wine, sweet wine,
Will make Elysian shades not too fair, too divine.

   Soon was God Bacchus at meridian height;
Flush'd were their cheeks, and bright eyes double bright:
Garlands of every green, and every scent
From vales deflower'd, or forest-trees branch-rent,
In baskets of bright osier'd gold were brought
High as the handles heap'd, to suit the thought
Of every guest; that each, as he did please,
Might fancy-fit his brows, silk-pillow'd at his ease.

   What wreath for Lamia? What for Lycius?
What for the sage, old Apollonius?
Upon her aching forehead be there hung
The leaves of willow and of adder's tongue;
And for the youth, quick, let us strip for him
The thyrsus, that his watching eyes may swim
Into forgetfulness; and, for the sage,
Let spear-grass and the spiteful thistle wage
War on his temples. Do not all charms fly
At the mere touch of cold philosophy?
There was an awful rainbow once in heaven:
We know her woof, her texture; she is given
In the dull catalogue of common things.
Philosophy will clip an Angel's wings,
Conquer all mysteries by rule and line,
Empty the haunted air, and gnomed mine—
Unweave a rainbow, as it erewhile made
The tender-person'd Lamia melt into a shade.

   By her glad Lycius sitting, in chief place,
Scarce saw in all the room another face,
Till, checking his love trance, a cup he took
Full brimm'd, and opposite sent forth a look
'Cross the broad table, to beseech a glance
From his old teacher's wrinkled countenance,

And pledge him. The bald-head philosopher
Had fix'd his eye, without a twinkle or stir
Full on the alarmed beauty of the bride,
Brow-beating her fair form, and troubling her sweet pride.
Lycius then press'd her hand, with devout touch,
As pale it lay upon the rosy couch:
'Twas icy, and the cold ran through his veins;
Then sudden it grew hot, and all the pains
Of an unnatural heat shot to his heart.
"Lamia, what means this? Wherefore dost thou start?
Know'st thou that man?" Poor Lamia answer'd not.
He gaz'd into her eyes, and not a jot
Own'd they the lovelorn piteous appeal:
More, more he gaz'd: his human senses reel:
Some hungry spell that loveliness absorbs;
There was no recognition in those orbs.
"Lamia!" he cried—and no soft-toned reply.
The many heard, and the loud revelry
Grew hush; the stately music no more breathes;
The myrtle sicken'd in a thousand wreaths.
By faint degrees, voice, lute, and pleasure ceased;
A deadly silence step by step increased,
Until it seem'd a horrid presence there,
And not a man but felt the terror in his hair.
"Lamia!" he shriek'd; and nothing but the shriek
With its sad echo did the silence break.
"Begone, foul dream!" he cried, gazing again
In the bride's face, where now no azure vein
Wander'd on fair-spaced temples; no soft bloom
Misted the cheek; no passion to illume
The deep-recessed vision:—all was blight;
Lamia, no longer fair, there sat a deadly white.
"Shut, shut those juggling eyes, thou ruthless man!
Turn them aside, wretch! or the righteous ban
Of all the Gods, whose dreadful images
Here represent their shadowy presences,
May pierce them on the sudden with the thorn
Of painful blindness; leaving thee forlorn,
In trembling dotage to the feeblest fright

Of conscience, for their long offended might,
For all thine impious proud-heart sophistries,
Unlawful magic, and enticing lies.
Corinthians! look upon that gray-beard wretch!
Mark how, possess'd, his lashless eyelids stretch
Around his demon eyes! Corinthians, see!
My sweet bride withers at their potency."
"Fool!" said the sophist, in an under-tone
Gruff with contempt; which a death-nighing moan
From Lycius answer'd, as heart-struck and lost,
He sank supine beside the aching ghost.
"Fool! Fool!" repeated he, while his eyes still
Relented not, nor mov'd; "from every ill
Of life have I preserv'd thee to this day,
And shall I see thee made a serpent's prey?"
Then Lamia breath'd death breath; the sophist's eye,
Like a sharp spear, went through her utterly,
Keen, cruel, perceant, stinging: she, as well
As her weak hand could any meaning tell,
Motion'd him to be silent; vainly so,
He look'd and look'd again a level—No!
"A Serpent!" echoed he; no sooner said,
Than with a frightful scream she vanished:
And Lycius' arms were empty of delight,
As were his limbs of life, from that same night.
On the high couch he lay!—his friends came round—
Supported him—no pulse, or breath they found,
And, in its marriage robe, the heavy body wound.

Woody Allen

COUNT DRACULA

⇒⊶⊷⊰⇐

Woody Allen is best known for his many classic films, such as *Play It Again, Sam, Sleeper, Bananas, Annie Hall, Hannah and Her Sisters, Radio Days*, and *Zelig*. Besides being a great actor and director, he also wrote most of his screenplays and even a couple of books. This story is from his 1971 book *Getting Even*.

SOMEWHERE IN TRANSYLVANIA, DRACULA the monster lies sleeping in his coffin, waiting for night to fall. As exposure to the sun's rays would surely cause him to perish, he stays protected in the satin-lined chamber bearing his family name in silver. Then the moment of darkness comes, and through some miraculous instinct the fiend emerges from the safety of his hiding place and, assuming the hideous forms of the bat or the wolf, he prowls the countryside, drinking the blood of his victims. Finally, before the first rays of his archenemy, the sun, announce a new day, he hurries back to the safety of his hidden coffin and sleeps, as the cycle begins anew.

Now he starts to stir. The fluttering of his eyelids are a response to some age-old, unexplainable instinct that the sun is nearly down and his time is near. Tonight, he is particularly hungry and as he lies there, fully awake now, in red-lined Inverness cape and tails, waiting to feel with uncanny perception the precise moment of darkness before opening the lid and emerging, he decides who

this evening's victims will be. The baker and his wife, he thinks
to himself. Succulent, available, and unsuspecting. The thought
of the unwary couple whose trust he has carefully cultivated ex-
cites his blood lust to a fever pitch, and he can barely hold back
these last seconds before climbing out of the coffin to seek his
prey.

Suddenly he knows the sun is down. Like an angel of hell, he
rises swiftly, and changing into a bat, flies pell-mell to the cottage
of his tantalizing victims.

"Why, Count Dracula, what a nice surprise," the baker's wife
says, opening the door to admit him. (He has once again assumed
human form, as he enters their home, charmingly concealing his
rapacious goal.)

"What brings you here so early?" the baker asks.

"Our dinner date," the Count answers. "I hope I haven't made
an error. You did invite me for tonight, didn't you?"

"Yes, tonight, but that's not for seven hours."

"Pardon me?" Dracula queries, looking around the room puzzled.

"Or did you come by to watch the eclipse with us?"

"Eclipse?"

"Yes. Today's the total eclipse."

"What?"

"A few moments of darkness from noon until two minutes after. Look out the window."

"Uh-oh—I'm in big trouble."

"Eh?"

"And now if you'll excuse me . . ."

"What, Count Dracula?"

"Must be going—aha—oh, god . . ." Frantically he fumbles for
the doorknob.

"Going? You just came."

"Yes—but—I think I blew it very badly . . ."

"Count Dracula, you're pale."

"Am I? I need a little fresh air. It was nice seeing you . . ."

"Come. Sit down. We'll have a drink."

"Drink? No, I must run. Er—you're stepping on my cape."

"Sure. Relax. Some wine."

"Wine? Oh no, gave it up—liver and all that, you know. And

now I really must buzz off. I just remembered, I left the lights on at my castle—bills'll be enormous . . .''

"Please," the baker says, his arm around the Count in firm friendship. "You're not intruding. Don't be so polite. So you're early."

"Really, I'd like to stay but there's a meeting of old Roumanian Counts across town and I'm responsible for the cold cuts."

"Rush, rush, rush. It's a wonder you don't get a heart attack."

"Yes, right—and now—"

"I'm making Chicken Pilaf tonight," the baker's wife chimes in. "I hope you like it."

"Wonderful, wonderful," the Count says, with a smile, as he pushes her aside into some laundry. Then, opening a closet door by mistake, he walks in. "Christ, where's the goddamn front door?"

"Ach," laughs the baker's wife, "such a funny man, the Count."

"I knew you'd like that," Dracula says, forcing a chuckle, "now get out of my way." At last he opens the front door but time has run out on him.

"Oh, look, mama," says the baker, "the eclipse must be over. The sun is coming out again."

"Right," says Dracula, slamming the front door. "I've decided to stay. Pull down the window shades quickly—*quickly*! Let's move it!"

"What window shades?" asks the baker.

"There are none, right? Figures. You got a basement in this joint?"

"No," says the wife affably, "I'm always telling Jarslov to build one but he never listens. That's some Jarslov, my husband."

"I'm all choked up. Where's the closet?"

"You did that one already, Count Dracula. Unt mama and I laughed at it."

"Ach—such a funny man, the Count."

"Look, I'll be in the closet. Knock at seven-thirty." And with that, the Count steps inside the closet and slams the door.

"Hee-hee—he is so funny, Jarslov."

"Oh, Count. Come out of the closet. Stop being a big silly." From inside the closet comes the muffled voice of Dracula.

"Can't—please—take my word for it. Just let me stay here. I'm fine. Really."

"Count Dracula, stop the fooling. We're already helpless with laughter."

"Can I tell you, I love this closet."

"Yes, but . . ."

"I know, I know . . . it seems strange, and yet here I am, having a ball. I was just saying to Mrs. Hess the other day, give me a good closet and I can stand in it for hours. Sweet woman, Mrs. Hess. Fat but sweet . . . Now, why don't you run along and check back with me at sunset. Oh, Ramona, la da da de da da de, Ramona . . ."

Now the Mayor and his wife, Katia, arrive. They are passing by and have decided to pay a call on their good friends, the baker and his wife.

"Hello, Jarslov. I hope Katia and I are not intruding?"

"Of course not, Mr. Mayor. Come out, Count Dracula! We have company!"

"Is the Count here?" asks the Mayor surprised.

"Yes, and you'll never guess where," says the baker's wife.

"It's so rare to see him around this early. In fact I can't ever remember seeing him around in the daytime."

"Well, he's here. Come out, Count Dracula!"

"Where is he?" Katia asks, not knowing whether to laugh or not.

"Come on out now! Let's go!" The baker's wife is getting impatient.

"He's in the closet," says the baker, apologetically.

"Really?" asks the Mayor.

"Let's go," says the baker with mock good humor as he knocks on the closet door. "Enough is enough. The Mayor's here."

"Come on out, Dracula," His Honor shouts, "let's have a drink."

"No, go ahead. I've got some business in here."

"In the closet?"

"Yes, don't let me spoil your day. I can hear what you're saying. I'll join in if I have anything to add."

Everyone looks at one another and shrugs. Wine is poured and they all drink.

"Some eclipse today," the Mayor says, sipping from his glass.

"Yes," the baker agrees. "Incredible."

"Yeah. Thrilling," says a voice from the closet.

"What, Dracula?"

"Nothing, nothing. Let it go."

And so the time passes, until the Mayor can stand it no longer and forcing open the door to the closet, he shouts, "Come on, Dracula. I always thought you were a mature man. Stop this craziness."

The daylight streams in, causing the evil monster to shriek and slowly dissolve to a skeleton and then to dust before the eyes of the four people present. Leaning down to the pile of white ash on the closet floor, the baker's wife shouts, "Does this mean dinner's off tonight?"

F. Scott Fitzgerald

THE VAMPIRES WON'T VAMPIRE FOR ME

Francis Scott Fitzgerald is considered one of the most important authors of the twentieth century. He symbolized the "lost generation" of the 1920s, and is primarily remembered as the chronicler of the jazz age, with such books as *The Great Gatsby, Tender is the Night*, and *This Side of Paradise*. His and his wife's extravagance kept them in constant debt. His wife had a nervous breakdown in 1930 and spent the rest of her life in and out of institutions. Fitzgerald's life continued sliding downhill until his death. This poem was published circa 1917, while he was still in college.

> *Percy and Sal*
> Often I have seen on the screen,
> Pictures living and snappy,
> Girls quite a fistful, ingenues wistful,
> Loving I look at that makes me unhappy;
> Tell me why are girls that I meet,
> Always simple and slow?
> I want a brunette like those I met,
> Back in the seven-reel show.
>
> Liking striking blondes as I do,
> Hair that's golden and rippling,

Why don't I meet a few that aren't sweet but
Act very much like the ladies in Kipling?
Dolls are very numerous now,
Many wonders I've seen;
But I'd like a wife early in life,
Someone who learned on the screen.

Chorus
Theda Bara they say,
Drives depression away,
What Olga Petrova knows
Won't go in the censored shows!
Why are ladies I meet
Never more than just sweet?
Girls seem to be Vampires,
But they won't vampire for me.

Guy de Maupassant

THE HORLA

———⟶✦⟵———

Henri René Albert Guy de Maupassant is considered the greatest of all French short-story writers. He was trained in writing fiction by Gustave Flaubert (author of *Madame Bovary*), and wrote seventeen volumes of short stories in thirteen years, plus additional novels, plays, and travelogues. "Le Horla," published in 1887 in a book by the same name, was one of his later stories and mirrors his own approaching insanity from syphilis. While researching this story, Maupassant told a doctor that he wished to die in the arms of a woman. The doctor felt that he was well on his way to doing so. In 1891, Maupassant was committed to an asylum in Paris, where he later died. This, one of his more well-known works, was made into a movie called *Diary of a Madman* (1963), starring Vincent Price. The name "Horla" comes from *hors-là*, which means "out there."

MAY 8. WHAT A lovely day! I have spent all the morning lying in the grass in front of my house, under the enormous plane tree that shades the whole of it. I like this part of the country and I like to live here because I am attached to it by old associations, by those deep and delicate roots which attach man to the soil on which his ancestors were born and died, which attach him to the ideas and usages of the place as well as to the food, to local expressions, to the peculiar twang of the peasants, to the smell of the soil, of the villages and of the atmosphere itself.

214

I love my house in which I grew up. From my windows I can see the Seine which flows alongside my garden, on the other side of the high road, almost through my grounds, the great and wide Seine, which goes to Rouen and Havre, and is covered with boats passing to and fro.

On the left, down yonder, lies Rouen, that large town, with its blue roofs, under its pointed Gothic towers. These are innumerable, slender or broad, dominated by the spire of the cathedral, and full of bells which sound through the blue air on fine mornings, sending their sweet and distant iron clang even as far as my home; that song of the metal, which the breeze wafts in my direction, now stronger and now weaker, according as the wind is stronger or lighter.

What a delicious morning it was!

About eleven o'clock, a long line of boats drawn by a steam tug as big as a fly, and which scarcely puffed while emitting its thick smoke, passed my gate.

After two English schooners, whose red flag fluttered in space, there came a magnificent Brazilian three-master; it was perfectly white, and wonderfully clean and shining. I saluted it, I hardly knew why, except that the sight of the vessel gave me great pleasure.

May 12. I have had a slight feverish attack for the last few days, and I feel ill, or rather I feel low-spirited.

Whence come those mysterious influences which change our happiness into discouragement, and our self-confidence into diffidence? One might almost say that the air, the invisible air, is full of unknowable Powers whose mysterious presence we have to endure. I wake up in the best spirits, with an inclination to sing. Why? I go down to the edge of the water, and suddenly, after walking a short distance, I return home wretched, as if some misfortune were awaiting me there. Why? Is it a cold shiver which, passing over my skin, has upset my nerves and given me low spirits? Is it the form of the clouds, the color of the sky, or the color of the surrounding objects which is so changeable, that has troubled my thoughts as they passed before my eyes? Who can tell? Everything that we touch, without knowing it, everything that we handle, without feeling it, all that we meet, without clearly distinguishing it, has a rapid, surprising and inexplicable effect upon us and upon our senses, and, through them, on our ideas and on our heart itself.

How profound that mystery of the Invisible is! We cannot fathom it with our miserable senses, with our eyes which are unable to perceive what is either too small or too great, too near to us, or too far from us—neither the inhabitants of a star nor of a drop of water; nor with our ears that deceive us, for they transmit to us the vibrations of the air in sonorous notes. They are fairies who work the miracle of changing these vibrations into sounds, and by that metamorphosis give birth to music, which makes the silent motion of nature musical . . . with our sense of smell which is less keen than that of a dog, . . . with our sense of taste which can scarcely distinguish the age of wine!

Oh! If we only had other organs which would work other miracles in our favor, what a number of fresh things we might discover around us!

May 16. I am ill, decidedly! I was so well last month! I am feverish, horribly feverish, or rather I am in a state of feverish enervation, which makes my mind suffer as much as my body. I have, continually, that horrible sensation of some impending danger, that apprehension of some coming misfortune, or of approaching death; that presentiment which is, no doubt, an attack of some illness which is still unknown, which germinates in the flesh and in the blood.

May 17. I have just come from consulting my physician, for I could no longer get any sleep. He said my pulse was rapid, my eyes dilated, my nerves highly strung, but there were no alarming symptoms. I must take a course of shower baths and of bromide of potassium.

May 25. No change! My condition is really very peculiar. As the evening comes on, an incomprehensible feeling of disquietude seizes me, just as if night concealed some threatening disaster. I dine hurriedly, and then try to read, but I do not understand the words, and can scarcely distinguish the letters. Then I walk up and down my drawing-room, oppressed by a feeling of confused and irresistible fear, the fear of sleep and fear of my bed.

About ten o'clock I go up to my room. As soon as I enter it I double-lock and bolt the door; I am afraid . . . of what? Up to the present time I have been afraid of nothing . . . I open my cupboards, and look under my bed; I listen . . . to what? How strange it is that a simple feeling of discomfort, impeded or heightened circulation, perhaps the irritation of a nerve filament, a slight congestion, a small disturbance in the imperfect delicate functioning of our living machinery, may turn the most light-hearted of men into a melancholy one, and make a coward of the bravest? Then, I go to bed, and wait for sleep as a man might wait for the executioner. I wait for its coming with dread, and my heart beats and my legs tremble, while my whole body shivers beneath the warmth of the bed-clothes, until all at once I fall asleep, as though one should plunge into a pool of stagnant water in order to drown. I do not feel it coming on as I did formerly, this perfidious sleep which is close to me and watching me, which is going to seize me by the head, to close my eyes and annihilate me.

I sleep—a long time—two or three hours perhaps—then a dream—no—a nightmare lays hold on me. I feel that I am in bed and asleep . . . I feel it and I know it . . . and I feel also that somebody is coming close to me, is looking at me, touching me, is getting on to my bed, is kneeling on my chest, is taking my neck between his hands and squeezing it . . . squeezing it with all his might in order to strangle me.

I struggle, bound by that terrible sense of powerlessness which paralyzes us in our dreams; I try to cry out—but I cannot; I want to move cannot do so; I try, with the most violent efforts and breathing hard, to turn over and throw off this being who is crushing and suffocating me cannot!

And then, suddenly, I wake up, trembling and bathed in perspiration; I light a candle and find that I am alone, and after that crisis, which occurs every night, I at length fall asleep and slumber tranquilly till morning.

June 2. My condition has grown worse. What is the matter with me? The bromide does me no good, and the shower baths have no effect. Sometimes, in order to tire myself thoroughly, though I am fatigued enough already, I go for a walk in the forest of Roumare. I used to think first that the fresh light and soft air, impregnated with the odor of herbs and leaves, would instill new blood into my veins and impart fresh energy to my heart. I turned into a broad hunting road, and then turned toward La Bouille, through a narrow path, between two rows of exceedingly tall trees, which placed a thick green, almost black, roof between the sky and me.

A sudden shiver ran through me, not a cold shiver, but a strange shiver of agony, and I hastened my steps, uneasy at being alone in the forest, afraid, stupidly and without reason, of the profound solitude. Suddenly it seemed to me as if I were being followed, that somebody was walking at my heels, close, quite close to me, near enough to touch me.

I turned round suddenly, but I was alone. I saw nothing behind me except the straight, broad path, empty and bordered by high trees, horribly empty; before me it also extended until it was lost in the distance, and looked just the same, terrible.

I closed my eyes. Why? And then I began to turn round on one heel very quickly, just like a top. I nearly fell down, and opened my eyes; the trees were dancing round me and the earth heaved; I was obliged to sit down. Then ah! I no longer remembered how I had come! What a strange idea! What a strange, strange idea! I did not in the least know. I started off to the right, and got back into the avenue which had led me into the middle of the forest.

June 3. I have had a terrible night. I shall go away for a few weeks, for no doubt a journey will set me up again.

July 2. I have come back, quite cured, and have had a most delightful trip into the bargain. I have been to Mont Saint-Michel, which I had not seen before.

What a sight, when one arrives, as I did, at Avranches toward the end of the day! The town stands on a hill, and I was taken into the public garden at the extremity of the town.

I uttered a cry of astonishment. An extraordinarily large bay lay extended before me, as far as my eyes could reach, between two hills which were lost to sight in the mist; and in the middle of this immense yellow bay, under a clear, golden sky, a peculiar hill rose up, somber and pointed in the midst of the sand. The sun had just disappeared, and under the still flaming sky appeared the outline of that fantastic rock which bears on its summit a fantastic monument.

At daybreak I went out to it. The tide was low, as it had been the night before, and I saw that wonderful abbey rise up before me as I approached it. After several hours' walking, I reached the enormous mass of rocks which supports the little town, dominated by the great church. Having climbed the steep and narrow street, I entered the most wonderful Gothic building that has ever been built to God on earth, as large as a town, full of low rooms which seem buried beneath vaulted roofs, and lofty galleries supported by delicate columns.

I entered this gigantic granite gem, which is as light as a bit of lace, covered with towers, with slender belfries with spiral staircases, which raise their strange heads that bristle with chimeras, with devils, with fantastic animals, with monstrous flowers, to the blue sky by day, and to the black sky by night, and are connected by finely carved arches.

When I had reached the summit I said to the monk who accompanied me: "Father, how happy you must be here!" And he replied: "It is very windy here, monsieur"; and so we began to talk while watching the rising tide, which ran over the sand and covered it as with a steel cuirass.

And then the monk told me stories, all the old stories belonging to the place, legends, nothing but legends.

One of them struck me forcibly. The country people, those belonging to the Mount, declare that at night one can hear voices talking on the sands, and then that one hears two goats bleating, one with a strong, the other with a weak voice. Incredulous people declare that it is nothing but the cry of the sea birds, which occasionally resembles bleatings, and occasionally, human lamentations; but belated fishermen swear that they have met an old shepherd wandering between tides on the sands around the little town. His head is completely concealed by his cloak and he is followed by a billy goat with a man's face, and a nanny goat with a woman's face, both having long, white hair and talking incessantly and quarreling in an unknown tongue. Then suddenly they cease and begin to bleat with all their might.

"Do you believe it?" I asked the monk. "I scarcely know," he replied, and I continued: "If there are other beings beside ourselves on this earth, how comes it that we have not known it long since, or why have *you* not seen them? How is that *I* have not seen them?" He replied: "Do we see the hundred-thousandth part of what exists? Look here; there is the wind, which is the strongest force in nature, which knocks down men, and blows down buildings, destroys cliffs and casts great ships on the rocks; the wind which kills, which whistles, which sighs, which roars—have you ever seen it, and can you see it? It exists for all that, however.''

I was silent before this simple reasoning. That man was a philosopher, or perhaps a fool; I could not say which exactly, so I held my tongue. What he had said had often been in my own thoughts.

July 3. I have slept badly; certainly there is some feverish influence here, for my coachman is suffering in the same way as I am. When I went back home yesterday, I noticed his singular paleness, and I asked him: ''What is the matter with you, Jean?'' ''The matter is that I never get any rest, and my nights devour my days. Since your departure, monsieur, there has been a spell over me.''

However, the other servants are all well, but I am very much afraid of having another attack myself.

July 4. I am decidedly ill again; for my old nightmares have returned. Last night I felt somebody leaning on me and sucking my life from between my lips. Yes, he was sucking it out of my throat, like a leech. Then he got up, satiated, and I woke up, so exhausted, crushed and weak that I could not move. If this continues for a few days, I shall certainly go away again.

July 5. Have I lost my reason? What happened last night is so strange that my head wanders when I think of it!

I had locked my door, as I do now every evening, and then, being thirsty, I drank half a glass of water, and accidentally noticed that the water bottle was full up to the cut-glass stopper.

Then I went to bed and fell into one of my terrible sleeps, from which I was aroused in about two hours by a still more frightful shock.

Picture to yourself a sleeping man who is being murdered and who wakes up with a knife in his lung, and whose breath rattles, who is covered with blood, and who can no longer breathe and is about to die, and does not understand—there you have it.

Having recovered my senses, I was thirsty again, so I lit a candle and went to the table on which stood my water bottle. I lifted it up and tilted it over my glass, but nothing came out. It was empty! It was completely empty! At first I could not understand it at all, and then suddenly I was seized by such a terrible feeling that I had to sit down, or rather I fell into a chair! Then I sprang up suddenly to look about me; then I sat down again, overcome by astonishment and fear, in front of the transparent glass bottle! I looked at it with fixed eyes, trying to conjecture, and my hands trembled! Somebody had drunk the water, but who? I? I without any doubt. It could surely only be I. In that case I was a somnambulist; I lived, without knowing it, that mysterious double life which makes us doubt whether there are not two beings in us, or whether a strange, unknowable and invisible being does not at such moments, when our soul is in a state of torpor, animate our captive body, which obeys this other being, as it obeys us, and more than it obeys ourselves.

Oh! Who will understand my horrible agony? Who will understand the emotion of a man who is sound in mind, wide awake, full of common sense, who looks in horror through the glass of a water bottle for a little water that disappeared while he was asleep? I remained thus until it was daylight, without venturing to go to bed again.

July 6. I am going mad. Again all the contents of my water bottle have been drunk during the night—or rather, I have drunk it!

But is it I? Is it I? Who could it be? Who? Oh! God! Am I going mad? Who will save me?

July 10. I have just been through some surprising ordeals. Decidedly I am mad! And yet! . . .

On July 6, before going to bed, I put some wine, milk, water, bread and strawberries on my table. Somebody drank—I drank—all the water and a little of the milk, but neither the wine, bread nor the strawberries were touched.

On the seventh of July I renewed the same experiment, with the same results, and on July 8, I left out the water and the milk, and nothing was touched.

Lastly, on July 9, I put only water and milk on my table, taking care to wrap up the bottles in white muslin and to tie down the stoppers. Then I rubbed my lips, my beard and my hands with pencil lead, and went to bed.

Irresistible sleep seized me, which was soon followed by a terrible awakening. I had not moved, and there was no mark of lead on the sheets. I rushed to the table. The muslin round the bottles remained intact; I undid the string, trembling with fear. All the water had been drunk, and so had the milk! Ah! Great God! . . .

I must start for Paris immediately.

July 12. Paris. I must have lost my head during the last few days! I must be the plaything of my enervated imagination, unless I am really a somnambulist, or that I have been under the power of one of those hitherto unexplained influences which are called suggestions. In any case, my mental state bordered on madness, and twenty-four hours of Paris sufficed to restore my equilibrium.

Yesterday, after doing some business and paying some visits which instilled fresh and invigorating air into my soul, I wound up the evening at the *Théâtre-Français*. A play by Alexandre Dumas the younger was being acted, and his active and powerful imagination completed my cure. Certainly solitude is dangerous for active minds. We require around us men who can think and talk. When we are alone for a long time, we people space with phantoms.

I returned along the boulevards to my hotel in excellent spirits. Amid the jostling of the crowd I thought, not without irony, of my terrors and surmises of the previous week, because I had believed—yes, I had believed—that an invisible being lived beneath my roof. How weak our brains are, and how quickly they are terrified and led into error by a small incomprehensible fact.

Instead of saying simply: "I do not understand because I do not know the cause," we immediately imagine terrible mysteries and supernatural powers.

July 14. Fête of the Republic. I walked through the streets, amused as a child at the firecrackers and flags. Still it is very foolish to be merry on a fixed date, by Government decree. The populace is an imbecile flock of sheep, now stupidly patient, and now in ferocious revolt. Say to it: "Amuse yourself," and it amuses itself. Say to it: "Vote for the Emperor," and it votes for the Emperor, and then say to it: "Vote for the Republic," and it votes for the Republic.

Those who direct it are also stupid; only, instead of obeying men, they obey principles which can only be stupid, sterile, and false, for the very reason that they are principles, that is to say, ideas which are considered as certain and unchangeable, in this world where one is certain of nothing, since light is an illusion and noise is an illusion.

July 16. I saw some things yesterday that troubled me very much.

I was dining at the house of my cousin, Madame Sable, whose husband is colonel of the 76th Chasseurs at Limoges. There were two young women there, one of whom had married a medical man, Dr. Parent, who devotes much attention to nervous diseases and to the remarkable manifestations taking place at this moment under the influence of hypnotism and suggestion.

He related to us at some length the wonderful results obtained by English scientists and by the doctors of the Nancy school; and the facts which he adduced appeared to me so strange that I declared that I was altogether incredulous.

"We are," he declared, "on the point of discovering one of the most important secrets of nature; I mean to say, one of its most important secrets on this earth, for there are certainly others of a different kind of importance up in the stars, yonder. Ever since man has thought, ever since he has been able to express and write down his thoughts, he has felt himself close to a mystery which is impenetrable to his gross and imperfect senses, and he endeavors to supplement through his intellect the inefficiency of his senses. As long as that intellect remained in its elementary stage, these apparitions of invisible spirits assumed forms that were commonplace, though terrifying. Thence sprang the popular belief in the supernatural, the legends of wandering spirits, of fairies, of gnomes, ghosts, I might even say the legend of God; for our conceptions of the workman-creator, from whatever religion they may have come down to us, are certainly the most mediocre, the most stupid and the most incredible inventions that ever sprang from the terrified brain of any human beings. Nothing is truer than what Voltaire says: 'God made man in His own image, but man has certainly paid Him back in his own coin.'

"However, for rather more than a century men seem to have had a presentiment of something new. Mesmer and some others have put us on an unexpected track, and, especially within the last two or three years, we have arrived at really surprising results."

My cousin, who is also very incredulous, smiled, and Dr. Parent said to her: "Would you like me to try and send you to sleep, madame?" "Yes, certainly."

She sat down in an easy chair, and he began to look at her fixedly, so as to fascinate her. I suddenly felt myself growing uncomfortable, my heart beating rapidly and a choking sensation in my throat. I saw Madame Sable's eyes becoming heavy, her mouth twitching and her bosom heaving, and at the end of ten minutes she was asleep.

"Go behind her," the doctor said to me, and I took a seat behind her. He put a visiting card into her hands, and said to her: "This is a looking-glass; what do you see in it?" And she replied: "I see my cousin." "What is he doing?" "He is twisting his mustache." "And now?" "He is taking a photograph out of his pocket." "Whose photograph is it?" "His own."

That was true, and the photograph had been given me that same evening at the hotel.

"What is his attitude in this portrait?" "He is standing up with his hat in his hand."

She saw, therefore, on that card, on that piece of white pasteboard, as if she had seen it in a mirror.

The young women were frightened, and exclaimed: "That is enough! Quite, quite enough!"

But the doctor said to Madame Sable authoritatively: "You will rise at eight o'clock tomorrow morning; then you will go and call on your cousin at his hotel and ask him to lend you five thousand francs which your husband demands of you, and which he will ask for when he sets out on his coming journey."

Then he woke her up.

On returning to my hotel, I thought over this curious seance, and I was assailed by doubts, not as to my cousin's absolute and undoubted good faith, for I had known her as well as if she were my own sister ever since she was a child, but as to a possible trick on the doctor's part. Had he not, perhaps, kept a glass hidden in his hand, which he showed to the young woman in her sleep, at the same time as he did the card? Professional conjurers do things that are just as singular.

So I went home and to bed, and this morning, at about half-past eight, I was awakened by my valet, who said to me: "Madame Sable has asked to see you immediately, monsieur." I dressed hastily and went to her.

She sat down in some agitation, with her eyes on the floor, and without raising her veil she said to me: "My dear cousin, I am going to ask a great favor of you." "What is it, cousin?" "I do not like to tell you, and yet I must. I am in absolute need of five thousand francs." "What, you?" "Yes, I, or rather my husband, who has asked me to procure them for him."

I was so thunderstruck that I stammered out my answers. I asked myself whether she had not really been making fun of me with Dr. Parent, if it was not merely a very well-acted farce which had been rehearsed beforehand. On looking at her attentively, however, all my doubts disappeared. She was trembling with grief, so painful was this step to her, and I was convinced that her throat was full of sobs.

I knew that she was very rich and I continued: "What! Has not your husband five thousand francs at his disposal? Come, think. Are you sure that he commissioned you to ask me for them?"

She hesitated for a few seconds, as if she were making a great effort to search her memory, and then she replied: "Yes . . . yes, I am quite sure of it." "He has written to you?"

She hesitated again and reflected, and I guessed the torture of her thoughts. She did not know. She only knew that she was to borrow five thousand francs of me for her husband. So she told a lie. "Yes, he had written to me." "When, pray? You did not mention it to me yesterday." "I received his letter this morning." "Can you show it me?" "No; no . . . no . . . it contained private matters . . . things too personal to ourselves . . . I burned it." "So your husband runs into debt?"

She hesitated again, and then murmured: "I do not know." Thereupon I said bluntly: "I have not five thousand francs at my disposal at this moment, my dear cousin."

She uttered a kind of cry as if she were in pain and said: "Oh! oh! I beseech you, I beseech you to get them for me. . . ."

She got excited and clasped her hands as if she were praying to me! I heard her voice change its tone; she wept and stammered, harassed and dominated by the irresistible order that she had received.

"Oh! oh! I beg you to . . . if you knew what I am suffering . . . I want them today."

I had pity on her: "You shall have them by and by, I swear to you." "Oh! thank you! thank you! How kind you are."

I continued: "Do you remember what took place at your house last night?" "Yes." "Do you remember that Dr. Parent sent you to sleep?'' ''Yes.'' ''Oh! Very well, then; he ordered you to come to me this morning to borrow five thousand francs, and at this moment you are obeying that suggestion.''

She considered for a few moments, and then replied: ''But as it is my husband who wants them—''

For a whole hour I tried to convince her, but could not succeed, and when she had gone I went to the doctor. He was just going out, and he listened to me with a smile, and said: ''Do you believe now?'' ''Yes, I cannot help it.'' ''Let us go to your cousin's.''

She was already half asleep on a reclining chair, overcome with fatigue. The doctor felt her pulse, looked at her for some time with one hand raised toward her eyes, which she closed by degrees under the irresistible power of this magnetic influence, and when she was asleep, he said:

''Your husband does not require the five thousand francs any longer! You must, therefore, forget that you asked your cousin to lend them to you, and, if he speaks to you about it, you will not understand him.''

Then he woke her up, and I took out a pocket book and said: ''Here is what you asked me for this morning, my dear cousin.'' But she was so surprised that I did not venture to persist; nevertheless, I tried to recall the circumstance to her, but she denied it vigorously, thought I was making fun of her, and, in the end, very nearly lost her temper.

There! I have just come back, and I have not been able to eat any lunch, for this experiment has altogether upset me.

July 19. Many people to whom I told the adventure laughed at me. I no longer know what to think. The wise man says: ''It may be!''

July 21. I dined at Bougival, and then I spent the evening at a boatmen's ball. Decidedly everything depends on place and surroundings. It would be the height of folly to believe in the supernatural on the Ile de la Grenouillière . . . but on top of Mont Saint-Michel? . . . and in India? We are terribly influenced by our surroundings. I shall return home next week.

July 30. I came back to my own house yesterday. Everything is going on well.

August 2. Nothing new; it is splendid weather, and I spend my days in watching the Seine flowing past.

August 4. Quarrels among my servants. They declare that the glasses are broken in the cupboards at night. The footman accuses the cook, who accuses the seamstress, who accuses the other two. Who is the culprit? It is a clever person who can tell.

August 6. This time I am not mad. I have seen . . . I have seen . . . I have seen! . . . I can doubt no longer . . . I have seen it! . . .

I was walking at two o'clock among my rose trees, in the full sunlight . . . in the walk bordered by autumn roses which are beginning to fall. As I stopped to look at a Géant de Bataille, which had three splendid blossoms, I distinctly saw the stalk of one of the roses near me bend, as if an invisible hand had bent it, and then break, as if that hand had picked it! Then the flower raised itself, following the curve which a hand would have described in carrying it toward a mouth, and it remained suspended in the transparent air, all alone and motionless, a terrible red spot, three yards from my eyes. In desperation I rushed at it to take it! I found nothing; it had disappeared. Then I was seized with furious rage against myself, for a reasonable and serious man should not have such hallucinations.

But was it an hallucination? I turned round to look for the stalk, and I found it at once, on the bush, freshly broken, between two other roses which remained on the branch. I returned home then, my mind greatly disturbed; for I am certain now, as certain as I am of the alternation of day and night, that there exists close to me an invisible being that lives on milk and water, that can touch objects, take them and change their places; that is, consequently, endowed with a material nature, although it is imperceptible to our senses, and that lives as I do, under my roof—

August 7. I slept tranquilly. He drank the water out of my decanter, but did not disturb my sleep.

I wonder if I am mad. As I was walking just now in the sun by the river side, doubts as to my sanity arose in me; not vague doubts such as I have had hitherto, but definite, absolute doubts. I have seen mad people, and I have known some who have been quite intelligent, lucid, even clear-sighted in every concern of life, except on one point. They spoke readily, clearly, profoundly on everything, when suddenly their mind struck upon the shoals of

their madness and broke to pieces there, and scattered and floun-
dered in that furious and terrible sea, full of rolling waves, fogs
and squalls, which is called *madness*.

I certainly should think that I was mad, absolutely mad, if I were
not conscious, did not perfectly know my condition, did not
fathom it by analyzing it with the most complete lucidity. I should,
in fact, be only a rational man who was laboring under an hallucination. Some unknown disturbance must have arisen in my
brain, one of those disturbances which physiologists of the present
day try to note and to verify; and that disturbance must have
caused a deep gap in my mind and in the sequence and logic of
my ideas. Similar phenomena occur in dreams which lead us
among the most unlikely phantasmagoria, without causing us any
surprise, because our verifying apparatus and our organ of control
are asleep, while our imaginative faculty is awake and active. Is it
not possible that one of the imperceptible notes of the cerebral
keyboard had been paralyzed in me? Some men lose the recollection of proper names, of verbs, or of numbers, or merely of
dates, in consequence of an accident. The localization of all the
variations of thought has been established nowadays; why, then,
should it be surprising if my faculty of controlling the unreality of
certain hallucinations were dormant in me for the time being?

I thought of all this as I walked by the side of the water. The
sun shone brightly on the river and made earth delightful, while
it filled me with a love for life, for the swallows, whose agility
always delights my eye, for the plants by the river side, the rustle
of whose leaves is a pleasure to my ears.

By degrees, however, an inexplicable feeling of discomfort
seized me. It seemed as if some unknown force were numbing
and stopping me, were preventing me from going further, and
were calling me back. I felt that painful wish to return which
oppresses you when you have left a beloved invalid at home, and
when you are seized with a presentiment that he is worse.

I, therefore, returned in spite of myself, feeling certain that I
should find some bad news awaiting me, a letter or a telegram.
There was nothing, however, and I was more surprised and uneasy than if I had had another fantastic vision.

August 8. I spent a terrible evening yesterday. He does not show
himself any more, but I feel that he is near me, watching me,

looking at me, penetrating me, dominating me, and more redoubtable when he hides himself thus than if he were to manifest
his constant and invisible presence by supernatural phenomena.
However, I slept.

August 9. Nothing, but I am afraid.

August 10. Nothing; what will happen tomorrow?

August 11. Still nothing; I cannot stop at home with this fear
hanging over me and these thoughts in my mind; I shall go away.

August 12. Ten o'clock at night. All day long I have been trying
to get away, and have not been able. I wish to accomplish this
simple and easy act of freedom—to go out—to get into my carriage in order to go to Rouen—and I have not been able to do it.
What is the reason?

August 13. When one is attacked by certain maladies, all the
springs of our physical being appear to be broken, all our energies
destroyed, all our muscles relaxed; our bones, too, have become
as soft as flesh, and our blood as liquid as water. I am experiencing
these sensations in my moral being in a strange and distressing
manner. I have no longer any strength, any courage, any self-
control, not even any power to set my own will in motion. I have
no power left to will anything; but someone does it for me and I
obey.

August 14. I am lost. Somebody possesses my soul and dominates
it. Someday orders all my acts, all my movements, all my
thoughts. I am no longer anything in myself, nothing except an
enslaved and terrified spectator of all the things I do. I wish to go
out; I cannot. He does not wish to, and so I remain, trembling and
distracted, in the armchair in which he keeps me sitting. I merely
wish to get up and to rouse myself; I cannot! I am riveted to my
chair, and my chair adheres to the ground in such a manner that
no power could move us.

Then, suddenly, I must, I must go to the bottom of my garden
to pick some strawberries and eat them, and I go there.

I pick the strawberries and eat them! Oh, my God! My God! Is
there a God? If there be one, deliver me! Save me! Succor me!
Pardon! Pity! Mercy! Save me! Oh, what sufferings! What torture!
What horror!

August 15. This is certainly the way in which my poor cousin
was possessed and controlled when she came to borrow five thou-

sand francs of me. She was under the power of a strange will which had entered into her, like another soul, like another parasitic and dominating soul. Is the world coming to an end?

But who is he, this invisible being that rules me? This unknowable being, this rover of a supernatural race?

Invisible beings exist, then! How is it, then, that since the beginning of the world they have never manifested themselves precisely as they do to me? I have never read of anything that resembles what goes on in my house. Oh, if I could only leave it, if I could only go away, escape, and never return! I should be saved, but I cannot.

August 16. I managed to escape today for two hours, like a prisoner who finds the door of his dungeon accidentally open. I suddenly felt that I was free and that he was far away, and so I gave orders to harness the horses as quickly as possible, and I drove to Rouen. Oh, how delightful to be able to say to a man who obeys you: "Go to Rouen!"

I made him pull up before the library, and I begged them to lend me Dr. Herrmann Herestauss' treatise on the unknown inhabitants of the ancient and modern world.

Then, as I was getting into my carriage, I intended to say: "To the railway station!" but instead of this I shouted—I did not say, I shouted—in such a loud voice that all the passersby turned round: "Home!" and I fell back on the cushion of my carriage, overcome by mental agony. He had found me again and regained possession of me.

August 17. Oh, what a night! What a night! And yet it seems to me that I ought to rejoice. I read until one o'clock in the morning! Herestauss, doctor of philosophy and theogony, wrote the history of the manifestation of all those invisible beings which hover round man, or of whom he dreams. He describes their origin, their domain, their power; but none of them resembles the one which haunts me. One might say that man, ever since he began to think, has had a foreboding fear of a new being, stronger than himself, his successor in this new world, and that, feeling his presence, and not being able to foresee the nature of that master, he has, in his terror, created the whole race of occult beings, of vague phantoms born of fear.

Having, therefore, read until one o'clock in the morning, I went and sat down at the open window, in order to cool my forehead and my thoughts, in the calm night air. It was very pleasant and warm! How I should have enjoyed such a night formerly!

There was no moon, but the stars darted out their rays in the dark heavens. Who inhabits those worlds? What forms, what living beings, what animals are there yonder? What can they do more than we can? What do they see which we do not know? Will not one of them, some day or other, traversing space, appear on our earth to conquer it, just as the Norsemen formerly crossed the sea in order to subjugate nations more feeble than themselves?

We are so weak, so defenseless, so ignorant, so small, we who live on this particle of mud which revolves in a drop of water.

I fell asleep, dreaming thus in the cool night air, and when I had slept for about three-quarters of an hour, I opened my eyes without moving, awakened by I know not what confused and strange sensation. At first I saw nothing, and then suddenly it appeared to me as if a page of a book which had remained open on my table turned over of its own accord. Not a breath of air had come in at my window, and I was surprised, and waited. In about four minutes, I saw, I saw, yes, I saw with my own eyes, another page lift itself up and fall down on the others, as if a finger had turned it over. My armchair was empty, appeared empty, but I knew that he was there, he, and sitting in my place, and that he was reading. With a furious bound, the bound of an enraged wild beast that springs at its tamer, I crossed my room to seize him, to strangle him, to kill him! But before I could reach it, the chair fell over as if somebody had run away from me—my table rocked, my lamp fell and went out, and my window closed as if some thief had been surprised and had fled out into the night, shutting it behind him.

So he had run away; he had been afraid; he, afraid of me!

But—but—tomorrow—or later—some day or other—I should be able to hold him in my clutches and crush him against the ground! Do not dogs occasionally bite and strangle their masters?

August 18. I have been thinking the whole day long. Oh, yes, I will obey him, follow his impulses, fulfill all his wishes, show myself humble, submissive, a coward. He is the stronger; but the hour will come.

August 19. I know—I know—I know all! I have just read the following in the *Revue du Monde Scientifique*: "A curious piece of news comes to us from Rio de Janeiro. Madness, an epidemic of madness, which may be compared to that contagious madness which attacked the people of Europe in the Middle Ages, is at this moment raging in the Province of San-Paolo. The terrified inhabitants are leaving their houses, saying that they are pursued, possessed, dominated like human cattle by invisible, though tangible beings, a species of vampire, which feed on their life while they are asleep, and who, besides, drink water and milk without appearing to touch any other nourishment.

"Professor Don Pedro Henriquez, accompanied by several medical savants, has gone to the Province of San-Paolo, in order to study the origin and the manifestations of this surprising madness on the spot, and to propose such measures to the Emperor as may appear to him to be most fitted to restore the mad population to reason."

Ah! Ah! I remember now that fine Brazilian three-master which passed in front of my windows as it was going up the Seine, on the 8th day of last May! I thought it looked so pretty, so white and bright! That Being was on board of her, coming from there, where its race originated. And it saw me! It saw my house which was also white, and it sprang from the ship onto the land. Oh, merciful heaven!

Now I know, I can divine. The reign of man is over, and he has come. He who was feared by primitive man; whom disquieted priests exorcised; whom sorcerers evoked on dark nights, without having seen him appear, to whom the imagination of the transient masters of the world lent all the monstrous or graceful forms of gnomes, spirits, genii, fairies and familiar spirits. After the coarse conceptions of primitive fear, more clear-sighted men foresaw it more clearly. Mesmer divined it, and ten years ago physicians accurately discovered the nature of his power, even before he exercised it himself. They played with this new weapon of the Lord, the sway of a mysterious will over the human soul, which had become a slave. They called it magnetism, hypnotism, suggestion—what do I know? I have seen them amusing themselves like rash children with this horrible power! Woe to us! Woe to man! He has come, the—the—what does he call himself—the—

I fancy that he is shouting out his name to me and I do not hear him—the—yes—he is shouting it out—I am listening—I cannot—he repeats it—the—Horla—I hear—the Horla—it is he—the Horla—he has come!

Ah! the vulture has eaten the pigeon; the wolf has eaten the lamb; the lion has devoured the sharp-horned buffalo; man has killed the lion with an arrow, with sword, with gunpowder; but the Horla will make of man what we have made of the horse and of the ox; his chattel, his slave and his food, by the mere power of his will. Woe to us!

But, nevertheless, the animal sometimes revolts and kills the man who has subjugated it. I should also like—I shall be able to—but I must know him, touch him, see him! Scientists say that animals' eyes, being different from ours, do not distinguish objects as ours do. And my eye cannot distinguish this newcomer who is oppressing me.

Why? Oh, now I remember the words of the monk at Mont Saint-Michel: "Can we see the hundred-thousandth part of what exists? See here; there is the wind, which is the strongest force in nature, which knocks men, and bowls down buildings, uproots trees, raises the sea into mountains of water, destroys cliffs and casts great ships on the breakers; the wind which kills, which whistles, which sighs, which roars—have you ever seen it, and can you see it? It exists for all that, however!"

And I went on thinking; my eyes are so weak, so imperfect, that they do not even distinguish hard bodies, as if they are as transparent as glass! If a glass without tinfoil behind it were to bar my way, I should run into it, just as a bird which has flown into a room breaks its head against the window-panes. A thousand things, moreover, deceive man and lead him astray. Why should it then be surprising that he cannot perceive an unknown body through which the light passes?

A new being! Why not? It was assuredly bound to come! Why should we be the last? We do not distinguish it any more than all the others created before us! The reason is, that its nature is more perfect, its body finer and more finished than ours, that ours is so weak, so awkwardly constructed, encumbered with organs that are always tired, always on the strain like machinery that is too complicated, which lives like a plant and like a beast, nourishing itself on air, herbs and flesh, an animal machine which is a prey to maladies, to malformations, to decay; broken-winded, badly regulated, simple and eccentric, ingeniously badly made, at once a coarse and a delicate piece of workmanship, the rough sketch of a being that might become intelligent and grand.

We are only a few, so few in this world, from the oyster up to man. Why should there not be one more, once that period is passed which separates the successive apparitions from all the different species?

Why not one more? Why not, also, other trees with immense, splendid flowers, perfuming whole regions? Why not other elements besides fire, air, earth, and water? There are four, only four, those nursing fathers of various beings! What a pity! Why are there not forty, four hundred, four thousand? How poor everything is, how mean and wretched! grudgingly produced, roughly constructed, clumsily made! Ah, the elephant and the hippopotamus, what grace! And the camel, what elegance!

But the butterfly, you will say, a flying flower? I dream of one that should be as large as a hundred worlds, with wings whose shape, beauty, colors and motion I cannot even express. But I see it—it flutters from star to star, refreshing them and perfuming them with the light and harmonious breath of its flight! And the people up there look at it as it passes in an ecstasy of delight!

What is the matter with me? It is he, the Horla, who haunts me, and who makes me think of these foolish things! He is within me, he is becoming my soul; I shall kill him!

August 19. I shall kill him. I have seen him! Yesterday I sat down at my table and pretended to write very assiduously. I knew quite well that he would come prowling round me, quite close to me, so close that I might perhaps be able to touch him, to seize him. And then—then I should have the strength of desperation; I should have my hands, my knees, my chest, my forehead, my teeth to strangle him, to crush him, to bite him, to tear him to pieces. And I watched for him with all my over-excited senses.

I had lighted my two lamps and the eight wax candles on my mantelpiece, as if with this light I could discover him.

My bedstead, my old oak post bedstead, stood opposite to me;

on my right was the fireplace; on my left, the door which was carefully closed, after I had left it open for some time in order to attract him; behind me was a very high wardrobe with a looking-glass in it, before which I stood to shave and dress every day, and in which I was in the habit of glancing at myself from head to foot every time I passed it.

I pretended to be writing in order to deceive him, for he also was watching me, and suddenly I felt—I was certain that he was reading over my shoulder, that he was there, touching my ear.

I got up, my hands extended, and turned round so quickly that I almost fell. Eh! well? It was as bright as at midday, but I did not see my reflection in the mirror! It was empty, clear, profound, full of light! But my figure was not reflected in it—and I, I was opposite to it! I saw the large, clear glass from top to bottom, and I looked at it with unsteady eyes; and I did not dare to advance; I did not venture to make a movement, feeling that he was there, but that he would escape me again, he whose imperceptible body had absorbed my reflection.

How frightened I was! And then, suddenly, I began to see myself in a mist in the depths of the looking-glass, in a mist as it were a sheet of water; and it seemed to me as if this water were flowing clearer every moment. It was like the end of an eclipse. Whatever it was that hid me did not appear to possess any clearly defined outlines, but a sort of opaque transparency which gradually grew clearer.

At last I was able to distinguish myself completely, as I do every day when I look at myself.

I had seen it! And the horror of it remained with me, and makes me shudder even now.

August 20. How could I kill it, as I could not get hold of it? Poison? But it would see me mix it with the water; and then, would our poisons have any effect on its impalpable body? No—no—no doubt about the matter—Then—then?—

August 21. I sent for a blacksmith from Rouen, and ordered iron shutters for my room, such as some private hotels in Paris have on the ground floor, for fear of burglars, and he is going to make me an iron door as well. I have made myself out a coward, but I do not care about that!

September 10. Rouen, Hôtel Continental. It is done—it is done—but is he dead? My mind is thoroughly upset by what I have seen.

Well then, yesterday, the locksmith having put on the iron shutters and door, I left everything until midnight, although it was getting cold.

Suddenly I felt that he was there, and joy, mad joy, took possession of me. I got up softly, and walked up and down for some time, so that he might not suspect anything; then I took off my boots and put on my slippers carelessly; then I fastened the iron shutters, and, going back to the door, quickly double-locked it with a padlock, putting the key into my pocket.

Suddenly I noticed that he was moving restlessly round me, that in his turn he was frightened and was ordering me to let him out. I nearly yielded; I did not, however, but putting my back to the door, I half opened it, just enough to allow me to go out backward, and as I am very tall my head touched the casing. I was sure that he had not been able to escape, and I shut him up alone, quite alone. What happiness! I had him fast. Then I ran downstairs; in the drawing-room, which was under my bedroom, I took the two lamps and I poured all the oil on the carpet, the furniture, everywhere; then I set fire to it and made my escape, after having carefully double-locked the door.

I went and hid myself at the bottom of the garden, in a clump of laurel bushes. How long it seemed! How long it seemed! Everything was dark, silent, motionless, not a breath of air and not a star, but heavy banks of clouds which one could not see, but which weighed, oh, so heavily on my soul.

I looked at my house and waited. How long it was! I already began to think that the fire had gone out of its own accord, or that he had extinguished it, when one of the lower windows gave way under the violence of the flames, and a long, soft, caressing sheet of red flame mounted up the white wall, and enveloped it as far as the roof. The light fell on the trees, the branches, and the leaves, and a shiver of fear pervaded them also! The birds awoke, a dog began to howl, and it seemed to me as if the day were breaking! Almost immediately two other windows flew into fragments, and I saw that the whole of the lower part of my house was nothing but a terrible furnace. But a cry, a horrible, shrill, heartrending cry, a woman's cry, sounded through the night, and two garret windows were opened! I had forgotten the servants! I saw their terror-stricken faces, and their arms waving frantically.

Then overwhelmed with horror, I set off to run to the village, shouting: "Help! help! fire! fire!" I met some people who were already coming to the scene, and I returned with them.

By this time the house was nothing but a horrible and magnificent funeral pile, a monstrous funeral pile which lit up the whole country, a funeral pile where men were burning, and where he was burning also, He, He, my prisoner, that new Being, the new master, the Horla!

Suddenly the whole roof fell in between the walls, and a volcano of flames darted up to the sky. Through all the windows which opened on that furnace, I saw the flames darting, and I thought that he was there, in that kiln, dead.

Dead? Perhaps?—His body? Was not his body, which was transparent, indestructible by such means as would kill ours?

If he were not dead? Perhaps time alone has power over that Invisible and Redoubtable Being. Why this transparent, unrecognizable body, this body belonging to a spirit, if it also has to fear ills, infirmities and premature destruction?

Premature destruction? All human terror springs from that! After man, the Horla. After him who can die every day, at any hour, at any moment, by any accident, came the one who would die only at his own proper hour, day, and minute, because he had touched the limits of his existence!

No—no—without any doubt—he is not dead—Then—then—I suppose I must kill myself! . . .

Alexandre Dumas

THE VAMPIRE OF THE
CARPATHIAN MOUNTAINS

—✦—

Alexandre Dumas the elder is probably the most widely read of all French authors. He was extremely prolific, with close to 800 titles to his credit. Most of them were romantic adventures and include *The Three Musketeers*, *The Corsican Brothers*, *The Man in the Iron Mask*, and *The Count of Monte Cristo*. His father was one of Napoleon's generals and his father's death in 1806 left the family destitute, forcing Dumas to forego a formal education. Dumas amassed an enormous fortune through his writing, most of which he squandered on a long succession of mistresses. By the end of his life, he was bankrupt. His son, Alexandre Dumas the younger, was the author of *Camile*. George Bernard Shaw said, "The elder Dumas was what Gounod called Mozart, a summit of art. Nobody ever could, or did, or will improve on Dumas' romances and plays." One of these plays was "Le Vampire," which was based on Dr. John Polidori's story, "The Vampyre." "The Vampire of the Carpathian Mountains" is actually a story told within the 1849 novel *Les Mille et un Fantômes: Una Journée a Fontenay-aux-Roses* (*A Thousand and One Phantoms: A Day's Journey at Fontenay-aux-Roses*). The framework of this book is similar to *The Decameron*, the fourteenth-century classic where 100 tales are told by ten people over ten days while they try to escape the plague by hiding out in the gardens and villas above the

This story was translated and adapted by Alan Hull Walton in his book *Horror at Fontenay*, 1975.

city. In Dumas's book, Dumas himself is invited by a friend to Fontenay-aux-Roses to hunt. He arrives to find that a quarryman has murdered his wife by cutting off her head, and the quarryman swears the head talked to him. Later, at the mayor's house, the guests begin telling stories involving corpses and other horrors. The final story is told by Madame Hedwig Gregorishka. In describing her earlier in the book, Dumas writes, "I felt it could not be a human woman I was looking at. . . . Her large dark eyes, contrasting sharply with the fairness of her hair, fixed themselves on mine with the strangest expression, and were rendered even more hypnotic by the deathly pallor of her skin. She must have been in her early thirties, and had once been unusually beautiful—would, indeed, have remained so, had not her cheeks lost their fullness and the warmth of living color. . . . she seemed more like a shadow floating beside me than any human creature made of flesh and blood." At the end of the evening, she tells her tale:

"YOU HAVE ALL TOLD your own stories, and this seems an opportune moment for the relation of mine, which is an unusual one by any standard. Moreover, I defy any of you to controvert its truth, for it is my own life-story, and it reveals the reason for this deathly pallor which no one can help but notice, on my hands and on my face."

At this moment a shaft of blue moonlight fell through one of the tall windows, encircling the lady as she lay on her sofa in a darkened area, away from the candles, so that she had all the appearance of a black marble statue resting on some elegant tomb.

Nobody replied to these introductory remarks. On the contrary, the curiously deep silence which filled the room was sufficient indication of the avidity with which the guests awaited her story.

The pale lady raised herself slowly and gracefully, fixed her cushions, unconcernedly rearranged the folds of her dress, and made herself thoroughly comfortable—during which prolonged moments one could have heard a pin drop. And then, in soft and gently magnetic tones which riveted one's attention, calmly began to relate the story of her life:

"I was born in Poland, where legends have the power of articles of faith, and where we accept tradition as firmly as we believe in the Gospel. We haven't a single castle without its ghost, not a cottage without its familiar spirit. Both rich and poor, from palace to isolated shack, accept the contrasting principles of good and evil, just as they do in the East. Now and again there are clashes between these principles, and they battle together in the invisible ether. At such times as these inexplicable sounds are heard in deserted corridors, hootings in the ruins of ancient towers, and even thick stone walls vibrate fearfully. So terrifying are these manifestations that people flee both castle and village, running to the nearest church for protection beneath the sacred cross, or cowering close within the proximity of holy relics.

"It may be difficult for sophisticated people of the Western world to understand such reactions; yet I can assure you that it is so . . ."

Here she paused for a moment and sighed, but almost immediately continued:

"Added to these circumstances are two still more implacable emanations of the same principles. By this I mean the yoke of tyranny and the urge to freedom. Which was why, during the year 1825, yet one more struggle broke out between Poland and Russia—a struggle which drained the life-blood of our people, and threatened to bring our country to naught. In other words, war . . .

"My father and my two brothers had joined the forces moving against the Czar, and stood firmly together under the flag of Polish independence. That tragic flag, so frequently torn down, yet so frequently raised on high once more.

"Then one day news was brought me that my youngest brother had been killed; and a few days later I heard that my elder brother had suffered fatal wounds. Some time after this I experienced the horror of a long afternoon, when the intolerable booming of the cannon came closer and closer; until my father rode into the courtyard with a hundred horsemen—the sole remnant of the three thousand he had set out with. Beaten and anguished, he had come back to close himself in our castle; to die, if necessary, beneath its ruins.

"Unafraid for himself, my father trembled at the danger surrounding me. For him death was the worst possibility. But for me, insult, rape, and slavery were almost certain.

"Therefore he chose ten men from the hundred left him, and, summoning his steward, gave into his care all the gold and jewels we possessed. He had not forgotten how, during the partition of Poland, my mother—then scarcely out of childhood—had found safety in the Monastery of Sastru, high in the distant Carpathian Mountains. And it was here that he instructed his steward and the ten selected men to take me, secretly.

"Our leave-taking was something like a hurried nightmare, because the Russians were expected within sight of the castle during the next twenty-four hours. Hastily I pulled on a riding habit, ran down to the courtyard, and mounted the best horse in our stables. Scarcely able to hold back his tears, my father kissed me, slid his two loaded pistols into my holsters, and within minutes we were galloping away at top speed.

"Throughout the night, and the following day we covered more than sixty miles, following the banks of a river whose name I've forgotten. Yet another day of travel, and we were safely beyond reach of the enemy, first setting our eyes on the enchanted beauty of the Carpathians in one of the loveliest sunsets I've ever known. On the third day we had reached their base, and were soon gradually ascending by way of a deep winding cleft in the hills.

"Perhaps I should point out here that the Carpathians are very different from your mountains in France, in Italy, or in England, for these are tamed and civilized by comparison. The snowy wind-swept peaks of the Carpathians lose themselves in mist and cloud, and have an uncontrolled majestic wildness, far beyond the imagination of those who've never traveled in this remote area of Central Europe. The lower slopes are thickly patched with woods of pine and fir, whose melancholy grandeur is reflected in the crystal mirror of lakes for ever undisturbed by boat or oar. The voice of man is rarely heard in these uniquely isolated regions, which echo only to the wind, the storm, and the strange sounds of those creatures whose natural habitat is the wilderness. Mile after mile one travels under the cathedral-like arches of the forests, knowing that danger hides everywhere; but one hasn't time to be afraid. In fact astonishment banishes fear, so sudden, so varied, so beautiful, or so harrowing are the sights one comes across, and the accidents one survives.

"Then, after these endless forests,. one enters the vast and boundless spaces of the steppes; bare, rugged, and unbelievably depressing in their monotony. Terror isn't possible here—only the numbing sensation of a desolate sadness. One climbs a great deal and descends a little, climbs again, and repeats the process over an endless waste which looks eternally the same. Yet, mercifully, the awful silence is now and then broken by the long shrill calls from small flocks of peculiar birds, circling overhead.

"Finally, thank God, one begins to descend again, turning southwards; and the landscape recovers all its magical grandeur. With delight one sees new ranges further off; ever higher, ever more impressive and inviting. Once again there are woods, streams, and cascades of water falling incredible distances from tall rocky promontories.

"With foliage and moist earth life returns to the surroundings. And occasionally, from the distance, the tinkling of a hermit's bell is borne on the breeze. Sometimes a tiny village can be seen, nestling in a valley, or clustered on the mountainside—the houses grouped closely together for protection from robber and bandit, wolf and bear. For wherever man dwells in these fastnesses, danger is there in plenty.

"Nevertheless, despite every threat, we were drawing nearer to our journey's end. Ten days of unremitting riding had passed without serious mishap, and the summit of Mount Pion was in sight. This is a giant of a mountain, impressive beyond description, and on its slopes the Monastery of Sastru is built. Within another two days, all being well, we should be there, and I cannot tell you how much I was looking forward to the possibility of relaxing completely, in absolute safety.

"The time was August, and the heat had been intense. You can imagine our joy when, stopping to rest by the moldering ruins of Niantzo, we felt the first cool breeze of evening. From here the view was magnificent. One could follow the course of the Bistrita just below, its banks liberally besprinkled with bright red poppies, many-petaled flowers of a delicate gold, and enormous white campanulas. Having eaten a little and refreshed ourselves, we made our way slowly along a narrow, precipitous track, which led steeply down to the river. So restricting was this stony path that we were obliged to proceed in single file, the guide going first, sitting side-saddle on his horse as he sang a melancholy song learnt long ago in the village of his childhood.

"Then suddenly a shot rang out, its echo fading rapidly in the distance. The song stopped instantly, in mid-verse, our guide falling dead, without even a cry, over the edge of the terrible precipice. His horse trembled on the brink, an almost human look of astonishment on its face, as it gazed questioningly into the depths.

"There was nothing for it but to move on down the slope, since the narrowness of the way excluded the possibility of turning. Nor could we tell whence the shot had come. Several minutes later the path disappeared round a slight bend. Having successfully encountered this, we discovered to our surprise that we were riding across a miniature plateau, the entire area of which was thickly scattered with giant shrubs, and which had two other pathways opening on to it. I noticed that our own road widened considerably at the far side. But at this instant we were deafened by a wild chorus of men, shouting vociferously and threateningly, and found ourselves completely surrounded by a troop of at least thirty husky brigands. It all happened so quickly that we scarcely had time to think.

"But my guardians, being some of the best of my father's soldiers, reacted automatically, and gave vigorous fire. Surprisingly enough I found myself grabbing my own pistols; and, digging in my spurs, goaded my horse at a fast gallop towards the more level country below.

"But it was useless. We were dealing with expert mountaineers, natives who knew the secret of leaping from one rock to another with the ease and accuracy of eagles swooping on their prey.

"We were cut off from behind, while just ahead, where the road widened, the young leader of the band awaited us, at the head of a dozen horsemen. It was this group that stopped me, charging forward to attack us, and killing three-quarters of our men in little more time than it takes me to utter these words. They wore jackets of sheepskin, hats freely decorated with wild flowers, and guns which they aimed with deadly accuracy. Their belts, moreover, were furnished with sabers and braces of pistols.

"The leader was about twenty-two, handsome, but forbidding,

with slanting dark eyes, and long black hair falling almost to his shoulders. He was wearing a full Moldavian gown, trimmed with fur, and gathered in at the waist by a shining belt heavily embroidered with gleaming gold thread. In his hand was a naked, curved saber, glinting brightly in the late sun; and as the battle raged he bellowed wild, incoherent cries, in a loud, uncanny baritone. These seemed to have some meaning, for the group closed in on us with answering calls. I felt my last moment had come, and closed my eyes briefly in prayer.

"Yet miracles happen; for when I opened them again it was to see another young man, handsome as a god, bounding with lightning speed from rock to rock as he descended to our level. Suddenly he froze into immobility, stopping in mid-flight on a nearby boulder, looking for all the world like a statue on its pedestal, as he glared down at us with devastating eye.

"Then in a voice of command pregnant with meaning, loudly and clearly, he shouted but a single word:

" 'Enough!'

"In a flash the enemy was transfixed and silent, every eye being cast up towards the newcomer. Only one man, already in the act of raising his gun, fired at us. One of our men gave an audible groan, for the bullet had broken his left arm. He moved towards the man who had injured him, but before his horse had taken more than a few paces a shot rang out, and his adversary fell, dead, his skull shattered, and his face streaming with blood.

"At this moment, weak with exhaustion and shock, I slipped from my horse and lost consciousness. When I recovered I found myself lying on the ground, my head resting on the knees of a man whose pale hands were covered with magnificent rings. But that was all I could see of him. Opposite me, his arms crossed defiantly over his chest, stood the young Moldavian brigand who had attacked us.

"The man supporting me, his voice, vibrant with authority, was the first to speak:

" 'Kostaki,' he said, 'withdraw your men immediately, and leave me to look after the girl!'

" 'Brother Gregor,' replied the leader, who was on the verge of losing his temper, 'don't go too far with me! The Castle is yours—

leave the mountains and the forest to me! At home you are the master, but here I am the rightful ruler.'

" 'I am the eldest, Kostaki! Which means that I am master everywhere—on the mountain and in the forest, equally as in the Castle. I am a Brankovan as you are, and being of royal blood I must be obeyed!'

" 'You can order your own servants, Gregor, but not my soldiers.'

" 'Your soldiers, Kostaki, are criminals acting outside the law. If they do not obey me I can have them hanged from the battlements of our Castle by sunset.'

" 'Try it then—give them orders, and see what they'll do!'

"At these words my protector drew away his knees and gently laid my head on a cloak rolled up as a pillow. I followed his movements with some anxiety, recognizing the agile young god who had fallen so opportunely from the skies within moments of our defeat.

"He wasn't more than twenty-five or six, tall, fair, and with enormous blue eyes full of strong determination. His pale gold hair shone with light, giving to his face something of the aspect of an archangel. But his lips were parted in a smile of disdain as he faced his brother. His glance was that of an eagle confronting the elements.

"His garb was immaculate, consisting of a beautifully-cut doublet of black velvet, a small pointed hat decorated with an eagle's feather, skin-tight breeches, and heavily embroidered riding-boots. A hunting-horn was slung round his shoulders on a thickly-twisted silk rope, and he carried the double-barreled carbine which had so effectively silenced the disobedient rebel.

"He raised his right arm with an imperious movement, which seemed to draw reverence even from his brother. Then he spoke briefly, but severely, to the crowd of men, in a local dialect which I could not understand. They looked humbled, almost servile, and at a signal he made, retired into formation behind us.

" 'Very well, Gregor,' exclaimed Kostaki; 'we shan't take the woman to our caves. But I swear to you that I'll have her. She's just to my taste—and since I captured her myself, she's mine by right!'

"With these words he took the few steps necessary to reach me, and seized me in a grip of iron.

" 'She shall be taken to the Castle and passed into my mother's care,' said Gregor, sternly. Then he continued, slowly, and with emphasis on every word: 'I intend, moreover, to see that this is done!'

"Then, looking round, he quickly seized the bridle of a riderless horse, and in a flash was sitting on its saddle.

"Kostaki, although he still held me in his arms, was on his own horse as quickly, and in a matter of seconds we were off at a mad gallop.

"Gregor's mount was a fiery well-trained creature, keeping neck by neck level with Kostaki's brute.

"It must have been a fantastic sight to see the two brothers riding with insane fury over rock and hill, through copse and wood—the whole scene drenched in the ruddy glow of the setting sun.

"Gregor's remarkable blue eyes never left mine for an instant. But Kostaki, noticing this, skillfully moved my position, so that all I could see was his own sinisterly brooding gaze as he stared down at me, like some impatient monster waiting to devour me. I was terrified; but even when I looked away I could still feel his searing glance burning its way to my inmost being. It must have been the intensity of my fear that produced the illusion, because at that moment I began to think I was the Lenore of Bürger's celebrated poem, being carried off by the ghostly horseman:

> "Is there a hundred miles between
>   Us and our bridal bed?
> Eleven has struck on the clock I ween,
>   And dawn will soon shine red."
> "Nay, look, my love, at the full moon's face:
>   We and the dead folk ride apace
> So before day with darkness meets
>   You shall press your bridal sheets."
>
> They ride, they ride, on either hand,
>   Too fast to see or know them
> Fly hedges, wastes, and pasture-land,

The rocks resound below them.
"Dost fear, my love! The moon shines bright.
   Hurrah! For the dead ride fast by night.—
Don't fear, my love, the dead! . . .
   Nay, let them rest, the dead!"

They flew to right, they flew to left,
   The hills, the trees, the sedges;
They flew to left, to right, to left,
   Townlets and towns and hedges.
"Don't fear, my love, the moon shines bright!
   Hurrah, for the dead ride fast by night—
Dost fear, my love, the dead?"
   "Ah, let them rest, the dead."

On, on they race by the moon's pale light;
   All things seem flying fast;
The heaven, the stars, the earth, the night
   In one wild dream flash past.
"Don't fear, my love—the moon shines bright.
   Hurrah, for the dead ride fast by night—
Dost fear, my love, the dead?"
   "Alas, let be the dead."

In a second's space came a wonder strange,
   A hideous thing to tell;
The rider's face knew a ghastly change,
   The flesh from the white bones fell.
A featureless skull glared down on her,
   No hair to feel, no lips to stir:
She was clasped by a skeleton!
   Yet the frightful ride went on.

"Some time later—though I could never gauge how long—
when the riders had slackened their speed to a trot, I opened my
eyes in absolute terror, certain that I should find myself in a graveyard, surrounded by open tombs and crumbling monuments.

"What I did see was scarcely more inviting. For I found that we
were in the inner courtyard of an enormous mountain castle; a

dark, and virtually impregnable stronghold, built some time during the fourteenth century, judging by its architecture.

"Kostaki let me slide to the cobbled ground, but in an instant was beside me. Yet I need not have feared, for Gregor was, as he had claimed, supreme master in his castle. It was then that I noticed the absence of the bandits, who must have left their leader to return to their secret hiding-place.

"We were not, however, alone, for a number of servants had gathered in the yard, automatically summoned by the noisy arrival of the young lords.

"Two women came up to us. Gregor said something to them in Moldavian, and gave me sign to follow them. Had it not been for the look accompanying this gesture, I should have been more apprehensive than ever; but so kindly were his features, so sincere his respect, that I found myself obeying him on the instant.

"A few minutes later I found myself in a roomy bedchamber, sparsely furnished, but reasonably well curtained. The waiting-women told me it was the best the castle could offer.

"It was so large and so high that I felt dwarfed by its vastness. The bed was an enormous divan, covered with a rich tapestry overlay, and littered with inviting cushions. There was a large, carved oak chest; two gigantic oak settles; a beautifully carved wardrobe, which must have been at least two centuries old; and, finally, a reasonably comfortable-looking easy chair. Several thick fur rugs were scattered over the stone-flagged floor.

"Scarcely had I had time to take all this in when my bags and trunks were brought up by some sturdy young lackeys. The women reappeared, and with a friendly, but reverential attitude, helped me unpack essentials. Then, during a half-hour of considerable difficulty, I managed to remove all traces of our nightmare journey. But I decided to continue wearing my long riding habit, since this seemed infinitely more in keeping with the attire of my hosts, and my bare and desolate surroundings, than any softly feminine evening gown could have been.

"I dismissed the women, and had only just completed my toilette, when I heard a gentle knocking on the heavily studded door.

" 'Please come in,' I called, automatically lapsing into French, which is our second tongue in Poland.

"Gregor entered, smiling as he walked across the room. Then, with the utmost graciousness and charm he spoke:

" 'It's a blessing, Mademoiselle, that you know French. It will make everything so much easier.'

" 'I'm also glad,' I replied; 'for that was the language you used when you saved me from your brother's inexplicable attention—and I'm equally delighted to employ it now, because I want to thank you with all my heart for your miraculous help.'

" 'That's very kind of you, Mademoiselle; but it was perfectly understandable that I should come to the aid of a woman in circumstances such as yours. Fortunately I was hunting in the mountains, and reasonably close when I heard the continued firing. Thank God I arrived in time . . . Yet what, may I ask, causes a distinguished lady such as yourself to travel in these wild and dangerously remote parts?'

"His solicitude increasing my confidence and warming my sense of gratitude, I felt obliged to tell him something of my previous life, and what had caused me to set out on this journey. Thus I told him that I was of the Polish nobility; that my two brothers were dead; that my father had probably been killed by this time in the defense of our castle; and that I was traveling to the monastery of Sastru, which had safely sheltered my mother throughout a similar period, during her girlhood.

" 'Good! The fact that you have suffered so much at the hands of the Russian armies will stand you in good stead here,' exclaimed my handsome young friend. 'I'm afraid *we* also may have trouble from that direction very soon; and the struggle will be long and bitter . . .

" 'But now, Mademoiselle, since you have acquainted me with the details of your own history, I think I had better tell you something about myself. This ancient stronghold is the Castle of the Brankovans—an illustrious name, and one probably not unknown to you.'

" 'My Christian name is Hedwig,' I interrupted, a little confusedly. Then, pulling myself together, I quickly added: '—Yes, of course—the fame and distinction of the Brankovans has reached us, even in Poland.'

"Gregor gave a broad grin, obviously amused and curious at the awkward way in which I had prefaced my reply with the introduction of my personal name—yet delighted with the compliment this might imply.

"Then, having considered me silently for several seconds, a look of the deepest sympathy in his eyes, he proceeded to tell me something of his own background.

"His mother, it seems, was the last Princess of the Brankovan line; indeed the last descendant of the family. Her first husband had been a Prince Waivady, who had been educated in Vienna, where he came to appreciate all the sophisticated refinements of civilized life.

" 'As a result,' my host continued, 'my father was intent that I also should become a perfect European; in learning and in thought, as well as in outward manner. Thus the years of my boyhood were passed, in company with my father, living in Germany, in Austria, in France, and in Italy. My mother, being averse to such indefinitely prolonged travel, remained here at Brankovan, where she managed the estates.'

"At this point Gregor gave a deep sigh, shaking back a lock of hair that had fallen over his brow.

" 'I know,' he resumed, 'that according to the unwritten laws of family loyalty I should not reveal the information I am about to disclose. Yet it is essential for your own safety that you should know all about us . . . During the long years of our absence from home, my mother, lonely and bored, indulged in a love affair with a Count Georgi Koproli, half Greek and half Moldavian. After some time she wrote to my father, admitting her guilt, and asking for a divorce—strengthening her position by saying that she could no longer continue to be the wife of a man who had needlessly, and for many years, stayed away from his home and his native land.

" 'My father, I regret to say, was never obliged to answer the letter. Indeed he didn't even cast eyes on it, for he died of a heart attack some days before its arrival. On reading it I considered the situation carefully, finally deciding that the best thing to do was to send my heartfelt wishes for my mother's happiness.

" 'This I did in a reply which told her of my father's death, and in which I also asked her permission to continue my travels abroad—a request which, not surprisingly, was immediately granted.

" 'Between you and me it had been my intention to settle permanently in Germany, so as to avoid meeting Koproli, a man who hated me, and whom I detested with equal fervor. Nevertheless, these arrangements were cut short by the news that he had been assassinated by some old friends of my father, within a year or two of the marriage.

" 'Although my mother had rarely shown any affection towards me, I still loved her more than I can say; and realized the extent of her suffering and loneliness in this sudden tragedy. As a result I traveled back to my homeland with the greatest possible speed. Then one day, unexpectedly, I arrived back at Brankovan, not having sent a single word to indicate the possibility of my return.

" 'You can imagine my surprise when I found the servants obeying a handsomely dressed young man, whom at first I took to be a temporary guest of unusual distinction. Very soon I learned that he was my brother, who had been born many years before, during the early days of my mother's illicit liaison. By now, of course, he had been legitimized by her second marriage. His name was Kostaki, and you have seen him—that wild, ungovernable fellow, whose only guides are his lusts, who recognizes nothing sacred apart from his mother, and who obeys me only as the tiger obeys the trainer who has broken him by absolute strength of will. I might add that deep within himself he nourishes a profound and bitter hatred of me, a secret hope that some day he may find a chance of getting rid of me. Nevertheless—and only for the sake of my mother's peace of mind—we have come to a kind of arrangement. Since I am the eldest son, it is understood that I remain supreme master in the Castle of the Brankovans and the Waivadys. But in the open country, beyond the impregnable walls of this straggling fortress, he is free to rule the depths of the forests, the open plains, and the rocky heights of the mountains. There he is able to bend everything beneath the ruthless iron of his evil will. And I cannot understand why, today, he gave way before my commands, or why his men followed my orders. I can only suspect that it was due to the shock of surprise. But I shouldn't like to put my authority to the proof of a second test!

" 'Listen to me carefully. Your only safety lies in remaining within the precincts of this castle. Stay in your room as much as you wish—but never leave the courtyard or stray beyond the gate.

Providing you do this I can guarantee you safety. Otherwise my sword and my life are your only defense; and a single man against that band would have little chance, save for a miracle.'

" 'You mean to say that I can't go on with my journey to the Monastery of Sastru, that I can't possibly leave this place?'

" 'You can attempt it if you must; and you can rely on me to carry out any orders you shall give. But the result would be my own death—you would be raped by Kostaki, and would certainly never reach the Monastery.'

" 'Then what on earth can I do?'

" 'Only one thing. Bide your time. Stay here and see what happens. Chance sometimes offers unusual circumstances. Once you can accept the fact that you have fallen into a nest of inhuman bandits, but that you are safe within these walls, then your courage will do the rest. And you will find my mother, though she is very fond of Kostaki, unusually generous and considerate of a Princess. You'll meet her soon, and you'll like her; because I know she'll protect you against the crude sexuality of her other son. Let her see you trusting her; and because you are beautiful, and of noble blood yourself, she will love you and guard you as a daughter. That I can promise you.'

"Gregor stopped and looked at me tenderly. In the half-light his rugged handsomeness became soft and warm.

" 'As a matter of fact,' he added, gently, 'I don't think anyone could look at you or be with you for more than a few minutes without loving you . . .'

"I turned away for a few seconds to hide my embarrassment. Then, rising to his feet, my host continued with more immediate matters: 'Come,' he said, 'dinner will almost be ready in the main hall, and my mother will be waiting for you with not a little curiosity. But show *no* sign of awkwardness or distrust. And speak only Polish. No one but myself understands that language here; and I shall translate all you say accurately to my mother. Finally— and it is a very important thing—do not breathe a word of our conversation to anyone; you can have no idea of the guile and frequent untrustworthiness of my fellow countrymen.'

"As he said this he walked towards the door and opened it. I followed him down the enormous staircase, which was now illuminated by torches held in skillfully fashioned iron hands protruding from the gray stone walls. We traversed a similarly lit gallery, and then Gregor threw open the door of a high, vaulted hall, announcing me as: 'The Stranger Lady.' At these words a most impressive woman rose from her high-backed chair near a blazing open fire, and came to meet us with slow dignity.

"This was the Princess Brankovan. Her hair was absolutely white, and coiled in thick plaits around her head, these being surmounted by an aigrette of costly diamonds, which scintillated with a thousand colors in the brilliant fire-light. She was dressed in a long full-skirted gown of gold material, richly peppered with carefully-matched pearls. Her sleeves, waist, and the base of her dress were tastefully trimmed with the purest white fur; and she carried a jeweled rosary, the beads of which passed regularly between her fingers as she approached us.

"Behind her was Kostaki, splendidly garbed in the superb traditional costume of the Magyars. The collar of a white silk shirt showed above a knee-length gown of bright green silk-velvet, the sleeves of which were unusually full.

His breeches were of red cashmere, and he wore slippers of soft Moroccan leather, with pointed, curling toes, the entire surface of which were covered with intricate embroidery in golden thread. His long blue-black hair fell about his shoulders, increasing the whiteness of his muscular neck. In this costume he looked even more exotic and more terrifying than when I first set eyes on him.

"He bowed with some awkwardness, muttering a few words in his own tongue. But I could not understand these. It was then that I noticed a curious thing. The gold light from the fire was casting our shadows, and those of the furniture, on the smooth pavement of the floor—but Kostaki had *no* shadow at all! I managed to repress a slight gasp as I bowed to my hosts.

"Then Gregor spoke: 'You can talk in French, Kostaki,' he said. 'Mademoiselle is Polish, but she understands that language as well.' Yet Kostaki's utterances in French were equally as unintelligible as his mutterings in Moldavian. At this point the Princess commanded them both to be silent and extended her hand with a regal air. I kissed it formally, after which she made a brief speech of welcome in her own tongue. The kindness of her features, and the subtle inflections and modulations of her voice, made perfectly clear the meaning of words which I couldn't possibly have understood otherwise.

"Then she indicated an enormous, heavily carved, and indescribably beautiful refectory table, laid for dinner; obviously suggesting that we should be seated. It was lit by four dozen candles set in twelve solid gold candelabra. The plates and cutlery were all of purest silver, and the wine glasses of exquisitely cut crystal. The tapestried walls were lit by torches flaring in ornamental polished silver sconces, each one set in a bare stone space between the magnificent hangings.

"After she was seated, the Princess made the sign of the cross in silence, then proceeded to repeat grace. I sat at her right hand, with Gregor beside me, whilst Kostaki was at her left. The conversation was quiet and subdued as the servants began to bring in numerous dishes of meats, local delicacies, and salads. It was then I learned that my hostess's Christian name was Smerande.

"The remainder of the household (apart from those who were waiting on us) dined at the same table, each taking his or her place according to superiority. But despite the excellence of the food and the comfort of the hall, the atmosphere at table was dismal and depressing. Kostaki didn't speak again; though Gregor did his best to keep up my spirits with conversation in French. The Princess Smerande helped me to every course with her own beautifully jeweled hands; but always with an attitude of religious solemnity, as though she were serving at a rite, rather than welcoming a guest.

"When we had finished eating Gregor explained to his mother that I must be extremely tired after my long journey, and that bed was perhaps the best place for me. She nodded her head in acquiescence, kissed me on the brow, and said that she wished me a good night, and a sound and dreamless sleep within the walls of her castle.

"The young man couldn't have chosen a better moment, for I was desperately tired, and most anxious to get to bed and be alone to sort out my thoughts. I thanked the Princess, who accompanied me to the hall door, where I found the two women who had previously waited on me. Bowing to Smerande and her sons I took my leave, retiring immediately to my room, accompanied by my attendants. Thanking them for their solicitude, I informed them in sign-language that I would prefer to undress myself. They left the room immediately, with marks of respect that made it very clear they had received orders to obey me implicitly in all ways.

"All I had to illumine the enormous apartment was a single candelabrum holding three candles. But the light was sufficient to make clear only the small area near my bed table. Picking it up I walked around the room—if it could be called that, for it was more like a small hall—exploring every nook and cranny. I was chilled by a strange sense of fear, increased by the oblique beams from a clouded moon as they fell through the open window in sinister competition with my candles.

"Besides the main door, which gave way to the staircase, there were two others in the chamber. But each was furnished with massive bolts, already shot, on the inside. These gave me renewed assurance. Next I looked at the entrance-door. This, too, had a pair of strong iron bolts, which I immediately pushed into place. Then I walked to the window and looked out of it before closing it. Beneath was a sheer precipice of some hundreds of feet.

"I sighed with relief, realizing clearly enough that Gregor must have chosen this particular room to keep me safe from any danger.

"Returning to my comfortable, almost luxurious bed, I found a sheet of notepaper lying on one of the pillows. Opening it I read the following words:

" 'My Dear Hedwig,

Forgive me for taking the liberty of using your first name— but sleep peacefully, assured of complete safety. You have nothing to fear, as I told you, so long as you remain within the castle boundaries.

> With my sincere respects,
> *Gregor.'*

"Somewhat gauche as the expression of this note may have seemed, I experienced an abiding sense of relief. My terrors vanished, and drowsiness overcoming every other sensation, I got into bed (it had been beautifully warmed with warming pans), and soon was fast asleep.

"When I awoke the sun was rising in a cloudless blue sky; an incredible variety of birds were singing joyously; far below, the green of the forest spread itself out, like a calm emerald sea, and all my anxieties had faded like a dream.''

The pale lady paused, sighed, and begged a glass of Monsieur Ledru's excellent sparkling Moselle to quench the dryness which had come into her throat. Then she continued with her tale:

''I must try and be a little more brief, since otherwise this story of mine will take up the entire night! And, after all, it is the essentials, the highlights, which matter most.

''I was very soon firmly established in the castle of Brankovan; all went well at first, but shortly afterwards the awful drama in which I was involved began to unfold itself.

''Needless to say, both brothers had fallen in love with me, each in his own peculiar manner. Kostaki's showed itself as the lust which burned in his devilish eyes; and in the sly, lascivious leer which occasionally overspread his features. Gregor's revealed itself in the gentleness of his glance, and emanated from his heart with a radiant purity of intention.

''Gregor delayed his declaration; but his brother did not wait more than a few days before explaining his feelings, emphatically telling me, not only that he loved me, but that I should belong to him or no one else. His emotion rising to mania, he blurted out that he would kill me rather than let me become the wife or mistress of any other man.

''Gregor realized what was going on, but was wise enough to say nothing. He remained friendly and considerate, spending most of his leisure with me, and doing everything in his power to keep me happy and contented. This was not difficult, since he was handsome, had the advantage of the best of educations, and a background of extraordinarily prolonged travel, during which he had resided as an honored guest at the most brilliant of European Courts.

''Within a few short weeks the mere sound of his voice made me feel he was the only man to whom I could ever belong. Looking deep within his eyes—as I often did—I knew without any doubt that he was my destined partner, my soul-mate, to put it romantically.

''During the subsequent three months Kostaki continually declared his insane passion for me (lust might have been a more appropriate expression), and equally repeated his disturbing threats. But his mere presence only increased the profound revulsion I experienced when he was anywhere within sight. Even his polite manners could do nothing to soften the indescribable feeling of panic which seized me when he entered a room. And I kept noticing his peculiar *absence of a shadow* in candlelight . . .

"As for Gregor, never once during this period did he so much as hint at the word 'love.' Yet I was fully aware that should he do so, I could do nothing but reply 'Yes!' with every fiber of my being.

"At this point Kostaki abandoned his out-door life as a bandit completely, temporarily conferring his authority on one of his aides, and mooching around the castle and its precincts in moody disconsolation.

"Then the mystery deepened. Smerande, who had always shown me the utmost consideration, not to say kindness, began to reveal a passionate concern for my welfare which virtually terrified me. This was shortly followed by her openly taking sides with Kostaki, whose praises she sang at any possible opportunity. In fact she seemed to become more jealous of me than her criminal son. Of course she knew only a few words of French, but she would kiss me from time to time on the forehead, and then slowly repeat, in a repulsively gentle whisper: 'Kostaki loves Hedwig . . . '

"In the midst of this awful situation I received some frightful news which temporarily abated my growing dread of the Princess. The few of my retainers who had survived the fight with Kostaki's men had been allowed to return to Poland. Four months afterwards one of them came back to Brankovan—as he had promised he would—only to bring me news of my father's death when the enemy had razed our castle to the ground.

"Thus I remained alone in the world, with only Gregor, and the two women who waited on me, as my friends.

"Kostaki increased his attempts, and Smerande her sugary kindness. But fortunately I was in the position of being able to interpose my grief at my father's death as an impassable obstacle— at least for several weeks. But eventually both son and mother began to belabor me with their opinion that, in my present depressed and lonely state, I needed love and protection more than ever.

"During my stay at Brankovan I had discovered the incredible power of the Moldavians to hide even the slightest vestige of their true feeling. This was not hypocrisy, but a kind of natural discretion or diplomacy, sometimes utilized for purposes of cunning. But it was also utilized to prevent embarrassing the feelings of others—which, I am sure, is why Gregor never betrayed by any word, sign, or gesture, the depths of love which I knew he felt for me. Instinct alone could have led Kostaki to any sensibility of his brother's possibility as a rival; just as only an interior revelation could have informed Gregor of my endless devotion to him.

"Yet this fantastic degree of self-control began to bother me. I knew, within myself, that he loved me; yet under such circumstances how could I be certain? I was aching for definite proof. I was in the throes of an agonizing mood such as this, having only recently retired to my room for the night, when I heard a gentle tapping at the other door I have described, and which had never been unbolted. Somehow I knew that the sounds were made by a friend, so I went quietly up to it, and in a whisper inquired who was there.

"It was Gregor, whose voice had a unique quality.

" 'What is it?' I asked, nervously, yet hopefully.

" 'If you feel you can trust me, will you grant me a favor?' he asked.

" 'Yes,' I replied; 'but what is it?'

"Extinguish your candles,' he said, 'and pretend you have retired for the night. Wait for half an hour; then unbolt this door and let me in.'

" 'I have no means of knowing the time,' I answered; 'but I shall do as you say, and will draw the bolts when you knock.'

"My heart was beating insensately, for I felt some desperate situation had arisen and that he had come to warn me of danger. The time passed so slowly that it seemed like hours; but as soon as I heard the gentle tapping I withdrew the bolts. Gregor came in, closing the door silently behind him, and making it fast again without the slightest suggestion of noise.

"He remained still for a few seconds, listening carefully. Then, certain that he had not been followed, and noting my state of near-collapse, he half-carried me to a chair by the light of the moon.

" 'In the name of God,' I gasped, 'what on earth's wrong with you—and why all this secrecy?'

" 'Because your life—not to mention my own—depends on what we are about to discuss, and what you personally decide.'

"I broke out in a cold sweat, grasping his hand in fear. He raised it to his lips and kissed it, looking into my eyes with a kindly smile which begged acceptance.

" 'I love you,' he said slowly, in a voice which was soft as the cadence of a song.

" 'And I love you,' I replied.

"He sighed with joy . . .

" 'Then you will marry me?'

" 'Whenever you wish!'

" 'And you will promise to come with me wherever I may choose to take you, whatever the danger?'

" 'I promise; no matter where; no matter what the danger!'

" 'I say this,' he continued, "because we can only find peace and contentment by getting away from this castle—even from this country . . . '

"I was so excited by the idea that I exclaimed, eagerly, and in rather a loud voice 'Oh! please help me to escape from Brankovan; do get me away from here and from your brother!—he terrifies me, and so does your mother!'

" 'Be quiet!' he murmured, sharply. 'On no account must you speak above a whisper . . . '

"I felt my flesh creep as I realized what Gregor implied.

" 'Let me explain myself,' he went on: 'If I have kept my love for you to myself it was only to be sure, first of all, that you returned it; and to save us both from the devilry of Kostaki, and my mother's misled designs in his favor.

" 'I'm a rich man, Hedwig; rich in land, property, and cattle. Recently I sold to the neighboring Monastery of Hango some land, villages, and herds to the value of a million. They paid for part of the purchase in valuable jewels, a large amount in gold, and the remainder in letters of credit payable at Vienna. Do you think that will do for us?'

"I squeezed his strong hand which was resting in mine. 'Your love is sufficient for me, Gregor,' I said, affected so deeply that I could say nothing further.

" 'Excellent! Now listen carefully. Tomorrow morning I am returning to the Monastery to make final arrangements with the Superior. He will have first-class horses ready for me, fitted with saddle-bags and all we shall need. These horses will be hidden in a secluded spot very near the castle by mid-evening.

" 'After dinner you must go up to your room, as you did tonight; and, following the same routine, blow out your candles and pretend to have gone to bed. I shall knock, in the same way, at the same door, and you will let me in. But tomorrow, instead of my leaving you, you will come with me. We shall leave by a little-used side-gate, mount our horses, and by dawn we should be a good fifty miles away.'

"He kissed me long and tenderly; then disappeared as he had come, warning me to bar the door carefully.

"The night seemed interminable. I was so possessed by love, and obsessed with the thought of escape, that sleep was an impossibility. The mad ride to the castle when I had been captured had been so sinister, so harrowing, that the thought of riding off with Gregor made me tremble with delight.

"Day came at last, and I went down to the hall. But Kostaki's morning greeting seemed odd, to say the least; while his smile contained something of an unspoken threat. The Princess Smerande was her usual self; yet something made me feel distinctly uncomfortable.

"After breakfast Gregor casually told one of the servants to see that his horse was got ready. He left about an hour later, asking us not to await him for dinner that evening, since he might be delayed. He was wise enough scarcely to take any notice of me, apart from a polite excuse as he strode from the room. As for Kostaki, he seemed completely uninterested in his brother's arrangements. Yet, as the door closed behind Gregor, I detected a malign flash of hatred in his eyes which not only made me shudder, but caused me to wonder if he had guessed at anything.

"The late morning and early afternoon dragged even more slowly than the night had done. The effort of remaining cool and behaving normally, in the face of such anxiety, can easily be imagined. I stayed alone as much as I could possibly manage, tormented by the ridiculous notion that everyone in the castle could read not only my thoughts, but knew even our secret intentions:

"Luncheon was absolute hell. It was unusually chilly and formal, a macabre silence descending on everyone. The only words spoken were by Kostaki, who appeared to grumble to his mother—in Moldavian—at infrequent intervals. And some inexpressible quality in the timbre of his voice increased my fears to an almost unbearable pitch; so much so that I experienced the utmost difficulty in swallowing each mouthful.

"As I left the table to go up to my room, the Princess gave me her usual kiss, and repeated, for the first time in weeks, a phrase I detested: 'Kostaki loves Hedwig.'

"The effect was so powerful that when, exhausted, I threw myself on my bed, her words kept echoing and re-echoing in my ears with all the intensity of a vituperous curse. And it was then I remembered something Gregor had told me: 'Kostaki's love, Kostaki's kiss, meant death!'

"Gradually I fell into a deep sleep, untroubled by dreams; only to wake with a sudden start just as twilight was creeping across the sky. I could hear faint but unusual noises rising to my window, presumably from the courtyard; and since the room adjoining my own had a view of this part of the castle, I took the risk of unbolting the door and entering it.

"Hiding myself within the window embrasure I peered out. Below, I could see Kostaki, walking with determined steps across the cobbled stones towards the stables. As he entered he gave a rapid backward glance at the window of my bedroom, probably to make certain I wasn't watching. Within a few minutes he emerged with his favorite horse, already accoutered and saddled for attack. He was wearing the identical clothes in which I had seen him on the day his band attacked our party, yet carried only a single weapon—a two-edged sword, which was belted round his waist.

"A torch was flaring in one of the side-entrances, and it was through this passage that Kostaki rode quietly into the starry night—in the direction of Hango!

"My heart began to pound in an absolute paroxysm of fear. I knew within myself—by intuition, or whatever else you like to call it—that Kostaki was intent on killing Gregor. Although I was well aware that I could do nothing, I continued to watch until the horseman vanished into the darkness of the forest, which was over half a mile away.

"I stayed in the embrasure as though frozen to stone. For how long I cannot say; but it must have been at least three-quarters of an hour. Finally exhaustion rebounded on itself, and renewed energy began to arise in my body and spirit. With this resurgence came the realization that whatever news arrived, it would reach the main hall long before it reached the privacy of my bedchamber.

"Therefore I pulled myself together, miraculously assuming the calmest of attitudes, and descended earlier than expected for attendance at dinner.

"Smerande was sitting, as usual, in her fireside chair. I looked at her with some curiosity; but her serene and quiet expression revealed not a sign of nervous tension. She greeted me in friendly fashion, and then continued giving instructions for dinner to a couple of men-servants who stood near her. This gave me an opportunity to glance at the table. It was laid in the habitual manner, with the customary places set for Gregor and Kostaki. Whatever was happening, it seemed clear that the Princess knew nothing of it. Nor could I ask her, for our knowledge of each other's languages was almost useless.

"I watched the castle clock which stood in the dining hall. My fears nagged ever more incessantly with each passing minute. As the loud bell rang out for eight-thirty I found myself silently questioning whether Gregor would return.

"Just before nine, which was the time set for the meal, I heard the loud hoof-beats of a horse riding furiously into the courtyard. The Princess heard it as well, and walked towards the tall windows. But the darkness had become too intense for her to distinguish anything. Fortunately she didn't look at me, or she might have wondered at my expression—for there was only the sound of *one horse*: and, momentarily I was unable to control the look of terror which passed across my face. Heavy, dragging steps were soon heard, slowly crossing the stone flags of the ante-chamber. Within a few moments the door opened, and I could make out the dim figure of a man, not clearly visible in the candle-light. He stood there without moving, for about half a minute. My heart began to thud unbearably. Then, as he stepped forward and began walking into the lighted room, I found myself breathing a great sigh of relief.

"It was Gregor who stood before us; but haggard and gray as a corpse. One glance at him, and it became obvious that something dreadful had happened only recently.

" 'Is that you, Kostaki?' asked Smerande.

" 'No, mother—it's Gregor,' he answered, in a hoarse, unrecognizable, and toneless voice.

" 'And how long do you expect me to await you for dinner?' she snapped back at him, irritable and disappointed.

" 'But, mother,' said Gregor, 'I told you I might be late; and it's barely nine o'clock, which is our regular time for eating!'

"As he uttered these words, the loud, slow ticking of the enormous clock was drowned by nine strokes on the resounding bell.

" 'I suppose that's right enough,' she replied, with an impatient shrug of her shoulders. '—But where's your brother? He went out earlier tonight; and I can't for the life of me tell either why, or where!'

"This was the question I myself was longing to ask; and for a horrible moment I found the story of Cain and Abel flitting through my mind.

"But Gregor did not reply.

" 'Hasn't *anyone* seen Kostaki?' demanded the Princess, imperiously.

"The Steward went to make inquiries. On returning he described events very similar to those I had witnessed from the upstairs window. It was at this precise instant that my eyes met those of Gregor. Looking at his face—whether it was reality or imagination I cannot tell—I seemed to see a large drop of blood running down the whiteness of his forehead.

"Keeping my eyes fixed on his, I slowly raised a forefinger to my brow. Gregor appeared to understand; and, taking out his handkerchief, began wiping the spot, as though trying to remove dirt and sweat.

"The Princess was gazing with annoyance at the Steward. 'Continue!' she exclaimed.

" 'He must have spotted a wolf, or perhaps a fox, and chased one or the other for the fun of it. Your Highness knows what he's like when the mood's on him . . . '

" 'That's no reason why he should keep us waiting,' murmured Smerande, angrily. Then, turning to her other son, 'Gregor,' she asked, 'where did you leave your brother? Was it many miles away?'

" 'Mother,' he replied, in a quietly controlled voice, 'Kostaki and I did not go out in each other's company. If you remember correctly, I left the castle much earlier in the day.'

" 'Yes, of course, that is so,' answered the Princess. Then she moved slowly to the dining-table, took her appointed seat, signaling the remainder of us to do likewise, and ordered dinner to be served.

"Just as the first dishes were brought in from the kitchen, a diabolical noise, accompanied by a blood-curdling neighing and stamping, arose from the direction of the main gateway. Seconds later a half-crazed servant rushed in, shouting at the top of his voice:

" 'Highness! Highness!—Kostaki's favorite horse has just galloped into the yard. It's riderless, covered in blood, and is stampeding as though all hell were after it.'

" 'God in Heaven!' gasped Smerande, rising to her feet, and growing visibly pale in the candlelight; 'it was like this that his father's horse returned, about ten o'clock one evening.'

"I was told, later, that Prince Koproli's horse had come back to the castle one night, without its master, the saddle drenched in blood. An hour or two afterwards, working by torchlight, his retainers found his body on a deserted track several miles away. It had been hacked virtually into pieces.

"A half-delicious, half-paralyzing admixture of relief and shock was pouring through me. Automatically my glance reverted to Gregor. His countenance was ashen; yet he seemed to command, from unknown resources deep within his being, the most admirable self-control.

"Smerande called for torches. Taking one from an obliging servant she held it high in her right hand; and, walking rapidly through the open doors, with a majesty which had to be seen to be believed, led the way down the rough steps into the open courtyard.

"Kostaki's horse, thrashing about and neighing insanely, was being held down—as much as was possible—by eight stable-men.

The Princess walked fearlessly up to them and began to examine the poor creature. Turning from the blood-soaked saddle, she immediately noticed a wound over the animal's muzzle.

" 'My son was killed by a single man,' she said, 'and he was stabbed or cut down by a thrust from the front.—Let every available male in the castle go and search for the body!'

"Immediately there was a scurrying hither and thither. Flares were brought, and shortly every man in the place was rushing down the steep incline towards the fields or the forest. As they vanished into the distance, they gave the impression of glow-worms lighting up minute portions of hedge on a dark night in summer.

"Smerande, cold as ice, rigid as a statue, remained motionless in the gateway, directly under the portcullis. Her pale cheeks bore not the trace of a tear; yet beneath this incredible display of regal dignity it was clear that her heart was breaking with despair—for her love-child meant infinitely more to her than the child of her marriage.

"Gregor was standing at her left, and I was behind him. Momentarily he attempted to give me the support of his arm, but, with a guilty look, withdrew it.

"After staring into the darkness for at least twenty minutes, a cold wind blowing through our hair, we noticed a solitary torch make its reappearance in the far distance, just where the road turns toward the forest. One by one each individual flame commenced to show up again. But instead of being scattered here and there, as in the beginning, they now formed what can only be described as a long, narrow rectangle—as though the men holding them were marching slowly homeward in equalized double-file.

"At last we could make out the details of this bizarre procession. At its center was a hastily constructed litter, with the body of a man stretched full length along it.

"The advance continued at a snail's pace, pausing momentarily at the castle gate. We stepped aside to let the bearers pass, following them across the yard and into the main hall, where, reverently, they set the body down in a convenient space, right at the very center of the room.

"Smerande, with a superb gesture, commanded everyone to draw back as far as possible. Calmly and sadly she approached the corpse, kneeling down before it. Without any sign of a tear she parted the long strands of thick dark hair which had blown around its face, kissed its lips, and gazed tenderly, but determinedly, at the blood-soaked shirt.

"The wound was a deep one, in the right side between the ribs, and had clearly been made by a double-edged weapon. I remembered with horror that, during breakfast the same morning, I had seen in Gregor's belt a hunting-knife which could have produced exactly this kind of fatal injury. Automatically I glanced at his waist—but it was no longer there . . .

"The Princess, calling for a bowl of water, soaked her handkerchief in it and carefully washed the swollen flesh. A gush of fresh red blood seeped up, overflowing the lips of the dreadful gash.

"The atmosphere was electric, and had attained a somber and almost epic grandeur. A few years previously I had been fascinated by the poetry of the *Nibelungenlied*; and here, I felt, was the counterpart of the death of Siegfried, with Smerande playing the sublime, if sinister role, of Kriemhilde. Yet, whereas Siegfried had been a hero and a demi-god, Kostaki reflected only the composite image of robber, sadist, and demon.

"The enormous, gloomy hall, with its giant flickering shadows, the strong smell of the pine torches, the grotesque peasant faces studded with ferocious, gleaming eyes, and the dazzlingly barbaric colors of the varied garments, all served to lend a fantastic and most impressive majesty to this incredible scene—which was further heightened by the icily tragic mother, kneeling by the body of her son, yet deaf to the continual sobbing of his band of cutthroats, as she attempted to guess how long he had been dead.

"Finally Smerande kissed Kostaki lightly on the forehead; and, standing regally, at her full height, she threw back the tresses of her long, white hair, as she called deeply, in full-throated voice:

" 'Gregor!—Come to me at once!'

"Gregor shuddered visibly, stepped forward, and said obediently:

" 'Here I am, mother!'

" 'Come closer! I wish to speak to you!'

"But the nearer he approached the body, the more freely the blood trickled from the open wound.

"Fortunately the Princess was looking at Gregor, and not at the corpse; otherwise the very sight of this accusatory flow would have informed her that there was no further need to seek the murderer.

" 'Gregor,' she continued, 'I am perfectly well aware that Kostaki and you detested each other. I know equally well that, by your different fathers, you are a Waivady, and he a Koproli. But since I gave you birth, you are both Brankovans. You are a sophisticated and educated man of the Western World; Kostaki was a wild child of these beautiful and rugged mountains, which keeps us so far removed from the luxuries of civilization. Yet you remain brothers! That is an incontrovertible fact . . . '

"Here she paused, looking at him with solemnity.

" 'I would like to know, Gregor,' she went on, 'if you intend carrying your brother's body into his father's tomb without making an oath of vengeance against his murderer? I should like to know if I can trust you to play your part as the man you have always appeared to be?'

"Give me the name of the man who murdered Kostaki, mother, and I promise you that within the next twenty-four hours he shall have ceased to breathe.'

"Smerande, who was standing with all the majesty of a Queen, looked the epitome of vengeance. 'Gregor,' she said, in a deep contralto which reverberated throughout the hall, '—Gregor, that is not enough!—You must promise me that you will seek out the murderer, his brothers, his sisters, his mother, his wife, his children, killing them all with your own sword. And then you must burn and demolish the house, or houses, in which they live, leaving not a single stone to tell the tale that these people ever existed. If you fail in this, then, by Heaven, you have on your head your mother's utmost curse, together with her wish for your everlasting damnation!'

"Gregor walked over and knelt before his brother's body. Laying his hand upon the head he softly murmured, almost like a child: 'I swear it shall be done!'

"Then something terrible happened. It may have been imagination; it may have been reality—I don't know . . . But Kostaki's eyes opened and bored into mine. It was as though a ray of white-hot light had flashed between us, searing itself through my brain.

"The last remnants of my strength failed me. The room began to turn and swim, and I fainted away into oblivion.

"Returning to my senses some hours later—or so it seemed—I found myself lying on the immense fur rug which covered my bed, propped up against several pillows, with another fur rug spread over me. My two women attendants were seated by me, one at each side of the couch; and the room was lit by several candles, flickering in the slight draught from the half-open window.

"At first I could not remember where I was, or what had happened. Then, memory slowly restoring itself, I asked what the Princess was doing, and how she was. She was kneeling in prayer, they said, beside the corpse of her favorite son.

"When I inquired about Gregor, they told me he had gone to the Monastery at Hango. This was a considerable relief; for I felt that, should my suspicions finally prove correct, he was safer in that supposedly inviolable sanctuary than in the castle.

"Thinking things over I realized that escape was no longer necessary, now that Kostaki was dead. But marriage seemed an impossibility, since Gregor was almost certainly responsible for his brother's death; and however much I loved him, I could never become the wife of a murderer.

"I spent three days and nights lying on my bed, tormented by wild, fantastic dreams. Whether awake or asleep I could never banish from my vision the indescribable sight of those two burning, living eyes, set in the head of a corpse. Piercing eyes filled with malice, which followed me everywhere . . .

"Kostaki's funeral was to take place three days later. Early on that morning I was given a complete set of widow's weeds. They were sent by the Princess, who must have been half crazy, and imagined me already married to her deceased son. In a disturbed state of mind I dressed myself, descending to the ground floor. The hall, and all the other rooms, were silent and empty. But there was a Chapel in the castle; and, trembling somewhat at the thought of the ceremony, I slowly made my way to its doors.

"As I entered, Smerande, whom I hadn't seen for almost three days, came forward to greet me. Her face and hands were white as marble. Her lips had the color of darkish blue; and she was garbed from head to foot in black velvet trimmed with sable fur,

with a triple necklace of finest pearls around her neck. Her movement, as she glided towards me, was that of a statue propelled by
unseen hands.

"To my horror she kissed my forehead passionately, with lips
as cold as ice; then, in a hollow voice, which appeared to echo
from the bowels of the earth, rather than from her throat, she
uttered her deadly phrase:

" 'Kostaki *still loves* you!'

"I was dumbfounded. It would be impossible for you to grasp
the depths of shock these words produced in me: for she had said:
'Kostaki *still loves* you,' using the present tense; instead of saying,
as one might have expected 'My dear, Kostaki *did* love you . . . '

"Immediately afterwards, as she swiftly moved away, a gently
sibilant whisper vibrated in my ear—coming, apparently, from
nowhere—and quietly informing me that the world of the dead
had chosen me from the living; that I was undeniably the wife of
the murdered man, and could never marry his living brother.

"Looking round I saw nobody close enough to have murmured
these words, so extremely softly, within my hearing. One of my
women was standing about four feet away, with her back to me.
I stepped over and asked if she had heard them, or any other
sound.

" 'No,' she said; 'all has been silence since the Princess spoke to
you.'

"I was at my wits' end. A feeling of panic was creeping over
me; and my eyes, despite my will, were repeatedly attracted towards the coffin, accompanied by the thought of the living eyes
which it enclosed. The only way I can clarify my reactions is to
say that I was something like a bird, or a tiny creature, fascinated
by a serpent.

"I began to search for Gregor among the large crowd, finally
discovered him standing with his back to a pillar, as if for support.
He was pale and haggard, his eyes dull and lifeless; and I cannot
say whether or not he was aware of my presence. Respecting his
despair I approached no further . . .

"The monks of the Hango Monastery were grouped around the
funeral bier, chanting prayers according to the Greek rite, but with
a monotony which I found unbearable.

"I was longing to pray—for Gregor, for myself, for all of us. But the possibility escaped me. My mind had become numb; and I felt myself surrounded by a horde of demons, rather than being supported by the fathers of the Church.

"When the coffin was lifted by the bearers I attempted to join the procession. But my strength gave way. My legs trembled beneath me, and I grasped the doorpost for support as the scene undulated before my eyes, like something seen through a distorting lens moved up and down.

"Smerande came up to me, accompanied by Gregor, and said something in Moldavian.

" 'My mother asks me to translate what she is saying,' he said, continuing with an exact rendering of her words:

" 'You are weeping for my son, Hedwig, because you loved him. You have my thanks, just as much as if you were married in reality. From this moment on you have a country, a mother, and a permanent home. We shall together remember our dignity, and reveal ourselves faithful mourners of that wonderful man who is no longer with us . . . I am his mother—you are his true wife . . . Now, take my advice—go back to your room and rest. I shall follow my son to his tomb; and when I return I shall have overcome my sorrow. Don't worry, for I shall conquer it—I have no intention of letting it conquer me!'

"My only reply was a prolonged, but irrepressible moaning sound, for self-control had almost entirely deserted me.

"I left the Chapel and climbed the long staircase to my room; where, from the window, I watched the slow procession make its way round the distant bend of the road towards the Hango Monastery—for it was in these precincts that the tombs and vaults of the Brankovans and Waivady were situated.

"By this time November was nearing its end, and the days were short and cold. By five, at the latest, it was almost dark. At seven I noticed torches in the distance, indicating the return of the mourners. Everything, thank God, was over, and Kostaki was lying for ever in the tomb of his fathers.

"Worn out by the emotions and tensions of the day, I felt more distressed than ever before. One after another I heard the hours booming from the enormous bell in the clock-tower of the castle. I have already told you of the strange, obsessive fancies which possessed my mind since that fatal evening and of those closed eyes which suddenly reopened and fixed themselves piercingly on mine.

"Just as eight forty-five was striking I began to shiver, and an extraordinary sense of horror permeated my entire body, seeming to paralyze every muscle, every conscious intention. Accompanying this was an enfeebling sense of drowsiness such as is occasionally produced by a strong sleeping-draught, or a drug prescribed by an over-zealous physician. I felt heavy and weak, and sitting on the edge of my bed I fell backwards in a half-fainting state. Yet I retained sufficient consciousness to hear a slow and heavy foot-step approaching the door of my room. After that I heard nothing more, not even the opening of the door—if ever it *did* open! Yet, before fainting into complete oblivion, I felt a sharp stab of pain at one side of my naked throat. I attempted, unsuccessfully, to open my eyes; but then passed into that state where one knows nothing more . . .

"I awoke just before midnight, and finding my candles still burning attempted to get up. But my general weakness was so great that several agonizing attempts were necessary before I succeeded in being able to stand on my feet, however unstably. There was a tender, painful, prickly feeling in my throat, followed immediately by the horrible memory of what had happened just before I lost consciousness.

"With some effort I slowly dragged myself to the long mirror on the wall opposite my bed; and, holding a candle close, examined my neck. A puncture, somewhat larger than a pin prick, was apparent over the carotid artery, and a trickle of blood was still flowing from it. Not being able to explain such a wound I took it for granted that some local insect, probably of the larger variety, had bitten me during my sleep.

"Still feeling as weak as some convalescent after a serious illness I crawled back to bed; and exhausted with worry and fatigue was soon asleep again. But my dreams were unwholesome, and of such a kind that I would prefer not to describe them.

"Next day I awoke at the usual time, attempting to jump out of bed in my habitual manner. The effort however, failed. I was absolutely without strength or energy, and weak as a kitten whose mother has failed to feed it. I glanced across at the mirror, and was dumbfounded at the ghastly whiteness of my features. So, unable to do anything, I simply lay back and tried to relax.

"The hours passed like interminable centuries. Alternately I dozed and then returned to awareness of my surroundings. But it was not until evening that my women appeared, explaining that the Princess felt it was best for me to be left undisturbed for a day. With them they brought my supply of candles for the night; but I asked for several more candelabra, dreading the gloomy shadows of the long, dark hours. These kindly middle-aged creatures offered to stay with me. Yet I refused their company, preferring silence to the exhausting strain of sympathetic chatter in a language of which I could understand barely fifty words.

"The minutes dragged on. Then, at the same time as on the previous night, I experienced the identical nervous and physical sensations of panic-terror and near-paralysis. Once again I attempted to rise and call for help. But I couldn't get even as far as the door. Remotely, in the background, as though muffled by heavy curtains, I could hear the sound of a bell striking the hour of quarter-to-nine. Stepping rapidly backwards, because the faculty of hearing had failed me, I collapsed on my bed. My eyes closed automatically; and the only thing I remember after this moment is that I felt something bite viciously at my throat. Then the pain was succeeded by utter blackness.

"Once more I came to my senses near midnight. But I was weaker, and even whiter than before.

"The next morning, disturbed beyond measure, and almost unable to stand, I decided to go down to Smerande and explain my situation. Just at that instant one of my women came in and announced Gregor, who entered the room almost immediately.

"I attempted to rise from the high-backed chair in which I had managed, with some difficulty, to seat myself. But it was impossible. The effort was beyond endurance . . .

"Gregor, who was still haggard, gasped at my appearance, and rushed forward to help me.

" 'What on earth has happened to you?' he asked, an anxious tremor manifesting in his voice, which was normally deep, strong, masculine, and calculated.

" 'I might ask you the same question,' I replied, 'especially since the murder of your brother, however much I detested him!'

" 'I have come to say good-bye,' he said. 'The events of the past few days have given me time to think very carefully, and I have decided to leave a world which would be meaningless without your love and your presence. The only alternative is that I should join the Monks at Hango, and occupy a cell in the Monastery there . . .'

" 'Under the circumstances,' I replied, 'I'm afraid we must part. Nevertheless, I still love you more than any words can express . . . But, after what has happened, such a love can only be criminal in its associations.'

" 'I understand, my dear,' he said. 'Yet I beg that you will pray for me day by day for the remainder of your life—even though we never meet again.'

" 'I couldn't do anything else,' I replied, 'since your memory will remain with me every minute of my life. But I'm afraid that from now my hours are numbered . . .'

"A look of incomprehensive horror crossed his face.

" 'What do you mean?' he gasped; 'and why are you so pale?— your skin is the color of ivory!'

" 'Perhaps God is taking care of me, and releasing me from this terrible situation,' I replied.

"Gregor came close to me, and kneeling by my chair took my hand in his own. I hadn't the strength to resist. Then, looking me straight in the eyes he said:

" 'This bloodlessness isn't natural, Hedwig! You haven't been ill . . . Tell me, for God's sake, what's behind it all! I have my suspicions; but I want to hear from your own lips exactly what has been happening during the past few days.'

"The atmosphere suddenly became electric. I scarcely knew where to begin, or what to say.

" 'If I even tried to explain, Gregor,' I said, 'you'd think me absolutely insane. To be quite honest, I've even thought so myself!'

" 'You must tell me, Hedwig,' he replied, in a voice which betrayed unusual trepidation.

"His anxiety frightened me even more than the events of the past few days. I began to suspect that I might be drugged, or even poisoned.

" 'Hedwig,' he exclaimed again, 'you *must* tell me! You don't realize the truth! You are living in a country very different from any other country in the world—and, what is more, in the midst of a family which is so fantastic that it's unlike any other group of people you've ever met!'

"Trusting Gregor, and fearing for my safety, I told him, in detail, of the strange physical sensations, the odd coldness, the inexplicable attacks of unconsciousness I experienced at precisely the hour when Kostaki must have been killed. I told him about the slow, dragging footsteps, and how I had sometimes heard the bolted door opening, just as I lost grip of my awareness. Above all I explained the bite in my throat, and the increasing weakness, day by day, as I showed him the punctures.

"He listened intently; but even after I had finished remained silent for a while. A new fear caused my heart to palpitate rapidly. What if he was thinking I was mad, and ready for the asylum? I grasped the arms of my chair to support myself.

" 'You tell me,' he said, 'that you fall asleep, or faint, every night at quarter-to-nine?'

" 'Yes,' I replied. 'And no effort I make can prevent what happens.'

" 'And sometimes you can hear the creaking of the door as it opens?'

" 'Yes!—But that must be imagination, because it is always securely bolted . . . '

" 'Then you feel a bite, or a stabbing pain in your neck?

" 'Let me look at your throat again,' he asked.

"I bent my head slightly backwards, slightly to one side, so that he could see more clearly. He bent very close, giving an involuntary gasp, followed by a subdued exclamation of: 'My God!' Then he lapsed into another brief silence, a look of anguish passing across his features.

" 'Hedwig,' he said firmly, 'can you really trust me?'

" 'How can you possibly doubt it?' I murmured, feeling irritated that such a thought could enter his head.

" 'Will you believe what I am going to tell you?'

" 'I can never disbelieve a word you speak, Gregor!'

" 'What I have to say, then, is this: Unless you agree to follow my instructions from now onwards, implicitly, and to the very letter, you will not live even for a week—and we must begin immediately!'

" 'I'll agree to anything you ask of me—anything!'

" 'Good!—Then perhaps we'll manage to save you.'

" 'Only perhaps?'

"He refused, however, to answer, a grim expression furrowing his brow.

" 'No matter what happens, Gregor, no matter how difficult it may be, I'll do whatever you tell me . . . '

" 'Then listen carefully,' he said; 'and don't let terror overcome you.'

"With this he looked deeply into my eyes, with a love that seemed to infuse me with immensely new strength.

" 'In your country, as in ours,' he continued, 'there are several unpleasant beliefs. I refer to one in particular . . . '

"My skin went icy, and felt like goose-flesh, for I instinctively knew the belief to which he was making reference. He realized this, for he said:

" 'I see that you understand what I mean!'

" 'Yes,' I replied; 'in Poland I remember seeing people who suffered this damnable curse.'

" 'And you are speaking of the vampire?'

" 'Yes! During childhood I was exposed to the most harrowing sight I've ever seen in my life.'

" 'What happened?'

" 'It was in a village cemetery on land belonging to my father. More than forty of our peasants had died within three weeks, quite inexplicably. No disease, no cause of death could be found. Owing to general dissatisfaction over these events the bodies were shortly exhumed for further examination. Seventeen revealed every sign of being vampires. Their bodies were as fresh, even as warm as in life. In fact they looked as though they were still living, apart from the absolute stillness in which they lay. The other bodies, apparently, had been their victims. And, as you know, the victim of a vampire frequently becomes one himself; though this is sometimes disputed. Anyway, I saw all this, because I accompanied my father; and it is a sight I shall never forget.'

" 'Can you tell me what method was used to save the countryside from this epidemic?'

" 'A wooden stake, sharp-pointed, was hammered through their hearts at a crossroad; and the bodies were burned on an enormous funeral pyre.'

" 'That is the most usual method,' said Gregor. 'But I doubt if it will be enough in the present situation.'

" 'Gregor, you're terrifying me!' I exclaimed.

" 'I've already told you that fear is your worst enemy,' he said. 'Conquer that, and half the battle is already won!

" 'Now listen carefully,' he continued. 'I don't know who, or what, is attacking you. But I have my suspicions. Did you ever notice anything peculiar about Kostaki?'

" 'Yes,' I replied. 'On at least two occasions he seemed to cast no shadow in bright light, while everyone else did! And on another occasion—although it may have been imagination on my part—he came into this room to ask if my women were sufficiently attentive. He was standing with his back to that mirror, and I could swear that his image was not reflected in it!'

" 'I have suspected this possibility for a long time,' Gregor said. 'I do not know if my mother is aware of it; but she loved him so much she would keep silent in any case.'

"He lapsed into thought for a moment, and then continued:

" 'Before God, whether it's my brother or not, I'm going to put an end to this! But you must give me your word of honor that you'll faithfully carry out every instruction I give you, no matter how unusual it seems . . . '

"With an extreme effort I hoarsely whispered: 'Yes!'

" 'You must overcome your terror, Hedwig,' he said; 'that is absolutely necessary. If *it* overcomes you, than all is lost . . . Now tonight, at seven, you must come alone to the castle Chapel. I shall be waiting for you, and we shall be married according to the rites of the Church.'

"I nodded my assent. But I couldn't resist exclaiming: 'Gregor, if it *is* Kostaki, surely he'll try to kill you!'

" 'Don't worry, Hedwig,' he said, in the softest of voices; 'all will be well. You only have to do what I tell you . . . '

"With this he rose to his feet, and wishing me good courage left the room.

"Fifteen minutes later I heard the sound of horse's hooves leaving the courtyard; and crawling to my window I saw a rider galloping furiously towards Hango. It was Gregor. Immediately he disappeared behind the trees I fell to my knees, and prayed as profoundly and fervently as I had ever prayed in my entire life. Then I lay down on my bed, sleeping now and again, waiting in a half-dazed state for seven o'clock to sound. Thus I remained, arising only with the first stroke of the hour.

"Looking at myself in the mirror I threw a long black gauze veil over my head to conceal the ivory pallor of my skin. The journey to the Chapel was slow and painfully difficult because of my weakness. Fortunately, however, I got there without meeting either the Princess or any of her domestics. Gregor was waiting for me, accompanied by the Superior of the Hango Monastery.

"At his side he wore an historic sword, a family heirloom which had come down to him from an ancestor who accompanied Villehardouin at the Crusades. It had been blessed, he told me, by a saintly old priest, centuries previously.

" 'My dear,' he said, grasping the hilt with his right hand, 'here is a weapon which can successfully avert the misfortune threatening you.'

"One after the other, contritely, we made our confessions. Then the marriage ceremony commenced.

"I cannot remember a more simple or moving wedding. There were only the three of us present. The priest himself placed the bridal crowns on our heads, and handed the ring to Gregor. Indeed there was only one sad aspect about it, and that was the fact that all of us were still dressed in mourning.

"Finally we were both given a lighted candle, which were instructed to hold as we knelt before the altar. Then Father Basil pronounced us man and wife, following this declaration with his own special blessing to bring us safely through what might follow:

" 'Now, my children you are joined in Holy Matrimony, and I pray God Almighty to bring you all the courage and fortitude you may need in overcoming the evil which surrounds you. Eternal justice is on your side; therefore go forth into the world in peace, with the Lord's every blessing to speed and protect you both . . . '

"He handed us the Bible to kiss, made the sign of the cross over us, and slowly and quietly left the Chapel.

"I leaned on Gregor's arm. We embraced; and with this contact new and vigorous life seemed to pour through me.

" 'Now all will be well, Hedwig,' he said.

"But an unexpected doubt crossed my mind, like a dark cloud: 'Won't Smerande be driven to frenzy when she discovers we're married?—She still, in her meandering state, thinks of me as Kostaki's wife!'

"Just then the castle bell tolled the hour of eight-thirty.

" 'She'll miss you at dinner,' I added. 'Besides, she might take it into her head to come and visit me in my room . . .

" 'That's not likely,' he answered. 'She hasn't left her own apartment since the burial . . . What little she eats is taken up to her there.'

"These words gave me some relief. Perhaps we could escape before any discovery was made; for I dreaded the wrath of the Princess of Brankovan. But Gregor broke into my thoughts again.

" 'Now,' he continued, 'you are to keep your promise, following my instructions exactly. But you have a choice in what to do . . . You can retire to your bed, allowing yourself to sink into the unnatural sleep you have described. Or, by sheer effort of will, you can force yourself to stay awake, watching the horror that follows. I shall be with you throughout, concealed in a suitable corner of the room.

" 'I shall stay awake,' I said; 'I want to solve the mystery and see what happens.'

"Gregor then took from his purse, which hung from the belt at his waist, a little sprig of box-tree, still damp with the holy-water with which the priest had consecrated it. Handing it to me he explained its purpose.

" 'Keep this sprig in your hand,' he said, 'never letting go of it for even a second. Hold it tightly! Now lie down on your couch. Repeat your usual prayers, asking protection for the night. Above all, keep fear from your mind, because with this holy box-wood you can hold even demons at bay. Finally, and this is very important, do not scream or make a noise of any kind. Just pray, and continue praying.'

"We ascended the stairs softly, entering my room and closely bolting the door. I lay on my bed in a half-seated position, reclining against an arrangement of enormous cushions, and clutching the precious twig to my bosom. Gregor disappeared behind the gigantic, heavily carved high-backed chair, which stood diagonally across a corner of the room, throwing it into deep shadow.

"Counting the minutes in an almost breathless state, I waited for the bell to strike the hour of eight forty-five. No sooner did I hear it than I felt the same strange sleepiness; the same cold chill of terror, creeping up from the base of my spine to the crown of my head. But I held the blessed box-leaves close to my heart and felt refreshed.

"A minute passed and I could hear the slow, heavy footsteps, coming closer and closer to my door. It opened gradually, without noise of any sort, as though operated by some hidden machine.

"Then, inexplicably, as though he had appeared from thinnest air, Kostaki was standing on the threshold . . .

"His long, black, shoulder-length hair fell lankly around his neck. It was dripping with blood. He was pale as a corpse; yet somehow living, somehow moving. He wore his customary dress, but the tunic was open at the front, and showed the gaping wound in his chest—which was still bleeding . . . There was no doubt but that this was a man from the tomb, because even his movements seemed those of an automaton; and the stench of the graveyard filled the room with its vile smell. Only the eyes—those piercing, burning eyes—were truly alive. Kostaki had come back, and *I* was his prey!

"It may seem peculiar, but instead of falling into panic at this unbelievable sight, I felt a distinct upsurge of strength and divine protection. Perhaps it was because I knew that Gregor was in the room with me. Perhaps it was the blessed sprig I grasped with such faith and trust. Perhaps both . . .

"The figure of the 'living-dead' took three slow and calculated steps towards my bed. I stared deep into its burning eyes, which were fixed on me with hypnotic and demoniac intent. At the same time I made the sign of the cross with the spray of leaves I held in my right hand.

"The evil creature hesitated and stopped, groaning deeply as an omnipotent power came between us.

"I rose to my feet; yet I could not withdraw my eyes from the unflinching gaze. This was, indeed, fortunate, since it kept his attention fixed while Gregor silently emerged from his hiding place, drawn sword in hand. Slowly he walked forward, the tip of his blade threatening the vampire. With his free hand he made the sign of the cross . . .

"Instantly Kostaki was aware of the presence of his brother. He drew his own sword and struck with all his force. But scarcely had steel struck steel than the dead bandit's blade splintered into several pieces, falling noiselessly as they scattered themselves over the thick fur rugs covering the floor. The dead man's arm dropped to his side, paralyzed, as he heaved an enormous sigh, pregnant with viciousness and loathing.

" 'What do you want, Gregor?' he asked his brother.

" 'I command you, in the name of the Living God, to answer my questions,' replied my husband.

" 'Circumstances oblige me to,' answered Kostaki; —continue!'

" 'On the evening I was at Hango, did I lie in ambush for you?'

" 'No, you did not!'

" 'Did I threaten, or attack you in any way whatsoever?'

" 'No!'

"The pestiferous odor of death and decay grew stronger as Gregor approached his brother face to face, demanding, in a resounding voice:

" 'Did I attempt to strike you with either sword or dagger?'

" 'No! You never made any attempt to strike or hurt me.'

" 'You are perfectly well aware as to what happened, Kostaki,' continued my husband. 'You lay in ambush for me!—and in your uncontrollable rage and jealousy you rushed out, tripping over a small projecting rock, and falling heavily on the point of my sword, which I was holding forward only for self-protection. I made no step towards you—in fact I tried to lower my weapon— but too late . . . Thus, in the eyes of God, as of men, I am innocent of the crime of murder. For these reasons your haunting is not that of a murdered soul seeking retribution, but of the accursed dead who feed on the blood of the living, infecting them with their own damnable vampirism! I command you, in the name of all that is holy, to return to your tomb, to remain there evermore; and may you rest at peace, in the name of the Lord.'

"At these words the living corpse replied, in a voice trembling with fury:

" 'Yes, Gregor, I shall return to my tomb—but only with this woman!'

"And as he uttered them I could see him doing his best, but unsuccessfully, to move a few steps nearer me.

" 'You shall go alone!' yelled Gregor: 'Hedwig is my wife!'

"As he said this he extended the point of his consecrated blade, so that it touched the open wound in his brother's chest. Kostaki shrieked, as though the raw flesh were being drenched with boiling oil. Then, once more like an automaton, he took several paces backward.

"Gregor advanced firmly, keeping time with the almost mechanical steps; his eyes remaining fixedly on those of the dead man; his sword still pointing at the half-naked breast.

"There was something indescribably horrible, something beastly and nauseating about this candle-lit scene. Both men were breathing deeply; both unbelievably pale. Yet, slowly but surely, Gregor was succeeding in forcing his brother's animated corpse to forsake the castle, causing it to move, however unwillingly, in the direction of the funeral vault which was now its permanent home . . . And it was moving *backwards*, as a man moves away from the altar in a Church . . .

"At this point I noticed, for the third time, Kostaki's complete inability to reflect a shadow. Gregor's, however, was outlined in gigantic proportions on the smooth stone of the walls—because, in our haste, we had set the two candelabra on low stools near the bed.

"Still on my feet, I felt movement creeping back into my body, and followed directly behind my husband.

"We passed along the gallery, and down the great staircase, still lit by guttering torches held in the hands of the curiously-human iron arms. All this while I was terrified that Smerande might appear. Just as we entered the hall a servant, crossing it, stopped dead in his tracks, dropped his candle, and stood gibbering like an idiot . . . We proceeded, at the same slow pace, over the courtyard and through the gates; Kostaki ever walking backward, and Gregor continually holding his sword, point forward.

"Not being on horseback we were able to take a shortcut to Hango. This took us just over an hour and a half. But the dead man *must* be got back to his tomb. That was vitally important. The darkness, as we passed through wood and copse, was profound. The moon was shrouded; yet by some strange power we could actually see. And we could see, too, Kostaki's eyes, which burned like glowing lamps in the blackness.

"At last we reached Hango and passed into the Monastery cemetery. That night, for some unknown reason, I found myself possessed of knowledge I had never previously had; of the exact appearance and location of places I had never seen. I cannot explain this. It just happened.

"For example, no sooner were we within the precincts, than I recognized the entrance to Kostaki's vault. When we reached it the door was open, and Gregor stopped. I remained standing behind him.

" 'Kostaki,' he said, 'if you repent and return to your tomb, promising never to leave it again, the powers of goodness will forgive you, and you will escape the damnation which you know must eventually overtake you.'

" 'I do not repent!' Kostaki shouted, trembling with unsurpassed rage.

"Twice Gregor repeated his request; and twice it was refused.

" 'Then call the devil to your assistance,' he replied, 'as I shall call God to mine! We shall see which shall conquer the other!'

"Kostaki still held the broken half of his sword in his right hand, and with two ear-piercing roars both men closed together in desperate combat.

"The fight can't have lasted more than thirty seconds or thereabouts. Yet it seemed an eternity . . .

"Then Kostaki fell on his back, the remnants of his sword shattered from his grip. Within a split second Gregor was standing astride him. I saw the holy blade raised in the air, watching in a delirium of relief and terror as it plunged down and straight through his heart, nailing him to the earth just beside the open doorway. There was an inhuman, blood-chilling shriek—then utter silence . . .

"Just as Gregor staggered, weak and shaken, to a nearby gravestone, using it as a support, the moon emerged from a veil of smoky cloud.

"Rushing forward I put my arms around him, kissing him fervently, my heart thudding like a drum.

" 'Are you hurt?' I asked, in desperation.

" 'No, Hedwig,' he replied; 'I'm not physically wounded. But in a struggle such as this the life-force is depleted. That is where the danger lies . . . '

" 'For God's sake,' I cried, 'let's get into the Monastery—there, at least, we shall be safe, and you can recover your strength before we leave this country for ever!'

" 'No, my dear,' he said quietly; 'there isn't time! And you must continue to follow my instructions immediately. Take in your hand a little soil mixed with the blood from my brother's wound. Then smear it over the bites he inflicted on your neck. This is the only certain means of protecting yourself against any remaining power he may have.'

"Almost stupefied with horror I did as he commanded. Kneeling by the body I could just make out a stream of thick, dark blood, slowly seeping into the earth. Mixing it into a small quantity of paste I rubbed it into the wounds on my throat.

"Gregor turned to me, his face lit by compassion, but his voice weak as that of a dying man:

" 'Hedwig,' he said, 'listen carefully to my last requirement. You are to leave this country at the earliest possible moment. Father Basil has my instructions, and he will help you in every way. Go to him now . . . But first, give me your final kiss and blessing.'

"As I kissed him he fell dead in my arms. I sank to my knees with the weight of his strong, muscular body; released my hold, and then literally ran to the door of the Monastery. Where I received the strength to do this I do not know, but God—and Gregor's prayers—must have been on my side.

"In desperation I clutched at the ring-shaped hammer of the enormous gargoyle-like knocker, and was just about to expend the last ounces of my energy in beating it, when the door opened as of its own accord. Within stood Father Basil, surrounded by a nimbus of light cast by many votary candles some distance behind him.

" 'Come in, my child,' he said, leading me to a welcome seat not far from the entrance.

" 'You must understand, Hedwig,' he continued, 'that those of us who lead a contemplative life, are sometimes aware of what is happening at the precise moment of their occurrence. I know what has just taken place, and we shall help you.'

"He called a dozen of the brothers together, each bearing a flaming torch; and two by two, led by father Basil, we returned to the open vault, the monks chanting the Mass for the dead.

"I looked down at Kostaki, whose face was contorted by a threatening leer—the evidence of his final agony. Gregor lay close by; yet his features were calm and peaceful, almost smiling, as in sleep.

"My husband had given instructions to the priest—should the worst happen—as to what was to be done. Thus the two brothers were laid to rest, side by side, in the same vault. Gregor, God's servant as it were, keeping watch over Kostaki, Satan's minion. This was done especially for my safety.

"Immediately the ceremony was over a message was sent, post haste, to the castle. The Princess Smerande arrived at the Monastery about two hours later, having traveled by the usual route in a small coach. I told her the sinister details of Kostaki's nightly visits to my bedroom; and, together with Father Basil, all the events of the night which had just passed.

"To my surprise she listened to all these fantastic details without any evidence of shock or disbelief. It was obvious, however, that she had lost her evil, almost insane obsession with Kostaki, and had once again become the same charming woman I had met on the evening of my arrival at the castle. Though she retained, understandably enough, the marks of grief in her features, and the indelible look of tragedy in her eyes.

"She gazed silently at me for a few seconds, and then said, in the gentlest of voices:

" 'Hedwig, you have just told me an exceptional story. Yet it remains the simple truth. The Brankovan family have been under a curse during four generations, because one of us once killed a priest. The curse, however, has now expired; since, though married to my son Gregor, you remain a virgin. And, as for me, I am the last of my line.

" 'Your husband, I am told, has left you a million. Take it, and God bless you. Moreover, when I am no longer here, I leave you my fortune, apart from a few legacies to the poor, and to this Monastery.

" 'It is vitally important that you should obey Gregor's instructions immediately, leaving this country early tomorrow. I should advise France as being one of the most suitable places for your welfare and safety.

" 'Do not worry about me, since I am self-sufficient, and need no one to help me. Forget me, and accept my heart-felt good-byes. My future is concerned only with God . . . '

"Then she kissed me on the forehead, as on the day she had welcomed me; and with admirable dignity took her leave, returning to Brankovan, where I am told she became a recluse in her enormous bed-chamber.

"The next day I commenced the long journey to France, where I have lived ever since.

"As Gregor had prayed, the hauntings ceased completely; and within a few months health and vigor returned. The only remaining sign of my terrible adventure being the ivory color of my skin—which, apparently, endures throughout life with every man or woman who has suffered the bite of a human vampire . . ."

With these words the mysterious creature lapsed into her usual silence, sinking back on her cushions with every sign of fatigue; for the narration had been lengthy.

Monsieur Ledru handed her a brandy, which she accepted gratefully. Just at that moment midnight sounded. The night had become sultry; a thunderstorm threatened; and I don't think there was a single guest who didn't feel the suggestion of a shiver tingling up his spine.

It was time to leave, and, one by one we paid our respects, thanking our host for his food, his excellent wine, and his unusual entertainment. . . .

As for myself, I never returned to Fontenay; nor did I ever come across the pale lady from the Carpathians again. It seems that she never frequented Parisian society.

Baudelaire

The Metamorphoses of a Vampire

(Translated by George Dillon)

——⊰●⊱——

"Les Métamorphoses du Vampire" ("The Metamorphoses of a Vampire") was originally included in Baudelaire's 1857 masterpiece, *Les Fleurs du Mal* (*Flowers of Evil*). Deemed as too offensive for publication, the French courts confiscated the first edition of the book, and Baudelaire was convicted of and fined for obscenity. The authorities allowed the book to be published after six poems were removed; the ban on these poems stood until 1949. This is one of them.

Meanwhile, from her red mouth the woman, in husky tones,
Twisting her body like a serpent upon hot stones
And straining her white breasts from their imprisonment,
Let fall these words, as potent as a heavy scent:
"My lips are moist and yielding, and I know the way
To keep the antique demon of remorse at bay.
All sorrows die upon my bosom. I can make
Old men laugh happily as children for my sake.
For him who sees me naked in my tresses, I
Replace the sun, the moon, and all the stars of the sky!
Believe me, learned sir, I am so deeply skilled

That when I wind a lover in my soft arms, and yield
My breasts like two ripe fruits for his devouring—both
Shy and voluptuous, insatiable and loath—
Upon this bed that groans and sighs luxuriously
Even the impotent angels would be damned for me!"

When she had drained me of my very marrow, and cold
And weak, I turned to give her one more kiss—behold,
There at my side was nothing but a hideous
Putrescent thing, all faceless and exuding pus.
I closed my eyes and mercifully swooned till day:
And when I looked at morning for that beast of prey
Who seemed to have replenished her arteries from my own
The wan, disjointed fragments of a skeleton
Wagged up and down in a new posture where she had lain
Rattling with each convulsion like a weathervane
Or an old sign that creaks upon its bracket, right
Mournfully in the wind upon a winter's night.

Conrad Aiken

EXCERPT FROM

THE DIVINE PILGRIM

—————>●<—————

Conrad Aiken won a Pulitzer Prize for his poetry in 1930 and the National Medal for Literature in 1969. While he is best remembered for his poetry, he also wrote novels, short stories, and literary criticism. He was born in Savannah, Georgia, and his father killed his mother and then committed suicide when he was ten years old. Aiken went on to graduate from Harvard the same year as T. S. Eliot, and later became a leading figure in the imagist and symbolist poetry movement. His poetry collections include *The House of Dust, Sheepfold Hills, The Morning Song of Lord Zero,* and *A Seizure of Limericks.* The following excerpt was originally published in 1916 as a part of *The Jig of Forslin: A Symphony.* Aiken later combined this with other "symphonies" and published them in 1949 as *The Divine Pilgrim: A Symphony.* The entire work runs in excess of 250 pages, but this section alone deals with vampires. In his preface, Aiken says, "The vampire narrative . . . is a free adaptation of the story of [Théophile] Gauntier—*La Morte Amoureuse* [*The Dead Lover*]." When he wrote the "program" for this "symphony," he titled this section, "The Belle Morte," which means "The Dead Woman."

Midnight it was, or just before;
And as I dipt for the hundredth time

The small white quill to add a rhyme
To the cold page, in candlelight,
Whereon my treatise slowly grew,—
Someone harshly knocked at the door;
And marvelling I became aware
That with that knock the entire night
Went mad; a sudden tempest blew;
And shrieking goblins rode the air.

Alarmed, not knowing why, I rose
And dropt my quill across the page.
What demon now, what archimage,
So roiled the dark? And my blood froze
When through the keyhole, with the wind,
A freezing whisper, strangely thinned,
Called my name out, called it twice . . .
My heart lay still, lay black as ice.
The candle trembled in my hands;
Between my fingers the dim light went;
Shadows hurried and shrank and blent,
Huddled, grotesque, in sarabands,
Amazed my eyes, till dumb I stood,
And seemed to see upon that air
Goblins with serpents in their hair,
Mouths contorted for soundless cries,
And hands like claws, and wounded throats,
And winking embers instead of eyes.
The blood went backward to my heart.
Thrice in the night a horn was blown.
And then it seemed that I had known,
For ages, even before my birth,
When I was out with wind and fire,
And had not bargained yet with earth,
That this same night the horn would blow
To call me forth. And I would go.
And so, as haunted dead might do,
I drew the bolt and dropped the chain,
And stood in dream, and only knew
The door had opened and closed again:

Until between my eyelids came
A woman's face, a sheath of flame,
The wink of opals in dusky hair,
And eyes that seemed to burn the air
So luminous were they with desire.
She laid one hand upon my arm
And straight a blaze was in my veins,
It pierced me so I feared a charm,
And shrank; whereat, pale hurriedly,
She whispered "Quickly! Come with me!
And shall be clear! But now make haste—
Four hours till dawn, no time to waste!"—
The amazing whiteness of her skin
Had snared my eyes, and now her voice
Seethed in my ears, and a ghost of sin
Died, and above it I heard rejoice
Loud violins, in chords ascending,
And laughter of virgins; I blew the light,
And followed her, heedless of the ending,
Into the carnival of that night.

(Make haste, beloved! the night passes,
The day breaks, the cock crows,
Mist slinks away in the sunlight,
And the thin blood drips from the rose.)

Black stallions rushed us through the air,
Their hooves upon the wind struck fire;
Rivers, and hills, and a moonlit spire
Glided beneath us, and then a flare
Of gusty torches beckoned us down
To a palace-gate in a darkened town.
She took my hand and led me in
Through walls of basalt and walls of jade,
And I wondered, to hear a violin
Sweetly within that marble played.
I heard it sing, a wandering tone,
Imprisoned forever in that deep stone.

*   *   *

And then upon a couch we lay,
And heard invisible spirits play
A ghostly music; the candles muttered,
Rose-leaves trembled upon the floor,
Lay still, or rose on the air and fluttered;
And while the moon went dwindling down
Poisoning with black web the skies,
She narrowed her eyelids, and fixed her eyes,
Fiercely upon me; and searched me so
With speeding fire in every shred
That I, consumed with a witching glow,
Knew scarcely if I were alive or dead:
But lay upon her breast, and kissed
The deep red mouth, and drank the breath,
And heard it gasping, how it hissed
To mimic the ecstasy of death.
Above us in a censer burning
Was dust of lotos-flowers, and there
Ghosts of smoke were ever turning,
And gliding along the sleepy air,
And reaching hands, and showing faces,
Or coiling slowly like blue snakes,
To charm us moveless in our places . . .
But then she softly raised her head
And smiled through brooding eyes, and said
"O lover, I have seen you twice.
You changed my veins to veins of ice.
The first time, it was Easter Eve,—
By the church door you stood alone;
You listened to the priests intone
In pallid voices, mournfully;
The second time you passed by me
In the dusk, but did not see . . ."
Her whisper hissed through every vein
And flowered coldly in my brain . . .

I slept, how long I do not know;
But in my sleep saw huge lights flare,
And felt a rushing of wild air,

And heard great walls rock to and fro . . .
Make haste, beloved! The cock crows,
And the cold blood drips from the rose . . .

. . . And then I woke in my own room,
And saw the first pale creep of sun
Drip through the dewed shutters, and run
Across the floor, and in that gloom
Marvelled to find that I had slept
In robe and sandals, and had kept
One bruised white rose-leaf in my hand—
From whom?—and could not understand.

For seven days my quill I dipt
To wreathe my filigrees of script:
For seven nights, when midnight came,
I swooned, I swept away on flame,
Flew on the stallions of the air,
Heard goblins laugh, saw torches flare,
And all night long, while music mourned,
Hidden under the vibrant floor,
I heard the insidious voice implore,
As one who speaks from under the earth,
Imploring music, imploring mirth,
Before the allotted time was done
And cock crew up the sullen sun.
Day by day my face grew pale,
Hollowed and purple were my eyes,
I blinked beneath too brilliant skies:
And sometimes my weak hand would fail,
Blotting the page whereon I wrought . . .
This woman is a witch! I thought . . .
And I resolved that night to find
If this were real, or in my mind.

Viol and flute and violin
Remote through labyrinths complained.
Her hand was foam upon my skin.
And then I closed my eyes and feigned
A sudden sleep; whereat her eyes

Peered, and darkened, and opened wide,
Her white brow flushed, and by my side
Laughing, with little ecstatic cries,
She kissed my mouth, she stroked my hair
And fed upon me with fevered stare.
"One little drop!" she murmured then—
"One little bubble from this red vein,
And safe I await the sun again—"

I heard my heart hiss loud and slow;
A gust of wind through the curtains came;
It flapped the upright candle-flame.
Her famishing eyes began to glow,
She bared my arm; with a golden pin,
Leaned and tenderly pricked the skin.
And as the small red bubble rose,
Her eyes grew bright with an evil light,
She fawned upon me; and my heart froze
Seeing her teeth so sharp and white.

Vampire! I cried. The flame puffed out.
Two blazing eyes withdrew from me.
The music tore discordantly.
The darkness swarmed with a goblin rout.
Great horns shattered, and walls were falling,
Green eyes glowed, voices were calling;
Stars above me paled in the sky,
Far off I heard one mournful cry—
Or under the earth—and then I found
I lay alone on leafy ground.
And when stars died, and the cock crowed,
The first pale gleam of sunlight showed
That it was on a grave I lay,
A new-made grave of sodden clay.

That night I took a priest with me;
And sharp at midnight, secretly,
By lantern-light, with spade and pick,
Striking on stones with metal click,
We laid a golden coffin bare,

And sprinkled the holy water there.
And straight we heard a sorrowful cry;
Something upon the air went by;
Far off, slowly, pealed a bell,
A voice sobbed, and silence fell.
And I grew sad, to think that I
Should make that marvelous spirit die.
Make haste, beloved! The night passes,
The clay creeps, the cock crows,
Mist slinks away in the pale sun,
And the opened grave must close.

Vampires, they say, blow an unearthly beauty,
Their bodies are all suffused with a soft witch-fire,
Their flesh like opal . . . their hair like the float of night.
Why do we muse upon them, what secret's in them?
Is it because, at last, we love the darkness,
Love all things in it, tired of too much light?

Here on the lamplit pavement, in the city,
Where the high stars are lost in the city's glow,
The eyes of harlots go always to and fro—
They rise from a dark world we know nothing of,
Their races are white, with a strange love—
And are they vampires, or do I only dream? . . .
Lamps on the long bare asphalt coldly gleam.

And hearing the ragtime from a cabaret,
And catching a glimpse, through turning doors,
Of a spangled dancer swaying with drunken eyes,
Applauded and stared at by pimps and whores—
What decadent dreams before us rise? . . .

The pulse of the music thickens, it glows macabre,
The horns are a stertorous breath,
Someone is dying, someone is raging at death . . .
Around a coffin they dance, they pelt dead roses,
They stand the coffin on end, a loud spring clangs,
And suddenly like a door the coffin uncloses:

And a skeleton leers upon us in evening dress,—
There in the coffin he stands,
With his hat in his white-gloved hands,
And bows, and smiles, and puffs at a cigarette.
Harlots blow kisses to him, and fall, forgotten,
The great clock strikes; soft petals drift to the floor;
One by one the dancers float through the door,
Hair is dust, flesh is rotten,
The coffin goes down into darkness, and we forget . . .
Who told us this? Was it a music we heard,
A picture we saw, a dream we dreamed? . . .
I am pale, I am strangely tired.
A warm dream lay upon me, its red eyes gleamed,
It sucked my breath . . . It sighed . . . It afflicted me . . .
But was that dream desired, or undesired?
We must seek other tunes, another fragrance:
This slows the blood in our hearts, and cloys our veins.
Open the windows. Show us the stars. We drowse.

Sir Thomas Malory

EXCERPT FROM

THE DEATH OF KING ARTHUR

Sir Thomas Malory was the author of the famous collection of Arthurian legends, *Le Morte D'Arthur* (*The Death of King Arthur*), which was based on legends that date back to the early sixth century A.D. and was first published fourteen years after his death. Malory spent much of his life in conflict with the law. He was charged with assault and theft in 1443, but what became of those charges is unknown. Two years later he became a member of Parliament. Five years after that, he was charged with a series of crimes that included extortion, raiding cattle, plotting to murder the Duke of Buckingham, and threatening Warwickshire's prior and monastery. This landed him in prison, but he soon escaped, and over the next two days he led a band that plundered Coombe Abbey twice. He pleaded innocent to all these crimes, but ended up spending most of the subsequent decade in various prisons. It's thought that Malory wrote *The Death of King Arthur* while incarcerated, for at the end of the book he says "pray for me while I am on live [alive] that God send me good deliverance." He completed the book in 1471—a year before he died—and it went on to be the most famous book on King Arthur. The excerpt presented here tells the story of Sir Galahad, Sir Bors, and Sir Percival's dealings with a vampiress. At this point in the story, the three knights are searching for the Holy Grail and they have come to "a waste forest." Travelling with them is Sir Percival's sister, who, the daughter of King Pelles, is also a princess.

. . . AND SO THEY CAME to a castle and passed by. So there came a knight armed after them and said: "Lords, hark what I shall say to you. This gentlewoman that ye lead with you is a maid?" "Sir," said she, "a maid I am." Then he took her by the bridle and said: "By the Holy Cross, ye shall not escape me to-fore ye have yolden [submitted to] the custom of this castle." "Let her go," said Percivale, "ye be not wise, for a maid in what place she cometh is free." So in the meanwhile there came out a ten or twelve knights armed, out of the castle, and with them came gentlewoman which held a dish of silver. And then they said: "This gentlewoman [meaning Percival's sister] must yield us the custom of this castle." "Sir," said a knight, "what maid passeth hereby shall give this dish full of blood of her right arm." "Blame have ye," said Galahad, "that brought up such customs, and so God me save, I ensure you of this gentlewoman ye shall fail while that I live." "So God me help," said Percivale, "I had liefer [rather] be slain." "And I also," said Sir Bors. "By my troth [word]," said the knight, "then shall ye die, for ye may not endure against us though ye were the best knights of the world."

Then let they run each to other, and the three fellows beat the ten knights, and then set their hands to their swords and beat them down and slew them. Then there came out of the castle a three score [sixty] knights armed. "Fair lords," said the three fellows, "have mercy on yourself and have not; ado with us." "Nay, fair lords," said the knights of the castle, "we counsel you to withdraw you, for ye be the best knights of the world, and therefore do no more, for ye have done enough. We will let you go with this harm, but we must needs have the custom." "Certes [certainly]," said Galahad, "for nought [nothing] speak ye." "Well," said they, "will ye die?" "We be not yet come thereto," said Galahad. Then began they to meddle together, and Galahad, with the strange girdles, drew his sword, and smote on the right hand and on the left hand, and slew what that ever abode him, and did such marvels that there was none that saw him but weened [thought] he had been none [not] earthly man, but a monster. And his two fellows halp [helped] him passing well, and so they held the journey everych [each one] in like hard till it was night: then must they needs depart.

So came in a good knight, and said to the three fellows: "If ye will come in to-night and take such harbour as here is ye shall be right welcome, and we shall ensure you by the faith of our bodies, and as we be true knights, to leave you in such estate to-morrow as we find you, without any falsehood. And as soon as ye know of the custom we dare say ye will accord therefore." "For God's love," said the gentlewoman, "go thither and spare not for me." "Go we," said Galahad; and so they entered into the chapel. And when they were alighted they made great joy of them. So within a while the three knights asked the custom of the castle and wherefore it was. "What it is," said they, "we will say you sooth [truthfully]."

"There is in this castle a gentlewoman which we and this castle is [are] hers, and many other. So it befell many years agone there fell upon her a malady; and when she had lain a great while she fell unto a measle [disease], and of no leech [doctor] she could have no remedy. But at the last an old man said an she might have a dish full of blood of a maid and a clean virgin in will and in work, and a king's daughter, that blood should be her health, and for to anoint her withal; and for this thing was this custom made." "Now," said Percivale's sister, "fair knights, I see well that this gentlewoman is but dead." "Certes [certainly]," said Galahad, "an ye bleed so much ye may die." "Truly," said she, an I die for to heal her I shall get me great worship and soul's health, and worship to my lineage, and better is one harm than twain. And therefore there shall be no more battle, but to-morn I shall yield you your custom of this castle." And then there was great joy more than there was to-fore, for else had there been mortal war upon the morn; notwithstanding she would none other, whether they wold [would] or nold [not].

That night were the three fellows eased with the best; and on the morn they heard mass, and Sir Percivale's sister bade bring forth the sick lady. So she was, the which was evil at ease. Then said she: "Who shall let me blood?" So one [Percival's sister] came forth and let her blood, and she bled so much that the dish was full. Then she lift up her hand and blessed her; and then she said to the lady: "Madam, I am come to the death for to make you whole, for God's love pray for me." With that she fell in a swoon. Then Galahad and his two fellows start up to her, and lift her up and staunched her, but she had bled so much that she might not live. Then she said when she was awaked: "Fair brother Percivale, I die for the healing of this lady, so I require you that ye bury me not in this country, but as soon as I am dead put me in a boat at the next haven, and let me go as adventure will lead me; and as soon as ye three come to the City of Sarras, there to enchieve the Holy Grail, ye shall find me under a tower arrived, and there bury me in the spiritual place; for I say you so much, there Galahad shall be buried, and ye also, in the same place."

Then Percivale understood these words, and granted it her, weeping. And then said a voice: "Lords and fellows, to-morrow at the hour of prime ye three shall depart everych [each one] from other, till the adventure bring you to the Maimed King [King Pelles]." Then asked she her Saviour; and as soon as she had received it the soul departed from the body. So the same day was the lady healed, when she was anointed withal. Then Sir Percivale made a letter of all that she had holpen [helped] them as in strange adventures, and put it in her right hand, and so laid her in a barge, and covered it with black silk; and so the wind arose, and drove the barge from the land, and all knights beheld it till it was out of their sight. Then they drew all to the castle, and so forthwith there fell a sudden tempest and a thunder, lightning, and rain, as all the earth would have broken. So half the castle turned up-so-down. So it passed evensong or [before] the tempest was ceased. . . .

Then they saw afore them a knight armed and wounded hard in the body and in the head, that said: "O God, succour [help] me for now it is need." After this knight came another knight and a dwarf, which cried to them afar: "Stand, ye may not escape." Then the wounded knight held up his hands to God that he should not die in such tribulation. "Truly," said Galahad, "I shall succour him for His sake that he calleth upon." "Sir," said Bors, "I shall do it, for it is not for you, for he is but one knight." "Sir," said he, "I grant." So Sir Bors took his horse, and commended him to God, and rode after, to rescue the wounded knight. Now turn we to the two fellows.

*   *   *

Now saith the story that all night Galahad and Percivale were in a chapel in their prayers, for to save Sir Bors. So on the morrow they dressed them in their harness toward the castle, to wit what was fallen of them therein. And when they came there they found neither man nor woman that he ne [not] was dead by the vengeance of Our Lord. With that they heard a voice that said: "This vengeance is for blood-shedding of maidens." Also they found at the end of the chapel a churchyard, and therein might they see a three score [sixty] fair tombs, and that place was so fair and so delectable that it seemed them there had been none tempest, for there lay the bodies of all the good maidens which were martyred for the sick lady's sake. Also they found the names of everych [each one], and of what blood they were come, and all were of kings' blood, and twelve of them were kings' daughters. Then they departed and went into a forest. Now, said Percivale unto Galahad, we must depart, so pray we Our Lord that we may meet together in short time: then they did off their helms and kissed together, and wept at their departing.

Thomas Hardy

THE VAMPIRINE FAIR

Thomas Hardy was the last of the great Victorian novelists. His masterpieces include *Tess of the D'Urbervilles*, *The Mayor of Casterbridge*, *The Return of the Native*, and *Far From the Madding Crowd*. After the turn of the century, his focus shifted from fiction to poetry. This poem is from *Time's Laughingstocks* (1909). In Hardy's original handwritten copy, this poem was titled "The Fair Vampire."

Gilbert had sailed to India's shore,
   And I was all alone:
My lord came in at my open door
   And said, "O fairest one!"

He leant upon the slant bureau,
   And sighed, "I am sick for thee!"
"My Lord," said I, "pray speak not so,
   Since wedded wife I be."

Leaning upon the slant bureau,
   Bitter his next words came:
"So much I know; and likewise know
   My love burns on the same!

"But since you thrust my love away,
   And since it knows no cure,

I must live out as best I may
   The ache that I endure."

When Michaelmas browned the nether Coomb,
   And Wingreen Hill above,
And made the hollyhocks rags of bloom,
   My lord grew ill of love.

My lord grew ill with love for me;
   Gilbert was far from port;
And—so it was—that time did see
   Me housed at Manor Court.

About the bowers of Manor Court
   The primrose pushed its head
When, on a day at last, report
   Arrived of him I had wed.

"Gilbert, my Lord, is homeward bound,
   His sloop is drawing near,
What shall I do when I am found
   Not in his house but here?"

"O I will heal the injuries
   I've done to him and thee.
I'll give him means to live at ease
   Afar from Shastonb'ry."

When Gilbert came we both took thought:
   "Since comfort and good cheer,"
Said he, "So readily are bought,
   He's welcome to thee, Dear."

So when my lord flung liberally
   His gold in Gilbert's hands,
I coaxed and got my brothers three
   Made stewards of his lands.

And then I coaxed him to install
   My other kith and kin,
With aim to benefit them all
   Before his love ran thin.

And next I craved to be possessed
  Of plate and jewels rare.
He groaned: "You give me, Love, no rest,
  Take all the law will spare!"

And so in course of years my wealth
  Became a goodly hoard,
My steward brethren, too, by stealth
  Had each a fortune stored.

Thereafter in the gloom he'd walk,
  And by and by began
To say aloud in absent talk,
  "I am a ruined man!—

"I hardly could have thought," he said,
  "When first I looked on thee,
That one so soft, so rosy red,
  Could thus have beggared me!"

Seeing his fair estates in pawn,
  And him in such decline,
I knew that his domain had gone
  To lift up me and mine.

Next month upon a Sunday morn
  A gunshot sounded nigh:
By his own hand my lordly born
  Had doomed himself to die.

"Live, my dear Lord, and much of thine
  Shall be restored to thee!"
He smiled, and said 'twixt word and sign,
  "Alas—that cannot be!"

And while I searched his cabinet
  For letters, keys, or will,
'Twas touching that his gaze was set
  With love upon me still.

And when I burnt each document
  Before his dying eyes,

'Twas sweet that he did not resent
  My fear of compromise.

The steeple-cock gleamed golden when
  I watched his spirit go:
And I became repentant then
  That I had wrecked him so.

Three weeks at least had come and gone,
  With many a saddened word,
Before I wrote to Gilbert on
  The stroke that so had stirred.

And having worn a mournful gown,
  I joined, in decent while,
My husband at a dashing town
  To live in dashing style.

Yet though I now enjoy my fling,
  And dine and dance and drive,
I'd give my prettiest emerald ring
  To see my lord alive.

And when the meet on hunting-days
  Is near his churchyard home,
I leave my bantering beaux to place
  A flower upon his tomb

And sometimes say: "Perhaps too late
  The saints in Heaven deplore
That tender time when, moved by Fate,
  He darked my cottage door."

Rod Serling

THE RIDDLE OF THE CRYPT

Rodman Serling created the TV anthology series *The Twilight Zone*, which he also hosted from 1959 to 1964. Serling was one of television's most respected writers, having won three Emmy Awards before he even started this series. The show won him two more, and spawned a movie, a magazine, and at least six books, most of which were written by Serling himself. He achieved playwright status through his many scripts, which include *Requiem for a Heavyweight*, *Seven Days in May*, and *The Planet of the Apes*. He also hosted the *Night Gallery* TV series, though he had little control over it. "The Riddle of the Crypt" is from Serling's first book, *The Twilight Zone* (1963), though it was never in the TV series. The story was adapted for the book by Walter Gibson, but just how much influence Gibson had on it is uncertain. Serling remains one of the most famous figures in the realm of supernatural fiction.

THE CABIN CRUISER *Rover* had just rounded Porpoise Point when Irene Morrow gained her first view of Cliff Island. Her brother Roy pointed it out as it loomed in sight, and Irene exclaimed, "How beautiful! How very, very beautiful!"

It was indeed a splendid sight, a mass of steep gray bluffs rising like the walls and towers of an enchanted palace floating on a clear blue sea. As the cruiser swung eastward of the island, the setting sun gave a scintillating touch to the granite heights, producing a scene straight from the pages of a fairy book.

As the boat sped closer, the island seemed to spread in size, creating another surprising illusion. Then, suddenly, a frowning headland cut off the sunlight and darkened the water with a sullen gloom, broken only by the tufted white of waves that crashed on the cold gray stones below. In a trice, all the sparkle was gone, and the face of the island became rugged and forbidding.

The transition struck Irene as she was repeating the enthusiastic words, forcing her to modify them:

"How very, very beautiful—and yet so weird and ghostly!"

In a sense, the change was fearful. The *Rover* seemed due to crash on the rocks. But Jerry Lane, the youthful skipper, deftly swung to port, almost skirting the spray of the treacherous breakers. Dead ahead, Irene saw a cleft in the rocky wall. It widened, and sunlight streamed through the jagged gap, transforming the moody black cliffs back to their glittering gray.

"We are coming into Middle Harbor," shouted Roy, above the tumult of the waves. "Don't let Jerry scare you. He really knows this channel."

The channel followed a fold between the high crags, and after a medley of sunlight and shadows, the cruiser hummed into a cozy cove where a few dozen speedboats and cruisers were moored alongside some trim sailboats and a motley lot of weatherbeaten fishing craft.

From a short pier, a gangplank ran down to a float where arriving craft could pull alongside regardless of the tide, which was heavy along this part of the New England coast. Soon Roy and Irene were ashore with their luggage, which was handled by a lanky man in overalls, whose face was as rugged as the island's cliffs. He carried the bags to a car old enough to mark its owner as one of the early settlers. It bore the crude legend:

J. CUPPY—TAXI

The settlement about the pier was a combination of a fishing and tourist haven, with a post office, some stores, sea food restaurants, and fishing shacks. But the slopes that funneled up from the harbor were studded with cottages of early twentieth century vintage. They were reached by zigzag roadways and paths with rock-hewn steps that served as shortcuts. Then Roy drew Irene back to the outer end of the pier and pointed to a ledge set back beyond the very top of the slope. On that dominant height, Irene could make out the front of a brand-new ranch house, ruddy in the sunlight's glow.

"That, I will have you know," said Roy, "is our humble abode. The most modern habitation on all Cliff Island with the best out-look."

Irene's round, enthusiastic face beamed an appreciative smile. She was starting to say that the place looked wonderful, even from a distance, when Mr. Cuppy put the last bag in the taxi. So they hurried to the ancient car and climbed in while Cuppy took the wheel and asked:

"Where to, Mr. Morrow?"

"To Castle Rock," returned Roy. "We're living in the new ranch house there."

Mr. Cuppy sat as if frozen behind the wheel. Then he slowly turned his thin red neck and gave his two passengers a long, beady look, turkey fashion. Next, he made a move as if to get out and remove the bags. Then, without a word, he looked ahead again, wheezed the old motor into action and headed the car up the hill.

The view was increasingly beautiful all the way up the long zigzag road. Middle Harbor was an ever-changing scene, with oc-casional glimpses of the ocean through the rocky walls of the channel. Then, at the top, the island became a saucer-shaped pla-teau, and Irene could see the ocean all around with an island-studded bay toward the west. There, the sun, going down beyond the mainland, blended crimson, gold and purple in one magnifi-cent splash.

The taxi gained new life down a slight, winding slope. It passed a stretch of barren, rocky ground, veered away from a thick clump of pine trees, and groaned up a slight, curving quarter-mile grade that brought it in back of the ranch house. Instead of using the driveway, Mr. Cuppy stopped on the road, unloaded the bags while his passengers alighted, and said:

"That'll be one dollar."

As Roy handed Cuppy a bill, the taxi man clambered back into the car, saying, "Got to get down to the dock right quick. The *Countess* is coming in."

With that he swung the car about and rattled away, as Irene asked:

"And who is the Countess?"

"A boat," replied Roy. "The steamer from the mainland. But she isn't due until nine o'clock tonight. I can't understand what's wrong with Cuppy."

"I can," came a cheery voice behind them. Irene turned and saw a smiling young man with a shock of light hair. "I've been watching from our ivory tower, expecting to see this happen."

"This is Alan Blount," introduced Roy, "who is helping me in my study of marine fossils. Go on, Alan. Why wouldn't Cuppy carry the bags?"

"Because no person living on Cliff Island will set foot on the blighted ground surrounding Castle Rock. That road is the dividing line. You'll see people walk by on the far side, looking at us as if we were saying, 'Shinny on your own side, this side is taboo.' A crazy superstition, that's all."

Irene smiled, recalling many places she had been where odd customs and strange superstitions were common; but they had never worried her. Besides, she didn't want to be bothered by visitors on Cliff Island. She was here on assignment for her company, International Metallurgics Associated. She had traveled through South America for I. M. A., and they had given her the job of translating and condensing all subsidiary reports from Spanish and Portuguese into English, a two-month job at least.

Roy, a professor of biology at a state university, had heard of the wonderful ranch house on Cliff Island and had rented it while making his fossil survey. So Irene had decided to come and do her work there. She liked the place as they entered the back door through a modern kitchen where Roy gestured to two bedrooms on the right and said:

"Those are bachelors' quarters for Alan and myself. You have the left wing, sis. It was planned as a garage, but nobody keeps a car on Cliff Island, or the taxi business would die. So they turned it into a studio with a glass window in place of a front door. Come and see it!"

It instantly became Irene's dream room. From the picture window, she could see the whole harbor, with the limitless ocean beyond, while a casement window at the side gave a view of the pine woods and the stretch of rocks beyond the curving road.

Each morning, Roy and Alan left early, and Irene went to work on her translations, pausing at intervals to look from the front window at a scene as varied as it was beautiful, for the moods of the clouds and the ocean were many. But at times, Irene found herself drifting into a dreamy state, in which the present faded and everything seemed as distant as the boundless sea. Always, she was jolted from such reveries by the sensation of watching eyes and a figure creeping behind her.

Then Irene would snap from the clutch of the unknown, often with an involuntary scream. All about, she would see floating blobs of blackness that would gradually dissolve. After such shocks, Irene felt an urge for human company. The fact that the Islanders regarded this ledge as taboo struck home with numbing force. Irene would rush out to the back road. There she felt safe, though no one was ever around.

Sometimes Irene regained her calm by walking down the road to the pine woods, which was beautifully shaped and exquisitely green, compared to the otherwise drab landscape of the plateau. In bright sunlight, the evergreens were restful. On cloudy days, or under the colorful tints of an early sunset, the grove took on a deeper green that absorbed Irene's worries with it.

The rocks beyond the grove were typical of the island's ruggedness. A hundred feet to the right of the evergreens, several hundred heavy stones were tumbled in a pile at least thirty feet across and half that high. The pile interested Irene, because it was manmade. She passed it late in the afternoons when she cut across to a path that led down among the cottages to the harbor. There she met Roy and Alan when they came in on the *Rover*. Often she stopped at an employment office to try to hire a woman to help with the housework. But when she said "Castle Rock" none was ever available.

Sometimes Irene had a fish or lobster dinner with Roy and Alan at one of the seafood places. Other times, she prepared dinner at the ranch house. Almost always, they went up the hill in Cuppy's taxi—until one afternoon when the whole ocean became a mass of white billows formed by a lowclinging fog that kept creeping up the island's craggy walls. By the time Irene reached the dock, she could just make out the bulk of a coast guard craft that was moored there. From it, a loudspeaker called off names, giving information about boats that were overdue. One announcement came:

"Miss Morrow—Miss Irene Morrow—message from the *Rover*. Fogbound at Port Clarion—will return to Middle Harbor tomorrow."

Irene ate alone at the pier restaurant and stayed late, hoping that the fog would clear, but it lessened only slightly. She found Cuppy asleep in his cab, wakened him, and they started up the hill, with Cuppy working his way slowly in low gear. Irene decided that this was a good time to get first-hand evidence on the Castle Rock taboo.

"I won't ask you to drive me to my door," she said, "but I would like to know why nobody on Cliff Island will come to Castle Rock."

"Well, the Rock has a curse on it," returned Cuppy. "Some sort of spell that has never worn off from long ago. People have seen strange critters up toward the Rock, the kind that change to giant bats."

"If you mean vampires," retorted Irene, "they are bunk. I have seen vampire bats in South America, but they prey on cattle, that's all."

Just then, a huge, swooping shape came into the glare of the car's bright headlights. Its wings were like mammoth arms as it loomed from the fog. Irene's nerves, which had been getting worse daily, were so raw that she started to scream, but rather than show weakness, she reduced it to an "Eeeek!" An answering "Eeeek!" came from the flitting shape, which was gone instantly, leaving only the whitish swirl of the fog. Irene decided it was an ordinary bat, magnified by the fog to gigantic proportions. As they neared Castle Rock, Cuppy suggested:

"Look, Miss Morrow. I'll back my car so the lights will guide you into the house, so nothing can come at you in the dark—"

"You mean a vampire?" broke in Irene. "Like the one we just saw?"

"I'm not sure what we did see," returned Cuppy. "The worst thing is the yellow eyes that people see up here. They come from that pine woods"—he gestured to an ominous bulk of blackness on his right—"but lookee, lady. If you get in the house and keep all the windows tight shut, nothing can sneak in with you, not even none of the fog. That's all I've got to say."

Cuppy used his bright lights as a path to the house, and Irene followed it. Once she was inside, Cuppy cut his headlights to dim, probably finding they reflected less glare from the fog. He started back down the road, and Irene went into her studio-garage, where she looked toward the pine grove, wondering if she would see those yellow eyes.

Then, suddenly, she did. Tiny, yellow beads, they squinted from the swirl of the fog and hovered as though coming closer. Irene wondered if Cuppy saw them from his creeping car. Then, just as her nerves reached the shrieking point, Irene gave a laugh that was hysterical but glad.

Those yellow eyes were the taillights of Cuppy's car. Their red lenses had gone to pieces years ago, leaving only little bright bulbs, like yellow, beady eyes. Irene realized that when Cuppy swung past the grove, because then, for the first time, his dim headlights showed and the taillights veered at a new angle.

Irene wished that this harrowing night was over; instead, it had just begun. When she opened the front door for air, fog billowed in. When it vanished after she slammed the door, it seemed all the more like a living thing. There was a magnetic force here, that created living phantasms, for when Irene looked from the window, she could see fog-faces form there, then dissipate in ghoulish swirls. She ran about clamping windows and bolting doors, until overwhelmed by mental and physical exhaustion, she collapsed in a big chair in the living room. All the lights were on, but she was still fearful until she fell into a sleep so deep that when she was finally roused from it, she started up, trembling.

All the lights were still on, but their glare was lost in the dazzle of broad daylight. There were no longer fog-faces peering at Irene, but real faces, those of her brother Roy and his assistant, Alan Blount. It was morning, the fog had lifted, and they had come back in the *Ranger*. When Irene told them what had happened, they nodded.

Their own work was so exacting, so limited on board the *Rover*, that Irene's talk of dazed moods and the floating blackness struck them as the result of her daytime intensity and isolation. One night alone had touched off Irene's accumulation of nervous tension. Roy and Alan stayed home that day. At night, they strolled beneath the stars with Irene and pointed out the constellations, which made earthly worries seem small.

The next day, Roy had another idea. He told Irene:

"We've been talking this over, Alan and I. We want you to come with us to Port Clarion, and while we're studying starfish instead of stars, you can go to the library and dig into the history of Cliff Island. There may be something behind this nonsense about Castle Rock, so let's get to the bottom of it."

Port Clarion was much like Middle Harbor but on a larger scale.

There, Irene saw the tubby *Countess*, a little steamer with its two decks sprouting tourists, as she came in from her morning tour of the islands of Fisherman's Bay, which included Cliff Island as the outermost. At the library Irene said that she was visiting Cliff Island—carefully avoiding any mention of which part—and that she was intensely interested in its history. When she joined Roy and Alan for dinner at one of the big pier restaurants, Irene was well briefed on her subject. But she waited until the *Rover* was speeding through the moonlit bay back to Cliff Island, with Jerry Lane at the helm. Then she sat in the cockpit with Roy and Alan while she went into her story.

"Apparently, Cliff Island was settled by the French in the early 1600's," stated Irene, "and they kept it clear up to the year 1715."

"That's not surprising," put in Roy. "The French had many outposts that they managed to keep from the British."

"In this case, they really held them off," Irene informed him. "The cliffs were like a fortress, and French peasants raised crops and cattle on the plateau, but occasionally their fishing was curtailed when the British occupied Middle Harbor. So about the year 1700, a French sea rover was appointed to take charge. He was called the Commandant Lesang, and he sailed into Middle Harbor on a ship called the *Aventure*.

"The first thing that Lesang and his crew did was build a citadel on the high rim of the plateau, right where we are living now. That is why it is called Castle Rock. He used to light beacons on a high point called *Cap Bec*, or Cape Beak, but which is now known as Signal Head."

"I know Signal Head," said Roy. "We'll show it to you when we get there. But go on with the story, sis."

"The arrival of the *Aventure* caused great joy," continued Irene, "but all changed to gloom when Lesang ruled the island like a tyrant. He and his evil crew committed murder, tortured helpless prisoners, and brought terror to the island. Finally, the British attacked, bombarded his citadel, and took over the island. The inhabitants were shipped away, and it was years before the island was settled again."

"And what happened to Commandant Lesang?" asked Roy.

"He disappeared," replied Irene. "Some say he escaped in a boat from one of the other harbors. Another account says that he was killed during the attack on the castle. It is even claimed that he was killed earlier but that his ghost returned and was still in command when the castle was demolished."

"That could be the groundwork for the vampire talk," agreed Roy. "Did you run across any of that stuff in the old archives?"

"Yes. Weird yellow eyes have been seen gleaming through the fog. People have been attacked by a gruesome monster that slashes their throats. Some persons have disappeared like Lesang himself."

"Disappeared completely? Without a trace?"

"In some instances, yes. But bodies have been found floating far out to sea and others have been discovered in the deep pit over which the old castle was built."

"Which is now our cellar," commented Roy grimly. "No wonder the place gives you the shakes. I can't blame people for not wanting to come near it."

"I'm sure I can stick it out now." Irene's tone was determined. "I should have laughed it all off when the yellow eyes turned out to be nothing but a taxi's taillights. However, keep a good grip on yourself while I tell you the most fearful legend of the lot. When the full of the moon arrives, the *Aventure* is sometimes seen sailing into Middle Harbor. Then things really cut loose."

"You mean all those things you've just mentioned?"

"And more. Once the ghost ship has been sighted, Lesang's own ghost is sure to appear. That's one legend that just won't die."

"It's a funny thing," put in Alan. "We've talked with a lot of characters around Middle Harbor, but they've never handed us any of this."

"Because that's the last place where they ever will talk about it," rejoined Irene. "The librarian, Miss Lacey, says that the Islanders are so afraid of its hurting the tourist trade that they've even suppressed all picture postcards dealing with it. Those used to be popular some twenty years ago, and Miss Lacey told me of a shop that was still bootlegging them. So I bought some."

Triumphantly, Irene produced a batch of picture postcards which Roy and Alan studied eagerly in the light of the cockpit. One card showed Castle Rock in its barren state; another, with an artist's conception of Lesang's citadel towering upon it. One card showed the pine woods, which was appropriately termed "The Haunted Grove," while another had the stone pile labeled "Old Norse Ruins." Another card depicted Signal Head, with its ancient beacon in full flare, and there was a closeup of a high ledge titled "Bat Roosts on Cliff Island" with bats hanging there.

"According to a book in the library," stated Irene, "those roosts were cleaned out long ago. Now the Islanders pretend they never heard of them."

"There would, of course, be some specimens remaining," declared Roy in his professorial style. "You saw one the other night, but Cuppy wouldn't admit it."

They were passing the *Countess* now, waddling in from her evening rounds, and ahead lay Cliff Island, more ghostly than ever, though Irene was ready to face its eerie heights with new confidence. Roy pointed out Signal Head, and Irene realized that the old beacon point was quite close to Castle Rock but off at a different angle than the road, which was why she had never noticed it. Then Irene remembered a postcard that she had been saving for the last. She brought it out and said:

"Here is the old *Aventure* herself, sailing into Middle Harbor. They've pasted her over a photo of the island, trying to make it look real ghostly."

They showed the picture of the *Aventure* to Jerry Lane. From her three tall square-rigged masts and high stern, he identified her as a French ship of the early 1700's. But the young skipper added that it looked like a stock picture from some old book and that it certainly was not a ghostly craft coming into the Cliff Island Channel, which was incorrectly shown in the composite photo.

When they finally arrived in Middle Harbor and docked at the float, Jerry ducked down into the cabin, then poked his head up and grinned at Irene.

"I hear you've been needing company up at the house, and I thought maybe I could help out," he said. With that, he brought a brown-and-white spotted cat into sight and handed it, purring, to Irene. "Her name is Ginger, and she came on board in Port Clarion. Maybe she'll be happier at Castle Rock than sailing in the *Rover*."

Irene thanked Jerry profusely and carried the contented cat to Cuppy's cab. Cuppy noticed Ginger, and while they were driving up the cliff road, he remarked:

"You may be needing that cat at your place. She looks like a good ratter."

"This cat," returned Irene, "still has all her nine lives, which is the same number as a baseball team. So she isn't a ratter; she is a batter. I may let her go after some of those bats that are still hanging around their old roosts under the cliffs. Like the one you and I saw in the fog, Mr. Cuppy."

That quip silenced Cuppy. For the next few days, everything was peaceful. Then, one mild evening, while Irene was doing translations in her study, and Roy was playing pinochle with Alan in the living room, a new scare struck. Irene had let Ginger out, and as the cat hadn't returned, Irene picked up a long five-cell flashlight and went out the back door to look for her new pet.

With the powerful beam, Irene spotted Ginger frisking halfway down to the haunted grove. Irene called and turned off the light as the cat came bounding toward her. Ginger's light color made her quite conspicuous in the moonlight that filtered through a film of wispy clouds. Irene was looking straight toward the blackish contour of the pine woods; and something she saw there made her laugh lightly. Then suddenly her throat closed up and she froze all over.

Coming straight from the woods were those yellow eyes! Irene's laugh, inspired by her recollection of Cuppy's taillights, faded as she realized his taxi wasn't anywhere around. The eyes grew larger as Irene stooped to snatch up Ginger. Then they were full upon her, and she was swinging the long flashlight wildly to ward off a clawing, jabbing fury that attacked her savagely from the dark. Half smothered by the monstrous thing, Irene kept clubbing with the flashlight as she raced to the house, screaming for Roy and Alan. They came out the back door just as Irene made a last valiant sweep with her improvised cudgel and stumbled into her brother's arms, still clutching Ginger. Roy and Alan identified the thing from the woods as it soared off.

It was a huge owl, the biggest that either had ever seen.

In the living room, Irene put salve on her scratched neck and wrists while Ginger stalked about gratefully. Then, with a forced laugh, Irene said, "Well, we have taken another chunk out of that vampire legend."

"And it's lucky the owl didn't take a chunk out of Ginger," declared Roy. "Considering that owls fly off with chipmunks, a cat isn't too big for them."

During the rest of that week, Irene found a new formula that helped her work and kept her cheerful. She broke those introspective spells by talking to Ginger. For variety, she took brisk walks across the fields. Soon she had found the perfect goal, Signal Head, which offered the best view of the island.

There was a strange fascination about that jutting point. Often, as she approached it, Irene heard voices calling, "Irene—Irene—" and she smiled as she identified them as the cries of seagulls off the point. By then, she could hear an echoing "Irene! Irene!" and she would look almost straight down to the booming breakers, hundreds of feet below. By craning a bit more, she could see the narrow strip of rocky beach where the reluctant surf shattered, foamed, and retreated after every crash.

As Irene became accustomed to the scene, it became more alluring, magnetically drawing her to the cliff edge that she no longer feared. Then, one day as she was staring downward, the whole world seemed to fade except for that captivating tumult far below. Eyes half closed, Irene felt herself swaying forward, forward, forward, until a voice spoke from behind her:

"You would be safer back here a little way."

Irene spun about with a frightened shriek. She almost lost her footing on the brink, but the man had anticipated that before he spoke. His quick hand caught Irene's arm in an iron grip and with a strong tug, he had her a dozen feet back from the treacherous rim before she gained a glance at his serious, yet kindly face. Irene was amazed to see that the man, despite his remarkable strength and youthful vigor, was really quite elderly. Vaguely, she recalled having seen him down at the dock.

"I am Dr. Felton," the elderly man said. "I am the island physician. This week, they gave me a nice new six-year-old station wagon, the only car on Cliff Island that isn't a taxi."

Irene saw the car as they left Signal Head and started walking back toward Castle Rock. It was parked near where Cuppy always stopped.

"I need a wagon as an ambulance," explained Dr. Felton, "but in your case, it wouldn't have helped. Those rocks are a long fall down."

"I know." Irene nodded. "I shouldn't have been so near the brink. But how did you realize that I was in danger?"

"I've been coming up here every day," returned the physician, "to see a sick farmer at the far end of the island. Each day I have returned at the same time, and I have seen you looking over the cliff. Always, you seemed to be getting closer to the edge. I knew it wouldn't do."

They reached the front door of the ranch house. "Won't you come in?" Irene asked, and when the doctor nodded, she exclaimed happily:

"Why, you're one person who isn't afraid to walk in here!"

"I'm not an Islander," Dr. Felton replied. "I retired a few years ago, and the township appointed me as resident physician here. But I've heard all about Castle Rock"—his gray eyes narrowed but remained as kindly as ever—"or perhaps I haven't heard all about it. You might be able to tell me more."

Irene sat down in a big chair and began to fondle Ginger, who nestled, purring, in her lap. Though willing to talk, she parried: "Like what?"

"Well, those scratches on your neck and wrists, for one thing," said Dr. Felton. "You certainly didn't get them from this amiable pet of yours."

"I got them from an owl," Irene informed him. "A big owl, while I was saving Ginger from it. I saw big yellow eyes, coming at me from the woods—"

"And you had heard of those eyes before. They must have frightened you."

"They did," returned Irene, grateful for the doctor's understanding. "I saw a bat one night, too. I've seen floating blackness by day, and I've watched the fog make faces by night. But I'm over all such things now—"

"Except cliff walking. Other people have felt that urge, too."

"You really mean there is—there is something uncanny here?"

"I mean, don't be frightened, whatever does happen. Have you ever seen a full-rigged ship come in by full moonlight? Like a ghost ship?"

"No, but I've heard of it," admitted Irene, "and I know what it signifies. Doctor, is there anything to this vampire talk involving a Frenchman named Lesang, who lived more than three hundred years ago—and yet—"

"And yet may still live today?" Dr. Felton shook his head slowly. "It's hard to tell where legend ends and fact begins. You're a sensible young lady, so I can tell you this: I have been in many parts of the world, and I have found the same taboos, the same superstitions, the same unexplainable ailments or accidents, so often attributed to the same strange causes, that it may be they have much in common. Here on Cliff Island there have been too many odd deaths."

"I know that," agreed Irene. "I was reading about some of those cases in an old book over at the Port Clarion Library."

"I'm not talking about what was in old books," rejoined Dr. Felton. "I'm talking about what was in the newspapers during recent years. One woman was found dead in the haunted pine grove, very badly clawed. From your own experience, an owl could have been responsible, though I think in her case, the wounds were worse than any owl could inflict.

"On three different occasions, people have walked off cliffs, one from the very brink where you were today. In every case, they were apparently drawn to their doom by some baleful, indefinable influence. People have seen mammoth bats; not just small ones that they imagined were large. Other persons have disappeared entirely from Cliff Island."

It was growing late in the afternoon, and the doctor noted that although Irene was by no means nervous, she was becoming restless. He asked the reason, and when she told him she would have to go to meet her brother and his assistant, Dr. Felton offered her a ride down to the harbor in his wagon. Irene accepted, and when the *Rover* came in, she introduced Roy and Alan to the physician. The result was that they all dined together in an outdoor corner of the pier restaurant, where spray from scudding speedboats occasionally flicked over the rail.

But their conversation, unlike the gay chitchat so common on the pier, concerned very serious matters. Much of the island's mystery, including the vampire angle, became more intriguing, but also more shuddery, the further they discussed it. When Dr. Felton learned that Irene had seen actual vampire bats in South America, he smiled slightly.

"So that was where you heard how vampires dissolve into black specks and fog," said Dr. Felton. "That means those experiences could have been your imagination. Still, I feel that a vampiric influence is at work and that after failing earlier, it resorted to methods unknown to you."

"You mean like luring me to Signal Head, to push me off?"

"Not to push you off. To hold you there, teetering between "Stop" and "Go," to put it in modern terms. The invisible creature—he could be the notorious Lesang—was waiting until dusk, when his powers grow to their full. Then he could materialize into a solid being and kill you, vampire fashion. After that, he would let you fall to the rocks below, as his alibi."

It was Roy who voiced a strenuous objection:

"Come now, doctor! Don't tell us that vampires need alibis!"

"Of course they do," rejoined Dr. Felton, more serious than ever. "How could a monster like Lesang go on living—I should say existing—except through ignorance on our part? In the Middle Ages, simple-minded peasants recognized such creatures for what they really were and proceeded to get rid of them. Today, we make foolish excuses. We blame these happenings on cliff bats, on broken taillights, on owls' eyes, on everything except what they really represent, the baleful influence of a vampire!"

Dr. Felton paused to let that unnerving statement strike home. Then, he turned to Irene and said calmly:

"Since you are already under the vampiric influence, it is waiting to claim you as its next victim. When it strikes, we must be ready."

"And that," said Irene, "means that I am just a guinea pig."

"You are a very wonderful guinea pig, who can lift the curse of three centuries and still remain unharmed, if we take due precautions. Believe me, Miss Morrow"—sincerity shone in Dr. Felton's gray eyes—"if I could make myself the bait for this experiment, I would do so gladly. You know how many lives have been lost already. I can assure you that as many more will be endangered, unless we stop this fiendish creature here and now. You understand?"

"I understand. If this influence is working on me as you say, I should be the one most interested in seeing it settled forever. But must I first see that ship come in?"

"It would be helpful," stated Dr. Felton, with a nod. "Real or imaginary, it would show that you are conditioned to become the vampire's prey."

Roy and Alan stayed close to Castle Rock from that evening on. During the day, one occasionally went out in the *Rover* with Jerry; but the other was always on hand. In the evenings, both were at the ranch house, helping Irene get dinner ready, for she had to stay right there to keep a lookout for the phantom ship that, in her mind, at least, was becoming very real.

At intervals each evening, Irene would stroll out in the brilliant moonlight, sometimes as far as Signal Head. She went alone, rather than risk breaking the spell. Roy and Alan would keep watching Irene from the picture window of her studio, ready to dash out if she ventured too close to the cliff edge, or if any other danger threatened. But always, Irene was duly cautious and soon returned to the house.

Then came the night when the rising moon was at the full. Irene's hopes—or were they fears?—had reached a high point when Jerry Lane arrived in Cuppy's taxi, with word for Roy and Alan.

"The fog warnings are out," informed Jerry. "Thought you ought to know in case you want anything in Port Clarion. The only way to get there is to head out tonight."

"Nobody's going to Port Clarion," rejoined Roy. "Send Cuppy's

taxi down the hill and join us in a game of three-handed pinochle."

"Because you're going to stay all night, Jerry," Alan added.
"Now that you're here, we'll need you to help watch for vampires.
When it's foggy, they are most apt to be around."

Irene shuddered at that recollection. Then she realized that if
the fog thickened, she would never see the phantom ship.

"I'm going out to take a last look at the moonlight," Irene told
the three men. "Don't worry. I'll be back."

"You'd better be," returned Roy, "and anyway, we'll watch."

The full moon had risen high enough above the hazy horizon
to show the harbor clearly and vividly, even to its tiniest boats,
though off shore the mist was thickening, playing odd tricks while
Irene watched. In the broad path of light that stretched from the
moon across the dancing wavelets to the foot of Signal Head, Irene
saw a billow of white that puffed like a balloon and floated onward. It was followed by another, then a third; and as those
mighty masses moved shoreward they became the great white
sails of a full-rigged ship!

It had to be a ship, because Irene could see a darkish line just
beneath that rose at one end to a long prow; and at the other, to
the high stern that marked it as the old *Aventure*. This could be no
illusion, for Irene could make out every detail of the old-square
rigger that Lesang and his cutthroat crew had sailed into Middle
Harbor three centuries ago!

Irene wanted to rush back to the house and tell the others, but
she couldn't take her eyes from the fantastic sight for fear of losing
it. On quick inspiration, she walked slowly, steadily—but know-
ingly—toward the edge of the cliff. That brought Roy and Alan
dashing to her rescue, as she knew it would. But before they arrived, the ship with the billowing sails had reached the channel
and gone out of sight within its cleft.

"I've seen the *Aventure*!" exclaimed Irene as they drew her
back. "Watch for it—you'll see it come from the channel into the
harbor!"

But the ship was slow in coming through, and now thick fog,
stirred by the wind that could not reach the cleft, was pouring in
from the sea. Then, as Irene pointed out the prow and foresail of

the *Aventure* nosing from the channel, the fog came with it, enveloping it so completely that only Irene really saw it.

"That was it," said Irene. "I saw enough of it to know."

"We saw enough to believe you, sis," declared Roy. "Let's go back to the house."

"Ship or no ship," added Alan, "we'll keep close watch tonight."

Half an hour later, Dr. Felton drove up in his station wagon and stopped at the ranch house. He was enthusiastic when Irene told him that she was sure she had sighted the phantom ship; and he was pleased because there were now three men on watch in the house.

"I'm going on over to see my patient," stated the doctor, as he was leaving. "I won't need to stop on the way back. You have everything under control."

After another hour, Irene went to the studio and tried to rest. She kept awakening fitfully, and each time, a glance at the big picture window showed that the moonlight was still clear, though fog was slowly working up over the edges of the cliff. For the dozenth time, she studied the side window and saw that its metal casements were firmly latched. Except for just a touch of fog, everything was as clearly defined as if by daylight, except that the scene was colorless.

The pine boughs were one massive black blot, though Irene could make out the tree trunks beneath them, as straight as penciled lines. To the right the rocky ground was tinted a splendid silver by the moonlight. That applied particularly to the pile of stones forming the misshapen mound, which one legend claimed was the remains of a tower built by roving Vikings on early visits to America.

Either the wisps of fog were causing the effect of motion among the silvered rocks, or Irene was seeing black spots again, for she saw something gliding, snakelike, from the rock pile toward the grove. Then she was studying the blackened trees again and under the moonlight's bewitchment, the world about Irene seemed to fade as she was fascinated by the sight of gleaming yellow eyes, emerging from that darkness.

They were growing, those eyes, moving upward, hovering above the level of the trees. Then Irene was horrified to see that the eyes belonged to a mammoth creature with outspread arms, batlike in its shape, but human in its action. For instead of flying, it was approaching in a series of long bounds, until it was at the window, filling it.

Then Irene's hands were on the sill and she was staring through the panes, not only eye to eye, but face to face with the monster from the dark. It was a man's face, tawny, shriveled like the shell of a dried coconut, with long, jagged yellow teeth showing from a lipless mouth beneath a snoutlike nose. Its hands were beside its face, scratching at the window panes with fingers that resembled claws, yet which, like the face, were of man-sized proportions.

Frozen by that leering visage, Irene could neither move nor even think. She was like a terrified bird transfixed by a serpent's gaze, for at this close range, the yellow, fiery eyes were more fearful than anything that Irene could have imagined in her worst and wildest dreams. The tightly clamped window was her one guarantee of safety; but as Irene watched, it began to yield.

Those clawish fingers were working like knife points between the sections of the metal frames. First, the long nails, then the thin fingertips, then the leathery hands gained a powerful grip. The lipless mouth leered more viciously as tinkles of breaking glass told that the panes were falling from the yielding metal, which was twisting like mere cardboard.

Now the window was gone, and the ghoulish creature was doubling up, edging its head, arms, and legs in through the gap. More overpowering than that sight was the moldy odor of decay that permeated the room with a stifling pungency, choking Irene as she tried voicelessly to scream. Then the thing was upon her, those claw hands at her neck, the fang-teeth wide, as though to deliver a ferocious bite.

At last, despite the suffocating effect, the touch of those fearful claws loosened Irene's vocal cords. Her scream echoed from the studio walls and was followed by the clatter of an opening door, which projected a shaft of light from the living room. Roy's face appeared there, then Alan's, with Jerry's behind them. They saw the studio bathed in the moonlight from the picture window, with Irene in its midst, struggling with an indefinable mass that identified itself when she tried to twist away.

That was when a gloating face looked up triumphantly, just long enough to deliver a hateful snarl. Savagely, the defiant creature flung Irene from its hideous embrace, squarely at her rescuers. As Roy and Alan caught the girl, the vampire reversed its course, sprang to the window and doubled itself through and outward.

Roy gestured to Jerry to take care of Irene. Then, with drawn revolver, Roy rushed out the front door, while Alan, also armed with a gun, took the back way. They saw the monster plop from the side window, spread its winglike arms, and take off with long zigzag bounds toward the woods. They blazed away and despite its crazy course, Roy must have clipped it in one flank, for it sprawled to one side, bobbed up again and bounded away at another angle.

But before it reached the grove, a small squad of men with shotguns surged out from beneath the trees. Seeing its course blocked, the bounding creature made for the broken rock pile ahead of the blasting shotguns. Roy and Alan closed in upon the monster there and were joined by the men from the woods, headed by Dr. Felton, who had evidently induced some farmers to set up an ambush for the vampire in the grove. But when they clambered about the rock pile, they could see no sign of the monstrous figure. The evil thing had completely disappeared.

Dr. Felton gave an anxious look, which Roy understood.

"The thing got Irene," he said, "but I am sure she is all right."

"That we had better find out."

Dr. Felton told his men to stand guard over the rock pile, while he went to the house with Roy and Alan. Irene was all right, but very faint, more from fright, however, than from loss of blood. Dr. Felton was pleased to find that her wounds were scratches only; none from the vampire's bite. He treated the wounds, and Irene soon felt well enough to go with the group to the rock pile.

On the way, Roy announced that he had shot the vampire, and Dr. Felton was highly pleased by the news.

"When these creatures take on human form," declared the physician, "they temporarily lose what might be termed their inhuman immunity. In short, in order to become solid and therefore formidable, they also become vulnerable. I am told that it takes some time for them to change from one state to another."

"Then where did Lesang go," demanded Roy, "if he didn't de-materialize?"

"He went down into that rock pile. That's where we saw him last."

"But why would he go into that old Norse ruin?"

"It isn't an old ruin," put in Alan, in answer to Roy's question. "I've talked to fishermen on other islands, and I find that some of their ancestors go way back to Lesang's time. They say it was the peasants on the island who tore the castle down and piled it stone by stone over Lesang's grave. Then they went their way of their own accord, even though the English wanted them to stay."

"So Lesang was buried here," Dr. Felton exclaimed. "You have seen snakes go into stone piles, and rats, too. We have just fought and trapped a creature that can squirm like any snake or rat. Look here!"

Dr. Felton took a long stick, thrust it down at various angles into the rocks and probed about, discovering gaps a foot or more in size.

"This rock pit," he announced, "is honeycombed with passages big enough for that monster to squirm through. We will find him under it."

No one doubted that now. They set a watch over the rock pile, day and night until the fog lifted and heavy highway construction equipment could be brought by ferry from the mainland. Then they began excavating the great stone pile. As the work proceeded, two points became apparent:

These actually were the stones from Lesang's old citadel on Castle Rock, for mortar was visible on many that were underneath. They also found a definite course of narrow but well-propped openings that twisted down through to form a tunneled route that only a rat or an inhuman vampire would have dared to follow. At last the heap was cleared, and they came across a broad, flat stone inscribed with the name, Lavignac. That rang a bell with Alan.

"The fishermen told me about the Lavignacs," he exclaimed. "They were the original family who owned the island over several generations. Lesang claimed that they had given him their title. So he was buried with them."

Beneath the slab, they found the old Lavignac family crypt, with a central burial chamber arched to form a low vault. There they identified the Lavignac family coffins, all broken apart and scattered about, their remains reduced to skeletons. That must have been the work of the usurper, for in the one unbroken coffin of the lot, lay the leathery thing with long sharp teeth and yellow eyes, that could only be Lesang the vampire, its batlike arms folded and claws clenched like fists.

From its glassy stare, Dr. Felton decided that the thing had been caught in the midst of one of its transmutations, unable to leave the near-human form that it had temporarily taken. He found the wound that Alan's bullet had inflicted and the physician pronounced the creature dead. Whether the next full of the moon would revive the vampire, Dr. Felton did not wait to learn.

Late that afternoon, the Morrows were leaving Cliff Island in the *Rover*, bound on a cruise which they hoped would help them forget the recent harrowing events. Alan Blount, who was with them, spoke quietly to Roy Morrow, who turned to Irene and said:

"Look back, sis, at Signal Head."

There, on the Head, smoke was rising. Puzzled, Irene exclaimed, "Why, somebody must have started the old beacon, the one that—"

"That once marked Lesang's arrival," completed Roy, when Irene hesitated. "But in this case, it is marking his departure."

"What do you mean by that, Roy?"

"Only that Dr. Felton, as health officer, has just decided to burn a lot of rubbish and with it, that thing we found in the old crypt."

The smoke billowed high against the afternoon sky, forming a thick black cloud that spread oddly into a weird, batlike form. A higher tuft of smoke was caught by a slight breeze and thinned sufficiently for the bright glare of the golden sun to shine through two momentary openings, giving them the semblance of a huge pair of yellow eyes.

Then the illusion faded, as did the dying smoke itself. All that remained of Lesang, the vampire from the Cliff Island crypt, was a smoldering beacon on Signal Head.

Goethe

THE BRIDE OF CORINTH

———◦◦◦———

Johann Wolfgang von Goethe has been called "the greatest of all German poets and the outstanding figure of world literature since the Renaissance." Besides being a poet, he was also a dramatist, novelist, lawyer, and scientist. His complete works take over 150 volumes. While he wrote in almost every field of science and his discoveries contributed to the theory of evolution, he is best known as the author of *Faust*, which he worked on for over thirty years and which has been described as "one of the greatest poetic and philosophic creations the world possesses." "Die Braut von Korinth" ("The Bride of Corinth") is one of his most famous poems. It was written in 1797 as part of a friendly contest between Goethe and Friedrich Schiller in the art of writing ballads, and was first published in Schiller's journal, *Die Horen*. Goethe based his poem on the story, from the second century A.D., of Philinnion, which I summarized in the introduction to this book (see pages xiv–xv).

A youth to Corinth, whilst the city slumbered,
   Came from Athens: though a stranger there,
Soon among its townsmen to be numbered,
   For a bride awaits him, young and fair.
      From their childhood's years
      They were plighted feres,
So contracted by their parents' care.

327

But may not his welcome there be hindered?
   Dearly must he buy it, would he speed.
He is still a heathen with his kindred,
   She and hers washed in the Christian creed.
      When new faiths are born,
      Love and troth are torn
Rudely from the heart, howe'er it bleed.

All the house is hushed;—to rest retreated
   Father, daughters—not the mother quite;
She the guest with cordial welcome greeted,
   Led him to a room with tapers bright;
      Wine and food she brought,
      Ere of them he thought,
Then departed with a fair good-night.

But he felt no hunger, and unheeded
   Left the wine, and eager for the rest
Which his limbs, forspent with travel, needed,
   On the couch he laid him, still undressed.
      There he sleeps—when lo!
      Onwards gliding slow,
At the door appears a wondrous guest.

By the waning lamp's uncertain gleaming
   There he sees a youthful maiden stand,
Robed in white, of still and gentle seeming,
   On her brow a black and golden band.
      When she meets his eyes,
      With a quick surprise
Starting, she uplifts a pallid hand.

"Is a stranger here, and nothing told me?
   Am I then forgotten even in name?
Ah! 'tis thus within my cell they hold me,
   And I now am covered o'er with shame!
      Pillow still thy head
      There upon thy bed,
I will leave thee quickly as I came."

"Maiden—darling! Stay, O stay!" and, leaping
  From the couch before her stands the boy:
"Ceres—Bacchus, here their gifts are heaping,
  And thou bringest Amor's gentle joy!
        Why with terror pale?
        Sweet one, let us hail
  These bright gods their festive gifts employ."

"Oh, no—no! Young stranger, come not nigh me;
  Joy is not for me, nor festive cheer.
Ah! such bliss may ne'er be tasted by me,
  Since my mother, in fantastic fear,
        By long sickness bowed,
        To heaven's service vowed
  Me, and all the hopes that warmed me here.

"They have left our hearth, and left it lonely,—
  The old gods, that bright and jocund train.
One, unseen, in heaven, is worshipped only,
  And upon the cross a Saviour slain;
        Sacrifice is here,
        Not of lamb nor steer,
  But of human woe and human pain."

And he asks, and all her words doth ponder,
  "Can it be that in this silent spot,
I behold thee, thou surpassing wonder!
  My sweet bride, so strangely to me brought?
        Be mine only now—
        See, our parents' vow
  Heaven's good blessing hath for us besought."

"No! thou gentle heart," she cried in anguish;
  " 'Tis not mine, but 'tis my sister's place;
When in lonely cell I weep and languish,
  Think, oh, think of me in her embrace!
        I think but of thee—
        Pining drearily,
  Soon beneath the earth to hide my face!"

"Nay! I swear by yonder flame which burneth,
　Fanned by Hymen, lost thou shalt not be;
Droop not thus, for my sweet bride returneth
　To my father's mansion back with me!
　　　Dearest, tarry here!
　　　Taste the bridal cheer,
For our spousal spread so wondrously!"

Then with word and sigh their troth they plighted
　Golden was the chain she bade him wear,
But the cup he offered her she slighted,
　Silver, wrought with cunning past compare,
　　　"That is not for me;
　　　All I ask of thee
Is one little ringlet of thy hair!"

Dully boomed the midnight hour unhallowed,
　And then first her eyes began to shine;
Eagerly with pallid lips she swallowed
　Hasty draughts of purple-tinctured wine;
　　　But the wheaten bread,
　　　As in shuddering dread,
Put she always by with loathing sign.

And she gave the youth the cup: he drained it,
　With impetuous haste he drained it dry;
Love was in his fevered heart, and pained it,
　Till it ached for joy she must deny
　　　But the maiden's fears
　　　Stayed him, till in tears
On the bed he sank, with sobbing cry.

And she leans above him—"Dear one, still thee!
　Ah, how sad am I to see thee so!
But, alas! these limbs of mine would chill thee:
　Love! they mantle not with passion's glow;
　　　Thou wouldst be afraid,
　　　Didst thou find the maid
Thou hast chosen, cold as ice or snow."

Round her waist his eager arms he bended,
  With the strength that youth and love inspire;
"Wert thou even from the grave ascended,
  I could warm thee well with my desire!"
        Panting kiss on kiss!
        Overflow of bliss!
  "Burn'st thou not, and feelest me on fire?"

Closer yet they cling, and intermingling,
  Tears and broken sobs proclaim the rest;
His hot breath through all her frame is tingling,
  There they lie, caressing and caressed.
        His impassioned mood
        Warms her torpid blood,
  Yet there beats no heart within her breast!

Meanwhile goes the mother, softly creeping
  Through the house, on needful cares intent
Hears a murmur, and, while all are sleeping,
  Wonders at the sounds, and what they meant.
        Who was whispering so?—
        Voices soft and low,
  In mysterious converse strangely blent.

Straightway by the door herself she stations,
  There to be assured what was amiss;
And she hears love's fiery protestations,
  Words of ardor and endearing bliss:
        "Hark, the cock! 'Tis light!
        But to-morrow night
  Thou wilt come again?" and kiss on kiss.

Quick the latch she raises, and, with features
  Anger-flushed, into the chamber hies.
"Are there in my house such shameless creatures,
  Minions to the stranger's will?" she cries.
        By the dying light,
        Who is't meets her sight?
  God! 'tis her own daughter she espies!

And the youth in terror sought to cover,
  With her own light veil, the maiden's head,
Clasped her close; but, gliding from her lover,
  Back the vestment from her brow she spread,
      And her form upright,
      As with ghostly might,
  Long and slowly rises from the bed.

"Mother! mother! wherefore thus deprive me
  Of such joy as I this night have known?
Wherefore from these warm embraces drive me?
  Was I wakened up to meet thy frown?
      Did it not suffice
      That in virgin guise,
  To an early grave you forced me down?

"Fearful is the weird that forced me hither,
  From the dark-heaped chamber where I lay
Powerless are your drowsy anthems, neither
  Can your priests prevail, howe'er they pray
      Salt nor lymph can cool,
      Where the pulse is full;
  Love must still burn on, though wrapped in clay.

"To this youth my early troth was plighted,
  Whilst yet Venus ruled within the land;
Mother! and that vow ye falsely slighted,
  At your new and gloomy faith's command.
      But no god will hear,
      If a mother swear
  Pure from love to keep her daughter's hand.

"Nightly from my narrow chamber driven,
  Come I to fulfill my destined part,
Him to seek to whom my troth was given,
  And to draw the life-blood from his heart.
      He hath served my will;
      More I yet must kill,
  For another prey I now depart.

"Fair young man! thy thread of life is broken,
  Human skill can bring no aid to thee.
There thou hast my chain—a ghastly token—
  And this lock of thine I take with me
      Soon must thou decay,
      Soon thou wilt be gray,
  Dark although to-night thy tresses be!

"Mother! hear, oh, hear my last entreaty!
  Let the funeral-pile arise once more;
Open up my wretched tomb for pity.
  And in flames our souls to peace restore
      When the ashes glow,
      When the fire-sparks flow,
  To the ancient gods aloft we soar."

Lenny Bruce

(UNTITLED)

Lenny Bruce (né Leonard Schneider; 1925–1966) was one of America's greatest social satirists. In an age that emphasized conformity, he had the ability to see right through society's hypocrisy and present it all in a humorous manner, while highlighting its ludicrous nature. Nothing was sacred. He openly discussed everything from racism and religion to sex and drugs. As a result, he was continually thrown in jail for obscenity, and harassed by the authorities for comedy routines that seem mild today. Arrested as many as seven times in a single city, by 1964 Bruce was under constant surveillance, and the only place he could perform was San Francisco. Abandoning his stage career, he entered the quagmire of the legal system to fight for free speech. Though he was finally exonerated, his legal battles destroyed him. He became "the sainted martyr of the counterculture." After his death, Dustin Hoffman played Bruce in the biographical movie *Lenny* and Bruce's influence continued to be felt through comedians ranging from Woody Allen to Cheech and Chong. During his life, he was often referred to as a "sick comic." Now he's considered a comic genius. The following piece was originally performed live. It was transcribed by John Cohen for *The Essential Lenny Bruce* (1967), and is uncensored.

Now, WE TAKE YOU to the town of Transylvania, and Boris does the narrating. Alright. Boris Karloff, Bela Lugosi. Oh—can you see my wrists stamped? The mark of the Golem. The *Dybbuk*! Alright.

NARRATOR [*hushed voice filled with mystery*]:   Soon, my friends, the town of Transylvania will be visited by Bela, who's looking for lodgings for the night. Soon Bela will be knocking at the door, and a woman will be answering . . .

tap tap tap tap

OLD WOMAN: [*Harsh, high, rasping voice*]:   Who are you young man? I've never seen you before. You're a stranger in Transylvania . . . I said, Who are you? Who are you?

DRACULA [*Hammy, fake-cultured East European*]:   Per-r-rmit me to introduce myself. Hahahahaha!

OLD WOMAN [*interested, voice softens*]:   Well, you sound pretty wild. Come in! What is your name?

DRACULA: My name, madam, is Count Dr-r-racula. And you see, ve are looking for lodgings for the night. Ve have been fortunate enough to br-r-reak down in your small town of Tr-r-r-ansylvania. Ve are but a small cir-r-rcus tr-r-roop, you see, and ve are ver-ry pleasant people. [*Aside*] It is getting light out, I am getting veak . . . Excuse me madam. There is yoost myself and my friend Igor.

IGOR [*British accent*]:   You promised to straighten out the hunch, master, you promised years ago when I came to the laboratory!

DRACULA: Shut up! I'll punch you in the hunch!

POCK!   And don bug me no more! You look gr-r-r-oovy that way. Look at the money ve made on the parties at Fire Island, looking at you . . . Now. Excuse, madam, for the small interr-r-ruption, but ah, ve vould like lodgings, yoost for a vile, you know.

OLD WOMAN [*Pushy*]:   Well, I know you show people, and it's usually customary that we get a little money first.

DRACULA: Vell, I'm a little hung for bread now, but, ah, I don't, ah—per-rhaps you'd like to punch Igor in the hunch?

OLD WOMAN [*interested*]:   Well, I've never done anything like that before . . .

DRACULA: Yes, there is a whole chapter on this in Kr-r-raft-Ebbing. Or maybe you vant to put on some high leather boots and choke some chickens? You like that? And you can talk dirty to them!

OLD WOMAN: Hahaha! *I'm* not a *freak*! Teeheehee. Oh yes. I remember years ago when Al Donohue was through here. Hahaha. I'll never be the same. No!

DRACULA: Alright. Vat is it you vant?

OLD WOMAN [*shrieking*]: Money! Money! That's what I want!

DRACULA: Alright, alright. Get off my back. Here. Here's ten cents. Now, get out of here . . . Now I vill take my family out of the boxes . . . [*Irritated*] I told you, don't bring your mother! . . . [*Fondly*] Bela Jr. . . .

BELA JR. [*popping out of box*]: Ah, Poppa, Poppa! Poppa, Poppa, Poppa!

DRACULA: Alright, shut up and dr-r-rink your blood. And bite Momma goodnight. You hear me? Don bug us no more! Go to the next room and eat your blackboard and crayons. And pr-r-ractice on sister's neck.

MRS. DRACULA [*nagging Jewish wife*]: Sure, that's a nice vay to talk to the child! Isn't it? Practice on sister's neck! That's all you tink about, you degenerate you! Aghh! I can't stand to look at you any more! Phah! You know vat it means ven a voman can't stand to look at a man any more? Our knot is all gone, Bela. The stake is burned out. You Fancy Dan vit the vaseline on the hair, dirtying up all the pillowcases. Ve are finished now.

DRACULA: Alright! Get off my back, you vitch you! You band rat! Sure, hanging around the Black Hawk, everybody freaked off vit you! And I was nice enough to take you avay from that—ugh! sure, that's appreciation!

MRS. DRACULA: Sure, you vit that vicious tongue, that never brought me any pleasures! No no. It is all over. Ve are finished! I'm going off.

DRACULA: Go ahead. Go off by yourself, you freak! Now, you hear? Ve are going into the next room now, and I don't vant to be disturbed.

MRS. DRACULA: Sure, you're going to get high! You're gonna smoke some shit, some of those crazy zigarettes again, and eat up the whole icebox!

DRACULA [*a beaten old Jewish man*]: I'm not getting high—a coupla pills . . . Vy don't you leave me alone?

MRS. DRACULA: Sure, you stupid pimp, you—*phah*! [*to Bela Jr.*] You like vat your daddy does for a living? He sucks people on the neck. Hm hm! You like dat? "Vat is my daddy doing?" "He sucks people's neck, for money." Hm hm! You degenerate, you freak you!

DRACULA: Look, you knew vat I vas ven you marr-ried me. Get off my back now. I'm no fr-r-reak.

MRS. DRACULA: Vat is a freak? You degenerate, you're sucking necks! Dot's all you do: "Hello. Vat does your daddy do for living?" "My daddy sucks a neck for a living." Hm hm hm! Dot's nice. Go head vit your friends, suck a neck, you pervert! *Ptu*! *Phah*!

DRACULA: Ohh, vill you stop? Vill you stop talking this vay in front of the kid?

SUPERINTENDENT [*Tough American voice*]: Mr. Lugosi, I hate ta interrupt ya, but I'm the super here. You gotta knock off this horseshit now. You wanna hear me? I mean, the people just aren't goin for it. I dunno where the hell you people lived before, but ya gotta move. I mean, I don like ta butt in on your personal business, but that suckin people onna neck is *disgusting*, now. I dunno where you people come fr—get your kid off my dog, Mr. Lugosi! God damn! The whole *family's* sick. Come on, son! Get off there! He don't like dat . . . Kid's *weird*, for Chrissake! Stop that, sonny! The dog isn't smiling, he don't like that. Mr. Lugosi, c'mon. I'm gonna give you the deposit back. You gotta get outta here. I mean, you're pushy about it! You never ask people—you're sucking their neck before you even say hello to them! C'mon, get outta here now. Damn fruit, you. You're not kiddin me. I don't want ya to do it to Father McGovern, either, trickin him into the confession booth and getting him onna neck like that, Damn weirdo . . .

T. S. Eliot

EXCERPT FROM

THE WASTELAND

Thomas Stearns Eliot (1888–1965) was one of the most influential poets of the twentieth century. For his work, he was awarded the Nobel
Prize in 1948, the British Order of Merit, also in 1948, and the American Medal of Freedom in 1964. His classic works include *The Four
Quartets*, "The Hollow Men," "Ash Wednesday," and "The Love Song
of J. Alfred Prufrock." Eliot was also a playwright, but it was one of
his books of poetry that eventually became the longest running musical in Britain and the second longest in America. That, of course, is
Cats, where Andrew Lloyd Webber put Eliot's *Old Possum's Book of Prac-
tical Cats* to music. The excerpt that appears here is from the first printed
version of Eliot's long poem *The Wasteland* (1922), and is a reference
to the scene in the novel *Dracula* where Jonathan Harker sees Dracula
crawling down the castle wall.

A woman drew her long black hair out tight
And fiddled whisper music on those strings
And bats with baby faces in the violet light
Whistled, and beat their wings
And crawled head downward down a blackened wall
And upside down in air were towers
Tolling reminiscent bells, that kept the hours
And voices singing out of empty cisterns and exhausted wells.

Edith Wharton

BEWITCHED

———◦———

Edith Wharton is probably the most well-known of America's classical novelists. Born into a wealthy New York family, she began making up stories to entertain herself during her lonely childhood. Her husband's mental illness apparently caused her to take up writing as a form of therapy. As a close friend of author Henry James, she was heavily influenced by his work. Wharton was eventually awarded the Pulitzer Prize for *The Age of Innocence*. Her other major works include *Ethan Frome, Twilight Sleep, The Children, Certain People*, and *A Backward Glance*. This story is from *Here and Beyond* (1926).

THE SNOW WAS STILL falling thickly when Orrin Bosworth, who farmed the land south of Lonetop, drove up in his cutter to Saul Rutledge's gate. He was surprised to see two other cutters ahead of him. From them descended two muffled figures. Bosworth, with increasing surprise, recognized Deacon Hibben, from North Ashmore, and Sylvester Brand, the widower, from the old Bear-cliff farm on the way to Lonetop.

It was not often that anybody in Hemlock County entered Saul Rutledge's gate; least of all in the dead of winter, and summoned (as Bosworth, at any rate, had been) by Mrs. Rutledge, who passed, even in that unsocial region, for a woman of cold manners and solitary character. The situation was enough to excite the curiosity of a less imaginative man than Orrin Bosworth.

As he drove in between the broken-down white gateposts topped by fluted urns the two men ahead of him were leading their horses to the adjoining shed. Bosworth followed, and hitched his horse to a post. Then the three tossed off the snow from their shoulders, clapped their numb hands together, and greeted each other.

"Hallo, Deacon."

"Well, well, Orrin—" They shook hands.

" 'Day, Bosworth," said Sylvester Brand, with a brief nod. He seldom put any cordiality into his manner, and on this occasion he was still busy about his horse's bridle and blanket.

Orrin Bosworth, the youngest and most communicative of the three, turned back to Deacon Hibben, whose long face, queerly blotched and moldy-looking, with blinking peering eyes, was yet less forbidding than Brand's heavily-hewn countenance.

"Queer, our all meeting here this way. Mrs. Rutledge sent me a message to come," Bosworth volunteered.

The Deacon nodded. "I got a word from her too—Andy Pond come with it yesterday noon. I hope there's no trouble here—"

He glanced through the thickening fall of snow at the desolate front of the Rutledge house, the more melancholy in its present neglected state because, like the gateposts, it kept traces of former elegance. Bosworth had often wondered how such a house had come to be built in that lonely stretch between North Ashmore and Cold Corners. People said there had once been other houses like it, forming a little township called Ashmore, a sort of mountain colony created by the caprice of an English Royalist officer, one Colonel Ashmore, who had been murdered by the Indians, with all his family, long before the Revolution. This tale was confirmed by the fact that the ruined cellars of several smaller houses were still to be discovered under the wild growth of the adjoining slopes, and that the Communion plate of the moribund Episcopal church of Cold Corners was engraved with the name of Colonel Ashmore, who had given it to the church of Ashmore in the year 1723. Of the church itself no traces remained. Doubtless it had been a modest wooden edifice, built on piles, and the conflagration which had burnt the other houses to the ground's edge had reduced it utterly to ashes. The whole place, even in summer,

wore a mournful solitary air, and people wondered why Saul Rutledge's father had gone there to settle.

"I never knew a place," Deacon Hibben said, "as seemed as far
away from humanity. And yet it ain't so in miles."

"Miles ain't the only distance," Orrin Bosworth answered; and
the two men, followed by Sylvester Brand, walked across the drive
to the front door. People in Hemlock County did not usually come
and go by their front doors, but all three men seemed to feel that,
on an occasion which appeared to be so exceptional, the usual
and more familiar approach by the kitchen would not be suitable.

They had judged rightly; the Deacon had hardly lifted the
knocker when the door opened and Mrs. Rutledge stood before
them.

"Walk right in," she said in her usual dead-level tone; and Bosworth, as he followed the others, thought to himself: "Whatever's
happened, she's not going to let it show in her face."

It was doubtful, indeed, if anything unwonted could be made
to show in Prudence Rutledge's face, so limited was its scope, so
fixed were its features. She was dressed for the occasion in a black
calico with white spots, a collar of crochet lace fastened by a gold
brooch, and a gray woolen shawl, crossed under her arms and tied
at the back. In her small narrow head the only marked prominence was that of the brow projecting roundly over pale specta-
cled eyes. Her dark hair, parted above this prominence, passed
tight and flat over the tips of her ears into a small braided coil at
the nape; and her contracted head looked still narrower from being perched on a long hollow neck with cord-like throat muscles.
Her eyes were of a pale cold gray, her complexion was an even
white. Her age might have been anywhere from thirty-five to
sixty.

The room into which she led the three men had probably been
the dining room of the Ashmore house. It was now used as a front
parlor, and a black stove planted on a sheet of zinc stuck out from
the delicately fluted panels of an old wooden mantel. A newly-lit
fire smoldered reluctantly, and the room was at once close and
bitterly cold.

"Andy Pond," Mrs. Rutledge cried to some one at the back of
the house, "step out and call Mr. Rutledge. You'll likely find him

in the woodshed, or round the barn somewheres.'' She rejoined her visitors. ''Please suit yourselves to seats,'' she said.

The three men, with an increasing air of constraint, took the chairs she pointed out, and Mrs. Rutledge sat stiffly down upon a fourth, behind a rickety beadwork table. She glanced from one to the other of her visitors.

''I presume you folks are wondering what it is I asked you to come here for,'' she said in her dead-level voice. Orrin Bosworth and Deacon Hibben murmured an assent; Sylvester Brand sat silent, his eyes, under their great thicket of eyebrows, fixed on the huge boot tip swinging before him.

''Well, I allow you didn't expect it was for a party,'' continued Mrs. Rutledge.

No one ventured to respond to this chill pleasantry, and she continued: ''We're in trouble here, and that's the fact. And we need advice—Mr. Rutledge and myself do.'' She cleared her throat, and added in a lower tone, her pitilessly clear eyes looking straight before her: ''There's a spell been cast over Mr. Rutledge.''

The Deacon looked up sharply, an incredulous smile pinching his thin lips. ''A spell?''

''That's what I said: he's bewitched.''

Again the three visitors were silent; then Bosworth, more at ease or less tongue-tied than the others, asked with an attempt at humor: ''Do you use the word in the strict Scripture sense, Mrs. Rutledge?''

She glanced at him before replying: ''That's how *he* uses it.''

The Deacon coughed and cleared his long rattling throat. ''Do you care to give us more particulars before your husband joins us?''

Mrs. Rutledge looked down at her clasped hands, as if considering the question. Bosworth noticed that the inner fold of her lids was of the same uniform white as the rest of her skin, so that when she drooped them her rather prominent eyes looked like the sightless orbs of a marble statue. The impression was unpleasing, and he glanced away at the text over the mantelpiece, which read:

The Soul That Sinneth It Shall Die.

"No," she said at length, "I'll wait."

At this moment Sylvester Brand suddenly stood up and pushed back his chair. "I don't know," he said, in his rough bass voice, "as I've got any particular lights on Bible mysteries; and this happens to be the day I was to go down to Starkfield to close a deal with a man."

Mrs. Rutledge lifted one of her long thin hands. Withered and wrinkled by hard work and cold, it was nevertheless of the same leaden white as her face. "You won't be kept long," she said. "Won't you be seated?"

Farmer Brand stood irresolute, his purplish underlip twitching. "The Deacon here—such things is more in his line. . . ."

"I want you should stay," said Mrs. Rutledge quietly; and Brand sat down again.

A silence fell, during which the four persons present seemed all to be listening for the sound of a step; but none was heard, and after a minute or two Mrs. Rutledge began to speak again.

"It's down by that old shack on Lamer's pond; that's where they meet," she said suddenly.

Bosworth, whose eyes were on Sylvester Brand's face, fancied he saw a sort of inner flush darken the farmer's heavy leathern skin. Deacon Hibben leaned forward, a glitter of curiosity in his eyes.

"They—*who*, Mrs. Rutledge?"

"My husband, Saul Rutledge . . . and her. . . ."

Sylvester Brand again stirred in his seat. "Who do you mean by *her*?" he asked abruptly, as if roused out of some far-off musing.

Mrs. Rutledge's body did not move; she simply revolved her head on her long neck and looked at him.

"Your daughter, Sylvester Brand."

The man staggered to his feet with an explosion of inarticulate sounds. "My—my daughter? What the hell are you talking about? My daughter? It's a damned lie . . . it's . . . it's . . ."

"Your daughter *Ora*, Mr. Brand," said Mrs. Rutledge slowly.

Bosworth felt an icy chill down his spine. Instinctively he turned his eyes away from Brand, and they rested on the mildewed countenance of Deacon Hibben. Between the blotches it had become as white as Mrs. Rutledge's, and the Deacon's eyes burned in the whiteness like live embers among ashes.

Brand gave a laugh: the rusty creaking laugh on one whose springs of mirth are never moved by gaiety. "My daughter *Ora*?" he repeated.

"Yes."

"My *dead* daughter?"

"That's what he says."

"Your husband?"

"That's what Mr. Rutledge says."

Orrin Bosworth listened with a sense of suffocation; he felt as if he were wrestling with long-armed horrors in a dream. He could no longer resist letting his eyes turn to Sylvester Brand's face. To his surprise it had resumed a natural imperturbable expression. Brand rose to his feet. "Is that all?" he queried contemptuously.

"All? Ain't it enough? How long is it since you folks seen Saul Rutledge, any of you?" Mrs. Rutledge flew out at them.

Bosworth, it appeared, had not seen him for nearly a year, the Deacon had only run across him once, for a minute, at the North Ashmore post office, the previous autumn, and acknowledged that he wasn't looking any too good then. Brand said nothing, but stood irresolute.

Well, if you wait a minute you'll see with your own eyes; and he'll tell you with his own words. That's what I've got you here for—to see for yourselves what's come over him. Then you'll talk different," she added, twisting her head abruptly toward Sylvester Brand.

The Deacon raised a lean hand of interrogation.

"Does your husband know we've been sent for on this business, Mrs. Rutledge?"

Mrs. Rutledge signed assent.

"It was with his consent, then—?"

She looked coldly at her questioner. "I guess it had to be," she said. Again Bosworth felt the chill down his spine. He tried to dissipate the sensation by speaking with an affectation of energy.

"Can you tell us, Mrs. Rutledge, how this trouble you speak of shows itself . . . what makes you think . . . ?"

She looked at him for a moment; then she leaned forward across the rickety beadwork table. A thin smile of disdain narrowed her colorless lips. "I don't think—I know."

"Well—but how?"

She leaned closer, both elbows on the table, her voice dropping. "I seen 'em."

In the ashen light from the veiling of snow beyond the windows the Deacon's little screwed-up eyes seemed to give out red sparks. "Him and the dead?"

"Him and the dead."

"Saul Rutledge and—and Ora Brand?"

"That's so."

Sylvester Brand's chair fell backward with a crash. He was on his feet again, crimson and cursing. "It's a God-damned fiend-begotten lie. . . ."

"Friend Brand . . . friend Brand . . ." the Deacon protested.

"Here, let me get out of this. I want to see Saul Rutledge himself, and tell him—"

"Well, here he is," said Mrs. Rutledge.

The outer door had opened; they heard the familiar stamping and shaking of a man who rids his garments of their last snow-flakes before penetrating to the sacred precincts of the best parlor. Then Saul Rutledge entered.

II

As he came in he faced the light from the north window, and Bosworth's first thought was that he looked like a drowned man fished out from under the ice—"self-drowned," he added. But the snow light plays cruel tricks with a man's color, and even with the shape of his features; it must have been partly that, Bosworth reflected, which transformed Saul Rutledge from the straight muscular fellow he had been a year before into the haggard wretch now before them.

The Deacon sought for a word to ease the horror. "Well, now, Saul—you look's if you'd ought to set right up to the stove. Had a touch of ague, maybe?"

The feeble attempt was unavailing. Rutledge neither moved nor answered. He stood among them silent, incommunicable, like one risen from the dead.

Brand grasped him roughly by the shoulder. "See here, Saul

Rutledge, what's this dirty lie your wife tells us you've been putting about?''

Still Rutledge did not move. "It's no lie," he said.

Brand's hand dropped from his shoulder. In spite of the man's
rough bullying power he seemed to be undefinably awed by Rutledge's look and tone.

"No lie? You've gone plumb crazy, then, have you?"

Mrs. Rutledge spoke. "My husband's not lying, nor he ain't
gone crazy. Don't I tell you I seen 'em?"

Brand laughed again. "Him and the dead?"

"Yes."

"Down by the Lamer pond, you say?"

"Yes."

"And when was that, if I might ask?"

"Day before yesterday."

A silence fell on the strangely assembled group. The Deacon at
length broke it to say to Mr. Brand: "Brand, in my opinion we've
got to see this thing through."

Brand stood for a moment in speechless contemplation: there
was something animal and primitive about him, Bosworth
thought, as he hung thus, lowering and dumb, a little foam bead-
ing the corners of that heavy purplish underlip. He let himself
slowly down into his chair. "I'll see it through."

The two other men and Mrs. Rutledge had remained seated.
Saul Rutledge stood before them, like a prisoner at the bar, or
rather like a sick man before the physicians who were to heal him.
As Bosworth scrutinized that hollow face, so wan under the dark
sunburn, so sucked inward and consumed by some hidden fever,
there stole over the sound healthy man the thought that perhaps,
after all, husband and wife spoke the truth, and that they were
all at that moment really standing on the edge of some forbidden
mystery. Things that the rational mind would reject without a
thought seemed no longer so easy to dispose of as one looked at
the actual Saul Rutledge and remembered the man he had been
a year before. Yes; as the Deacon said, they would have to see it
through. . . .

"Sit down then, Saul; draw up to us, won't you?" the Deacon
suggested, trying again for a natural tone.

Mrs. Rutledge pushed a chair forward, and her husband sat

down on it. He stretched out his arms and grasped his knees in his brown bony fingers; in that attitude he remained, turning neither his head nor his eyes.

"Well, Saul," the Deacon continued, "your wife says you thought mebbe we could do something to help you through this trouble, whatever it is."

Rutledge's gray eyes widened a little. "No; I didn't think that. It was her idea to try what could be done."

"I presume, though, since you've agreed to our coming, that you don't object to our putting a few questions?"

Rutledge was silent for a moment; then he said with a visible effort: "No; I don't object."

"Well—you've heard what your wife says?"

Rutledge made a slight motion of assent.

"And—what have you got to answer? How do you explain . . . ?"

Mrs. Rutledge intervened. "How can he explain? I seen 'em."

There was a silence; then Bosworth, trying to speak in an easy reassuring tone, queried: "That so, Saul?"

"That's so."

Brand lifted up his brooding head. "You mean to say you . . . you sit here before us all and say. . . ."

The Deacon's hand again checked him. "Hold on, friend Brand. We're all of us trying for the facts, ain't we?" He turned to Rutledge. "We've heard what Mrs. Rutledge says. What's your answer?"

"I don't know as there's any answer. She found us."

"And you mean to tell me the person with you was . . . was what you took to be . . ." the Deacon's thin voice grew thinner, "Ora Brand?"

Saul Rutledge nodded.

"You knew . . . or thought you knew . . . you were meeting with the dead?"

Rutledge bent his head again. The snow continued to fall in a steady unwavering sheet against the window, and Bosworth felt as if a winding sheet were descending from the sky to envelop them all in a common grave.

"Think what you're saying! It's against our religion! Ora . . . poor child! . . . died over a year ago. I saw you at her funeral, Saul. How can you make such a statement?"

"What else can he do?" thrust in Mrs. Rutledge.

There was another pause. Bosworth's resources had failed him, and Brand once more sat plunged in dark meditation. The Deacon laid his quivering finger tips together, and moistened his lips.

"Was the day before yesterday the first time?" he asked.

The movement of Rutledge's head was negative.

"Not the first? Then when . . . ?"

"Nigh on a year ago, I reckon."

"God! And you mean to tell us that ever since—?"

"Well . . . look at him," said his wife. The three men lowered their eyes.

After a moment Bosworth, trying to collect himself, glanced at the Deacon. "Why not ask Saul to make his own statement, if that's what we're here for?"

"That's so," the Deacon assented. He turned to Rutledge. "Will you try and give us your idea . . . of . . . of how it began?"

There was another silence. Then Rutledge tightened his grasp on his gaunt knees, and still looking straight ahead, with his curiously clear unseeing gaze: "Well," he said, "I guess it begun away back, afore even I was married to Mrs. Rutledge. . . ." He spoke in a low automatic tone, as if some invisible agent were dictating his words, or even uttering them for him. "You know," he added, "Ora and me was to have been married."

Sylvester Brand lifted his head. "Straighten that statement out first, please," he interjected.

"What I mean is, we kept company. But Ora she was very young. Mr. Brand here he sent her away. She was gone nigh to three years, I guess. When she come back I was married."

"That's right," Brand said, relapsing once more into his sunken attitude.

"And after she came back did you meet her again?" the Deacon continued.

"Alive?" Rutledge questioned.

A perceptible shudder ran through the room.

"Well—of course," said the Deacon nervously.

Rutledge seemed to consider. "Once I did—only once. There was a lot of other people round. At Cold Corners Fair it was."

"Did you talk with her then?"

"Only a minute."

"What did she say?"

His voice dropped. "She said she was sick and knew she was going to die, and when she was dead she'd come back to me."

"And what did you answer?"

"Nothing."

"Did you think anything of it at the time?"

"Well, no. Not till I heard she was dead I didn't. After that I thought of it—and I guess she drew me." He moistened his lips.

"Drew you down to that abandoned house by the pond?"

Rutledge made a faint motion of assent, and the Deacon added: "How did you know it was there she wanted you to come?"

"She . . . just drew me. . . ."

There was a long pause. Bosworth felt, on himself and the other two men, the oppressive weight of the next question to be asked. Mrs. Rutledge opened and closed her narrow lips once or twice, like some beached shellfish gasping for the tide. Rutledge waited.

"Well, now, Saul, won't you go on with what you was telling us?" the Deacon at length suggested.

"That's all. There's nothing else."

The Deacon lowered his voice. "She just draws you?"

"Yes."

"Often?"

"That's as it happens. . . ."

"But if it's always there she draws you, man, haven't you the strength to keep away from the place?"

For the first time, Rutledge wearily turned his head toward his questioner. A spectral smile narrowed his colorless lips. "Ain't any use. She follers after me. . . ."

There was another silence. What more could they ask, then and there? Mrs. Rutledge's presence checked the next question. The Deacon seemed hopelessly to resolve the matter. At length he spoke in a more authoritative tone. "These are forbidden things. You know that, Saul. Have you tried prayer?"

Rutledge shook his head.

"Will you pray with us now?"

Rutledge cast a glance of freezing indifference on his spiritual adviser. "If you folks want to pray, I'm agreeable," he said. But Mrs. Rutledge intervened.

"Prayer ain't any good. In this kind of thing it ain't no manner of use; you know it ain't. I called you here, Deacon, because you remember the last case in this parish. Thirty years ago it was, I guess; but you remember. Lefferts Nash—did praying help *him*? I was a little girl then, but I used to hear my folks talk of it winter nights. Lefferts Nash and Hannah Cory. They drove a stake through her breast. That's what cured him.''

"Oh—" Orrin Bosworth exclaimed.

Sylvester Brand raised his head. "You're speaking of that old story as if this was the same sort of thing?"

"Ain't it? Ain't my husband pining away the same as Lefferts Nash did? The Deacon here knows—"

The Deacon stirred anxiously in his chair. "These are forbidden things," he repeated. "Supposing your husband is quite sincere in thinking himself haunted, as you might say. Well, even then, what proof have we that the . . . the dead woman . . . is the specter of that poor girl?"

"Proof? Don't he say so? Didn't she tell him? Ain't I seen 'em?" Mrs. Rutledge almost screamed.

The three men sat silent, and suddenly the wife burst out: "A stake through the breast! That's the old way; and it's the only way. The Deacon knows it!"

"It's against our religion to disturb the dead."

"Ain't it against your religion to let the living perish as my husband is perishing?" She sprang up with one of her abrupt movements and took the family Bible from the whatnot in a corner of the parlor. Putting the book on the table, and moistening a livid finger tip, she turned the pages rapidly, till she came to one on which she laid her hand like a stony paperweight. "See here," she said, and read out in her level chanting voice:

" *'Thou shalt not suffer a witch to live.'*

"That's in Exodus, that's where it is," she added, leaving the book open as if to confirm the statement.

Bosworth continued to glance anxiously from one to the other of the four people about the table. He was younger than any of them, and had had more contact with the modern world; down in Starkfield, in the bar of the Fielding House, he could hear himself laughing with the rest of the men at such old wives' tales. But it was not for nothing that he had been born under the icy shadow of Lonetop, and had shivered and hungered as a lad through the bitter Hemlock County winters. After his parents died, and he had taken hold of the farm himself, he had got more out of it by using improved methods, and by supplying the increasing throng of summer boarders over Stotesbury way with milk and vegetables. He had been made a Selectman of North Ashmore; for so young a man he had a standing in the county. But the roots of the old life were still in him. He could remember, as a little boy, going twice a year with his mother to that bleak hill farm out beyond Sylvester Brand's, where Mrs. Bosworth's aunt, Cressidora Cheney, had been shut up for years in a cold clean room with iron bars in the windows. When little Orrin first saw Aunt Cressidora she was a small white old woman, whom her sisters use to "make decent" for visitors the day that Orrin and his mother were expected. The child wondered why there were bars to the window. "Like a canary bird," he said to his mother. The phrase made Mrs. Bosworth reflect. "I do believe they keep Aunt Cressidora too lonesome," she said; and the next time she went up the mountain with the little boy he carried to his great-aunt a canary in a little wooden cage. It was a great excitement; he knew it would make her happy.

The old woman's motionless face lit up when she saw the bird, and her eyes began to glitter. "It belongs to me," she said instantly, stretching her soft bony hand over the cage.

"Of course it does, Aunt Cressy," said Mrs. Bosworth, her eyes filling.

But the bird, startled by the shadow of the old woman's hand, began to flutter and beat its wings distractedly. At the sight, Aunt Cressidora's calm face suddenly became a coil of twitching features: "You she-devil, you!" she cried in a high squealing voice; and thrusting her hand into the cage she dragged out the terrified bird and wrung its neck. She was plucking the hot body, and squealing "she-devil, she-devil!" as they drew little Orrin from the room. On the way down the mountain his mother wept a great deal, and said: "You must never tell anybody that poor Auntie's crazy, or the men would come and take her down to the asylum at Starkfield, and the shame of it would kill us all. Now promise." The child promised.

He remembered the scene now, with its deep fringe of mystery, secrecy and rumor. It seemed related to a great many other things below the surface of his thoughts, things which stole up anew, making him feel that all the old people he had known, and who "believed in these things," might after all be right. Hadn't a witch been burned at North Ashmore? Didn't the summer folk still drive over in jolly buckboard loads to see the meetinghouse where the trial had been held, the pond where they had ducked her and she had floated? . . . Deacon Hibben believed; Bosworth was sure of it. If he didn't, why did people from all over the place come to him when their animals had queer sicknesses, or when there was a child in the family that had to be kept shut up because it fell down flat and foamed? Yes, in spite of his religion, Deacon Hibben knew. . . .

And Brand? Well, it came to Bosworth in a flash: that North Ashmore woman who was burned had the name of Brand. The same stock, no doubt; there had been Brands in Hemlock County ever since the white men had come there. And Orrin, when he was a child, remembered hearing his parents say that Sylvester Brand hadn't ever oughter married his own cousin, because of the blood. Yet the couple had had two healthy girls, and when Mrs. Brand pined away and died nobody suggested that anything had been wrong with her mind. And Vanessa and Ora were the handsomest girls anywhere round. Brand knew it, and scrimped and saved all he could to send Ora, the eldest, down to Starkfield to learn bookkeeping. "When she's married I'll send you," he used to say to little Venny, who was his favorite. But Ora never married. She was away three years, during which Venny ran wild on the slopes of Lonetop; and when Ora came back she sickened and died—poor girl! Since then Brand had grown more savage and morose. He was a hard-working farmer, but there wasn't much to be got out of those barren Bearcliff acres. He was said to have taken to drink since his wife's death; now and then men ran across him in the "dives" of Stotesbury. But not often. And between times he labored hard on his stony acres and did his best for his daughters. In the neglected graveyard of Cold Corners there was a slanting headstone marked with his wife's name; near it, a year since, he had laid his eldest daughter. And sometimes, at dusk, in the autumn, the village people saw him walk slowly by, turn in between the graves, and stand looking down on the two stones. But he never brought a flower there, or planted a bush; nor Venny either. She was too wild and ignorant. . . .

Mrs. Rutledge repeated: "That's in Exodus."

The three visitors remained silent, turning about their hats in reluctant hands. Rutledge faced them, still with that empty pellucid gaze which frightened Bosworth. What was he seeing?

"Ain't any of you folks got the grit—?" his wife burst out again, half hysterically.

Deacon Hibben held up his hand. "That's no way, Mrs. Rutledge. This ain't a question of having grit. What we want first of all is . . . proof . . ."

"That's so," said Bosworth, with an explosion of relief, as if the words had lifted something black and crouching from his breast. Involuntarily the eyes of both men had turned to Brand. He stood there smiling grimly, but did not speak.

"Ain't it so, Brand?" the Deacon prompted him.

"Proof that spooks walk?" the other sneered.

"Well—I presume you want this business settled too?"

The old farmer squared his shoulders. "Yes—I do. But I ain't a sperritualist. How the hell are you going to settle it?"

Deacon Hibben hesitated; then he said, in a low incisive tone: "I don't see but one way—Mrs. Rutledge's."

There was a silence.

"What?" Brand sneered again. "Spying?"

The Deacon's voice sank lower. "If the poor girl does walk . . . her that's your child . . . wouldn't you be the first to want her laid quiet? We all know there've been such cases . . . mysterious visitations. . . . Can any one of us here deny it?"

"I seen 'em," Mrs. Rutledge interjected.

There was another heavy pause. Suddenly Brand fixed his gaze on Rutledge. "See here, Saul Rutledge, you've got to clear up this damned calumny, or I'll know why. You say my dead girl comes to you." He labored with his breath, and then jerked out: "When? You tell me that, and I'll be there."

Rutledge's head drooped a little, and his eyes wandered to the window. "Round about sunset, mostly."

"You know beforehand?"

Rutledge made a sign of assent.

"Well, then—tomorrow, will it be?"

Rutledge made the same sign.

Brand turned to the door. "I'll be there." That was all he said. He strode out between them without another glance or word. Deacon Hibben looked at Mrs. Rutledge. "We'll be there too," he said, as if she had asked him; but she had not spoken, and Bosworth saw that her thin body was trembling all over. He was glad when he and Hibben were out again in the snow.

III

They thought that Brand wanted to be left to himself, and to give him time to unhitch his horse they made a pretense of hanging about in the doorway while Bosworth searched his pockets for a pipe he had no mind to light.

But Brand turned back to them as they lingered. "You'll meet me down by Lamer's pond tomorrow?" he suggested. "I want witnesses. Round about sunset."

They nodded their acquiescence, and he got into his sleigh, gave the horse a cut across the flanks, and drove off under the snow-smothered hemlocks. The other two men went to the shed.

"What do you make of this business, Deacon?" Bosworth asked, to break the silence.

The Deacon shook his head. "The man's a sick man—that's sure. Something's sucking the life clean out of him."

But already, in the biting outer air, Bosworth was getting himself under better control. "Looks to me like a bad case of the ague, as you said."

"Well—ague of the mind, then. It's his brain that's sick."

Bosworth shrugged. "He ain't the first in Hemlock County."

"That's so," the Deacon agreed. "It's a worm in the brain, solitude is."

"Well, we'll know this time tomorrow, maybe," said Bosworth. He scrambled into his sleigh, and was driving off in his turn when he heard his companion calling after him. The Deacon explained that his horse had cast a shoe; would Bosworth drive him down to the forge near North Ashmore, if it wasn't too much out of his way? He didn't want the mare slipping about on the freezing snow, and he could probably get the blacksmith to drive him back and shoe her in Rutledge's shed. Bosworth made room for him under the bearskin, and the two men drove off, pursued by a puzzled whinny from the Deacon's old mare.

The road they took was not the one that Bosworth would have followed to reach his own home. But he did not mind that. The shortest way to the forge passed close by Lamer's pond, and Bosworth, since he was in for the business, was not sorry to look the ground over. They drove on in silence.

The snow had ceased, and a green sunset was spreading upward into the crystal sky. A stinging wind barbed with ice flakes caught them in the face on the open ridges, but when they dropped down into the hollow by Lamer's pond the air was as soundless and empty as an unswung bell. They jogged along slowly, each thinking his own thoughts.

"That's the house . . . that tumble-down shack over there, I suppose?" the Deacon said, as the road drew near the edge of the frozen pond.

"Yes: that's the house. A queer hermit fellow built it years ago, my father used to tell me. Since then I don't believe it's ever been used but by the gypsies."

Bosworth had reined in his horse, and sat looking through pine trunks purpled by the sunset at the crumbling structure. Twilight already lay under the trees, though day lingered in the open. Between two sharply-patterned pine boughs he saw the evening star, like a white boat in a sea of green.

His gaze dropped from that fathomless sky and followed the blue-white undulations of the snow. It gave him a curious agitated feeling to think that here, in this icy solitude, in the tumble-down house he had so often passed without heeding it, a dark mystery, too deep for thought, was being enacted. Down that very slope, coming from the graveyard at Cold Corners, the being they called "Ora" must pass toward the pond. His heart began to beat stiflingly. Suddenly he gave an exclamation: "Look!"

He had jumped out of the cutter and was stumbling up the bank toward the slope of snow. On it, turned in the direction of the house by the pond, he had detected a woman's footprints; two;

then three; then more. The Deacon scrambled out after him, and they stood and stared.

"God—barefoot!" Hibben gasped. "Then it *is* . . . the dead. . . ."

Bosworth said nothing. But he knew that no live woman would travel with naked feet across that freezing wilderness. Here, then, was the proof the Deacon had asked for—they held it. What should they do with it?

"Supposing we was to drive up nearer—round the turn of the pond, till we get close to the house," the Deacon proposed in a colorless voice. "Mebbe then. . . ."

Postponement was a relief. They got into the sleigh and drove on. Two or three hundred yards farther the road, a mere lane under steep bushy banks, turned sharply to the right, following the bend of the pond. As they rounded the turn they saw Brand's cutter ahead of them. It was empty, the horse tied to a treetrunk. The two men looked at each other again. This was not Brand's nearest way home.

Evidently he had been actuated by the same impulse which had made them rein in their horse by the pondside, and then hasten on to the deserted hovel. Had he too discovered those spectral footprints? Perhaps it was for that very reason that he had left his cutter and vanished in the direction of the house. Bosworth found himself shivering all over under his bearskin. "I wish to God the dark wasn't coming on," he muttered. He tethered his own horse near Brand's, and without a word he and the Deacon ploughed through the snow, in the track of Brand's huge feet. They had only a few yards to walk to overtake him. He did not hear them following him, and when Bosworth spoke his name, and he stopped short and turned, his heavy face was dim and confused, like a darker blot on the dusk. He looked at them dully, but without surprise.

"I wanted to see the place," he merely said.

The Deacon cleared his throat. "Just take a look . . . yes . . . we thought so. . . . But I guess there won't be anything to *see*. . . ." He attempted a chuckle.

The other did not seem to hear him, but labored on ahead through the pines. The three men came out together in the cleared space before the house. As they emerged from beneath the trees they seemed to have left night behind. The evening star shed a luster on the speckless snow, and Brand, in that lucid circle, stopped with a jerk, and pointed to the same light footprints turned toward the house—the track of a woman in the snow. He stood still, his face working. ''Bare feet. . . .'' he said.

The Deacon piped up in a quavering voice: ''The feet of the dead.''

Brand remained motionless. ''The feet of the dead,'' he echoed.

Deacon Hibben laid a frightened hand on his arm. ''Come away now, Brand; for the love of God come away.''

The father hung there, gazing down at those light tracks on the snow—light as fox or squirrel trails they seemed, on the white immensity. Bosworth thought to himself: ''The living couldn't walk so light—not even Ora Brand couldn't have, when she lived. . . .'' The cold seemed to have entered into his very marrow. His teeth were chattering.

Brand swung about on them abruptly. ''*Now!*'' he said, moving on as if to an assault, his head bowed forward on his bull neck.

''Now—now? Not in there?'' gasped the Deacon. ''What's the use? It was tomorrow he said—'' He shook like a leaf.

''It's now,'' said Brand. He went up to the door of the crazy house, pushed it inward, and meeting with an unexpected resistance, thrust his heavy shoulder against the panel. The door collapsed like a playing card, and Brand stumbled after it into the darkness of the hut. The others, after a moment's hesitation, followed.

Bosworth was never quite sure in what order the events that succeeded took place. Coming in out of the snow dazzle, he seemed to be plunging into total blackness. He groped his way across the threshold, caught a sharp splinter of the fallen door in his palm, seemed to see something white and wraithlike surge up out of the darkest corner of the hut, and then heard a revolver shot at his elbow, and a cry—

Brand had turned back, and was staggering past him out into the lingering daylight. The sunset, suddenly flushing through the trees, crimsoned his face like blood. He held a revolver in his hand and looked about him in his stupid way.

''They *do* walk, then,'' he said and began to laugh. He bent his head to examine his weapon. ''Better here than in the churchyard. They shan't dig her up *now*,'' he shouted out. The two men caught him by the arms, and Bosworth got the revolver away from him.

IV

The next day Bosworth's sister Loretta, who kept house for him, asked him, when he came in for his midday dinner, if he had heard the news.

Bosworth had been sawing wood all the morning, and in spite of the cold and the driving snow, which had begun again in the night, he was covered with an icy sweat, like a man getting over a fever.

"What news?"

"Venny Brand's down sick with pneumonia. The Deacon's been there. I guess she's dying."

Bosworth looked at her with listless eyes. She seemed far off from him, miles away. "Venny Brand?" he echoed.

"You never liked her, Orrin."

"She's a child. I never knew much about her."

"Well," repeated his sister, with the guileless relish of the unimaginative for bad news, "I guess she's dying." After a pause she added: "It'll kill Sylvester Brand, all alone up there."

Bosworth got up and said: "I've got to see to poulticing the gray's fetlock." He walked out into the steadily falling snow.

Venny Brand was buried three days later. The Deacon read the service; Bosworth was one of the pallbearers. The whole countryside turned out, for the snow had stopped falling, and at any season a funeral offered an opportunity for an outing that was not to be missed. Besides, Venny Brand was young and handsome— at least some people thought her handsome, though she was so swarthy—and her dying like that, so suddenly, had the fascination of tragedy.

"They say her lungs filled right up. . . . Seems she'd had bronchial troubles before . . . I always said both them girls was frail. . . . Look at Ora, how she took and wasted away! And it's colder'n all outdoors up there to Brand's. . . . Their mother, too, *she* pined away just the same. They don't ever make old bones on the mother's side of the family. . . . There's that young Bedlow over there;

they say Venny was engaged to him. . . . Oh, Mrs. Rutledge, excuse *me*. . . . Step right into the pew; there's a seat for you alongside of grandma. . . ."

Mrs. Rutledge was advancing with deliberate step down the narrow aisle of the bleak wooden church. She had on her best bonnet, a monumental structure which no one had seen out of her trunk since old Mrs. Silsee's funeral, three years before. All the women remembered it. Under its perpendicular pile her narrow face, swaying on the long thin neck, seemed whiter than ever; but her air of fretfulness had been composed into a suitable expression of mournful immobility.

"Looks as if the stonemason had carved her to put atop of Venny's grave," Bosworth thought as she glided past him; and then shivered at his own sepulchral fancy. When she bent over her hymn book her lowered lids reminded him again of marble eyeballs; the bony hands clasping the book were bloodless. Bosworth had never seen such hands since he had seen old Aunt Cressidora Cheney strangle the canary bird because it fluttered.

The service was over, the coffin of Venny Brand had been lowered into her sister's grave, and the neighbors were slowly dispersing. Bosworth, as pallbearer, felt obliged to linger and say a word to the stricken father. He waited till Brand had turned from the grave with the Deacon at his side. The three men stood together for a moment; but not one of them spoke. Brand's face was the closed door of a vault, barred with wrinkles like bands of iron.

Finally the Deacon took his hand and said: "The Lord gave—"

Brand nodded and turned away toward the shed where the horses were hitched. Bosworth followed him. "Let me drive along home with you," he suggested.

Brand did not so much as turn his head. "Home? What home?" he said; and the other fell back.

Loretta Bosworth was talking with the other women while the men unblanketed their horses and backed the cutters out into the heavy snow. As Bosworth waited for her, a few feet off, he saw Mrs. Rutledge's tall bonnet lording it above the group. Andy Pond, the Rutledge farm hand, was backing out the sleigh.

"Saul ain't here today, Mrs. Rutledge, is he?" one of the village elders piped, turning a benevolent old tortoise head about on a loose neck, and blinking up into Mrs. Rutledge's marble face.

Bosworth heard her measure out her answer in slow incisive words. "No. Mr. Rutledge he ain't here. He would 'a' come for certain, but his aunt Minorca Cummins is being buried down to Stotesbury this very day and he had to go down there. Don't it sometimes seem zif we was all walking right in the Shadow of Death?"

As she walked toward the cutter, in which Andy Pond was already seated, the Deacon went up to her with visible hesitation. Involuntarily Bosworth also moved nearer. He heard the Deacon say: "I'm glad to hear that Saul is able to be up and around."

She turned her small head on her rigid neck, and lifted the lids of marble.

"Yes, I guess he'll sleep quieter now. And *her* too, maybe, now she don't lay there alone any longer," she added in a low voice, with a sudden twist of her chin toward the fresh black stain in the graveyard snow. She got into the cutter, and said in a clear tone to Andy Pond: " 'S long as we're down here I don't know but what I'll just call round and get a box of soap at Hiram Pringle's."

H. P. Lovecraft

THE HOUND

⊰⊱

The works of Howard Philips Lovecraft originally appeared in pulp magazines or amateur presses, and he remained virtually unknown until well after his death. It was through the persistent efforts of his friends and admirers that he finally received a wider, and ever-growing, audience. Two fellow-writers tried to convince publishers to reprint posthumous collections of Lovecraft's work. When their efforts failed, they formed Arkham House Publishers, and published the books themselves. Soon many major publishers came out with collections of his stories. He is now one of the best-known authors of horror and supernatural fiction. Lovecraft was the creator of the "Cthulhu Mythos," a collection of stories that are widely imitated and supplemented. His most famous stories are "The Call of Cthulhu" and "The Dunwich Horror." Many of his stories have been made into movies, and even some fantasy role-playing and computer games are based on his stories. His works are now continually in print and have been anthologized countless times. He wrote this story in September 1922, and it first appeared in the February 1924 issue of *Weird Tales* magazine.

IN MY TORTURED EARS there sounds unceasingly a nightmare whirring and flapping, and a faint, distant baying as of some gigantic hound. It is not dream—it is not, I fear, even madness—for too much has already happened to give me these merciful doubts. St. John is a mangled corpse; I alone know why, and such is my knowledge that I am about to blow out my brains for fear I shall be mangled in the same way. Down unlit and illimitable corridors of eldritch phantasy sweeps the black, shapeless Nemesis that drives me to self-annihilation.

May heaven forgive the folly and morbidity which led us both to so monstrous a fate! Wearied with the commonplaces of a prosaic world, where even the joys of romance and adventure soon grow stale, St. John and I had followed enthusiastically every aesthetic and intellectual movement which promised respite from our devastating ennui. The enigmas of the Symbolists and the ecstasies of the pre-Raphaelites all were ours in their time, but each new mood was drained too soon of its diverting novelty and appeal. Only the sombre philosophy of the Decadents could hold us, and this we found potent only by increasing gradually the depth and diabolism of our penetrations. Baudelaire and Huysmans were soon exhausted of thrills, till finally there remained for us only the more direct stimuli of unnatural personal experiences and adventures. It was this frightful emotional need which led us eventually to that detestable course which even in my present fear I mention with shame and timidity—that hideous extremity of human outrage, the abhorred practice of grave-robbing.

I cannot reveal the details of our shocking expeditions, or catalogue even partly the worst of the trophies adorning the nameless museum we prepared in the great stone house where we jointly dwelt, alone and servantless. Our museum was a blasphemous, unthinkable place, where with the satanic taste of neurotic virtuosi we had assembled an universe of terror and decay to excite our jaded sensibilities. It was a secret room, far, far underground; where huge winged dæmons carven of basalt and onyx vomited from wide grinning mouths weird green and orange light, and hidden pneumatic pipes ruffled into kaleidoscopic dances of death the lines of red charnel things hand in hand woven in voluminous black hangings. Through these pipes came at will the odours our moods most craved; sometimes the scent of pale funeral lilies, sometimes the narcotic incense of imagined Eastern shrines of the kingly dead, and sometimes—how I shudder to recall it!—the frightful, soul-up-heaving stenches of the uncovered grave.

Around the walls of this repellent chamber were cases of antique mummies alternating with comely, life-like bodies perfectly stuffed and cured by the taxidermist's art, and with headstones snatched from the oldest churchyards of the world. Niches here and there contained skulls of all shapes, and heads preserved in various stages of dissolution. There one might find the rotting, bald pates of famous noblemen, and the fresh and radiantly golden heads of new-buried children. Statues and paintings there were, all of fiendish subjects and some executed by St. John and myself. A locked portfolio, bound in tanned human skin, held certain unknown and unnamable drawings which it was rumoured Goya had perpetrated but dared not acknowledge. There were nauseous musical instruments, stringed, brass, and woodwind, on which St. John and I sometimes produced dissonances of exquisite morbidity and cacodæmoniacal ghastliness; whilst in a multitude of inlaid ebony cabinets reposed the most incredible and unimaginable variety of tomb-loot ever assembled by human madness and perversity. It is of this loot in particular that I must not speak—thank God I had the courage to destroy it long before I thought of destroying myself.

The predatory excursions on which we collected our unmentionable treasures were always artistically memorable events. We were no vulgar ghouls, but worked only under certain conditions of mood, landscape, environment, weather, season, and moonlight. These pastimes were to us the most exquisite form of aesthetic expression, and we gave their details a fastidious technical care. An inappropriate hour, a jarring lighting effect, or a clumsy manipulation of the damp sod, would almost totally destroy for us that ecstatic titillation which followed the exhumation of some ominous, grinning secret of the earth. Our quest for novel scenes and piquant conditions was feverish and insatiate—St. John was always the leader, and he it was who led the way at last to that mocking, that accursed spot which brought us our hideous and inevitable doom.

By what malign fatality were we lured to that terrible Holland churchyard? I think it was the dark rumour and legendry, the tales of one buried for five centuries, who had himself been a ghoul in his time and had stolen a potent thing from a mighty sepulchre. I can recall the scene in these final moments—the pale autumnal moon over the graves, casting long horrible shadows; the grotesque trees, drooping sullenly to meet the neglected grass and the crumbling slabs; the vast legions of strangely colossal bats that flew against the moon; the antique ivied church pointing a huge spectral finger at the livid sky; the phosphorescent insects

that danced like death-fires under the yews in a distant corner;
the odours of mould, vegetation, and less explicable things that
mingled feebly with the nightwind from over far swamps and seas;
and worst of all, the faint deep-toned baying of some gigantic
hound which we could neither see nor definitely place. As we
heard this suggestion of baying we shuddered, remembering the
tales of the peasantry; for he whom we sought had centuries before been found in this selfsame spot, torn and mangled by the
claws and teeth of some unspeakable beast.

I remember how we delved in this ghoul's grave with our
spades, and how we thrilled at the picture of ourselves, the grave,
the pale watching moon, the horrible shadows, the grotesque
trees, the titanic bats, the antique church, the dancing death-fires,
the sickening odours, the gently moaning night-wind, and the
strange, half-heard, directionless baying, of whose objective existence we could scarcely be sure. Then we struck a substance
harder than the damp mould, and beheld a rotting oblong box
crusted with mineral deposits from the long undisturbed ground.
It was incredibly tough and thick, but so old that we finally pried
it open and feasted our eyes on what it held.

Much—amazingly much—was left of the object despite the
lapse of five hundred years. The skeleton, though crushed in
places by the jaws of the thing that had killed it, held together with
surprising firmness, and we gloated over the clean white skull and
its long, firm teeth and its eyeless sockets that once had glowed
with a charnel fever like our own. In the coffin lay an amulet of
curious and exotic design, which had apparently been worn
around the sleeper's neck. It was the oddly conventionalised figure of a crouching winged hound, or sphinx with a semi-canine
face, and was exquisitely carved in antique Oriental fashion from
a small piece of green jade. The expression on its features was repellent in the extreme, savouring at once of death, bestiality, and
malevolence. Around the base was an inscription in characters
which neither St. John nor I could identify; and on the bottom,
like a maker's seal, was graven a grotesque and formidable skull.

Immediately upon beholding this amulet we knew that we
must possess it; that this treasure alone was our logical pelf from
the centuried grave. Even had its outlines been unfamiliar we
would have desired it, but as we looked more closely we saw that
it was not wholly unfamiliar. Alien it indeed was to all art and

literature which sane and balanced readers know, but we recognised it as the thing hinted of in the forbidden *Necronomicon* of the mad Arab Abdul Alhazred; the ghastly soul-symbol of the corpse-eating cult of inaccessible Leng, in Central Asia. All too well did we trace the sinister lineaments described by the old Arab dæmonologist; lineaments, he wrote, drawn from some obscure supernatural manifestation of the souls of those who vexed and gnawed at the dead.

Seizing the green jade object, we gave a last glance at the bleached and cavern-eyed face of its owner and closed up the grave as we found It. As we hastened from that abhorrent spot, the stolen amulet in St. John's pocket, we thought we saw the bats descend in a body to the earth we had so lately rifled, as if seeking for some cursed and unholy nourishment. But the autumn moon shone weak and pale, and we could not be sure. So, too, as we sailed the next day away from Holland to our home, we thought we heard the faint distant baying of some gigantic hound in the background. But the autumn wind moaned sad and wan, and we could not be sure.

II

Less than a week after our return to England, strange things began to happen. We lived as recluses; devoid of friends, alone, and without servants in a few rooms of an ancient manor-house on a bleak and unfrequented moor; so that our doors were seldom disturbed by the knock of the visitor. Now, however, we were troubled by what seemed to be frequent fumblings in the night, not only around the doors but around the windows also, upper as well as lower. Once we fancied that a large, opaque body darkened the library window when the moon was shining against it, and another time we thought we heard a whirring or flapping sound not far off. On each occasion investigation revealed nothing, and we began to ascribe the occurrences to imagination alone—that same curiously disturbed imagination which still prolonged in our ears the faint far baying we thought we had heard in the Holland churchyard. The jade amulet now reposed in a niche in our museum, and sometimes we burned strangely scented candles before it. We read much in Alhazred's *Necronomicon* about its properties, and about the relation of ghouls' souls to the objects it symbolised; and were disturbed by what we read. Then terror came.

On the night of September 24, 19—, I heard a knock at my chamber door. Fancying it St. John's, I bade the knocker enter, but was answered only by a shrill laugh. There was no one in the corridor. When I aroused St. John from his sleep, he professed entire ignorance of the event, and became as worried as I. It was that night that the faint, distant baying over the moor became to us a certain and dreaded reality. Four days later, whilst we were both in the hidden museum, there came a low, cautious scratching at the single door which led to the secret library staircase. Our alarm was now divided, for besides our fear of the unknown, we had always entertained a dread that our grisly collection might be discovered. Extinguishing all lights, we proceeded to the door and threw it suddenly open; whereupon we felt an unaccountable rush of air, and heard as if receding far away a queer combination of rustling, tittering, and articulate chatter. Whether we were mad, dreaming, or in our senses, we did not try to determine. We only realised, with the blackest of apprehensions, that the apparently disembodied chatter was beyond a doubt *in the Dutch language*.

After that we lived in growing horror and fascination. Mostly we held to the theory that we were jointly going mad from our life of unnatural excitements, but sometimes it pleased us more to dramatise ourselves as the victims of some creeping and appalling doom. Bizarre manifestations were now too frequent to count. Our lonely house was seemingly alive with the presence of some malign being whose nature we could not guess, and every night that dæmoniac baying rolled over the windswept moor, always louder and louder. On October 29 we found in the soft earth underneath the library window a series of footprints utterly impossible to describe. They were as baffling as the hordes of great bats which haunted the old manor-house in unprecedented and increasing numbers.

The horror reached a culmination on November 18, when St. John, walking home after dark from the distant railway station, was seized by some frightful carnivorous thing and torn to ribbons. His screams had reached the house, and I had hastened to the terrible scene in time to hear a whir of wings and see a vague black cloudy thing silhouetted against the rising moon. My friend was dying when I spoke to him, and he could not answer coherently. All he could do was to whisper, "The amulet—that damned thing—." Then he collapsed, an inert mass of mangled flesh.

I buried him the next midnight in one of our neglected gardens, and mumbled over his body one of the devilish rituals he had loved in life. And as I pronounced the last dæmoniac sentence I heard afar on the moor the faint baying of some gigantic hound. The moon was up, but I dared not look at it. And when I saw on the dim-litten moor a wide nebulous shadow sweeping from mound to mound, I shut my eyes and threw myself face down upon the ground. When I arose trembling, I know not how much later, I staggered into the house and made shocking obeisances before the enshrined amulet of green jade.

Being now afraid to live alone in the ancient house on the moor, I departed on the following day for London, taking with me the amulet after destroying by fire and burial the rest of the impious collection in the museum. But after three nights I heard the baying again, and before a week was over felt strange eyes upon me whenever it was dark. One evening as I strolled on Victoria Embankment for some needed air, I saw a black shape obscure one of the reflections of the lamps in the water. A wind stronger than the night-wind rushed by, and I knew that what had befallen St. John must soon befall me.

The next day I carefully wrapped the green jade amulet and sailed for Holland. What mercy I might gain by returning the thing to its silent, sleeping owner I knew not; but I felt that I must at least try any step conceivably logical. What the hound was, and why it pursued me, were questions still vague; but I had first heard the baying in that ancient churchyard, and every subsequent event including St. John's dying whisper had served to connect the curse with the stealing of the amulet. Accordingly I sank into the nethermost abysses of despair when, at an inn in Rotterdam, I discovered that thieves had despoiled me of this sole means of salvation.

The baying was loud that evening, and in the morning I read of a nameless deed in the vilest quarter of the city. The rabble were in terror, for upon an evil tenement had fallen a red death beyond the foulest previous crime of the neighbourhood. In a squalid thieves' den an entire family had been torn to shreds by an unknown thing which left no trace, and those around had heard all night above the usual clamour of drunken voices a faint, deep, insistent note as of a gigantic hound.

So at last I stood again in that unwholesome churchyard where a pale winter moon cast hideous shadows, and leafless trees drooped sullenly to meet the withered, frosty grass and cracking slabs, and the ivied church pointed a jeering finger at the unfriendly sky, and the night-wind howled maniacally from over frozen swamps and frigid seas. The baying was very faint now, and it ceased altogether as I approached the ancient grave I had once violated, and frightened away an abnormally large horde of bats which had been hovering curiously around it.

I know not why I went thither unless to pray, or gibber out insane pleas and apologies to the calm white thing that lay within; but, whatever my reason, I attacked the half-frozen sod with a desperation partly mine and partly that of a dominating will outside myself. Excavation was much easier than I expected, though at one point I encountered a queer interruption; when a lean vulture darted down out of the cold sky and pecked frantically at the grave-earth until I killed him with a blow of my spade. Finally I reached the rotting oblong box and removed the damp nitrous cover. This is the last rational act I ever performed.

For crouched within that centuried coffin, embraced by a close-packed nightmare retinue of huge, sinewy, sleeping bats, was the bony thing my friend and I had robbed; not clean and placid as we had seen it then, but covered with caked blood and shreds of alien flesh and hair, and leering sentiently at me with phosphorescent sockets and sharp ensanguined fangs yawning twistedly in mockery of my inevitable doom. And when it gave from those grinning jaws a deep, sardonic bay as of some gigantic hound, and I saw that it held in its gory, filthy claw the lost and fateful amulet of green jade, I merely screamed and ran away idiotically, my screams soon dissolving into peals of hysterical laughter.

Madness rides the star-wind . . . claws and teeth sharpened on centuries of corpses . . . dripping death astride a Bacchanale of bats from night-black ruins of buried temples of Belial. . . . Now, as the baying of that dead, fleshless monstrosity grows louder and louder, and the stealthy whirring and flapping of those accursed web-wings circles closer and closer, I shall seek with my revolver the oblivion which is my only refuge from the unnamed and unnamable.

Bram Stoker

DRACULA'S GUEST

As the author of *Dracula*, Bram Stoker is the king of vampire literature, having created the most popular vampire of all time. Originally from Dublin, Stoker was best known in his own day as the partner of actor Henry Irving, with whom he ran the famous Lyceum Theatre in London from 1878 to 1905. Today, his name is synonymous with Count Dracula. Stoker's creation of this cult hero has proven to be an endless cornucopia for movie makers, writers, and playwrights. *Dracula* is now considered to be one of the all-time classics of horror literature. Interestingly, Stoker's vampire love story, *The Lady of the Shroud* (1909), has largely been ignored. He probably intended it to be a companion book to *Dracula* (1897) since it is also written as a collection of letters, notes, and journal entries. Unfortunately, almost all available editions have been heavily abridged, which seriously reduces the book's effectiveness. Stoker's other novels include *The Mystery at Sea*, *The Lair of the White Worm*, and *The Jewel of Seven Stars*. "Dracula's Guest" was originally a part of *Dracula*, but was cut from the novel at the request of Stoker's publishers. Stoker's wife published it two years after his death as part of a short story collection titled *Dracula's Guest and Other Weird Stories* (1914). In 1936 it was made into the movie *Dracula's Daughter*.

WHEN WE STARTED FOR our drive the sun was shining brightly on Munich, and the air was full of the joyousness of early summer. Just as we were about to depart, Herr Delbrück (the maître d'hôtel

of the Quatre Saisons, where I was staying) came down, bare-
headed, to the carriage and, after wishing me a pleasant drive,
said to the coachman, still holding his hand on the handle of the
carriage door:

"Remember you are back by nightfall. The sky looks bright but
there is a shiver in the north wind that says there may be a sudden
storm. But I am sure you will not be late." Here he smiled, and
added, "for you know what night it is."

Johann answered with an emphatic, "Ja, mein Herr," and,
touching his hat, drove off quickly. When we had cleared the
town, I said, after signalling to him to stop:

"Tell me, Johann, what is tonight?"

He crossed himself, as he answered laconically: "Walpurgisnacht." Then he took out his watch, a great, old-fashioned
German silver thing as big as a turnip, and looked at it, with his
eyebrows gathered together and a little impatient shrug of his
shoulders. I realised that this was his way of respectfully protesting
against the unnecessary delay, and sank back in the carriage,
merely motioning him to proceed. He started off rapidly, as if to
make up for lost time. Every now and then the horses seemed to
throw up their heads and sniffed the air suspiciously. On such
occasions I often looked round in alarm. The road was pretty
bleak, for we were traversing a sort of high, windswept plateau.
As we drove, I saw a road that looked but little used, and which
seemed to dip through a little, winding valley. It looked so inviting
that, even at the risk of offending him, I called Johann to stop—
and when he had pulled up, I told him I would like to drive down
that road. He made all sorts of excuses, and frequently crossed
himself as he spoke. This somewhat piqued my curiosity, so I
asked him various questions. He answered fencingly, and repeatedly looked at his watch in protest. Finally I said:

"Well, Johann, I want to go down this road. I shall not ask you
to come unless you like; but tell me why you do not like to go,
that is all I ask." For answer he seemed to throw himself off the
box, so quickly did he reach the ground. Then he stretched out
his hands appealingly to me, and implored me not to go. There
was just enough of English mixed with the German for me to
understand the drift of his talk. He seemed always just about to
tell me something—the very idea of which evidently frightened

him; but each time he pulled himself up, saying, as he crossed himself: "Walpurgisnacht!"

I tried to argue with him, but it was difficult to argue with a man when I did not know his language. The advantage certainly rested with him, for although he began to speak in English, of a very crude and broken kind, he always got excited and broke into his native tongue—and every time he did so, he looked at his watch. Then the horses became restless and sniffed the air. At this he grew very pale, and, looking around in a frightened way, he suddenly jumped forward, took them by the bridles and led them on some twenty feet. I followed, and asked why he had done this. For answer he crossed himself, pointed to the spot we had left and drew his carriage in the direction of the other road, indicating a cross, and said, first in German, then in English: "Buried him—him what killed themselves."

I remembered the old custom of burying suicides at crossroads: "Ah! I see, a suicide. How interesting!" But for the life of me I could not make out why the horses were frightened.

While we were talking, we heard a sort of sound between a yelp and a bark. It was far away; but the horses got very restless, and it took Johann all his time to quiet them. He was pale, and said: "It sounds like a wolf—but yet there are no wolves here now."

"No?" I said, questioning him; "isn't it long since the wolves were so near the city?"

"Long, long," he answered, "in the spring and summer; but with the snow the wolves have been here not so long."

While he was petting the horses and trying to quiet them, dark clouds drifted rapidly across the sky. The sunshine passed away, and a breath of cold wind seemed to drift past us. It was only a breath, however, and more in the nature of a warning than a fact, for the sun came out brightly again. Johann looked under his lifted hand at the horizon and said:

"The storm of snow, he comes before long time." Then he looked at his watch again, and, straightway holding his reins firmly—for the horses were still pawing the ground restlessly and shaking their heads—he climbed to his box as though the time had come for proceeding on our journey.

I felt a little obstinate and did not at once get into the carriage.

"Tell me," I said, "about this place where the road leads," and I pointed down.

Again he crossed himself and mumbled a prayer, before he answered: "It is unholy."

"What is unholy?" I enquired.

"The village."

"Then there is a village?"

"No, no. No one lives there hundreds of years." My curiosity was piqued: "But you said there was a village."

"There was."

"Where is it now?"

Whereupon he burst out into a long story in German and English, so mixed up that I could not quite understand exactly what he said, but roughly I gathered that long ago, hundreds of years, men had died there and been buried in their graves; and sounds were heard under the clay, and when the graves were opened, men and women were found rosy with life, and their mouths red with blood. And so, in haste to save their lives (aye, and their souls!—and here he crossed himself) those who were left fled away to other places, where the living died, and the dead were dead and not—not something. He was evidently afraid to speak the last words. As he proceeded with his narration, he grew more and more excited. It seemed as if his imagination had got hold of him, and he ended in a perfect paroxysm of fear—white-faced, perspiring, trembling and looking round him, as if expecting that some dreadful presence would manifest itself there in the bright sunshine on the open plain. Finally, in an agony of desperation, he cried:

"Walpurgisnacht!" and pointed to the carriage for me to get in. All my English blood rose at this, and, standing back, I said:

"You are afraid, Johann—you are afraid. Go home; I shall return alone; the walk will do me good." The carriage door was open. I took from the seat my oak walking stick—which I always carry on my holiday excursions—and closed the door, pointing back to Munich, and said, "Go home, Johann—Walpurgisnacht doesn't concern Englishmen."

The horses were now more restive than ever, and Johann was trying to hold them in while excitedly imploring me not to do anything so foolish. I pitied the poor fellow, he was so deeply in earnest; but all the same I could not help laughing. His English was quite gone now. In his anxiety he had forgotten that his only means of making me understand was to talk my language, so he jabbered away in his native German. It began to be a little tedious. After giving the direction, ''Home!'' I turned to go down the cross-road into the valley.

With a despairing gesture, Johann turned his horses towards Munich. I leaned on my stick and looked after him. He went slowly along the road for a while; then there came over the crest of the hill a man tall and thin. I could see so much in the distance. When he drew near the horses, they began to jump and kick about, then to scream with terror. Johann could not hold them in; they bolted down the road, running away madly. I watched them out of sight, then looked for the stranger, but I found that he, too, was gone.

With a light heart I turned down the side road through the deepening valley to which Johann had objected. There was not the slightest reason, that I could see, for his objection; and I dare-say I tramped for a couple of hours without thinking of time or distance, and certainly without seeing a person or a house. So far as the place was concerned, it was desolation itself. But I did not notice this particularly till, on turning a bend in the road, I came upon a scattered fringe of wood; then I recognised that I had been impressed unconsciously by the desolation of the region through which I had passed.

I sat down to rest myself, and began to look around. It struck me that it was considerably colder than it had been at the com-mencement of my walk—a sort of sighing sound seemed to be around me, with, now and then, high overhead, a sort of muffled roar. Looking upwards I noticed that great thick clouds were drift-ing rapidly across the sky from North to South at a great height. There were signs of a coming storm in some lofty stratum of the air. I was a little chilly, and, thinking that it was the sitting still after the exercise of walking, I resumed my journey.

The ground I passed over was now much more picturesque. There were no striking objects that the eye might single out; but in all there was a charm of beauty. I took little heed of time and it was only when the deepening twilight forced itself upon me that I began to think of how I should find my way home. The brightness of the day had gone. The air was cold, and the drifting of clouds high overhead was more marked. They were accompanied by a sort of far-away rushing sound, through which seemed to come at intervals that mysterious cry which the driver had said came from a wolf. For a while I hesitated. I had said I would see the deserted village, so on I went, and presently came on a wide stretch of open country, shut in by hills all around. Their sides were covered with trees which spread down to the plain, dotting, in clumps, the gentler slopes and hollows which showed here and there. I followed with my eye the winding of the road, and saw that it curved close to one of the densest of these clumps and was lost behind it.

As I looked there came a cold shiver in the air, and the snow began to fall. I thought of the miles and miles of bleak country I had passed, and then hurried on to seek the shelter of the wood in front. Darker and darker grew the sky, and faster and heavier fell the snow, till the earth before and around me was a glistening white carpet the further edge of which was lost in misty vagueness. The road was here but crude, and when on the level its boundaries were not so marked, as when it passed through the cuttings; and in a little while I found that I must have strayed from it, for I missed underfoot the hard surface, and my feet sank deeper in the grass and moss. Then the wind grew stronger and blew with ever increasing force, till I was fain to run before it. The air became icy cold, and in spite of my exercise I began to suffer. The snow was now falling so thickly and whirling around me in such rapid eddies that I could hardly keep my eyes open. Every now and then the heavens were torn asunder by vivid lightning, and in the flashes I could see ahead of me a great mass of trees, chiefly yew and cypress all heavily coated with snow.

I was soon amongst the shelter of the trees, and there, in comparative silence, I could hear the rush of the wind high overhead. Presently the blackness of the storm had become merged in the darkness of the night. By-and-by the storm seemed to be passing away: it now only came in fierce puffs and blasts. At such moments the weird sound of the wolf appeared to be echoed by many similar sounds around me.

Now and again, through the black mass of drifting cloud came a straggling ray of moonlight, which lit up the expanse, and showed me that I was at the edge of a dense mass of cypress and yew trees. As the snow had ceased to fall, I walked out from the shelter and began to investigate more closely. It appeared to me that, amongst so many old foundations as I had passed, there might be still standing a house in which, though in ruins, I could find some sort of shelter for a while. As I skirted the edge of the copse, I found that a low wall encircled it, and following this I presently found an opening. Here the cypresses formed an alley leading up to a square mass of some kind of building. Just as I caught sight of this, however, the drifting clouds obscured the moon, and I passed up the path in darkness. The wind must have grown colder, for I felt myself shiver as I walked; but there was hope of shelter, and I groped my way blindly on.

I stopped, for there was a sudden stillness. The storm had passed; and, perhaps in sympathy with nature's silence, my heart seemed to cease to beat. But this was only momentarily; for suddenly the moonlight broke through the clouds, showing me that I was in a graveyard, and that the square object before me was a great massive tomb of marble, as white as the snow that lay on and all around it. With the moonlight there came a fierce sigh of the storm, which appeared to resume its course with a long, low howl, as of many dogs or wolves. I was awed and shocked, and felt the cold perceptibly grow upon me till it seemed to grip me by the heart. Then while the flood of moonlight still fell on the marble tomb, the storm gave further evidence of renewing, as though it was returning on its track. Impelled by some sort of fascination, I approached the sepulchre to see what it was, and why such a thing stood alone in such a place. I walked around it, and read over the Doric door, in German—

COUNTESS DOLINGEN OF GRATZ
IN STYRIA
SOUGHT AND FOUND DEATH
1801

On the top of the tomb, seemingly driven through the solid marble—for the structure was composed of a few vast blocks of stone—was a great iron spike or stake. On going to the back I saw, graven in great Russian letters:

"The dead travel fast."

There was something so weird and uncanny about the whole thing that it gave me a turn and made me feel quite faint. I began to wish, for the first time, that I had taken Johann's advice. Here a thought struck me, which came under almost mysterious circumstances and with a terrible shock. This was Walpurgis Night!

Walpurgis Night, when, according to the belief of millions of people, the devil was abroad—when the graves were opened and the dead came forth and walked. When all evil things of earth and air and water held revel. This very place the driver had specially shunned. This was the depopulated village of centuries ago. This was where the suicide lay; and this was the place where I was alone—unmanned, shivering with cold in a shroud of snow with a wild storm gathering again upon me! It took all my philosophy, all the religion I had been taught, all my courage, not to collapse in a paroxysm of fright.

And now a perfect tornado burst upon me. The ground shook as though thousands of horses thundered across it; and this time the storm bore on its icy wings, not snow, but great hailstones which drove with such violence that they might have come from the thongs of Balearic slingers—hailstones that beat down leaf and branch and made the shelter of the cypresses of no more avail than though their stems were standing corn. At the first I had rushed to the nearest tree; but I was soon fain to leave it and seek the only spot that seemed to afford refuge, the deep Doric doorway of the marble tomb. There, crouching against the massive bronze door, I gained a certain amount of protection from the beating of the hailstones, for now they only drove against me as they ricocheted from the ground and the side of the marble.

As I leaned against the door, it moved slightly and opened inwards. The shelter of even a tomb was welcome in that pitiless tempest, and I was about to enter it when there came a flash of forked lightning that lit up the whole expanse of the heavens. In the instant, as I am a living man, I saw, as my eyes were turned into the darkness of the tomb, a beautiful woman, with rounded cheeks and red lips, seemingly sleeping on a bier. As the thunder broke overhead, I was grasped as by the hand of a giant and hurled out into the storm. The whole thing was so sudden that, before I could realise the shock, moral as well as physical, I found the hailstones beating me down. At the same time I had a strange, dominating feeling that I was not alone. I looked towards the tomb. Just then there came another blinding flash, which seemed to strike the iron stake that surmounted the tomb and to pour through to the earth, blasting and crumbling the marble, as in a burst of flame. The dead woman rose for a moment of agony, while she was lapped in the flame, and her bitter scream of pain was drowned in the thundercrash. The last thing I heard was this mingling of dreadful sound, as again I was seized in the giant grasp and dragged away, while the hailstones beat on me, and the air around seemed reverberant with the howling of wolves. The last sight that I remembered was a vague, white moving mass, as if all the graves around me had sent out the phantoms of their sheeted dead, and that they were closing in on me through the white cloudiness of the driving hail.

Gradually there came a sort of vague beginning of consciousness; then a sense of weariness that was dreadful. For a time I remembered nothing; but slowly my senses returned. My feet seemed positively racked with pain, yet I could not move them. They seemed to be numbed. There was an icy feeling at the back of my neck and all down my spine, and my ears, like my feet, were dead, yet in torment; but there was in my breast a sense of warmth which was, by comparison, delicious. It was as a nightmare, if one may use such an expression; for some heavy weight on my chest made it difficult for me to breathe.

This period of semi-lethargy seemed to remain a long time, and as it faded away I must have slept or swooned. Then came a sort of loathing, like the first stage of sea-sickness, and a wild desire to be free from something—I knew not what. A vast stillness enveloped me, as though all the world were asleep or dead—only broken by the low panting as of some animal close to me. I felt a warm rasping at my throat, then came a consciousness of the awful truth, which chilled me to the heart and sent the blood surging up through my brain. Some great animal was lying on me and now licking my throat. I feared to stir, for some instinct of prudence bade me lie still; but the brute seemed to realise that there was now some change in me, for it raised its head. Through my eyelashes I saw above me the two great flaming eyes of a gigantic wolf. Its sharp white teeth gleamed in the gaping red mouth, and I could feel its hot breath fierce and acrid upon me.

For another spell of time I remembered no more. Then I became conscious of a low growl, followed by a yelp, renewed again and again. Then, seemingly very far away, I heard a "Holloa! holloa!" as of many voices calling in unison. Cautiously I raised my head and looked in the direction whence the sound came; but the cemetery blocked my view. The wolf still continued to yelp in a strange way, and a red glare began to move round the grove of cypresses, as though following the sound. As the voices drew closer, the wolf yelped faster and louder. I feared to make either sound or motion. Nearer came the red glow, over the white pall which stretched into the darkness around me. Then all at once from beyond the trees there came at a trot a troop of horsemen bearing torches. The wolf rose from my breast and made for the cemetery. I saw one of the horsemen (soldiers by their caps and their long military cloaks) raise his carbine and take aim. A companion knocked up his arm, and I heard the ball whizz over my head. He had evidently taken my body for that of the wolf. Another sighted the animal as it slunk away, and a shot followed. Then, at a gallop, the troop rode forward—some towards me, others following the wolf as it disappeared amongst the snow-clad cypresses.

As they drew nearer I tried to move, but was powerless, although I could see and hear all that went on around me. Two or three of the soldiers jumped from their horses and knelt beside me. One of them raised my head, and placed his hand over my heart.

"Good news, comrades!" he cried. "His heart still beats!"

Then some brandy was poured down my throat; it put vigour into me, and I was able to open my eyes fully and look around. Lights and shadows were moving among the trees, and I heard men call to one another. They drew together, uttering frightened exclamations; and the lights flashed as the others came pouring out of the cemetery pell-mell, like men possessed. When the further ones came close to us, those who were around me asked them eagerly:

"Well, have you found him?"

The reply rang out hurriedly:

"No! no! Come away quick—quick! This is no place to stay, and on this of all nights!"

"What was it?" was the question, asked in all manner of keys. The answer came variously and all indefinitely as though the men were moved by some common impulse to speak, yet were restrained by some common fear from giving their thoughts.

"It—it—indeed!" gibbered one, whose wits had plainly given out for the moment.

"A wolf—and yet not a wolf!" another put in shudderingly.

"No use trying for him without the sacred bullet," a third remarked in a more ordinary manner.

"Serve us right for coming out on this night! Truly we have earned our thousand marks!" were the ejaculations of a fourth.

"There was blood on the broken marble," another said after a pause—"the lightning never brought that there. And for him—is he safe? Look at his throat! See, comrades, the wolf has been lying on him and keeping his blood warm."

The officer looked at my throat and replied:

"He is all right; the skin is not pierced. What does it all mean? We should never have found him but for the yelping of the wolf."

"What became of it?" asked the man who was holding up my head, and who seemed the least panic-stricken of the party, for his hands were steady and without tremor. On his sleeve was the chevron of a petty officer.

"It went to its home," answered the man, whose long face was pallid, and who actually shook with terror as he glanced around him fearfully. "There are graves enough there in which it may lie. Come, comrades—come quickly! Let us leave this cursed spot."

The officer raised me to a sitting posture, as he uttered a word of command; then several men placed me upon a horse. He sprang to the saddle behind me, took me in his arms, gave the word to advance; and, turning our faces away from the cypresses, we rode away in swift, military order.

As yet my tongue refused its office, and I was perforce silent. I must have fallen asleep; for the next thing I remembered was finding myself standing up, supported by a soldier on each side of me. It was almost broad daylight, and to the north a red streak of sunlight was reflected, like a path of blood, over the waste of snow. The officer was telling the men to say nothing of what they had seen, except that they found an English stranger, guarded by a large dog.

"Dog! that was no dog," cut in the man who had exhibited such fear. "I think I know a wolf when I see one."

The young officer answered calmly: "I said a dog."

"Dog!" reiterated the other ironically. It was evident that his courage was rising with the sun; and, pointing to me, he said, "Look at his throat. Is that the work of a dog, master?"

Instinctively I raised my hand to my throat, and as I touched it I cried out in pain. The men crowded round to look, some stooping down from their saddles; and again there came the calm voice of the young officer:

"A dog, as I said. If aught else were said we should only be laughed at."

I was then mounted behind a trooper, and we rode on into the suburbs of Munich. Here we came across a stray carriage, into which I was lifted, and it was driven off to the Quatre Saisons— the young officer accompanying me, while a trooper followed with his horse, and the others rode off to their barracks.

When we arrived, Herr Delbrück rushed so quickly down the steps to meet me, that it was apparent he had been watching within. Taking me by both hands he solicitously led me in. The officer saluted me and was turning to withdraw, when I recognised his purpose, and insisted that he should come to my rooms. Over a glass of wine I warmly thanked him and his brave comrades for saving me. He replied simply that he was more than glad, and that Herr Delbrück had at the first taken steps to make all the searching party pleased; at which ambiguous utterance the maître d'hôtel smiled, while the officer pleaded duty and withdrew.

"But Herr Delbrück," I inquired, "how and why was it that the soldiers searched for me?"

He shrugged his shoulders, as if in depreciation of his own deed, as he replied:

"I was so fortunate as to obtain leave from the commander of the regiment in which I served, to ask for volunteers."

"But how did you know I was lost?" I asked.

"The driver came hither with the remains of his carriage, which had been upset when the horses ran away."

"But surely you would not send a search-party of soldiers merely on this account?"

"Oh, no!" he answered; "but even before the coachman arrived, I had this telegram from the Boyar whose guest you are," and he took from his pocket a telegram which he handed to me, and I read:

Bistritz

Be careful of my guest—his safety is most precious to me. Should aught happen to him, or if he be missed, spare nothing to find him and ensure his safety. He is English and therefore adventurous. There are often dangers from snow and wolves and night. Lose not a moment if you suspect harm to him. I answer your zeal with my fortune.—*Dracula*.

As I held the telegram in my hand, the room seemed to whirl around me; and, if the attentive maître d'hôtel had not caught me, I think I should have fallen. There was something so strange in all this, something so weird and impossible to imagine, that there grew on me a sense of my being in some way the sport of opposite forces—the mere vague idea of which seemed in a way to paralyse me. I was certainly under some form of mysterious protection. From a distant country had come, in the very nick of time, a message that took me out of the danger of the snow-sleep and the jaws of the wolf.

ACKNOWLEDGMENTS

My thanks to the following, who have granted permission to reprint copyrighted material. Every effort has been made to reach owners of copyrighted material. I apologize for any inadvertent omissions and will be grateful if such are brought to my attention.

"Bewitched" by Edith Wharton. © 1925 The Pictorial Review Co., renewed © 1953 The Hearst Corp. Reprinted by permission of the Hearst Corp.

"Count Dracula" by Woody Allen. From *Getting Even* by Woody Allen, copyright © 1971 by Woody Allen. Reprinted by permission of Random House, Inc.

"The Homecoming" by Ray Bradbury. Reprinted by permission of Don Congdon Associates, Inc. Copyright © 1946, renewed 1974 by Ray Bradbury.

"The Hound" by H. P. Lovecraft. © 1924. Reprinted by permission of the author's estate and its agents, JABberwocky Literary Agency, P.O. Box 4558, Sunnyside, NY 11104-0558.

"The Master of Rampling Gate" by Anne Rice. Copyright © 1983 by Anne O'Brien Rice. Originally published in *Redbook*. Reprinted by permission of the author.